"FREEZE. DROP YOUR WEAPONS."

Their surprise yielded to arrogance and belligerence. One, holding an Uzi, snarled.

"Who you jerking, old man? There's four of us and one of you. Let's burn him, homes," he said to the others, "and be gone."

"You'll take me down," said Tracy. "But I'll take at least two of you down with me, and the two who get away will be cop killers and there won't be anywhere for you to run. Or you can drop your weapons and your lawyers will have you back on the street in no time at all. Call it."

DICK TRACY

THE SECRET FILES

edited by

Max Allan Collins and Martin H. Greenberg

TOR

A TOM DOHERTY ASSOCIATES BOOK
NEW YORK

DICK TRACY: THE SECRET FILES

Copyright © 1990 by Tribune Media Services

A Tor Book
Published by Tom Doherty Associates, Inc.
49 West 24th Street
New York, N.Y. 10010

Cover art by Dick Locher

ISBN: 0-812-51010-0

First edition: June 1990

Printed in the United States of America

0 9 8 7 6 5 4 3 2 1

• CONTENTS •

DICK TRACY: THE SECRET FILES

an introduction
by
Max Allan Collins

It's been my privilege, since 1977, to write the internationally syndicated DICK TRACY comic strip. When Tracy's creator Chester Gould retired, I was given the opportunity to "try out" for the strip—that is, to write a sample TRACY story, after my work as a mystery novelist was called to the attention of editor Don Michel at Tribune Media Services.

I could not have been more thrilled, because DICK TRACY was my favorite comic strip, growing up. Actually, it was more than just my favorite—it was my obsession; I spent much of my childhood avidly collecting the comic books and strips, drawing my own strips, compiling scrapbooks, corresponding with Chester Gould himself. My specific interest in TRACY eventually led to a more general interest in detective fiction; it's not a great leap, really, for a seven-year-old reading DICK TRACY to become a thirteen-year-old reading Dashiell Hammett, Raymond Chandler, and Mickey Spillane.

While my youthful ambition to become a cartoonist

evolved into the realized goal of becoming a mystery writer, I never lost my interest in, or my love for, DICK TRACY. In fact, shortly after my first novel (BAIT MONEY, 1973) was published, I got back in contact with Chet Gould, and a wonderful friendship blossomed.

Now I've been the caretaker of Chet's strip for almost thirteen years—thus far, the only writer other than its creator ever to script the famous feature, working first with Chet's final assistant Rick Fletcher, and currently with another former Gould assistant, Pulitzer Prize–winning political cartoonist Dick Locher (who, I am pleased to say, provided the cover for this volume). The seven-year-old obsessive DICK TRACY fan has grown into (some would say "lucked out" into) being at least a footnote in the popular culture chapter Gould wrote.

I realize, however, that I am not unique in my love for TRACY; mystery writers of several generations have been influenced by the jut-jawed sleuth, who no less an expert than Ellery Queen termed "the world's first procedural detective of fiction, in the modern sense."

As the sixtieth anniversary of TRACY approaches, and a new major motion picture production starring and directed by Warren Beatty heads into the theaters, it seems appropriate to celebrate America's most famous fictional detective by inviting a few new faces to the party.

Last year I was invited by Martin Greenberg, in my (and just about anybody's) estimation the foremost anthologist in the country, to contribute a prose short story about the comic-book character Batman to an original collection, THE FURTHER ADVENTURES OF BATMAN (Bantam). The point was to invite top writers from the mystery, science-fiction and horror fields to do their "take" on the Caped Crusader. (I was the only writer in the collection who had ever written the character before, by the way—having done just under a year's worth of the monthly DC comic book.)

The BATMAN collection was well-received—readers

liked it, and in numbers sufficient to place the book on the *New York Times* bestseller list.

It occurred to me that a similar collection of original TRACY stories was apropos—and I contacted Martin Greenberg himself, to put it in motion. With the cooperation of Tribune Media Services (specifically, Elyce Small-Goldstein), we placed the book with Tor, and began approaching writers.

As I suspected, many TRACY fans were lurking among my contemporaries in the mystery field. We asked twenty-some writers, figuring a few would turn us down; we had a secondary list, with many other talented writers on it, ready to go—but we never got to it. Everyone we approached accepted, eagerly. (Almost everyone: Donald E. Westlake and Isaac Asimov reluctantly declined because of time constraints.)

You hold the results in your hands, a collection of TRACY stories that just about marks the first time Chester Gould's classic American detective has appeared in adult prose fashion. (I qualify that with ''just about,'' because there was a Dell paperback in the 1940s, entitled DICK TRACY AND THE WOO WOO SISTERS, which purported to be for adults, but wasn't really. Also, concurrently with this collection, my own novelization of the DICK TRACY movie should be appearing, from Bantam Books.)

I am extremely pleased with the resulting anthology. The writers herein make an impressive list, and they have come through to a man, and woman. A number of these stories are set in Chester Gould's glory days of the '30s through the '50s; others reveal Tracy's durability and credibility in a contemporary setting.

A number of villains from the strip rear their grotesque heads in the pages ahead. Best-selling horror novelist F. Paul Wilson brings Mumbles back from the dead, and along the way recreates a vivid 1950s milieu. Like Wilson, cartoonist Terry Beatty and his western-novelist wife Wendi Lee reveal an abiding familiarity with, and love for, the TRACY characters, in their collaboration; they too mount a '50s tale with a classic villain—Blowtop—and showcase such great Gould supporting players as B.O. Plenty, Gravel Gertie, their daughter "leetle" Sparkle, and ham actor Vitamin Flintheart. Mystery writer John Lutz, master of both the novel and short story, offers a wry comic caper, including one of my own villains, Putty Puss.

A number of writers have chosen to create their own Gould-style, larger-than-life grotesques: short-story virtuoso Ed Hoch has created master thief Chessboard; science-fiction legend Barry Malzberg gives us Crystal Freezum, in a chilling fable of drug abuse; Ric Meyers brings his cinematic, actionful touch to the tale of no less than three modern horrors—"Whirlpool, Sizzle, and The Juice."

There are also, I am pleased to report, several stories that focus on characters other than Tracy himself. My wife Barbara Collins—who is my assistant on the DICK TRACY strip, and has written the "Crimestoppers Textbook" Sunday feature for a number of years now—gives us a story told from the point of view of Tess (Trueheart) Tracy. Rex Miller, that powerhouse who melds detective fiction with horror like no one else, gives Junior center-stage in an unusual '40s story; and best-selling science-fiction author Mike Resnick does the same thing for none other than Chester Gould, in the warm, apocryphal "Origins."

Other writers bring a pop-culture touch to their tales. Ron Goulart, renowned for bringing off-center humor to both the mystery and science-fiction fields, takes Tracy to a vividly portrayed Hollywood in the '40s; while suspense master Henry Slesar harks back to the '30s in a tale that deals with the business of comic strips, and a young Dick Tracy.

Two stories emphasize the thinking detective within Tracy. Perhaps surprisingly, one of the current rising stars of the two-fisted hardboiled private eye story—Wayne

Dundee—emphasizes Tracy's role as a modern Sherlock Holmes in what is at least partially an updating of *The Hound of the Baskervilles*. Short-story specialist Josh Pachter and historian/mystery-novelist Mike Nevins collaborate on a tale that shows Tracy working effectively in an Ellery Queen mode.

Several stories eschew, to some extent, the comic-strip roots of the character and present Dick Tracy as a tough modern cop. Ed Gorman—who is equally adept in the mystery, western and horror fields—proves for the umpteenth time that he is one of the best short story writers around, with an evocative tale of Tracy being stalked. Novelist and short-story writer Steve Mertz presents one of the hardest-hitting yarns in this book, a modern tale that explores the older Tracy having to deal with his own legendary status, as well as a deteriorating urban landscape where street gangs and drug deals are commonplace.

Stories about drugs have been a taboo in the strip in recent years (and I am delighted to see Malzberg and Mertz—which sounds a little like a law firm, doesn't it?— tackling that problem in tough modern tales). For my own contribution to this anthology, I chose to write a story that explored another sort of crime that is off limits to me within the purview of the syndicated strip.

For readers who may not have access to the current strip, and whose notion of TRACY is either a vague nostalgic memory or perhaps the colorful one of the current Warren Beatty film, I'd like to offer a refresher course in the world of DICK TRACY.

The setting here is a major U.S. city, patterned upon (but not specifically) Chicago; it was Chester Gould's intention that readers in any major city might imagine this city to be their own.

Dick Tracy is the Chief of Detectives, working out of Central Headquarters; he heads up the Major Crime Squad, which consists of himself and partner Sam

Catchem, as well as policewomen Lizz Grove and Lee Ebony. (In the '30s to late '40s, Tracy's partner was Pat Patton, who is now chief of police, replacing Chief Brandon.)

Like Batman, Tracy's war on crime is fueled by a core of revenge. Tracy joined the force when his fiancée's father, a delicatessen owner, was shot down by thieves. Tracy's wife of many years, Tess, is a good mother and homemaker, very supportive of her husband's law enforcement career; but no wallflower: prior to their marriage, Tess often got involved in cases and was an amateur-sleuth version of policewoman Lizz. Tess and Tracy have a grown daughter, Bonnie Braids, a teacher; and a young son, Joe. Also, Tess is the adoptive mother of Dick Tracy, Jr., better known as Junior, now the police artist at Central HQ.

This information, and a well-oiled sense of wonder, are all you need to join the eighteen writers in the sixteen stories in this book, in their celebration of America's most famous fictional sleuth.

My thanks to my co-editor Marty Greenberg, as well as Tom Doherty, Heather Wood, and Robert Legault (at Tor Books), and all of the writers for helping throw the party.

And especially to you, for attending.

—Max Allan Collins
Muscatine, Iowa
January 3, 1990

ORIGINS

by
Mike Resnick

There is a beginning, an origin, to all things. This is one of them. Only the facts have been changed, since they sometimes get in the way of the Truth.

The visitor looked down at the drawing board.

"Funny animals?" he said distastefully.

The cartoonist sighed and turned to his visitor, who was looking over his shoulder.

"No choice," he replied wearily. "Nobody seems to want crime strips."

"*I* do," said the visitor.

"You're not an editor, more's the pity."

"I thought your strip was excellent. Why did they turn it down?"

The cartoonist shrugged. "If I knew, I could change it. Maybe it's not realistic enough, maybe they don't like my drawing style, maybe it's too grim. Who knows?"

"Well, I thought it was realistic," said the visitor.

"Especially that part about the jewel robbery. I thought it was brilliant."

"Thanks, Melvin. I wish somebody with a budget would agree with you."

"I keep asking you not to call me Melvin," said the visitor irritably.

"Sorry," said the cartoonist. "What was it you wanted to be called again?"

"Nimrod."

"Okay . . . but I don't know what you have against your real name."

"Nimrod *is* my real name. My middle name."

"Whatever makes you happy," said the cartoonist.

"I don't think it's too much to ask. After all, you ask people to call you Chet and not Chester."

"You have a point," agreed Chet. "Nimrod it is."

"Well," said Nimrod, looking at his wristwatch, "I gotta go. Anything I can do for you?"

"You might keep your radio a little softer after midnight," said Chet with a smile. "Even unemployed cartoonists need their sleep."

"You won't hear a sound tonight," said Nimrod with an odd grin. "I promise it."

"Thanks," said Chet. "Just let yourself out." A moment later he was oblivious to the rest of the world as he painstakingly drew a horde of funny animals doing funny things, and wondered, for the hundredth time, why he'd ever wanted to get into this profession in the first place.

He awoke early, shaved and dressed, and walked into the living room to examine the work he'd done the previous night. Not bad, he concluded—but also not what he'd had in mind when he had trained to become a cartoonist.

"Still," he muttered, "even an artist has to eat."

And, he reminded himself grimly, no one was beating down his door for funny animal strips, any more than they had lined up to buy his crime strip.

He spent a few more minutes checking last night's drawings, changing some shading here, darkening a line there, then put on his overcoat and went around the corner to the local delicatessen for coffee and a roll. Along the way he picked up a copy of the morning paper.

He entered the deli, seated himself in a booth, and immediately turned to the comic page. There was *Krazy Kat*, and *Tarzan*, and *Mutt and Jeff*, fine comics all, but, damn it, the paper really *needed* something realistic and contemporary. He shook his head in bewilderment and decided that one of these days he'd have to take another shot at the crime strip.

He turned to the sports section next, and finally checked the front page.

DARING JEWEL ROBBERY! the headline blared out at him. Well, the more data he collected, the more realistic his strip would appear when he finally went back to work on it; so he sighed, sipped his coffee, and began reading.

A solitary thief had broken into the biggest jewelry store in town, and had made off with almost half a million dollars' worth of rare gems, literally under the noses of the police force. So brilliant and innovative was the crime that authorities speculated that it might very well have been the work of a professional psychologist.

First the thief had entered five neighboring shops, all sharing the same roof, and tripped the alarms in each. All hell had broken loose as the air filled with bells and sirens, and the police were on the scene less than two minutes later. They realized almost instantly that no one had taken anything, and decided that the situation was due to faulty wiring among the connected buildings. Then, as all the alarms were blaring away, the thief had entered the jewelry store . . . and no one had paid any special attention to one more alarm. While the police were looking for a way to turn the alarms off, he had taken what he wanted and then blended in with the huge crowd of onlookers.

The cartoonist frowned and read the account of the

robbery once more. Then, deeply disturbed, he got up without finishing his coffee, tucked the paper under his arm, and returned home.

"Hi, Chet!" said Nimrod, sticking his head into the cartoonist's apartment. "Have a good day?"

"Not especially," answered Chet.

"Well, maybe a nice dinner will cheer you up," said Nimrod. "My treat."

"I thought you were looking for work," said Chet.

Nimrod grinned. "I found some."

"They paid you the first day on the job?"

"It was piece work," said Nimrod. Suddenly he laughed uproariously, as if at a private joke. "Get your coat and come on. I'll even pop for champagne."

"I wish I could," answered Chet. "But I didn't get much work done today. I think I'd better stay here and plug away."

"I'd take that as a personal insult," said Nimrod ominously.

"No insult is intended," explained the cartoonist, "but I've got to try to make a living."

"Come on, Chet," said Nimrod, now almost pleading. "You're the only person in the building who's ever been nice to me. Now that I'm in the chips, I want to pay you back."

"In the chips—from one day's work?"

Nimrod grinned again. "I have prospects." He paused. "So how about it? You gonna come out with me?"

"I really can't . . . and you don't owe me anything, Melvin—excuse me: Nimrod."

"Don't you want to be my friend?" persisted Nimrod.

"Of course I do."

"Then come out with me."

"I just can't," said Chet with a sigh. "I've got too much work to do."

"Can I still drop by and visit you?"

"When I'm not working."

"And we're still friends?"

"Of course."

"And I can still read your comic strips?"

"If you want to," said Chet with a sigh. "Hell, so far you're the *only* one who does."

"I especially like the crime strip."

"I know."

"I loved that story about the jewel robbery."

"It wasn't as original as I thought," replied Chet. "Last night someone pulled the very job I described."

"Really?" said Nimrod. "He must have been some kind of genius." He paused. "They never caught the thief in your strip, did they?"

"No," admitted the cartoonist. He smiled. "That's why it's a crime strip and not a detective strip. But I'm no criminal mastermind, and this is real life—I'm sure the cops'll catch this guy before too long."

"A guy smart enough to pull that kind of job?" said Nimrod. "I wouldn't bet on it, Chet." He paused. "Well, I'm off. You sure you don't want to come along?"

Chet shook his head. "No. I really have to get back to work. If Disney can sell a mouse, maybe I can sell *my* animals."

"Disney loved that mouse, Chet. You love crime. You ought to stick to what you love."

"Tell that to the landlord and the phone company," replied Chet wearily.

It was two days later that the cartoonist came home in midafternoon after another unsuccessful sales pitch to the comic syndicate and found his door unlocked. Frowning, he cautiously entered his apartment and found Nimrod sitting on the floor, a number of drawings spread out in front of him.

"What the hell are you doing here?" demanded the cartoonist.

"Oh, hi, Chet," said Nimrod, looking up with a

smile. "I didn't have anything to do, so I thought I'd stop by and read some more of your stuff."

"Did you ever hear of breaking and entering?"

"I didn't think you'd mind. After all, we're friends, aren't we?"

"Of course I mind!" snapped Chet. "This is my apartment, not a public library." He paused. "How did you get in here anyway?"

"I picked your lock."

"Where did you learn to pick locks?"

"From you, Chet," answered Nimrod easily.

"From *me*?"

"Well, from one of your crime strips. It's harder than you made it look, but it worked. You really know your stuff, Chet. You're some kind of genius."

"I'm also a private citizen who resents having his apartment broken into."

"I didn't mean to upset you, Chet," said Nimrod. He got to his feet. "I'll leave, if that's what you want."

"That's what I want."

"You want me to put these strips away first?"

"I'll take care of it."

Nimrod shrugged. "I hope you're not mad at me, Chet. I didn't mean any harm, really I didn't."

"I don't ever want you to do it again."

"Whatever you say. You're my only friend, Chet. Everyone else hates me. I don't want to do anything to make you mad, not a genius like you." Nimrod walked to the door, then turned. "Dinner tonight?"

"I don't think so."

Nimrod's face turned sullen. "I'm trying to be a nice guy, Chet. You don't appreciate me."

"You broke into my apartment," repeated Chet coldly.

"I already apologized for that," said Nimrod. "You really should be my friend, Chet. You wouldn't want me for an enemy. I can be very nasty to people I don't like."

"I'm sure you can be."

Suddenly Nimrod's expression softened. "You're just upset, Chet. We'll talk again tomorrow, okay?"

"We'll see," said the cartoonist noncommittally.

"We'll be friends again," said Nimrod confidently. "I'm going to make you proud of me. You'll see."

Then he was gone, and the cartoonist picked up his rejected strips and began filing them away.

The next morning the headlines all related to a particularly ingenious bank robbery. The criminal had disguised himself as a bank officer, explained to the head teller that he had reason to suspect that certain safety deposit boxes had been looted, had the teller unlock them while he inspected them, faked a coughing seizure, and managed to appropriate almost $200,000 in bearer bonds while the teller briefly left the vault to bring him a glass of water, never suspecting that he wasn't helping an old and trusted member of the bank's governing board. The thief had then helped the teller lock the boxes and expressed relief that his fears had been unfounded.

Two hours later the robbery had been discovered when an elderly businessman was going through his box's papers . . .

. . . and twenty minutes after he read the news story, the cartoonist presented himself at the local police station and asked to see someone in authority.

After a brief delay he was ushered into a small office, where he found himself facing a well-dressed young officer with dark hair, piercing gray eyes, a finely-chiseled nose, and a firm jaw.

"I'm Detective Richards," said the policeman. "Won't you please have a seat, Mr. . . . ah?"

"Gould," said the cartoonist. "Chet Gould."

"All right, Mr. Gould," said Richards. "What seems to be your problem?"

The cartoonist sighed. "I don't know exactly how to begin . . ."

"At the beginning, perhaps," suggested Richards with a smile.

"Let me start at the end," said Chet. "If you haven't thrown me out as some kind of crackpot, we can go back to the beginning and the middle."

"All right."

Chet took a deep breath. "I think I know who robbed that bank last night. And I think it's the same person who pulled off the big jewel heist three nights ago."

"The methods don't have much in common," commented Richards.

"You're wrong," said Chet. "They have one very important thing in common."

"Oh? And what is that?"

"*I* invented them."

Richards frowned. "Would you care to explain that?"

"I'm a cartoonist," said Chet. "Or, at least, I'm trying to be a cartoonist."

"What has that got to do with the robberies?" asked Richards.

"One of the strips that I tried to sell was a crime strip. In it, I described exactly the methods that were used to rob the jewelry store and the bank."

"You *tried* to sell it, you say?"

"That's right."

"But it's never appeared in print?"

"No."

Richards frowned again. "Do you realize what you're saying, Mr. Gould? If anyone is implicated by what appears in this unpublished comic strip, it's *you*."

Gould shook his head. "I have a neighbor. He just moved into the building a month ago. At first I thought he was merely eccentric, but over the past few days I've become convinced that he's actually psychotic."

"He's seen the strips?"

"Yes."

"And you think he's the thief?"

"Yes, I do."

"Why him?" asked Richards. "After all, if they've been rejected, at least a few editors have also seen them."

"Because he was absolutely penniless until the day after the jewel robbery, and then he offered to take me to dinner."

Richards smiled. "And from this, you deduce that he's a jewel thief?"

"He also offered to buy me a bottle of champagne."

"Generosity isn't a crime, Mr. Gould. Have you got anything else?"

"It's something I *haven't* got."

"I don't understand."

"Yesterday I caught him in my apartment. He had picked the lock, and when I found him he was going through the pages of my unsold crime strip." Gould paused. "I was upset, of course, but it wasn't until I read the papers this morning that I realized what was happening."

"I still don't understand."

"The strip in which the safety deposit box holdup is shown is missing," said Chet.

"And you think he took it?"

"I know he did. It was there three days ago." He paused. "I thought I had just misfiled it, but I checked again before I came over here, and it's gone."

"No one's been in your apartment since you caught this man reading the strips?"

"Starving cartoonists don't hire cleaning ladies," said Chet wryly.

"Of course, if it's missing, then you can't prove that you actually described the bank robbery," offered Richards.

"No," said Chet. "But I can show you that my plot for the jewel robbery was followed step by step."

He tossed a large manila envelope onto the officer's desk. Richards reached inside it, pulled out the contents, and began studying them.

"All right, Mr. Gould," he said at last. "You've convinced *me*—but this will never stand up in a court of law. The police can't touch him yet.''

''Maybe you can keep him under observation,'' suggested Chet.

Richards considered the notion for a moment, then suddenly smiled. ''I think I've got a better idea.''

''Oh?''

The officer nodded. ''But I'll need your help.''

''I'll do anything I can,'' said Chet promptly. ''But I warn you—I'm no policeman.''

''I've got all the policemen I need,'' answered Richards. ''I need you to do what you're best at.''

Chet looked puzzled. ''What's that?''

Richards chuckled. ''You're a cartoonist, Mr. Gould.''

''A *hopeful* cartoonist,'' Chet corrected him.

Richards looked down at the strips laid out on his desk. ''Striking art, good dialogue, intricate plotting. You're going to be a very successful one. I can tell.''

''I wish I could get some editors to agree with you.''

''You will—as soon as you get the proper hero. Right now all your villains are outwitting the police. That doesn't happen very often in real life.'' Richards shrugged. ''However, that's neither here nor there. What I need to know is: are you willing to draw another crime adventure?''

''I suppose so,'' replied Chet. ''But how will that help?''

''Simple,'' said Richards. ''In *this* strip, you'll choose the only furrier in town who's licensed to import sables from Russia. And, just in case our friend has any trouble figuring out who you're writing about, you'll draw in the street sign and the address.''

''And then what?''

''And then invite our culprit for dinner, or a drink, or to listen to the baseball game, and make sure the strip's lying around where he can see it, and at some point during his visit, find an excuse to leave the room for five minutes.''

"What if the strip's still there after he leaves?" asked Chet.

"Then it means that he's got a good memory—which is possible, since he didn't steal the jewelry strip—or else it means that I'm going to be wasting a lot of your time and the taxpayers' money."

Chet shrugged. "I'm willing to try it if you are."

Richards withdrew a card from his wallet and handed it to the cartoonist. "Call me at this number as soon as you know he's seen the strip and left your apartment."

"I will, Officer Richards," said Chet, getting to his feet.

"Oh, one more thing, Mr. Gould," said Richards.

"Yes?"

"What's our suspect's name?"

"His real name is Melvin Head, but he likes to be called Nimrod. I gather that's his middle name."

"Melvin Nimrod Head," mused the policeman. "Doesn't ring a bell." Suddenly he smiled. "Mel N. Head. Melonhead. Maybe you ought to write *him* into your strip."

"It's a thought," agreed Chet.

He drew the strip—three weeks' worth—that night, and invited Nimrod over the next afternoon.

The police staked out the furrier the same evening. For two nights nothing happened, but the third night Nimrod showed up, sneaking in through the back entrance, just as Chet had drawn it, and Richards was waiting for him.

The next morning there was a knock at Chet's door. The cartoonist got up from his drawing board, walked over, and opened it.

"Good morning, Mr. Gould," said Richards, stepping into the apartment. "I just dropped by to tell you that we apprehended your friend Nimrod in the act of robbing the furrier. When we found the comic strip in his coat pocket he confessed to all three crimes."

"Wonderful!"

"Actually, I should have known not to waste my time the first two nights," added Richards with a rueful smile.

"Oh?"

The policeman nodded. "To lend verisimilitude, you put the day of the week on each strip."

"Sure," answered Chet. "That keeps 'em in order."

"Well, the day the actual break-in began in your strip was a Thursday . . ."

". . . and last night was Thursday night!"

"Right," said Richards. "Poor Melonhead never had an original thought in his life. He not only needed you to show him how to rob a store, but he even had to be told what day to do it."

"Fascinating!" mused Chet.

"Commonplace," said Richards with a shrug. "You should see some of the *really* strange criminals I've had to bring in."

"I'd love to."

"You'd love to *what*?" asked Richards, confused.

"I'd love to talk to you from time to time about your work."

"You'd probably find it deadly dull."

"Not at all. In fact, I've decided to go back to working on my crime strip again." He grimaced. "I never did like funny animals."

"Well," said Richards, after giving the matter some thought, "if you really think it might help you . . ."

"I'm sure it would," said Chet. "Also, I've been thinking about what you said in your office the other day, about the strip needing a hero. What's your first name?"

"Tracy," said Richards. "But if you're going to pattern a cop after me, don't use my real name. The guys down at the station would tease me from now until Doomsday."

"Whatever you say."

"Also, don't use your friend Melonhead until after his trial. A good lawyer could claim you were prejudicing the jury."

"What a pity," replied Chet. "It was such a good name."

"Why not call him Pruneface?" suggested Richards. "It comes to the same thing, and this way some shyster won't put him back on the streets because of your new strip."

"All right," agreed Chet. "Though I hasten to point out that I haven't even written my new strip, let alone sold it."

"I have confidence in you, Mr. Gould," said Richards. "If you can draw a comic strip convincingly enough to trap Melonhead, you can draw one that editors will want to buy."

"I hope you're right," said Chet.

"I know I am." Richards looked at his watch. "I've got to be going. Melonhead was just a small fry. This week I'm after the biggest of the big boys."

"Big Boy," repeated Chet. "That would make a nice name for a villain, wouldn't it?"

"There's nothing nice about this particular villain, I assure you," said Richards grimly, as he opened the door and prepared to leave.

"Good luck," said Chet.

"Thanks. I have a feeling I'll be needing it."

Then he was gone, and Chet walked back to the drawing board. He looked at what he had done, crumpled it in a ball, and threw it in the wastebasket. Then he began outlining the panels for the first day of his new strip.

"Tracy Richards, Tracy Richards," he mused.

And then, carefully, meticulously, he began lettering the masterhead:

THE ADVENTURES OF PLAINCLOTHES TRACY.

DICK TRACY AND THE SYNDICATE OF DEATH

by
Henry Slesar

"Cheer up!" Chief Brandon said to Dick Tracy's dour profile, raising the volume of his voice to compensate for the roar of the elevated train over their heads. "Look at it this way. Now there's one less rat on the streets."

"All I see is a dead man," Tracy said glumly, his eyes fixed on the shattered body leaning against the El pillar. It had taken a formidable number of .45 slugs from a Thompson submachine gun to reduce a human form to this agglomerate of bone, tissue and bloody cloth, and Tracy, only in his second year in Homicide, hadn't yet developed the carapace which shields police professionals from the sentient assaults of violent death.

It was a good eight hours before the mop-up squad was able to produce identification of the body, but it confirmed Brandon's educated guess. The victim was William Mappe, better known as "Curly" Mappe, the nickname resulting from a thick mane of black ringlets which had been wound round many a feminine finger in his twenty-five years of life. With the exception, of course, of two years in juvenile detention and three-and-a-half in Sing Sing, Curly had compiled most of his criminal history out of state, which gave the police a problem. What was he doing in Chicago? And who was he doing it for?

Chief Brandon thought he had a partial answer when the envelope arrived containing Curly's effects: a shattered Rolex Oyster, a gold cigarette case with two bullet holes shredding the Twenty Grands, a demolished wallet, and a scrap of torn paper bearing one handwritten word: *Syndicate*.

The scrap fascinated Dick Tracy. He knew that the word had been coined by reporters to describe the "business arrangements" between crime bosses like Charlie Luciano, Louis (Lepke) Buchalter, Meyer Lansky and the rest. But it was a journalist's word, not criminal jargon. And what was it doing in the pocket of this small-time hoodlum? It was exactly the kind of cryptic clue that intrigued Dick Tracy, and it was reason enough for him to ask Chief Brandon to be assigned to the case.

Brandon's answer was as blunt as the cigar he was chewing.

"Forget it! We've got innocent people being murdered in this town. I'm not wasting my best investigator on a mob killing!"

Tracy wasn't flattered. His mouth was a grim line when he walked into the squad room, in sharp contrast to the ear-to-ear grin on the face of his friend Pat Patton, who greeted him with a happy outburst.

"I'm on the Curly hit," he said proudly. Pat was even newer in the Department than Tracy, and the assignment was like a benediction. Tracy didn't tell him about Brandon's low valuation of the case. He slapped Pat's shoulder and said: "Go get 'em, kid. And if you need any help, just give me a call."

That night, in Tess Trueheart's dining room, his lips were just as thinly delineated, despite the necessity of passing roast beef and baked potato between them. To her credit, Tess didn't press for explanations until it was time for coffee.

"It's nothing," Tracy said. "Just police business. Not worth talking about."

"I've got news for you," Tess answered dryly. "If I'm dating a cop, he'll have nothing *but* police business to talk about."

"Sorry," Tracy said, the mouth relaxing for the first time. Then he told her about Curly Mappe, and Tess watched him with her large blue eyes, but there was still puzzlement in them when Tracy stopped talking and concentrated on the apple pie.

"I wish I could understand," she said. "What makes this case so important to you?"

"I don't really know," Dick admitted grudgingly. "Maybe it was seeing that man's body. Or maybe it's just an intuition."

"Please," Tess said, sitting on his lap. "That word is reserved for women. You men have enough words that belong to you."

Yes, Dick Tracy was thinking. *Like . . . "Syndicate."*

He resisted the urge to query Pat Patton about his progress on the case for the next eight days. And the Chief was right, of course; there were more than enough homicide cases to keep Dick Tracy busy without worrying why an out-of-town hood was worth so many rounds of ammunition.

But on the ninth day, it was Pat himself who gave Tracy a report, and it was a gloomy one. They went to the Hawthorne Inn, Tracy's favorite spot because the bartender never looked injured when he ordered his usual seltzer-and-lime. Pat wasn't so abstemious; he downed a double shot of rye and said:

"I've got nothing, Dick. Nothing, nothing, nothing—not to mention absolutely nothing."

"What about our stoolies?" Tracy asked. "There must

be someone out there who can link Curly to a local gang.''

"No," Pat said, shaking his head. "They've never heard of the guy. He still had his training wheels on. He was too new in town to get himself a rep.''

"He was here long enough to get himself killed.''

"Maybe there was another motive, maybe it was an old grudge from another time and place . . . I'm standing in front of a stone wall, Dick, and I don't know where to go from here.''

"Just keep the file open and hope for the best," Tracy said encouragingly. "Sometimes all we can do is wait for a break.''

"What do I tell the Chief? If he asks how I'm doing?''

"I don't think he'll ask," Tracy said cynically.

Tracy wasn't sure why the idea hit him that night. It was after two A.M. when he arrived home from the South Side, from the scene of still another shootout, this time no mystery since both combatants managed to kill each other—all for the sake of a fifty-dollar debt. He fell across his bed and dropped into an exhausted sleep with his clothes on, and when he awoke, the idea was already in his head. He had it shaped and ready to fly by the time he fixed himself breakfast. Before he left the house, he dialed the number of a shoeshine parlor on Taylor Street. He was glad when the old man answered, not the son. He had good reason. The son was Dick Tracy's stoolie, and telephone conversations with him were something of an ordeal. He was known as Stuttering Stan.

He met Stan at their customary rendezvous point, the pre-Columbian room of the Art Institute, an unlikely place to run into underworld rats. Stan started complaining the moment they met. He didn't have anything for Tracy; he didn't know who hit Curly Mappe— Tracy stopped his stammering protest by banging both elbows on the table. Then he said:

"I don't need any information from you Stanley. I want *you* to give some information to the Boys.''

"M-m-m-me?" Stan said. "L-like what kind of—" He tried to say the word, but Tracy didn't wait.

"I want you to spread the news that Curly Mappe didn't die broke. There was an envelope on his body, an envelope containing ten thousand dollars in cold cash. And it was marked 'Boss.' Have you got that, Stanley?"

"B-b-b-b-b-b-b-Boss!" Stanley said triumphantly.

Tracy smiled.

It wasn't more than thirty-six hours before Pat Patton's phone rang, and the piping voice of a child said:

"You the bull handling the Curly Mappe case?"

"That's right, sonny," Pat said. "What can I do for you?"

"You can stop calling me 'sonny,' you—" He terminated the sentence with a string of expletives that burned up the detective's ears. Then he demanded that Pat meet him at a nearby diner.

Pat, sitting with an empty folder marked MAPPE, had to oblige. He went to the Loop Diner and looked down a row of empty booths. Then he finally realized that one booth was occupied, by a man whose head barely reached the top of the table. His face was all scowl when Pat slipped into the opposite booth, and the midget identified himself.

"They call me Little Buttons," he said, lighting a cigar. "I work for Spats Minifee, you know him?"

It was like asking a priest if he knew who the Pope was.

"Of course I know Spats," Pat said grimly. "How many suits does he own now? A hundred, two hundred?"

Little Buttons ignored the question. "This guy Curly worked for Spats, too," he said. "He just hired him about three weeks ago, as a rent collector. There was any dough on the guy, it belongs to the Minifee Real Estate Company. How soon can we pick it up?"

Pat, not having attended the meeting at the Art Institute, was completely baffled. He was even more perplexed when he saw Dick Tracy strolling into the diner. He grinned amiably at Pat, acting as if the meeting was sheer coincidence. He offered his hand to the midget when Pat introduced them, but Little Buttons jammed his tiny mitts into the pockets of his camel's-hair coat and said:

"We want the ten grand! It belongs to us!"

Dick gave him a toothy grin. "Why didn't you take it from the body when Curly was shot?"

"We had nothing to do with that!" the midget screeched, rage turning his little face as purple as a plum. "The guy was just a collector! We wouldn't waste ammo on a nobody!"

"Come on, Buttons," Tracy said smoothly. "Tell us the truth. We know Spats's real estate company is just a front for his protection racket. What did Curly do? Hold out on him? Skim some off the top?"

"You can't prove nothing against Spats!" the midget said fiercely. "Just try it!"

"And can you prove that ten grand belonged to him?" Dick said, grinning back.

Little Buttons looked daggers between the two police officers, and then a light went on in his eyes brighter than the glowing tip of his cigar.

"I get it," he said. "This is all a gag. There wasn't any money in Curly's pocket. It's your idea of a practical joke."

"Practical is the word," Dick Tracy said.

After Little Buttons had stormed out of the diner, Tracy looked at Pat and saw that his friend wasn't entirely pleased with the sudden developments.

"I guess I should have told you about it," Tracy said, a bit shamefaced. "I just thought a rumor about unclaimed funds was a good way of flushing out the truth about Curly's connection."

"Okay," Pat said sullenly. "So now we know Curly worked for Spats. What makes you think we can pin it on him?"

"It's a starting point, right? You said you were facing a stone wall, Pat, I just wanted to get you by it."

"Right," Pat said. "Which means my next step is paying a call on Spats himself." He frowned and answered the question Dick Tracy hadn't asked yet. "No," he said flatly. "You don't have to go with me. I'll handle this alone."

Tracy brought another worried face to Tess's dinner table that night, but this time his concern was for his friend. He knew Pat could handle himself; if anything, his bravery bordered on the foolhardy.

"I've heard of Spats Minifee," Tess said. "But isn't he one of those 'legitimate' criminals?"

"Meaning he's barricaded himself behind a lot of 'legitimate' enterprises," Tracy said bitterly. "He owns laundries, movie houses, a brickworks. He operates a hotel on the West Side, and he's a slum landlord . . . But he finances all his companies with money from the rackets. At least, what he doesn't spend on clothes."

"Then it's true what they write about him? In the Sunday newspaper sections?"

"I don't read that stuff," Tracy said.

"They say he has the biggest wardrobe in the country. That he's the best-dressed gangster in the world." She laughed. "Just like Natty Bumpof."

"Who?"

"I see you don't read the Sunday funnies, either."

The phone rang jarringly, and Tess picked it up. When the roses faded quickly from her cheeks, Tracy knew the call was bad news, and his instincts told him it had something to do with Pat Patton. She handed him the receiver, and he listened grimly to the report from German Deaconess Hospital.

"No bones broken," Chief Brandon told him. "Just a mild concussion and enough bruises to keep him out of action for the next two weeks."

"Can we nail Spats for this?"

"It doesn't sound like it. Pat was heading for his car

after seeing Spats when two guys jumped him and dragged him into the alley. I'm sure they were Minifee's muscle, but how do we prove it?''

Dick felt sick, and not a little guilty.

"I want this case, Chief," he said. "Maybe this is our chance to change Spats's wardrobe to striped suits.''

He held his breath until Brandon gave his reply.

"You got it," the Chief said.

Spats Minifee's apartment was in the Lakefront's newest luxury building, and from the moment he was admitted, Dick Tracy knew that someone else's taste had been responsible for the decor. It was an Art Deco museum, its furniture by Ruhlmann, its glass by Lalique, its walls and windows by Erté. But its most decorative item was the statuesque brunette who had her long limbs stretched out on a twelve-foot white sofa. Tracy could only blink at her twice before Spats himself made his appearance, gorgeously attired in a velvet smoking jacket. There was so much padding in it that Dick wondered how much of Spats Minifee really filled out his famous suits.

"Sorry to hear about your friend," Spats said, smoothing back his patent-leather hair. "I understand he got roughed up a little yesterday, after we had our chat.''

"He was cute, too," the woman said from the sofa as she manicured her nails. It earned her a murderous look, but Spats introduced her anyway, obviously proud of his acquisition. "Jet Adore," he said, boastfully. "Maybe you've seen her on stage.''

"I don't go to strip shows," Dick said, smiling thinly. "I just came by to find out what you told Detective Patton, since his vocal cords aren't working so well at the moment.''

"What could I tell him?" Spats said, fixing himself a drink. "I don't know anything about Curly's murder, and I didn't have anything to do with your buddy's beating. You want me to prove it?''

He pushed a button on the bar, and two men entered the room. They were both well over six feet, with barn-door shoulders that didn't require any padding.

"These are my associates," Spats said. "Danny G. and Willie D. They were with me when your cop buddy was here, and we all played a little poker after he left. Satisfied?"

"Spats," Dick Tracy said cordially, "I'm not going to be satisfied until you and all your plug-uglies are playing poker in the Big House."

Spats's thin little face went dark. "All right, copper," he said with a snarl. "You've made your little speech. Now why don't you take yourself and that cheap suit of yours out of here?"

"I think he looks terrific," Jet Adore said, giving Tracy a sultry look over her nail buffer. "He looks better in a cheap suit than you look in your expensive ones."

The explosion came so suddenly that Tracy had no time to react. Spats sprang across the room and his hand slammed against the woman's face with the force of a triphammer. She shrieked as blood spurted from her nose and encrimsoned the white sofa, a desecration that seemed to anger Spats even more. He started using his fists, but by then Tracy was on him, twisting Spats's arms behind him like velvet pretzels. Spats screamed out a wordless command, and Tracy found himself pressed between two snub-nosed revolvers, icy cold on both temples.

"Now get out of here!" Spats added, panting. "And next time you want to see me, Tracy, you better have a warrant!"

"You can bet your silk underwear on it," Dick Tracy said.

He knew it was only bravado. Legitimate warrants for crime bosses like Minifee were getting to be as rare as the Magna Carta. The underworld kingpins had developed the processes of legal immunity into a fine art.

Tracy and Tess visited Pat at the hospital the next day,

and found him improving slowly. His bruised throat only allowed him to emit a few croaks, but Tracy knew he meant them to be encouraging. It didn't make much difference in Tracy's mood. That night, he sat alone in his living room, hoping that Jack Benny's jokes would cheer him up, but the effect was negligible. The phone rang on the final punch line, but the caller was even more of a surprise.

"Detective Tracy?" the woman's voice said. "This is Jet Adore. Remember me?"

Ten minutes later, Tracy was on his way back to the Lakefront, this time to Jet Adore's own apartment in a residential hotel called the Prince Albert, owned by Minifee Management. He didn't even speculate about why Spats's mistress had invited him there. He simply hoped that her bloodied nose might have inspired her to disclose some useful information. What was that old quotation about a woman scorned? How about a woman socked?

The apartment wasn't big. It was a small suite, with a cramped living room, a smaller bedroom, and a kitchen whose stove had probably never been lit. The drinks and sandwiches she offered Tracy were obviously from hotel room service, but Jet Adore served them wearing nothing more than a thin houserobe with a fluffy ermine collar and cuffs. The robe seemed to have only one button, strategically placed, but the effect was still disturbing to a masculine eye. Tracy began to wonder if it was deduction or seduction that had brought him here.

"You were so terrific this afternoon!" Jet Adore said. "I mean, nobody's ever stood up for me like you did. They're all too afraid of that bozo Spats!"

"I'm a cop," Tracy said. "I can't stand around and watch people get beaten up."

"Still, it was like . . . chivalry! You know what I mean? That's why I thought I should find some way to thank you." Her voice hardened, and she touched her bruised nose. "And to pay that bozo back. Pay him back good!"

Tracy tried to hide his elation. He nibbled at a finger sandwich and tried to sound casual.

"Did you ever hear Spats mention Curly Mappe?"

"Are you kidding? That was all I heard about! Curly this, Curly that. And why? All because the guy was *nice* to me. All because he held the *door* for me. All because he gave me one little kiss when we all got drunk one night . . ."

"Wait a minute," Tracy said. "Are you saying Spats was jealous of Curly?"

A tear glinted in the corner of Jet Adore's eye. "He was crazy about me," she said. "Of course, he couldn't do anything about it, since Spats was paying his salary and all that. But he really loved me! He even gave me a picture of him . . . See?" She reached into the drawer of an end table and took out a silver frame. But to Tracy's surprise, the portrait of Curly Mappe wasn't a photograph. It was a pen-and-ink drawing, a caricature in the manner of comic-strip art. Tracy was no connoisseur of the medium, but the style looked familiar, and so did the initials of the artist at the base of the drawing: D.L.S.

"Who did this?" he asked. "It looks familiar."

"Of course it does," Jet said, taking the picture back and regarding it lovingly. "It was done by that famous cartoonist. You know, the one who draws *Ace Adams*. I forget him name."

"Shecter," Tracy said. "Doug Shecter. Only why did he make the drawing? Did Curly ever tell you?"

"No," the woman said. "I guess he was just a friend of his." She tried to take the portrait out of Tracy's hand, but he held on to it, puzzled by the peculiar inking of the dead hoodlum's curls. "Give it back," Jet said protestingly. "It's all I've got to remember him by."

Tracy handed her the picture, and she replaced it carefully in the drawer.

"You're pretty sentimental," he said.

"You bet I am," Jet Adore said. The she slipped a white arm around Tracy's neck and pushed her sizeable bosom against him. "Of course, I don't like to overdo it."

To Tracy's relief, the doorbell rang. Jet answered it, first checking out the peephole. The person outside didn't appear to be any Spats-related threat, because she slipped off the chain and opened the door. When Tracy heard the familiar voice, he could feel the blood draining from his face all the way down to his socks.

"My name is Tess Trueheart," the voice said. "I had a message to meet Detective Tracy here . . ."

"A *message*?" Jet said. "From who?"

"I really don't know," Tess said hesitantly, and for one wild moment Tracy thought of ducking into a closet. Then he reconsidered it on the grounds of dignity, and stood up.

"I'm here, Tess," he said, aware that his blood supply had decided to rush back upstairs. He felt the hot blush on his cheeks, and obviously Tess saw it, like a bright flag of embarrassment.

"Dick," she said softly. Then she looked at Jet Adore, whose single button had somehow parted from its buttonhole. Without another word, she turned and left.

"Tess, wait!" Tracy shouted. He tried to get past Jet, who grabbed his elbow and stammered something about not sending any "message" to anybody—she just didn't understand! But Tracy was more interested in catching up with his girl than hearing Jet's denials of guilt. He pushed her away and went out into the hall, racing down the corridor, but only in time to see the elevator doors close on Tess's stony expression.

Tracy groaned, and leaned against the wall. He tried to think about where he was and how he had gotten there. He was sure that no one at Headquarters knew of his visit to Jet Adore's hotel; what he didn't know was whether or not Jet herself had mentioned the fact to anyone. But what was the point of summoning Tess there? Was it only some kind of malicious prank?

Then he remembered the words "practical joke." Was this Little Buttons's way of paying him back?

The sound of a gunshot ended his speculation.

It was a loud, unmistakable sound that Dick Tracy had heard far too often in his lifetime, and it had come from the other end of the corridor, perhaps behind the closed door of Jet's suite. Tracy hurried back and seized the knob, but the door was locked. He didn't wait another fraction of a second to lift his right foot and smash his heel against the lock, snapping it on the first try. The door flew open and Tracy crashed into the room, hoping that it was nothing more serious than an accidental firing causing no bodily harm, rejecting the idea that Jet had tried to take her own life . . . When he saw her crumpled body on the carpet, his hopes were dashed. As soon as he lifted her, the bloodsoaked robe falling away to reveal the gaping wound in her chest, he knew that Jet Adore had breathed her last. He looked around for the smoking gun that had been responsible, but there was nothing there. Nothing.

Jet Adore had been shot to death by an unknown assailant, while Detective Dick Tracy stood right outside her one and only door.

It was a staggering realization, an unacceptable one. He drew in his breath and made a hasty search of the apartment, opening every closet door, even opening the windows that looked out upon a view of the lakefront from a height of nineteen stories. It was an impossible crime, but "impossible" wasn't a word in the police manual Dick Tracy knew by heart. There was only one explanation, and he simply had to accept it. Tracy had been so preoccupied with his personal problems that he had allowed a clever killer to make a swift, successful escape.

He picked up the telephone. Even as he dialed Headquarters, he was visualizing the screamer headlines in tomorrow's newspapers.

They proved to be as damning as he imagined them.

The *News* was the least offensive, but it was bad enough. It read:

GANGLAND MISTRESS SLAIN; HOMICIDE DETECTIVE FAILS TO SPOT KILLER.

The *Tribune* took a deeper bite out of his hide.

STRIP QUEEN SHOT TO DEATH WHILE DETECTIVE STANDS BY HELPLESSLY.

The *Post* couldn't resist carrying the story right to its editorial page.

> *With our city in a state of siege, with gang wars raging all around us claiming innocent victims, can our Police Department afford officers who can't seem to function without Seeing Eye dogs?*

The Commissioner himself fired off an angry letter to the *Post* publisher, an old enemy both personal and political, and the rebuttal, citing Dick Tracy's outstanding record, dutifully appeared in a *Letter to the Editor* section that nobody ever read.

It was definitely a low point in Dick Tracy's career, and he wasn't allowed to forget it. The day after Jet Adore's death, an uncomfortable silence greeted him at Police Headquarters. But there was nothing "silent" about Chief Brandon's response. He called Tracy on the carpet and demanded to know how he could have been so derelict in his duty. Was he drunk? Was he too infatuated with Spats Minifee's beautiful mistress? When he told the Chief about Tess Trueheart's intrusion, the Chief's frown only deepened. Was that the reason? Was Tracy so preoccupied with his love life that he could let a killer slip by him without even tipping his hat?

"I'm sure I know *why* she was killed," Tracy said grimly. "I'm sure Spats was the one who ordered the hit.

Jet Adore was giving him the business, and his pride was hurt. I think he had Jet murdered for the same reason he had Curly Mappe blown apart.''

''Prove it,'' Brandon said, slapping the desk. ''That's all I'm asking of you guys. Don't give me theories. Give me facts!''

Tracy's dark day had two silver linings. One was the return of Pat Patton, released from the hospital with nothing but a sore throat to show for his injuries. And later that afternoon, his telephone rang, and Tess's sweet voice made his heart leap.

''I thought you might want to take me out to dinner,'' she said. ''Unless you've got other plans, of course.''

''I'd break a dinner date with FDR for you,'' Tracy said.

They went to McBride's, a new restaurant on Michigan, and the service proved to be like a Chinese fire drill. But it didn't matter; Tracy was too happy to see forgiveness and understanding in Tess's big blue eyes. He held both her hands and told her:

''Take my word for it. The call was strictly business. Jet Adore was trying to spike Spats Minifee's wheels, but it looks like Minifee got to her first.''

''I felt so awful when I read the newspaper stories,'' Tess said. ''I know it wasn't your fault, Dick, you're much too good a detective.''

''Thanks,'' Tracy said wryly. ''I'm afraid most of the world doesn't share your opinion. Including, for that matter, me.''

''But isn't it obvious that someone was *watching* that woman all the time? That someone *knew* you were with her? That's why they were able to get me over there! To make me jealous!''

''Were you?'' Tracy asked.

''You're darned right I was! But then I thought about it, and realized that you were set up for this, Dick—and so was I.''

''Just the same, that girl *was* murdered right under my

nose," Tracy said ruefully. "I can't deny that, Tess. And the worst thing is, I still can't explain it." He looked down miserably, just as a waiter deposited a dish of corned beef and cabbage in front of him, and slid away. "Wait a minute," Tracy said. "I ordered the roast beef!"

Tess laughed. "And I ordered the chicken. But this looks like veal shank to me."

"That dumb waiter," Tracy growled. He waved his arm in the air, but every eye seemed to be looking in other directions. Suddenly, he gave up the battle and stared into space with a blankness of expression that alarmed his companion.

"Dick, what is it? What's the matter?"

"Nothing," he said, still not focusing. "I just had a thought, that's all. Something that I have to check out." He rose suddenly and said: "Tess, would you mind? If I just excused myself for a little while? I'll catch the waiter on the way out and make sure he gets you your chicken."

"But where are you going? When will you be back?"

"With any luck, in time for my roast beef. And with an appetite for it!"

He kissed her on the cheek and hurried out into the street. There was a cab on the corner, and a stout lady already had the door opened when Tracy slid inside and pulled the door out of her hand.

"Sorry, ma'am," he said, lifting his hat. "Police business."

She said something unladylike, but Tracy didn't hear it. He was too busy directing the driver to the Prince Albert Hotel.

Brandon had assigned a patrolman to guard the murder scene, and fortunately it was a cop who knew Tracy well enough not to make a fuss about the unauthorized visit.

He let himself into Jet Adore's apartment, casting only one grim look at the chalked outline of the body on the living room floor. Then he went into the kitchen. Within thirty seconds, he found what he was looking for, examined it, and made his determination of feasibility.

Then, with his heart pounding like a drum in a victory parade, he picked up the phone and called Chief Brandon's home telephone number.

Brandon didn't sound happy to be interrupted. Fred Allen was on the air, and the Chief would rather have missed a meal than ''Allen's Alley.'' But he could detect the excitement in Tracy's voice, so he gruffly agreed to meet him at the murder scene.

He regretted it the moment Tracy explained his theory, and showed him the small door in the kitchen wall that concealed a dumbwaiter.

''It's not in use anymore,'' Tracy said. ''I spoke to the hotel manager, and he told me that it dates back to the beginning of the century, when the Prince Albert used to send up meals to its guests from the kitchen. Most of the dumbwaiter doors have been sealed shut, but as you can see—this one works fine!''

''Why *this* one?'' the Chief growled.

''Because Spats Minifee owns the joint,'' Tracy said. ''Because he *wanted* this one to work.''

He opened the door, and the Chief shook his head so hard that the cigar in his mouth jiggled from side to side.

''You're nuts,'' he said flatly. ''Nobody could ride in that thing, not even a contortionist!''

''How about a midget?'' Tracy grinned.

He called McBride's to apologize to Tess, but there was no way he was going to finish their dinner that evening. He had an arrest to make, he said and he was going to enjoy making it.

But the apprehension of Little Buttons proved more complicated than Tracy assumed. He knew the little man's hangouts; they were on the record. His favorite nightspot was a billiard parlor called Vic's on South Ashland Avenue, where Little Buttons stood on a stool and trounced every opponent with the deadly accuracy of his scaled-down cuestick. Little Buttons loved that custom-made stick, but the moment he saw Dick Tracy and Pat Patton enter Vic's waving the warrant for his arrest, he flung it at them like a javelin and made them duck, affording him just enough time to scramble under the table into a forest of human legs. Both Tracy and Pat were startled; they hadn't expected Little Buttons to resist arrest. Even though it was further proof of his guilt, they were still dismayed to be involved in an unexpected pursuit.

The midget mobster turned out to be as cunning as a hunted fox. He was out the back door of Vic's before the detectives could grab him, and on the street his undersized form was hard to follow in the bustling crowd. Suddenly, there was no further sight of him, until Tracy realized that Little Buttons had decided to take to the vertical.

"There he goes!" Tracy yelled, pointing to the stairs of the elevated station.

"Look at him move," Pat said, almost admiringly.

Little Buttons was, indeed, proving his athletic abilities, his short legs pumping like a machine as he ascended the stairs, well ahead of his pursuers. Tracy and Patton were panting by the time they reached the upper level and leaped over the turnstiles, Pat waving his badge at the change-booth attendant. They could hear a train approaching—two of them, in fact, one from each direction—but there was no sign of Little Buttons.

Then Tracy realized what the escape plan was. Little Buttons had hopped down onto the track itself, and was crossing it nimbly to the other side. If he made it, he would have no problem boarding the uptown-bound train, debarking at the next local stop, and leaving his pursuers in the dust. They could almost hear the little man's high-pitched cackle of triumph.

But if Little Buttons was making gleeful noises, they soon became squeals of terror. From the edge of the platform, Tracy and Pat looked on in horror as they saw the midget on the other side, trying desperately to climb to safety. It was no more than six feet away, but Little Buttons was only four feet tall. His outstretched arms were only inches too short. His tiny fingers groped help-lessly for purchase on the concrete. He bounced up and down with all his might, but to no avail. They saw him turn his frightened face toward the oncoming train, but the motorman had seen this bizarre obstruction too late. The screech of his brakes wasn't as loud as Little Buttons's screech of fear as he ran back towards the down-town platform, hoping to find a place of refuge between the two trains.

No one prayed harder for his success than the detec-tives who watched the grim drama. For one thing, they both knew that Little Buttons's testimony would be vital if they were going to nail the real killer of Jet Adore, the crime boss who had hired him as an assassin.

But the little man had miscalculated again. There was only one place to go, and it was just as deadly. He stepped directly onto the electrified third rail. There was an awesome flash of white sparks, a terrible crackle, and a scream that no one heard over the roar of train wheels . . .

Tracy felt no sense of satisfaction as he went about the business of making up his homicide report. With his usual diligence, he returned to the Prince Albert Hotel to obtain testimony from the kitchen employees as to how Little Buttons employed the obsolete elevator system to murder Spats Minifee's mistress. He went back into the suite itself and had the dumbwaiter dusted, certain that he would find the killer's tiny fingerprints. Just before he left, he made a final desultory check of the living room, looking into closets, opening drawers.

It was then he realized that something was missing.

It was Curly Mappe's portrait—the cartoon caricature drawn by Doug Shecter.

Little Buttons hadn't only committed the crime of murder. He was also a thief.

But why?

What was so significant about the drawing of a dead man?

It was one of those puzzles that kept Dick Tracy awake half the night. When he arose groggily the next morning, he could think of only two people who might supply him with the answer. One was Spats Minifee. The other was the cartoonist himself.

Assuming he would fare better with the latter, Tracy looked up Doug Shecter's address. It turned out to be a three-story brownstone on Pine Grove Avenue. It was a fine residential street (the late criminal florist, Dion O'Bannion, had lived there) but Tracy soon discovered that Shecter's home was also his place of business.

A young man with hornrimmed glasses and ink-stained fingers answered the door. He seemed unnerved when Dick Tracy flashed his gold badge, so Tracy gave him a friendly smile to go with it and asked for his name.

"Joe Higgins," he said. "I work for Mr. Shecter. Is there any problem?"

"Just routine," Tracy said.

Higgins led the detective past a front room that had been converted into a studio; Tracy saw drawing boards and filing cabinets and three other young men, two of them in shirtsleeves. The other one, a thick-necked type in need of a shave, wore a suit, and didn't seem preoccupied with his work.

There was a small elevator that led to Doug Shecter's private quarters on the top floor. It was just big enough for two, and slow enough to allow Tracy to ask a few questions.

"Just what is it you do here, Mr. Higgins?"

"Me? I'm an inker."

"And what does an 'inker' do?" Tracy said, grinning as he realized he sounded like Jimmy Durante.

"I do *Ace Adams, Crime Buster.*"

"I thought Mr. Shecter did that."

"Mr. Shecter draws the strip in pencil, and then I do the inking. We also have somebody else who does the lettering. His name is Phil Bodoni."

"Quite a little factory operation, isn't it?"

A minute later, he was in the presence of the cartoonist himself, who proved to be a surprise. Tracy didn't follow the feature, but he knew that the *Ace Adams* strip was a hard-nosed detective story, reflecting the violence of the times. But the pudgy, soft-featured man responsible looked more like a country storekeeper than the creator of crime melodrama.

When they shook hands, Shecter's palm felt cold and sweaty, and the fingers trembled. No wonder he needed someone else to do his inking.

"I know quite a few detectives," the cartoonist said, trying to maintain a smile. "The police have been very helpful in my research on the strip. But I don't think we've ever met, Mr. Tracy."

"Well, I'm doing a little research myself, Mr. Shecter. And I was wondering if you ever met a man named William Mappe, also known as 'Curly.' "

Shecter's paper-white complexion became a shade lighter.

"Well, yes. I did know the man. Slightly."

"How did you meet?"

Shecter's small hands fumbled among the objects on the tabouret beside him, pencils and paper clips, bits of kneaded erasers. The nervous movements didn't escape Tracy's attention.

"He was a fan of the strip," the cartoonist said. "He used to visit me often, to talk about it. I try to be polite to the fans, you know. I wouldn't be in business without them."

"Yes, of course," Tracy said. "And do you also do drawings of the fans, when they request them?"

"I have, on occasion. I did one for Mr. Mappe, actually."

"I'm sure you're aware that Mr. Mappe is no longer among the living?"

"Yes," Shecter said. "I was shocked when I read about it. I'm not really fond of violence, Mr. Tracy, no matter what you might see in my work. It's all make-believe for me. It has nothing to do with real life, nothing at all!''

His voice rose into a contralto, suggesting that the issue was important to him. But his agitation subsided into apathy when the elevator door opened, and the bull-necked young man stepped into the hallway and interrupted them.

''Just reminding you of your appointment, Mr. Shecter.''

''Yes, that's right,'' Shecter said. ''It's almost time for my appointment, isn't it? I'll be right down, Arnold.''

''I'll have the car out front in five minutes.''

''Thank you, Arnold.''

The cartoonist started to rise, but Tracy put a hand on his arm.

''Just one more question, Mr. Shecter. Would you do a drawing of me, too?''

''What?''

''I admired the other portrait you made. I especially liked the way you did his hair. Couldn't you do a quick sketch, right now?''

Shecter glanced at the bull-necked man, whose neck seemed to be getting fuller and redder by the second. Then he glanced quickly at his watch, and said:

''I still have a few minutes, don't I, Arnold? Just a few minutes, that's all it'll take.'' He managed another smile. ''We have to be nice to our friends in the police department, don't we?''

He picked up a drawing pad, and then dipped a fine-pointed brush into an ink bottle. With swift, assured strokes, he captured Dick Tracy's sharply-delineated profile, the aquiline nose, the square jaw, the tight but good-humored line of his mouth. He put Tracy's hat on his head, even though it was now in Tracy's lap. He turned up the collar of his trenchcoat, and scribbled a pattern on his tie. Then he signed it with a flourish: ''D.L.S.'' The whole process hadn't taken more than three minutes.

"There!" Doug Shecter said, ripping the page out of the pad. "It's all yours, Detective! I hope you like it."

"If it's anything like the other one," Tracy said significantly, "I'm sure I will."

When Pat Patton arrived at headquarters that afternoon, he found his friend at his desk, staring at a cartoon caricature. He went up behind him, but Tracy didn't even seem to notice his presence.

"What is this?" Pat asked. "Narcissus time?"

"It's a clue," Tracy answered. "It may be a key to the whole Curly Mappe case."

"How about letting a pal in on it?"

Tracy swiveled his chair about and looked up at him.

"You remember the drawing I told you about, the sketch of Curly made by the cartoonist? When Jet Adore showed it to me, I noticed something peculiar about it, something that I couldn't quite figure out. It had to do with the way the hair was rendered."

"What was it?"

"I can't be absolutely sure, of course, since the drawing is gone, probably destroyed by Little Buttons. But I have the feeling that Doug Shecter wasn't only drawing 'curls.' He was drawing a *message* in Curly Mappe's hair!"

"A message? Saying what?"

"Probably the same thing he wrote in this drawing of *me*."

He handed Pat the drawing and smiled as Pat studied it, scratching his head.

"I don't see anything!"

"Because you're not looking hard enough. I'll give you a hint," Tracy said. "Turn it upside down. And take a good long look at the tie I'm wearing."

Pat turned the drawing at several angles, and finally it dawned on him.

"He's scribbled something into the design! It's the word 'HELP'!"

"That's right." Dick Tracy grinned. "Shecter understood exactly what I asked him to do, to convey the same idea to me that he put into the drawing of Curly. The man is in trouble, Pat!''

''But what kind of trouble? Why didn't he just tell you about it? Why didn't he just call the cops?''

''I don't know. But it's obvious that he's afraid to make a public cry for help. All he can do is hint about it! That's what he did, right in his drawing . . . Pat, didn't you once tell me you had a friend at the *Daily News*?''

''Sure, I do. Simey Wilson, the features editor.''

''Great,'' Tracy said. ''Then do me a favor right now. Call your friend Wilson, and ask him to send over the last eight, nine, ten weeks of the *Ace Adams* comic strip. And I mean pronto!''

Tess in the kitchen, cutting up salad greens, was determined to make this the best dinner she had ever prepared for Dick Tracy. She still felt guilty about her lack of faith in him, and she was also aware of the disappointment he was feeling in his failure to wind up the Curly Mappe case. When her doorbell rang, a good hour earlier than expected, she was flustered and irritated, especially since her hair was a mess and there was biscuit flour all over her face and hands. She was about to launch her complaints, when Dick stopped her mouth with a crushing kiss that was more celebratory than amorous.

''Wait till you hear this!'' Tracy said. ''I could have had this case solved a month ago, if I had only listened to you!''

''To *me*?'' Tess said, astonished.

''Yes! It was only when I was looking at a bunch of Sunday comics that I remembered what you said to me, the day Pat went to see Spats Minifee and ended up in the hospital. You mentioned somebody named 'Natty Bumpof'!''

''But I thought almost everybody knew Natty Bumpof!''

''I didn't,'' Tracy said wryly. ''Maybe if I had, I would

have made the connection. Jet Adore might still be alive, and Little Buttons might be serving time in the Big House. Or the Little House—if that's where they put midgets who go up the river.''

"Dick Tracy, I have *no* idea what you're babbling about!''

"Then look at these!''

He had a manila envelope with him, and he withdrew a stack of tearsheets from the Sunday funnies section of the *News*. They were all front-page adventures of *Ace Adams, Crime Buster*, and featured prominently in many of the bright-colored panels was a man dressed in a double-breasted suit with exaggerated shoulders and wide lapels. There was a neatly-folded handkerchief in his breast pocket and a carnation in his buttonhole. When he was depicted in shirtsleeves the shirt cuffs were French with gleaming links, and the left breast pocket was neatly monogrammed NB.

"Natty Bumpof!'' Tracy said. "The racket boss Ace Adams is trying to stop, and having a hard time doing it!''

"I know,'' Tess said. "The man is really very smooth. Did you see the one about his wardrobe?'' She flipped through the sheets until she found it. "There it is! Natty is showing his girlfriend how many suits he has—so many that he had to rent an apartment next door, just for his clothes!'' Tess laughed. "Of course, everybody knows that Natty Bumpof is modeled after your friend Spats.''

"That's right,'' Tracy said with a tight grin. "Everybody knows that, especially the crooks and tinhorns who do business with Spats Minifee. He must have been very flattered—especially since Natty keeps getting the better of that idiot Ace Adams!''

"He *has* been getting the better of him,'' Tess said thoughtfully. "But that's only temporary, of course. In the end, Ace Adams will win. I mean, he always does, doesn't he?''

"Maybe this story is an exception to the rule. Maybe

this is the comic strip which is going to prove that crime *does* pay!''

Tess looked at him without comprehension, but Tracy put his arms around her waist and drew her close. Then he said:

''I hate to do this to you, Tess, but—could we make that dinner some other night?''

''Of course,'' Tess sweetly. ''I've only been preparing it since early this morning. Don't give it another thought.''

''I knew you'd understand,'' Dick Tracy said.

He arrived at Doug Shecter's brownstone just as the staff was preparing to leave for the night. Joe Higgins was slipping his ink-stained fingers into a pair of gloves—the weather was turning colder—and the lettering man, Phil, was on the phone, confirming a date. The man with the bull neck was tying a woolly scarf around it, and when he saw Dick Tracy at the door, he frowned and tried to pass him by.

''Just wait a few moments,'' Tracy said amiably. ''I've wanted to talk to you boys for some time. I'm really interested in the work you do for Mr. Shecter.''

''But I told you what I do,'' Higgins said. ''I ink in the pencil drawings he makes.''

''My job's pretty easy to describe,'' Phil Bodoni said. ''Mr. Shecter writes the dialogue for the balloons, and I letter them in.''

Tracy smiled at the third man.

''And what do you do exactly—is it Arnold?''

''Yes,'' the man said gruffly. ''My name is Arnold. And I'm kind of like a business manager.''

''I see,'' Tracy said. ''And I guess that explains why you always wear a suit. So you can carry your 'business' equipment wherever you go.''

His hand darted out suddenly and dived into Arnold's left breast pocket. Arnold cried out a protest, but it was cut short when Tracy's hand emerged clutching a small revolver.

"You're not going to need this anymore, Arnold," Tracy said with a humorless grin. "Because you're through intimidating Doug Shecter—and so is your boss."

He couldn't see Arnold's thick neck under the woolen muffler, but he was sure that it was brick red.

Tracy noticed that the neck of Danny G. was also formidable. When Spats Minifee's bodyguard answered the door, he gave Tracy his patented deadeye look, meant to convey the idea that the visit wasn't welcome. Tracy didn't even bother to flash his gold badge. He simply nodded pleasantly and walked by him, almost hoping that he would try to stop him. Danny G. must have respected his audacity. He didn't move one of his many muscles.

The door to Spats's bedroom was open, and Tracy could hear a one-sided conversation that indicated a telephone call. Tracy breezed inside and saw Spats in his underwear, reflected in three mirrors of his dressing room, and it was all he could do to keep from laughing out loud. Because Jet Adore had been right. Without the padded shoulders, the double-breasted suits, the custom-made shirts, the built-up heels, there was almost no recognizing Spats. He was hardly more than five foot five; his shoulders were like wire coathangers; his ribcage was bony and his legs were pipe racks. He was a perfect illustration of the old adage that clothes make the man. In the case of Spats Minifee, there wasn't much man without them.

"What the hell are you doing here?" he snarled, slamming down the receiver. "Who the hell let you in here, Tracy?"

"Why, I thought your door was always open, Spats."

"Not to you, copper! Now get out of here before I have you thrown out!"

"You don't want to do that," Tracy said, holding up

a large manila envelope. "I'm sure you'd like to see this, since it concerns a very good friend of yours."

"What friend?" Spats said suspiciously. "What kind of game are you playing now, Tracy?"

"I'm talking about your personal hero—Natty Bumpof. You know who he is, don't you?"

"I've heard the name," Spats said gruffly, reaching for his robe. "It's that comic-strip character, in the Sunday paper."

"Not just any old character, however. Everybody seems to think it's *you*, Spats. He looks like you, talks like you, dresses like you. He's been giving poor old Ace Adams a bad time, too. People tell me there hasn't been such a *successful* villain as Natty Bumpof in the history of the comic strip. How do you feel about that?"

"How should I feel? It makes no difference to me."

"Oh, good," Dick Tracy said. "Then this strip that's running next Sunday won't make any difference either."

He held out the page, and Spats hesitated before snatching it from his hands. His eyes grew wider and wider as he moved through each panel until he reached the final, cataclysmic denouement. Then the long fuse of his temper reached the explosive point.

"What the hell is this! He's gunned down! Ace Adams shoots Natty—and in his underwear!"

"Quite a coincidence, isn't it?" Dick Tracy grinned. "Of course, he has good reason to shoot, since Natty is firing at him. But you know Ace—he always gets his man."

Spats pulled the robe around him, his eyes blazing.

"It stinks!" he said gratingly. "He's made Natty look like a bum—a cheap little hoodlum! And in his underwear! He can't do that, understand? This strip will never run, not if I have to buy the whole damned newspaper!"

"I'm afraid that won't be possible," Tracy said. "You see, you're going to be too busy for that, Spats. You'll be too busy talking to lawyers and judges and people like that."

He took a folded document out of the same envelope and dangled it in front of him, waving it like a small battle flag.

"Here's that paper you never thought you'd see, Spats. It's a warrant for your arrest. The charges are extortion, blackmail, and—oh, yes—murder. Now pick out your best suit. You'll want to look real nice for the police photographer."

"Can you imagine the *ego* of the guy?" Pat Patton said wonderingly. "To intimidate a cartoonist, just to make himself look good in the funny papers?"

Tess cut him a second slice of blueberry pie, not waiting for him to ask. "What I'd like to know is, why did Doug Shecter let him get away with it for so long? He could have called the police!"

"He was a frightened man," Dick Tracy said, "but not just for himself. Shecter has a sick wife at home; Spats threatened to do her harm if he didn't make Natty Bumpof a hero instead of a bum."

"So that was Curly Mappe's first job with the gang," Pat said. "To keep Shecter in line at his studio, to make sure that the strip went the way Spats Minifee wanted it to go."

"Right," Tracy said. "But unfortunately, Spats's lady friend liked Curly's curls too much, and Spats had him rubbed out. And when Jet Adore decided to talk to me, Spats had *her* taken care of, too." He took Tess's hand and said: "That night at the Prince Albert Hotel—it wasn't just a 'practical joke' that made Little Buttons call you, Tess. He wanted to get me out of there before Jet Adore said anything incriminating about his boss. Then he made sure she wouldn't be able to talk to me again . . ."

"There's still one thing I don't understand," Pat said. "This whole thing started because of that word we found in Curly Mappe's pocket. What does the *Syndicate* have to do with this case?"

Tracy chuckled.

"Nothing," he said. "Absolutely nothing. Shecter told me that his boss at the newspaper was complaining about the way the strip was going. He said it was time for Ace Adams to pull the plug on Natty Bumpof. So Spats sent Curly to talk to the guy, to lean on him if necessary. All Curly Mappe had in his pocket was an address—of the Daily News Syndicate. Boy!" Dick Tracy said. "Anybody who can bake a blueberry pie like this ought to be married! How about it?"

"I thought you'd never ask," Tess Trueheart said.

DICK TRACY GOES HOLLYWOOD

by
Ron Goulart

Neither one of them likes to talk about this particular case.

Tracy because he had no jurisdiction out there and shouldn't have been solving a murder or shooting up gangsters. Hix because he prefers to recount biographical anecdotes in which he's the undisputed star.

It happened in Southern California back in 1941, in the summer just before America entered World War II. Hix was putting in time in the Writers Department at the Lugom Brothers Studio in Burbank, and Dick Tracy was on the lot consulting on the movie Lugom was making based on one of his most famous police cases.

Hix it was who discovered the body. That happened because he hadn't written the Tracy script.

It commenced at the tail end of a hot, sultry Tuesday in August. Hix was pacing the small office of his current scriptwriting partner. Hix was a moderate-sized man, compact, in his early thirties. His dark, crinkly hair seemed to have a life of its own, crackling and fluttering

as he strode back and forth across a narrow patch of
worn, dirt-colored linoleum.

"A major injustice," he was saying to the fresh-faced
Mac Snilloc, a novice scriptwriter recently arrived from
the Midwest, where he'd been a moderately successful
novelist. "Nope, make that two injustices—or at least a
major injustice and a half. First the halfwit Lugom Brothers didn't hire me to pen the initial script of *The Dick
Tracy Story*. A dumb move, followed by the latest news
that they intend to pass me over for the rewrite, too. Now
if—"

"Hix," put in his sandy-haired partner, "the matter
at hand is"—Snilloc tapped the battered portable typewriter sitting before him on his lame desk—"the three
remaining scenes we need so we can finish this *The
Gringo Kid Rides Again* script."

"Okay, the villain gets trapped in a sheep stampede."
Hix paused at the tiny room's only window to glower out
at the waning day. "Here's a chance for you to strut your
stuff by soloing on these scenes while I—"

"You used a stampede to end *Lightning Slim Rides
Again*."

Hix blinked. "In the Lightning Slim opus it was a
herd of *buffalo* that tromped the bad guy into the sod.
But here our fresh, clever variation involves *sheep*. A vast
difference, lad."

"It's not me who suggested you quit sticking the same
ending on all your Western scripts," reminded Snilloc.
"It's the head of the Story Department who—"

"Okay, okay. He falls off the railroad bridge."

"What railroad bridge?"

Hix was pacing again. "I should have had that damn
Tracy assignment in the first place. Somebody with my
fabled knowledge of criminology is perfect for this true
crimes stuff."

"I never knew you had any knowledge of—"

"Did I not write five Mr. Woo scripts over at Twen-
tieth? Not to mention three Ravens for RKO, two In-

spector Quick of Scotland Yards, a half a Charlie Chan
and three terrific scenes that got cut out of a Thin Man?''
Hix bounced a few times on his heels before returning
to his pacing. ''I also have a deep, thorough knowledge
of the particular case the Tracy flicker is based on. Somewhere in a shoebox I possess a wad of clippings about
that Redrum guy who—''

''There isn't any railroad.''

Cupping a hand to his ear, Hix inquired, ''Hm?''

''In the period that this Gringo Kid story takes place,
Hix, the railroad hadn't reached that far west.''

''Okay, instead of the bridge, it's a shack, and the bad
guy gets shot by his own men as he comes out of it. See,
he'd set up an ambush for the Kid and his saddle pardner,
Crusty. Irony is what that'll be, something dearly prized
by the sweaty, acne-dappled youths who flock to the
movie palaces to savor our sagas of the Old West whilst
consuming Crackerjacks—box and all.'' He suddenly
snapped his fingers. ''Lola. Yes, Lola Punip. Sure, she's
playing Tess Trueheart in this epic. She's not in the scenes
they're shooting today, but I know she's on the lot. Remember the cordial greeting she gave me in the commissary just this noon?''

''She threw you the finger, then—''

''You don't understand passion, lad. At least not as
practiced in Hollywood and environs. Nope, Lola and I
were, for six giddy weeks back in 1939 or thereabouts,
an item. And despite her good-natured kidding, she still
harbors a deep and abiding passion for me.''

''I read in the columns a couple weeks ago that she's
engaged to Tim Athens.''

''Naw, all publicity tripe,'' Hix assured him. ''In real
life Athens resides in a Malibu love nest with a lifeguard
from Oxnard.''

''Even so, she—''

''Why didn't I think of this earlier? I'll simply per-
suade the fair Lola to nudge Sam Lugom into getting me
the rewrite job on *The Dick Tracy Story*. I hear they can't

shoot the damn thing much beyond mañana unless they haul in a new writer.''

''Rodent,'' recalled his partner. ''Lola called you a rodent and a jerk. While she was making the obscene gesture, Hix.''

Hix pointed an accusing finger at the typewriter. ''You haven't been assimilating enough about the true nature of partnership from this script, my boy.'' Hix shook his head sadly. ''Crusty, the Kid's devoted and loyal saddle pal, would never remind him that a bimbo had recently dubbed him, even in jest, a rodent and a jerk.'' He moved to the doorway. ''Now, while you're doing a rough draft of that swell ambush stuff I just invented, I'll pay a cordial social call on Lola.'' He went lurching into the dim corridor.

Hix hustled across the twilight studio grounds, his frazzled hair crackling. A warm wind had started up and was rattling the palm trees along the wide roadway. A man in a gorilla suit came shambling by from the opposite direction, gorilla head tucked under his arm and an unlit cigar in his mouth.

''Got a light, Hix?''

''In a hurry.'' Fishing a matchbook out of a pocket of his maroon slacks, he tossed it to the shaggy actor. ''Keep 'em.''

''Only one match left.''

''Keep 'em anyway.'' Hix kicked up his pace.

A gaggle of nuns exited one of the sound stages. Two of them gave Hix the finger as he hurried by, another yelled, ''Where's my five bucks, Hix?''

''Payday,'' he promised, breaking into a trot.

Dusk was closing in as he neared the row of cottages that was his destination. All but one of the shingle-roofed little buildings was dark. But light showed at the curtained windows of Lola's place, radio music was spilling out into the approaching night.

Bounding up the three red-brick steps, Hix gave a few

polite whaps on the imitation oaken door with both fists. After a faint creak, the door swung open inward.

Hix frowned, hesitating on the threshold. ''The old open door business,'' he murmured. He'd used that most recently in *Mr. Woo Visits a Wax Museum.* ''Lola, honey? It's Hix, commonly known as the Bard of Burbank. You at home?''

The unseen radio went on playing a Count Basie tune.

Sniffing the air, Hix entered the parlor of the actress's cottage. ''Smell of gunpowder in the air,'' he observed, his frown deepening and his hair jiggling. ''Lola?''

Something crunched under his bright orange loafers as he entered the small combination bedroom and office beyond the parlor. Some sort of brownish crumbs.

The actress was sprawled on the white carpeting at the center of the room, facedown, her left hand clutching the leg of the low coffee table next to the wicker armchair she'd apparently been sitting in. Beside her on the floor lay a snubnosed .32 revolver.

The gun had been used on Lola. The right side of her head wasn't all there any longer. Her platinum-blonde hair was blackened, stained with blood.

Hix paused, took a deep breath. He circled the body, noticing that Lola was wearing a frilly white dressing gown and nothing else. He scowled at the scatter of stuff atop the coffee table—an empty coffee cup, a small glass cat, a menu from the restaurant Lola owned over in Santa Monica, a stub of yellow pencil, the blank .45 bullet that she kept around as a memento of her first starring movie, an open pack of Camels.

Then he noticed the typewriter on her desk in the corner. There was a sheet of paper in the machine.

''Message in the typewriter business?'' He'd used that six months ago in *The Raven Needs An Alibi.*

The neatly typed message read *Forgive me. I can't go on living without Tim. Goodbye to all my friends in the industry and to my adoring fans.*

"Hooey," concluded Hix, bending to get a closer look at the sheet of cream-colored paper.

It had Lola Punip's initials embossed in the upper left-hand corner in pale blue. There was a peach-colored stain of something across the righthand side of the page, just above where the farewell message started.

"Makeup," decided Hix. He looked over at the dead actress. "But it ain't Lola's."

He scrutinized the room again, then returned to the parlor. "The studio cops, and the local law, are halfwits. They're certain to write this off as a suicide and ignore me if I try to tell them otherwise," he said to himself. "And what's worse—now I don't have anybody to put in a good word for me on the Tracy rewrite job."

Hair flickering, Hix bounced over to the small marble-topped table that held the phone.

"Even so, I'll have to call in the cops. But first . . ." He grabbed up the receiver. When he heard the voice of one of the studio switchboard girls, he said, "Myrt, get me Dick Tracy."

The studio cop chuckled as the studio troubleshooter took hold of Hix by the collar of his lime-green polo shirt and the seat of his maroon slacks. "No more kibbitzing, Hix," advised the husky blond man, urging the writer out of Lola's bedroom.

In the parlor Hix had to execute a tricky sidestep to avoid being tossed smack into the arriving Lieutenant Jake Blunt of the Burbank police.

"Underfoot yet again, Hix?" he asked, swinging out a hefty hand to halt Hix's progress.

"I discovered this murder." Hix eased himself free of the police lieutenant's grasp. "While I was awaiting your arrival, sahib, I jotted down a couple dozen pertinent—"

"It's a pure and simple suicide," put in Ballard, the burly troubleshooter. "The poor kid was real high-strung, Jake, like most actresses. When Tim Athens gave her the brushoff, why she naturally—"

"Malarkey," mentioned Hix. "That suicide note's a fake." He fished a folded-up old laundry list from his hip pocket. "Let me explain why it's as phoney as—"

"Your problem, Hix," said Blunt. "Well, one of them anyway. The problem is you suffer from a common Hollywood malady. You can't tell reality from make believe. This isn't one of your third-rate Mr. Woo quickies or—"

"Second-rate," corrected Hix. "And Lola sure as hell wouldn't knock herself off over a pansy only the publicity department thought she was in love with."

"Hell, I just saw in Hedda Hopper's column yesterday that Lola was devastated about Athens breaking off their engagement," said the cop.

"Yoicks." Hix executed a commendable slow burn. "Run that business about fantasy and reality by me again, loot."

Ballard said, "It's suicide, Jake. Take a look for yourself—you and your crew'll agree."

Two more plainclothes men, one a photographer, had just come barging into the small parlor.

"See you around, Hix." Blunt started for the dead girl's bedroom.

"The typing," called Hix.

"What?"

"It's much too good."

Ballard moved closer to him. "Go away, Hix. Scoot," he suggested. "Didn't I hear that you're incredibly late on some horse opera script?"

"Actually, we're six days ahead of schedule. Plus which, seeing that justice is done takes precedent over—"

"Scram." He reached for Hix again.

"There's no need for that," said Dick Tracy as he came in from the night outside. He wore a dark suit and a yellow snapbrim hat, had his yellow trenchcoat folded over his arm. "You're Hix?"

"Right, Richard," replied Hix. "We met outside one of the Lugom Brothers' offices few weeks ago."

Tracy nodded, turning to the troubleshooter. "Would

it be all right, Ballard, if I poked around here a little? Hix got me interested.''

Hesitating, Ballard ran his tongue over his lower lip. "Sure, I don't see why not, and I imagine Blunt won't mind," he said finally. "Though I assure you, Dick, you're going to find this is a routine suicide. You're not familiar with things here in California, but actresses and starlets are doing the Dutch quite often and—''

"She's the one," Tracy asked Hix, "who was playing the part of Tess Trueheart, wasn't she?''

"The same. And, trust me, Lola isn't the kind of broad who'd blow her brains—such as they were—out.''

"I'll have a look," said Tracy.

"The suicide note?" Hix backed toward the exit door. "The makeup smear.''

Hix located Tracy in the studio commissary the next morning. It was raining today; the small high windows were dotted with raindrops.

The detective was sitting alone at a small table in a far corner of the vast dining room, drinking a cup of coffee.

Hix, with several morning newspapers tucked under his arms, wended his way through the tables toward the detective. "Hiya, Akim. Thought you were working over at Paramount this week. Morning, Eve, my love. You're looking fetching. Or is that just a hangover? Another porter part, Willie?" He took, uninvited, a seat opposite Tracy. "I'm disappointed.''

"How so, old man?" Tracy glanced up and smiled.

Depositing the newspapers on the table top, Hix slapped them with his palm. "If you couldn't come up with any snappy dialogue on your own, Richard, you should've asked me," he said, giving a forlorn shake of his head. " 'When asked his opinion of the case, noted visiting detective Dick Tracy said, "No comment," ' No comment? And so those nitwit cops wrote it off as a suicide.''

"Possible suicide so far," Tracy pointed out. "And

notice that important word *visiting*. I'm from out of town and I don't have authority here. Nor do I want to interfere in another man's investigation.''

Hix's hair seemed to grow as he jiggled in his seat. "Don't tell me you think Lola actually did kill herself?"

"No." The detective picked up a menu.

"Listen, Richard, almost all the chow here is wretched," warned Hix. "However, I can tout you onto a couple of items that aren't as vile as . . . Ah, but that ain't the commissary menu." He'd noticed the words *Lola's Deli* in platinum letters on the menu front. "You glommed that from her room, from the scene of the alleged suicide."

"Borrowed it with Lt. Blunt's permission."

"Does Lola's restaurant in Santa Monica tie in?" He lifted his backside so he could ease the old laundry list out of the hip pocket of his ocher slacks. "I don't have that jotted down in my—"

"The crumbs on the floor of her bedroom." Tracy set the menu aside. "Reminded me of something. They weren't from anything she'd eaten."

"Bread crumbs, weren't they?"

"Graham cracker crumbs."

Hix's hair crackled as he frowned deeply. "Graham crackers . . . delicatessens," he murmured. "Jeez, I hate to think that I, of all people, am obtuse, yet—"

"I'm looking into a few things, in a purely unofficial way," said Tracy. "In fact, last night I made some telephone calls back home, to Pat Patton and some others."

"About what?"

"I'll fill you in when I have more information, old man."

Hix was sorting through the newspapers, each of which he had folded open to an account of Lola's death. "Did you catch the business with the suicide note?"

"The makeup stain that wasn't hers, you mean?"

"Sure, and the typing."

"I missed that."

Hix leaned forward. "Lola's typing was what is technically known as lousy. In fact, she was drummed out of not one but two business colleges back in her native Tucson, Arizona. Had she not developed a knack for looking sensational on camera whilst not wearing a stitch of underwear beneath her clothes, Lola would've been unemployed. During our torrid, and mercifully brief, romance a couple years ago, she typed several love missives to me." He paused to sigh. "Lola was strictly a two-finger typist and she hit—on her best day—maybe about seventy-five percent of the keys she aimed at. She couldn't have batted out that suicide note left in her machine, since the copy didn't have one damn mistake."

Tracy said, "I mentioned to Lt. Blunt that it would be helpful to determine what sort of makeup that was smeared on the note."

Hix suddenly exclaimed, "Yreka."

"What is it?"

Hix's forefinger tapped a photo in one of the papers. "A dying message," he said excitedly. "Gee, I love those and have used dying messages in at least seventeen of my Oscar-deserving screenplays. I think Lola was maybe trying to reach something on that coffee table. So as to leave us a clue to the identity of her killer." He whapped the side of his head with the heel of his hand. "Why didn't I notice this ere now?"

"You mean the black cartridge?"

Hix sagged. "Well, yeah," he admitted. "The name that Redrum, the chief villain in your film, was known by was the Blank. Chiefly because he appeared to have nothing much in the way of a face."

"That occurred to me, too," said the detective. "As a matter of fact, I know the actor who's playing the part of the Blank."

"Sure, Matt Idol hails from your part of the country, doesn't he?"

"A very gifted young actor, once he got himself straightened out."

"Could be that Matt bumped her off and that she was reaching for that blank to convey—"

"Matt Idol was on the set during the hours when she had to have been killed."

"And I suppose you were on the set then, too, and saw him?"

"Not the entire time, but I was there for at least an hour," answered Tracy. "The coroner estimates she was shot sometime between four and six in the afternoon."

Hix said, "Well, don't despair, Richard. We'll crack this case yet."

Hix came doubletiming into his partner's office. "Just the chap I wanted to see."

"Likewise," said Snilloc, looking up hopefully from his typewriter. "I'm stuck for a way for Dumler to lure the Gringo Kid into the shed."

"Who's Dumler?"

"Ace Dumler, our villain."

"Oh, him." Hix sat on the edge of the only other chair in the tiny room. "He convinces the Kid that Betsy is trussed up in there with a load of dynamite that's about to explode."

"You think his horse will fit into a small shed like that?"

"I thought Betsy was the name of the schoolmarm," said Hix. "Anyway, whatever her name is, she's about to become smithereens. Now to business—did you know Matt Idol when you dwelled in the Midwest?"

"Not personally, but I saw him in a few plays around—"

"Before that, was there anything shady in his background?"

After thinking a moment, the younger writer answered, "I did hear once that Idol'd made a couple of blue movies early in his career. That was only a rumor, though. Why, Hix, would the Kid believe Lisa Mae was in the shed when he was just now at the barn dance with her?"

"They had a quarrel . . . she thought he was flirting with . . . with our other broad . . . Rosita."

"Carmelita."

"Exactly. So Lisa Mae walks away in a huff, jumps in her buggy, takes off. Later the Kid gets a note—'Thought you might like to know that your girlfriend is shacked up with a load of TNT. Signed, Concerned Citizen.' What do graham cracker crumbs remind you of, my lad?"

"Cheesecake."

"Hum?"

"You use them to make the crust of certain kinds of cheesecake."

"Of course. Now if I can link Matt Idol with cheesecake, I should be able to—"

"That's funny, because the guy he was supposedly making those sex films for back in the Midwest was called Cheesecake. Sort of a double-barreled nickname, since the guy produced cheesecake movies and also loved to bake real cheesecake. He sold it in the string of delis he—"

"That might put it all together."

"What together?"

"The solution to the crime of the century, among other things." Hix stood. "Just a little while ago I broke Idol's alibi—but I wasn't clear on motive."

"His alibi?"

"The point being that the Blank doesn't have a face."

"True, but what—"

"I do believe I'll drop in on Idol."

"You sure this shack-blowing-up thing is going to work?"

"It always has," assured Hix, making his exit.

Approximately an hour and a quarter later Hix was climbing a tree in the heart of Hollywood.

As he'd approached the sound stage where the Tracy film was lensing, Matt Idol had slipped out of a side door and gone sneaking off toward the parking lot.

Unseen, Hix trailed him. When the actor took off in his Cord, Hix followed in his disreputable Plymouth coupe.

Idol drove into Hollywood, parked in front of a restaurant that was shaped like a gigantic coffee pot, and hurried inside.

Hix left his car a block beyond Cheesecake's Deli #2, utilizing a space in front of a fireplug. He skulked along the afternoon street, ducking into the weedy field that lay next to the newly reopened delicatessen.

"So Cheesecake himself is now in the West," he mused as he moved in among the stand of high trees that faced the spout side of the enormous coffee pot. "That ties in, sure enough."

Over at Republic a year or so ago Hix had written the first six chapters of a jungle serial, and he was confident he could climb any tree around. He wasn't certain exactly what sort of trees these were growing close to Cheesecake's, but they seemed to offer sufficient branches for climbing. He jumped up, caught a low branch and began making his way upward.

In under ten minutes he was swinging into the large hollow plaster and lathe spout of the coffee cup. It was about the size of a phone booth, and there was a small dusty window inset in the wall he found himself facing.

From inside the coffee cup came voices. Moving as deftly as he could under the circumstances, Hix worked his way over to the window and cautiously peered in.

He looked down into a huge kitchen. Idol was standing next to a long raw wood table on which were stacked hundreds of graham crackers. An impressively fat man in a black pinstripe suit and a floppy chef's hat was facing the actor, a rolling pin dangling from one pudgy hand. That must be Cheesecake himself.

"It's not a problem," Cheesecake was telling Idol.

"But Hix has been nosing around too much. He knows my stunt double did all the action scenes yesterday—meaning I had time to slip away to take care of Lola for you."

"So kill Hix."

"How—another suicide?"

Out in the spout Hix scowled, rubbing at the side of his head.

"I hear he tomcats around a lot. Make it look like a jealous dame bumped him off."

"And what about Dick Tracy?"

Cheesecake tapped himself on his broad front with the rolling pin. "I'll take care of him."

"He suspects you, I think, because of those crumbs I let drop."

"Yeah, and I told you not to stand so close while I'm making my cheesecakes. You get crumbs in your cuffs."

The anxious actor said, "Look, Cheesecake, you and I are quits. I killed Lola, so you could buy her place cheap from her heirs. You, in turn, are supposed to give me the prints and the negatives of those two unfortunate and embarrassing stag films I—"

"Listen, you're not talking to one of the Lugom Brothers."

"You gave me your word."

"You take care of Hix and we'll talk about the movies."

"I'm an actor, damn it, not a torpedo."

"Too bad all the critics don't see it that way, kid."

"Okay, all right. Suppose—"

Idol was interrupted by a loud ripping, cracking noise.

The noise was produced by the spout Hix was hunkered in suddenly breaking loose from the rest of the building.

Hix awoke to find himself swinging gently. He felt warm, became aware of the strong scent of spices all around him.

"Yikes." He realized he was suspended directly above a huge boiling vat of soup, dangling upside down from a rope that was rigged over a metal catwalk at the top of the big kitchen.

His nose wrinkled. "Borscht," he decided, squinting at the bubbling liquid ten feet beneath his head.

"You saved me a lot of trouble coming here on your own, jerk."

"I wish people would quit calling me that." Hix twisted his head until he got a glimpse of Cheesecake grinning up at him.

"What I'm going to do," explained the chef-hatted gangster, "is have you lowered, very slowly, into the borscht. It's made, by the way, from an old family recipe handed down to me by my sainted mom. You'll be boiled alive, which'll pretty thoroughly fix your wagon."

"Cheesecake, if I may call you that," said Hix. "Cheesecake, you've obviously got an inventive mind. Why not let me get you a lucrative job in the scenario department of some major Hollywood—"

"Nix on that crap, Hix."

He cleared his throat. "Okay, let's try another angle," he said. "You won't be able to convince the cops I was a suicide. Mainly because very few people end their lives by boiling themselves in beet soup."

"Yeah, but I like these bizarre ways of bumping off jerks. Once, back in the Midwest, if that jerk Tracy hadn't stopped me, I was going to barbecue the whole Greenberg Mob."

"He's right," put in Idol. He was sitting uneasily in a straight-back chair.

"Precisely," seconded Hix.

The actor said, "You've got to kill the guy in a more commonplace way, really."

"Jack, lower the rope about a foot or so," the huge Cheesecake ordered the henchman who was holding the other end of the rope.

Hix jerked closer to the hot soup.

Cheesecake giggled. "Let him down another . . . Holy Moses!" Cheesecake grew even paler than usual. He spun on his heel, went waddling toward a metal ladder. He grabbed the railing with one pudgy hand, started climbing up for the catwalks high above.

"Attach that rope to something safe," ordered Dick Tracy to Jack.

The hawknosed detective had just come bursting into the big kitchen. There was a .45 automatic in each fist.

"Yes sir, Mr. Tracy." Jack obliged, attached the tail of the rope to a handy pipe, and then raised both hands high.

"Come on down, Cheesecake," Tracy ordered.

"In a pig's valise," called the fat crook from up on a swaying catwalk. "You chased me out of the Midwest, forcing me to set up here in Southern California and try my deli racket again. I'm not going to retreat any—"

"I'll count to five."

"Go to hell, copper." Cheesecake started to reach into his coat for his shoulder holster.

Tracy fired twice.

The first slug sliced through the expensive pinstripe fabric of the fat gangster's coat, digging into the hand that was clutching the handle of the .38 revolver.

The second bullet drilled a neat hole square in the middle of Cheesecake's pasty forehead.

The fat man swayed, wobbled, teetered, fell.

He came plummeting down, slushing to a stop in the vat of boiling soup intended for Hix.

The purple liquid splashed up at the dangling writer. "Yow," he observed.

"I'll have you down in a minute," Tracy told him. "Good thing for you, Hix, I decided to look Cheesecake up once I knew for sure he was out here on the coast."

"It was," agreed Hix.

"From now on, see if you can keep away from poking into murder cases."

"Well, I suppose I could," said Hix. "Thing is, I'd

need something to occupy my mind. For example, if I had the job of rewriting *The Dick Tracy Story* I'm pretty sure I could do—"

"I'll talk to the Lugoms," promised the detective.

And that's how Hix added another screen credit to his long list.

THE CEREAL KILLER

by
Rex Miller

It is just after dusk, but in the small lab near Crown Western Broadcasting, where the fat man works, time has little meaning.

The fingers are those of a human who has devoted his life to gluttony in all its multifarious shapes. Disgustingly fat, repulsively soft fingers probe at the bottom of a rectangular package. The digits appear to be of a consistency that suggests nothing firmer than Jell-O. Flabby appendages on the doughy hands of a person who lives only for gratification.

But these hands move with the grace of a concert pianist, and the touch of the revolting fingers is remarkably sure. These are in fact the hands of a fiend who has taken many lives, and who will kill again.

The box, rectangular and cellophane-wrapped, is in his left hand. In the right he holds a tool that resembles a hobbyist's putty knife, or an artist's palette knife, but it is neither.

Gross, bloated fingers move with a surgeon's precision. Eyes squint through the eyepiece of a high-magnification loupe, as he peers at the bottom of what appears to be a box of Kraklies Breakfast Food—"The morning choice of winners!" The right hand carefully places the spatulette down. Gripping the box with both hands by its top, the fiend suspends the container over a small kettle of water that bubbles from a ringed stand atop a bunsen burner.

A moment passes as the water boils above the intense blue flame. He emits a tiny sigh of contentment. Removes the box from the path of the hot steam, and makes a quick, careful probe with the spatulette. Cellophane parts at the join, as the law of molecular adhesion is violated.

He makes the first incision. Steamed cardboard separates, as mucilage, applied by auto-insertion machine, relinquishes its tenuous hold. The interior package is methodically penetrated from its base. Blubbery arms quiver as he reaches for the nicotine sulfate.

Morning. An icy wind whips through the city. The fat man's soft, flabby hand slaps the metal doorplate as he puts his weight behind it, and shoves the IN door of the grocery story open wide. A blast of cold air comes in with him, and in back of the counter near an ornate brass register the clerk shudders.

"B-R-R-R! She cold enough for ya this morning?" The vastly corpulent figure ignores him, hunching down deeper into his voluminous overcoat in response. The clerk shrugs, grateful for the wool sweater he wears under his white apron, and turns back to the paper. Gratefully, he notes that the weatherman is calling for warmer weather.

The clerk turns to the sports page and a story on the Brooklyn Dodgers taking game three of the series. He turns the page, glancing at a follow-up story on the European emergency. Truman is telling people not to eat meat on Tuesdays, and to give up poultry and eggs on

Thursdays. He turns to the latest adventures of the Dragon Lady.

The fat man glides past the Campbell's Oxtail Soup, and the rows of Van Camp's chili and Mother's canned tamales. He passes under the large, hand-lettered sign that hangs from butcher's twine: CHILI TODAY, HOT TAMALE. He slows down at the packaged breakfast foods.

Enormously round, grotesquely obese, his body under the heavy, shape-concealing topcoat is a short, obscene mound of quivering protoplasm that jiggles, bounces, and shakes with every movement. Both his upper body and his head are perfect O's.

At first glance he appears to be a freak without eyes. His face, absolutely round and almost featureless under a shiny, bald dome, looks like a pie crust from certain angles, and where human eyes should be one sees only fork indentations of the baker. Small cuts made into the circle of pasty dough.

He reaches the cereals now and the slits widen slightly, as soulless eyes of evil scan the shelves.

Kellogg's Pep. Mother's Oats. Rice Krispies. Coco-malt. Rye Pops. Kix. Cheerios. Bosco. Barley Cornies. Wheaties. Munchos. Quaker Puffed Wheat. Quaker Puffed Rice. Oaties. Cheerioats. Crackle Bran. Kraklies.

He stops in front of the distinctive red and yellow package of Kraklies Breakfast Food. From the side or from the rear all movements are blocked to the onlooker by five feet of blubber and the immense overcoat. The fingers of the grossly fat man move deftly, and he moves to another aisle to make a purchase.

At the counter the clerk has finished reading about the latest machinations of the Dragon Lady and is going over the ads. Peter Pain has just been knocked on his can by Ben-Gay, and Sam Spade is wading through the bad guys to get at the Wildroot Cream Oil, when a blimp-shaped thing in a coat blocks out most of the reading light.

"Will that be all this morning?" the clerk asks, and

then he looks up at the tub of blubber in front of him, having to check himself from saying "*Holy*-moley!" out loud. "Uh . . . sir?"

The fat man does not speak. Perhaps there is a sigh of breath. The clerk has to wrench his eyes off the vision that confronts him to ring up the items on the register. That *face*! Perfectly round, like a huge dinner plate. And featureless. Where were the man's nose and mouth? He'd seen bald men before, but never someone quite so totally hairless. No eyebrows, no facial hair. Not even the suggestion of sideburns or the hint of a beard's shadow. A massive, featureless face, sickeningly white; flesh the color of solidified Crisco, reclaimed in a Mason jar and chilled for reuse in the Fridge.

Woodenly the clerk begins counting out the man's change. Later he will try to recall what had been purchased: a box of Rinso perhaps, and a Sky-bar? Mundane items that will not stay in his mind the way the face will. He looks up as he hands the change across the counter. If one looks closely one can discern eye-slits, a tiny bump of a nose, and perhaps the trace of a mouth. The fat man's face is like a large, unbaked pie waiting to be placed in the oven.

"Thank you," he says, omitting the usual "come again." Truthfully he hopes he will never have to lay eyes on this spooky personage again.

The stuffed overcoat turns as if on oiled wheels and appears almost to glide toward the door.

The inhumanly pale, flab-puffed hand of the fat man pushes against the metal plate of the OUT door, and he propels himself through its opening and back out onto the wind-whipped city street.

At last, as he moves in the direction of his gleaming new 1948 Chevy Sedan, he permits himself a mirthful sigh of pleasure.

Inside Mid-City Groceries, on the third shelf of the cereal products section, where, only minutes before, eight boxes of Kracklies Breakfast Food stood, there are now nine.

With great difficulty he wedges himself behind the wheel of the Chevy and inserts a key into the ignition slot, bloated fingers starting the vehicle and pulling easily out into the flow of traffic.

He turns on the radio to get the morning news and dials to another station as the tubes slowly warm up and he hears a woman talking about "Oxydol's Ma Perkins."

It amuses him to think of his actions as a kind of reverse kleptomania. He goes into stores and—when nobody is watching—he *leaves* things. Nasty things. Deadly things to hurt, and cripple, and kill. These pleasurable thoughts help dispel the nausea that he feels at having had contact, however brief, with a human.

The man with the face like an unbaked pie has a lethal allergy. He is allergic to people.

Nearly Midnight. Just outside the three-mile limit, a thick veil of fog clings tenaciously to the dark face of the sea. The fog, wet and blanketing like a blood-soaked shroud, drapes the gently rolling waters.

At the stroke of twelve, in a cascade of crashing water, a frightening apparition from the deep suddenly breaks through the waves, and a towering prow of deadly gunmetal-steel knifes out of the ocean.

U-Boat! Just the name can send a shiver down one's spine. But here is the genuine article: an enormous U-Boat has penetrated the surface of the dark sea in a noisy Niagara of water, its conning tower smeared with the murderous symbol of evil—the dreadful Nazi swastika.

The hatch of the conning tower slams open with a resounding metallic clang as a German officer emerges, quickly scanning the surrounding fog and sneering to someone below.

"Ach! Ze Americans are fools. We haff taken zem by

zurprize. It is choost as I haff planned. Zis attack has been perfectly timed.'' The Nazi officer sneers a cruel, twisted smile.

As if in response, from out of nowhere, a high-powered engine growls its sudden warning through the chill, murky fog.

High above the ocean, in an opening between the cloudbanks, a winged messenger of justice peels off into a screaming power dive, machine guns spitting down in a staccato promise of vengeance.

Somewhere along the nearby shore a bell ominously chimes Midnight as the roar of the mighty aircraft thunders out of the sky; the snarling engines, tolling bell, angry barking of the fifty-caliber guns all screaming their death-knell at the vicious Nazi invaders below.

Junior Tracy's arms and legs are covered with pin-pricks of excitement as soon as he hears the sound of the tolling Midnight hour, and the snarl of the mighty aircraft. The moment the distinctive resonance of Pierre André slashes out of the radio he is virtually jumping out of the chair on the first word:

"Captainnnnnnnn." Just the one word is enough. The response is so deeply engrained and automatic. It is the Pavlovian reaction to years of after-school, after-basketball, after-homework quarter-hours of vicarious thrills and chills. It is the formula-proven, involuntary, dyed-in-the-wool gut-reaction of a true serial fan, as basic as breathing in and breathing out. Every "tune in tomorrow," every "dime and a box-top," every secret message, and every magic carpet ride across the airwaves cuts through the ether on the nasal "nnnnnnn" of the Captain's first name. The second spoken word is almost an anti-climax.

"MID-niiiiiiiigggggggghhhhhhhhhhhttttttttttt!" (BONGGGGGG-G-G-G-G-G! *RRRRRRROOOOO-AAAARRRRRRRRRR!*) "Brought to you by the makers of Ovaltine!"

Junior listens with his ears of course, with his mind,

in the physiological auditory manner one hears and comprehends sound. But there is no way to accurately translate the words from nine-year-old into adult. The language offers no word for the invisible appendage that transmits adventure plotlines to a kid's brain.

Alone, but far from lonely, Junior listens in a near-rapturous cocoon of isolation. Other boys and girls, all across the country, are similarly enmeshed in a rich web of gossamer fantasy a million miles beyond reality. Junior, like all of his peers from coast to coast, is truly in another world. The world of Nazi warlords, U-Boats, and Captain Midnight.

Radio was a dark spawning-ground for chimerical demons that slithered out of the glowing box to grab a kid where he lived. Although Junior could be considered an extremely precocious youngster, he was still just a boy, and like any boy or girl, he could instantly be transported into fantasy-land by those action-packed serials that came blasting through the air like blazing tracers. But there was one thing he liked even better than comics, movie chapters, or adventure serials, and that was being around a real-life hero, his mentor and adoptive father, ace G-man Dick Tracy.

"Junior!" The familiar, warm baritone voice rang through the house, bringing the boy back to reality. He ran to meet his pop, not concealing his excitement.

"Hi!" The two Tracys were glad to see each other. The real Dick Tracy, the celebrated sleuth with the lantern jaw and chisel-edged nose, whose exploits were first chronicled by Mr. Gould some decade-and-a-half earlier, had not adopted *his* son until 1939. But in a case of life imitating art, as a way of showing homage to the man who'd made his name a household word, Tracy decided to name the boy Junior, after the kid in the comic strip.

The real Junior had become all that Dick had ever hoped for, in just the few years they'd been together. The boy was loyal, honest, stalwart, and smart as a whip.

Moreover, he showed indications that one day he'd grow up to be a fine, decent citizen, and make a meaningful contribution to society. What more could any father want?

There was a danger in letting one's life be treated as a comic strip. A fellow G-Man colleague of Tracy's had let his life come apart over just that kind of constant publicity. So the genius detective had thought about it long and hard before he gave his adopted son the same name as that of a child who existed only on paper.

For his part, Junior seemed marvelously levelheaded. He was intrigued by the idea that he had a namesake who was nearly as famous as his father was, but on some level he couldn't explain, the boy appeared to be aware that there was a serious weight and responsibility that came with the name "Junior Tracy."

It was a name he would have to earn, he sensed. And the mystique that went with being the son of the world's most famous crimefighter was not something any kid could just shrug off.

The first artifact of the fictional Tracy that Junior had been allowed to have, as a kid, was a fat little book called *Dick Tracy and the Spider Gang*. It was called a Big Little Book, not much larger than a cigarette case but thick, and with a brightly colored cover. The book had been published a year before the real Junior had even been born, and it fascinated him in an odd kind of way to see his name and imaginary exploits in the book.

One of the local neighborhood theaters had recently revived the first Dick Tracy serial from 1937, and was showing it to postwar audiences as if it were a new chapter play. It was then that Junior realized for the first time this his treasured Big Little Book was the story of a movie, and that the Tracy he saw on film or in the comic strips, and the man who had named him Junior, were not the same man at all.

The Tracy in the comics sometimes used machine guns, and the movies had a way of emphasizing this. The effect was to make Dick Tracy appear to be a violent man, but Junior knew this wasn't true. Why, nobody was kinder or more gentle than his pop. Sure, he had to shoot a bad guy now and then, but he didn't like it. Violence was ''a last resort,'' and Junior had already learned to differentiate fantasy from reality by applying this lesson.

However, Junior was still just a boy, so he enjoyed the far-out adventures of Sky King and the radio Dick Tracy, The Shadow and The Green Hornet, and favorite comic books like Plastic Man and Sub-Mariner.

''I got away a little early today, Junior.'' Tracy was in his study, surveying a mound of paperwork. ''How was school?''

''Okay,'' Junior said, in a tone that meant it wasn't too okay at all.

''But, you know, history n' stuff. It's so *boring*. I wish I could study crime detection instead of all that dull stuff they teach at school.''

''Junior,'' Tracy said with a smile, ''I'm going to show you something I'm sure you'll find of interest. Look at this.'' Getting up from his desk and walking over to the wall full of framed displays, he pointed to a frayed, ink-stained document that was framed on the wall.

Junior had looked at the wall a thousand times, but he'd never really read all the stuff. It was mostly awards Tracy had received, or pictures from old newspapers, things like that. Tracy was pointing at a beat-up looking chart of some kind. It looked like some sort of dull measuring table or something. How could anything like that be interesting?

''There's more excitement captured in those lines of ancient history than in any case I've ever worked, I'll guarantee you.''

''Huh? You're kidding.'' It occurred to Junior that he was missing Captain Midnight. He tried to read the faded document in the frame.

''No. I'm not kidding. You're looking at a piece of history more dramatic, more vividly exciting, than any I

can imagine. In fact, all the walls in the study here have
many similar documents. Prime visuals, I call them.
Striking examples of quantitative graphic displays.'' Junior's face scrunched up at the big words and unfamiliar
phrases; but Dick Tracy did not believe in talking down
to children.

''These are visuals that track great, dramatic moments
in history. There is a precise parallel between the study
of military history, for example, and the science of crime
detection. That's just one reason why history is such a
dynamic subject for study.''

''No lie?''

''No lie. This one happens to be a *carte figurative*. It
was drawn by a fellow named Minard, and it depicts
Napoleon Bonaparte's 1812 invasion of Russia. You remember who Napoleon was, don't you?''

''Sure,'' Junior said, scowling. ''We don't like him
'cause he shot the Sphinx's nose off.''

''Okay.'' Tracy chuckled. ''Not him personally, but
that's close enough. This is a prime visual because it
renders all the known variables of time, place, troop
strength, routes of attack and retreat, into a graphic display. But look, Junior! Minard shows us a table that re-
lates all these facts, not just to each other, but to the
vicious frigidity of the Russian winter. See?'' Tracy
pointed across the bottom of the chart. ''This is called a
tableau graphique. It means—like a visual table. And
because of the way the facts are visualized and interre-
lated, you and I can tell something about a military operation that took place over a century ago. There's the
time-line. Those are the cities. There's the temperature.
The width of this line is Napoleon's troop strength. What
do you see?''

''I see that the cold weather was a fact—uh, was an
important factor in er—um, Napoleon's army. In the SIZE
of the army!''

''Excellent. That's great! Good boy.'' Tracy hugged
Junior affectionately.

"Okay. History can be interesting, if the teacher is Dick Tracy. But Mrs. Burke is boring. And anyway, what's this got to do with crime fighting?"

"This has *everything* to do with crime fighting. The process of thinking we used in our talk about the chart was two-fold: it was eduction, and deduction. I'll explain to you later how these thought processes work. But just remember this for now: eduction and deduction are the most important ways a good detective solves a case."

"Yeah?"

"Um hm. And Mrs. Burke may *seem* boring, but she knows things about history that will be extremely valuable lessons to you later, if you decide you want a career in law enforcement. So think of Mrs. Burke as a challenge. And when you sit in your history class, imagine that Mrs. Burke is playing a game with you. She wants to disguise those important nuggets, the facts that you will need to educe/deduce conclusions about great historical events, by speaking in a monotonous tone or by hiding the nuggets in a series of other, less meaningful statistics. Your job is to stay alert and sort out the important truths. That skill will be vitally important to you if you join the crusade against crime." Tracy was at his most serious, his dark eyes boring into Junior.

"Okay."

"Good." Tracy went back to the desk. "Well, don't let me interrupt your programs."

"Yeah. I wanna hear Tom Mix next. Hey—" he called as he was walking out of the study, "you didn't happen to see Spot outside, did you? I thought I had him tied up good, but he got loose."

"You probably won't find Spot for a while," Tracy told him.

"How come?"

"I'll show you." Tracy got up again and headed for the backyard. "Come on," he said unnecessarily, since

Junior was right behind him. "This will be a good time to test your powers of observation." They stepped into the yard.

"Great! You mean we can do some detective work together?"

"Precisely." Tracy knelt down where the dog had been tied. "What do you notice about the rope?"

"It hasn't been cut or chewed. It might have been untied, though. Do you think Spot's been stolen?"

"Look here," Tracy told him by way of an answer, pointing at the ground. "Notice anything?"

"Nothing. Just the ground."

"Look closely. This is rabbit sign. And here—look!" Junior followed his mentor as he slowly looked around the backyard. "Here by the gate, and there by the center of the fence. Paw prints and rabbit tracks."

"Spot saw a rabbit and worked at the rope until he could pull loose!"

"Maybe. Maybe not. But one thing is certain." Dick Tracy lifted his sharp features toward the clear, cold sky. At this moment he was exactly the image Chester Gould had drawn, and Ralph Byrd had portrayed. "Whenever you've got hounds and hares, you can expect a chase scene."

"Is that a Dick Tracy Crimestopper?"

"No, that's just common sense. Hey, hold it. We've got company." A marked scout car was pulling up by the side of the house. Dick waved at the familiar sight of his friend and sidekick Pat Patton, and headed for the street.

"No rest for the wicked," Patton said.

"Trouble?"

"Another poisoning," Pat told him, getting out of the police car.

"Oh, my God. No!"

"A lady in Brookhaven Heights. Ate breakfast this morning. Complained of being violently ill. Husband rushed her to County Gen. They pumped her but apparently couldn't get it in time.''

"What was the time of death?''

"Little after ten this morning. I know. Don't ask. Why weren't we notified by County? It was a snafu in the records. Lab just got it half an hour ago. They called me. We didn't even have an incident report on it in Homicide!'' Patton shook his head. "We gotta do something about the paperwork bottleneck.''

"I know, Pat. But right now we've got a more immediate problem. We've either got one of the worst poisoners in history on our hands, or somebody's started a series of copycats.''

"You mean you still think it's remotely possible these are different poisoners?''

"No. Of course not. But because every poison used has been different, or at least of a different origin if not class, we have to consider the possibility of one or two copycats as well as our main killer.''

"But off the record—?''

"Off the record I think we've got a serial killer. Somebody as dangerous as a psycho can get, and who fancies himself or herself a modern-day Jack the Ripper. Only this time the Ripper uses chemicals.''

"You know it'd be one thing if they were just using one or two variations of arsenic or common rat poison. But you got a perpetrator or perpetrators who *know* poisons. Everything from dope to weed eradicator. Number six—the young guy in Cortland Park. They think it was *fire extinguisher fluid*. I mean somebody is going to a lot of work to make sure we can't get a handle on 'em. Almost makes you wonder about a crime cartel like Murder, Inc.''

"And we certainly can't exclude a consortium of criminals. But the one commonality appears to be breakfast foods. So far as I know one of the few areas in which organized crime has yet to find a stranglehold is the milling business. But . . .''

"You got your people loading the cereal boxes. Your truckers. Your plant and factory workers."

"And if it was the mob they'd be hitting Battle Creek, Checkerboard Square—all the big boys. You don't see the poisoner compromising any Wheaties, or Ralston, or any of the big half-dozen. Instead the poison is turning up in Toast-Chex, Zippy, and Wheat-O-Rama. The obscure brands, most of which are produced regionally."

"So maybe it's somebody around this area."

"Or somebody who wants us to rush to that conclusion so they're conspicuously not touching the big guys. I think we need to triple our manpower and really exhaust the disgruntled-employee angle. Anybody who left one of the regional milling companies in any kind of confrontational dispute. Someone got fired or laid off or passed over for a big promotion. If you put that into play with a disturbed sociopath you have a volatile potential for creating a murderer. We can continue to trim the list to those who have sufficient knowledge of chemistry and poisons—so we can at least be dealing with manageable numbers of suspects."

"Right."

"How old was the Brookhaven Heights victim?"

"I think they said thirty-six. Married. Husband with a good executive position out at Robidoux Brothers. Three kids. No priors. Ordinary household."

"No ties to any of the other twelve victims?"

"None that jumped out at me," Patton said.

"No common threads of age, background, family, occupation. Nothing that they share? No common enemy to bond them in a group or cause?" Tracy started around the car, turning toward the house. "HEY, JUNIOR, BRING ME MY—" Junior materialized with his yellow trenchcoat. "—coat. Thanks. Good lad. I've got to go back downtown."

"Sure. Okay. See ya later. So long, Pat!"

"Fine kid, that Junior," Patton said to his old friend as he waved at the flame-haired youngster.

"Yes, he's a good boy. I'm very proud of him. Well—let's head for the morgue," Tracy said.

In the ensuing week that had passed since the murder of the suburban housewife, there'd been three more cases of breakfast-food poisonings. Sixteen containers tampered with in a period of just a few weeks. The quick feedback from the FBI lab had indicated that the Kraklies Breakfast Food box had contained lethal nicotine sulfate. The next two victims, a student and a blue-collar worker who lived in the city, had not ingested sufficient amounts of poison to bring fatal results, but each of them had become seriously ill. The toxic agents had been "Spanish Fly" and ordinary radiator cleaner. Each had been inserted into a breakfast product: the former into a box of Branola, the latter into a vanilla-flavored drink preparation called Fair Shake.

Then, exactly one week following the death of the Brookhaven Heights woman, poisoned breakfast food claimed the life of the seventeenth person, and nearly killed three more persons. For the first time, by pure coincidence, an entire family had eaten breakfast food from the same container. The father was dead on arrival at Mercy Hospital, the mother and two children violently ill. The initial lab report indicated that it was probably parathion in the Shredded Oats. Only the fact that the man of the house had immediately shown signs of poisoning had saved the other family members from consuming more than a spoonful or two.

Junior Tracy came home from school that afternoon and read about the latest spate of poisonings in the late edition of the paper. He knew Dick would solve this terrible case soon. He turned to the radio listings and selected his favorite serials, turned on the big living-room Philco, and settled down on the sofa to hear Buzz Bradshaw, King of the Sky. When 4:45 P.M. showed on the living-room wall clock, he heard the staff announcer intone:

"This is WCWB, your fifty-thousand-watt voice of Crown Western Broadcasting. 'Buzz Bradshaw, King of the Sky,' normally heard at this time, will not be heard today due to unforeseen circumstances. Instead, we invite you to stay tuned for a quarter hour of Uncle Ed's Organ Magic, a pleasant interlude of uninterrupted organ melodies. Keep listening at five o'clock for 'Poetry Recital,' today featuring a special reading by Mrs. Carol Spangberg, from her book *Soothing Sonnets*." Junior switched over to Hop Harrigan. At least Hop was still on the air.

Like most of the other kids listening to the radio at that moment, he knew what "unforeseen circumstances" had befallen Buzz Bradshaw, King of the Sky. Buzz's main sponsor had been Shredded Oats. Another sponsor had bailed out on one of the after-school shows.

Obviously people were afraid to buy breakfast cereals now. And the breakfast-food companies sponsored all the children's shows on radio. Junior had heard Dick talking about the poisoner or poisoners being "serial killers." But he had interpreted it to mean "cereal killers," since in fact the cereal companies were in bad trouble. Now, Junior thought, they had become radio-serial killers as well. Yesterday his favorite show, King Neptune of Atlantis, had been replaced by another stupid program of dreary organ music.

Dick had taught him not to think of his own needs first, and Junior's conscience nudged him hard. He had no business worrying about radio shows when people were being poisoned.

The paper didn't report it, but he'd heard his pop say that security was stepped up in all the grocery stores and breakfast-food plants. Anyone from an average-appearing housewife to a respectable businessman could be substituting the tampered-with cereals and breakfast drinks.

Junior couldn't get into Hop's adventures today. The poisonings were all he could think about. He got up and went into Tracy's study and looked at the chart thing again. The one about Napoleon's cold-weather campaign in Russia.

What if Junior could create his own "prime visual" of the poisonings? He could solve the case and truly earn the proud name Junior Tracy! He grabbed some paper and a pencil out of Dick's desk and began charting out all the known data about the killings. Making neat columns of all the names of the cereals, and of the serials they sponsored. Maybe this was an angle they hadn't covered. Only a kid would think of the radio shows. He *could* solve this case!

He carefully printed all the cereals and shake-up drinks beginning with Mother's Oats and ending with Shredded Oats. Gee, maybe it was somebody who hated oats! He put down all of the brand names: Rye Pops, Munchos, Oaties, Crackle Bran, Rye Cream, Barley Cornies, Break-Fast, Crunchies, Kraklies, Twin-Crisps, Wheat-O-Rama, Zippy, Toast-Chex, Fair Shake, Branola, Sweet Snaps, so many cereals! He had missed a couple. He got Dick Tracy's file out and corrected the list.

Next Junior started on all the radio serials the various companies sponsored: Dr. Fearless, The Adventures of Pirate Pete, Captain Trouble, Big Dave and Winky, Buzz, Flip, Chick, Whiz, Buck, Flash, Lance, Rip, Yukon Queen and King Neptune of Atlantis, The Yellow Beetle and the Blue Racer, Mighty Mongoose and Wonder Cat, The Gumps, The Schnertzes, and The Jerks From Wisconsin! All kids' shows sponsored over the various "juvenile blocks" of the regional networks. And these were serials that Junior knew as well as he knew his own name.

Then he went back and made a column that listed each date, each day of the week the poisonings occurred, the location and name of the store where the contaminated merchandise had been purchased, and every other known fact about the victims and the crimes.

He drew a rough outline of the city and, using a ruler

and Crayolas, connected each column to its respective location with color-coded lines. What would Dick Tracy put on this chart? Would he find out what the temperature was at the time of each poisoning? How much wood *could* a woodchuck chuck?

It was meaningless to him. Just a series of random names, numbers, places, and colored markings. The Napoleonic chart told you something when you looked at it—this told you nothing. Junior sighed and plopped down in his pop's big leather chair. He closed his eyes and tried to remember everything he'd heard Dick Tracy say about solving murder cases.

"The application of logic is an important tool in the fight against crime . . . Very little of a detective's work involves violence . . . The science or art of war may be neither of those things, but there are similarities between war and law enforcement . . . The military man, like the policeman, spends much of his time in paperwork and preparation . . . very little in violent confrontation . . . Eduction and De-deck-shun . . . Prime visuals . . . *Everything* to do with crime fighting!"

It felt so good to close his eyes and snuggle down in the soft chair. Just a short nap. In his mind's eye Junior saw the mysterious image of the spider on the yellow-green spine of his Dick Tracy Big Little Book. It crawled off the edge of the book and started down his hand and up his arm.

NO! He shook it off—a poisonous black widow! He stomped it to death, his heart pounding. In that instant he had seen the connection between the killings, and it came to him like a Whiz-Bang lightning bolt. He could solve this case!

No time to waste. He had to have proof for the capture of the poisoner. He ran upstairs to his room and got his Dick Tracy Camera and made sure it was loaded with film. He undressed rapidly, throwing his school clothes on the bed, and pulling a thick sweater over the lanyard around his neck, which held a miniature Tracy Flip-Top

Pocket Flashlight. It had cost a dime and a Quaker Oats box-top, and it worked like a charm. He wouldn't wear his official Crimestopper suspenders. This was a job for his Lone Ranger belt with the Secret Silver Bullet Buckle. He tested it, by sliding back the bas-relief bullet, revealing a hidden compartment. It was just big enough for one of pop's old Gem razor blades ("avoid the Five O'Clock Shadow! Buy Gem Blades!"), a bit of fishing line, and a hook.

He pulled on Red Ryder jeans with the secret coin pocket, into which he tucked his Neptun-Nife with its miniature hacksaw. He loaded a coin for a pay phone into the top of his Green Hornet Secret Signal Ring, checked the pointing needle on his Nabisco compass ring to make sure it hadn't become magnetized, and determined his Sky King Lockpick Ring was in working order. Satisfied, he put the rings on.

Junior buckled his Official Dick Tracy 2-Way Wrist Radio to his left wrist. It was no toy. Dick had taken the crystal diode wrist radio obtained by Junior through the pages of Zoot Comics, and had the lab boys at work install one of Diet Smith's 2-way units inside. What appeared to be merely a kid's plastic toy concealed a sophisticated 2-way communications unit.

He filled a Plastic Man Utility Belt with his Wheaties Sun-Watch, Sgt. Preston Distance Finder, and Jack Armstrong Hike-O-Meter, and wrapped this around his left ankle, covering it with an argyle sock and the rolled-down cuff of his jeans.

Junior debated taking his Dick Tracy Rapid-Fire Tommy Gun ($3.95 from Ranger Comics), but this was no kid adventure he was going on. He finished dressing, picked up the camera, and headed out of the house.

Some twenty minutes later Junior was outside the building he always thought of as the Black Castle, after the radio serial Sky King, whose nemesis, a sinister character named Dr. Shade, lived in just such a rundown old mausoleum of a house.

Summoning up all his courage, he flipped open the glow-in-the-dark top of the Sky King Lockpick Ring and opened one of the picks. At that moment, with the winter sun almost under, he felt a shiver run through his body, and the boy suddenly had to go to the bathroom very badly. They never talked about *that* on any of the serials or in the comics—how a crime fighter could get scared and have to do number one so bad he'd almost go in his pants. Nobody ever had to stop and go to the bathroom in the comics or on the air. But Junior did. So he went over and took a leak behind a big bush, and just as he was zipping up, something hard and metallic smashed into the back of his head, and he was dead to the world.

When he came to, it was in darkness and he was very much alone. Alone and lonely and frightened. He could not remember being so cold or so afraid. His hands were tied behind him tightly, and he felt like his neck had been broken. He began to cry, wishing he hadn't done this stupid thing. He would give anything if his pop would find him. If only he could turn back time. Why had he come alone? He was just a dumb kid.

It was freezing cold and he hurt. He strained to see but he couldn't make out any shapes. It was totally black, wherever they'd taken him. The camera was gone, of course, and soon he'd be gone as well. He wished his feet weren't trussed up so he could kick himself!

He moved his leg. Again. The other one. His legs *weren't* tied. His back was against something hard and cold. Was he tied to it? No! He could stand. He tried to get his feet under him but he was still groggy from the blow to his head, and he lost his balance and smashed to the hard floor. Concrete, it felt like. The smell in the room was wet and—awful—like the smell of slime. He felt dirty.

This time Junior managed to stand. His hands were tied tightly but not to a post or wall, so he could move his arms a little. Junior tried to remember the yoga trick he'd read about in the Mandrake The Magician Illusion Book he'd sent away for. "Yogic posture #4: hands tied behind back." He forced himself to think very skinny, and began trying to work his tied wrists down below his bottom. He willed his shoulder blades to compress. It felt like his back was breaking.

Slowly, struggling with all his might, concentrating as hard as he could, Junior finally managed to slip his bound hands down to the back of his knees. From there it was a relatively simple maneuver to kneel back down on the floor very slowly, drop to his side, and inch by inch force one of his hands to the tip of a foot. At that point he stepped through his tied hands, and he now had his hands in front of him.

He pulled the heavy sweater up and flipped the top on the Dick Tracy Flashlight, and suddenly he could see. Junior blinked as he flashed the light quickly around. He was in what appeared to be a stone basement. Windowless. Canned foods on the shelves along one wall. A heavy wooden door.

He slid the belt buckle open and removed the blade. It proved plenty sharp enough for the ropes and Junior was soon free. He had felt like something was missing but only now, on his feet and looking for a way out, did he realize what it was. Whoever had knocked him unconscious had been clever enough to take his wrist radio. Another icy jolt of fear shot through him. He wouldn't be able to call for help.

Junior flashed the light down on his left hand—great! They hadn't taken his secret rings. He flipped open the pick and started to work on the door, but the lock was different. He couldn't pick this one. He kept trying but the batteries were fading in the little flashlight and he could feel himself beginning to panic. He'd been crazy to try to solve this case—he was only a kid. A stupid little kid.

Noise. The sound of heavy footsteps on the other side of the door. Junior snatched up the cut length of rope and held it behind him, scrambling back over to where he'd come to, against the cold wall. He also held the used blade in his hand. "Violence is a last resort" echoed loudly in his ears as he flashed the small light off and slipped it under him.

He was in darkness as the door opened, his eyes shut tight in feigned unconsciousness. He'd have one chance. Cut and run.

Even without seeing he knew a powerful man was in the room with him. He could sense the physical power before it touched him. But from the second the hands grabbed him he knew his idea of escape was hopeless. His hand with the blade was pinned by a strength many times superior to his, and it was shaking him hard enough to snap his neck. Junior was done for.

"So long, Pop," was what he said. His eyes were filled with tears. He hoped he'd be helpful in the solving of the case. Maybe they'd use his chart to educe and deduce who'd been poisoning the innocent people.

"Wake up, Junior," Tracy said again, shaking the boy by the shoulders. "I've never seen anybody can sleep as soundly as you can."

"It's *you*!" Junior rubbed his eyes. His neck felt like it was broken from where he'd fallen asleep, wedged down in the leather chair in the study.

"Yep. I've got some great news, too, Son. Hey—what's this? You've been drawing a table, eh?"

"I think I've solved the case. Look!" Junior pointed to where he'd dreamed about converging lines. Vectors that would prove the evil mastermind Dr. Shade was wiping out the breakfast foods. His big solution had been nothing more than a pipe dream. The lists of names and dates and places were just that—random and unconnected. He felt like a fool. "I guess I dreamed the part about solving the case."

"This is good, though, Junior. You were on the right

track. But you'll be happy to know we just broke the case. The poisoner is behind bars.''

''Wow! That's great! When did you get 'im?''

''Just a short time ago. I had to come back here and get some files, and I'm on my way back downtown. We have some paperwork to wrap up, a few loose ends, and then we'll be drafting a statement for the press and radio, so you're getting an exclusive report.''

''How did you break the case? Who was it? Why did they do it? Where was—''

''Whoa! One thing at a time. Okay—we got him through a tip. As you know, Junior, many crimes are solved by police informants and witnesses. In this case it was somebody who thought a man 'looked suspicious,' and he told the security officer, who made the arrest right there in the store. The killer had a box of Wheat Treats Cereal under his overcoat. We got an immediate confession. It was laced with a chemical called sodium monofluoracetate,'' Tracy told the child, reading the tongue-twister name from a sheet of paper.

''Who was he?''

''The man is Edward Morgan, A/K/A 'Pieface.' Very sad, Junior. This fellow was once a brilliant chemist, but he had the most beautiful voice, and he switched careers to work on radio. For many years he had the most popular afternoon show on the Crown Western Broadcasting network. People loved to listen to him tell stories because of his wonderful, deep voice.

''The audience was always sending him gifts. A mentally ill woman sent him a case of Sparkle Cola once, and he drank some from one of the bottles, not knowing she had put a lye solution in some of the soft drinks. He recovered but was never able to speak again. It warped his mind.

''Morgan was quite obese, with a round, hairless face, and as he turned to criminal pursuits and gained even more weight, he began to be known as Pieface. The fact that his once-beautiful speaking voice was now gone, together with his appearance, eventually pushed him over the brink.

"He'd been a fairly accomplished organist, so the people at Crown Western felt sorry for him and let him stay on as a studio player. They gave him little quarter-hour programs of organ music now and then: Uncle Ed's Organ Magic, as his show was called."

"I've heard that name on the radio!"

"Right. Perhaps inside his twisted mind he thought if he made it impossible for the breakfast-food sponsors, who kept all the other afternoon shows on the air, to continue sponsoring radio serials, he'd be rid of all his competition and his program of organ music would be popular. Who knows? He claims he put the poisoned containers in the stores 'just to get even.' He hates the world, and of course he's completely mad."

"Will he get the chair for killing all those people?"

"I imagine he'll go to a place that treats the criminally insane until he's well enough to be moved to death row."

"You mean he can't be put in the electric chair as long as he's insane?"

"That's right, Junior. It's the law. Pieface will have to be treated for his mental illness first. It doesn't appear to make sense, I know, but we do not believe that insane murderers should be punished for their crimes. Basically it's a humane law, but one that can be abused."

"Gosh! I thought I was going to solve this case. I wanted to make a prime vigil for you like the one on Napoleon's army."

"Prime visual. Yes." Tracy looked at the Crayola marks. "And you were well on your way. Look at this . . ." Dick Tracy leaned over the chart with genuine interest. "If you substitute the name carbon tet for phosgene, and U-4d for this, and Cantharides for that one—look what you get!" He made some scrawls on the paper.

"What? What do you get?" Junior couldn't see what the big deal was.

Cyanide
Arsenic
Thallium
Cyanogen chloride
Hyoscyamine
Methyl bromide
Ethyl mercury
Ipral
Fowler's solution
U-4d
Carbon tetrachloride
Atropine
Nicotine sulfate
Cantharides
Oxalic acid
Parathion
Sodium monofluoracetate

The column of names looked pretty much the same. Just a bunch of big words. Chemical names. His list was boring.

"Pieface used some trade names and some generic names when he was planning his campaign of terror and murder. It won't make any difference to the innocent victims or their families, but you see if you look at the list chronologically, with the first letter of each name emphasized the way you did it on your excellent visual display, you see that the madman sent us a secret message. *You* caught that, Junior. You turned up a clue the rest of us missed. We'll frame this page as a piece of memorabilia from Junior Tracy's first case."

Junior looked at the list again. He couldn't seem to get his mind to slip back into gear. Cat-something? Tracy saw the dilemma and took a pencil and helped his son, marking a line between each of the word groups. The boy's mouth dropped open as he read the secret communication from the brain of a warped madman.

CATCH ME IF U CAN, COPS, it read. Junior was glad

the insane killer hadn't been able to have the last word. "Uncle Ed" would not be heard from again, due to unforeseen circumstances.

In the distance, Junior heard Spot baying somewhere outside the window. Like his master, the hound was not beyond chasing imaginary quarry. But he was awestruck by the notion that a few marks on a sheet of paper had brought *him* into the world of a serial killer.

Happily this case was closed.

AULD ACQUAINTANCE

by
Terry Beatty
and Wendi Lee

Dick Tracy kept a strong grip on his wife Tess's arm as they carefully made their way down the icy sidewalks toward the Towne Theater.

"I'm so excited, Dick," Tess said, her breath coming out in white clouds. "It was nice of the boys in your department to give us this night out."

Tracy smiled at her. He remembered when he'd gotten the call on his two-way wrist radio a week ago. Chief Patton had wanted him to come back to Central Head-quarters before he went home for the weekend.

"Can't it wait until Monday, Pat?" Tracy had asked. He was only a few blocks from his house and wanted to get home a little early so he could take his adopted son, Junior, sledding before dinner.

"No. It's important," the chief said shortly and signed off.

When the detective walked into headquarters, Chief Pat Patton was there with Tracy's partner Sam Catchem and the rest of the boys on the force, all of them grinning like Santa Claus. In Sam's hand was a small pale-gold envelope, which he handed to his partner. "This is from all of us, Tracy—a combination Christmas gift and anniversary present for you and Tess."

Pat cleared his throat and began his speech. "It's been a tough year for you, Dick. Your honeymoon was interrupted by the Wormy Marrons case. You lost your home to an explosion ordered by Blowtop Jones. You were nearly killed tracking down the kidnapper, T.V. Wiggles. It seems to us that you're overdue for a little rest and relaxation, so, we all chipped in and bought you and Tess tickets for the Orphans' Fund concert on New Year's Eve."

Tracy opened the envelope. With tickets priced at one hundred dollars apiece, the Orphans' Fund concert was the talk of the town. He felt overwhelmed. In a little over a week, he'd be taking Tess to the social event of the year.

"I don't know what to say except thanks," Tracy said. He could feel a lump forming in the back of his throat as he looked up at his friends and co-workers and added, "If there's ever anything I can do for you . . ."

His friends came up to shake his hand and clap him on the back before Tracy could finish his sentence.

Dick and Tess Tracy paused to look up at the lighted marquee with the names "Sparkle Plenty" and "Vitamin Flintheart" in large red letters. All the wealthiest people in town were flocking toward the lobby doors. It was a pickpocket's dream. Tracy was thankful to see a pair of off-duty police officers standing guard on either side of the theater's entrance.

Considering what had happened to Tracy and Tess this year, it was hard to believe that they were ending it by attending this exclusive and expensive event. They had rebuilt their house in time to celebrate Christmas and their first wedding anniversary, but on a detective's salary, Tracy and Tess were having a hard time making ends meet. They had borrowed heavily against their mortgage in order to add improvements to, and to furnish the new house. Nineteen fifty-one would be a lean year as they attempted to pay off their debt to the bank. But Tracy was thankful that his family—Tess, Junior, and their faithful police dog, Mugg—had survived Blowtop's attempt on their lives.

Tracy held the theater door open for his wife and presented his tickets to a tuxedoed man who, in turn, gave them the once-over as if he was wondering how the Tracys had ever scratched together enough dough for this event. Tracy surveyed the bevy of wealthy patrons in the lobby.

Silk and satin finery rustled quietly as the wealthy greeted each other in hushed tones. Even in the low lighting, the number of diamonds worn tonight made Tracy wish he'd brought along sunglasses.

The collar of Tracy's tuxedo pressed tightly against his neck. He pulled at the stiff fabric, trying to position the collar so he could breathe more easily, with no luck. Tracy longed for the comfort of his black suit with the red-and-black striped tie and yellow fedora. The only part of his usual wardrobe that he wore tonight was his two-way wrist radio. Absently, he touched the gadget and hoped that this was one time he could enjoy an evening out with Tess without being called away via the two-way to a crime scene.

As if she'd been reading his thoughts, Tess sighed and said, "It would be nice if just this once, your wrist radio wouldn't interrupt our evening." She looked mournfully at it and added, "But I suppose it would be too much to ask."

Tracy agreed. "Let's keep our fingers crossed, honey." He slipped his arm around her shoulders and helped his wife out of her coat.

It was New Year's Eve, Tracy thought to himself, and the chances of making it through the entire concert without an interruption were slim.

He heard his wife's sharp intake of breath.

"Oh, Dick," she whispered, smoothing the long skirt of her black velvet dress. "I don't know if I'm appropriately dressed!" Her eyes scanned the crowd, which was aglow with gemstones. "Thank goodness for your anniversary present. They dress up my plain black frock."

She touched the plain string of pearls around her neck. Tracy had given her the necklace in celebration of their first wedding anniversary this Christmas eve.

He squeezed her elbow affectionately and said, "Honey, you look beautiful."

"Oh, Dick." Tess blushed, then leaned over and brushed her lips lightly against his cheek.

Tess could wear a flour sack and she'd still be a knockout, Tracy thought proudly. He was quite aware of the envious looks that men were throwing his way as he and Tess wound their way through the crowded lobby.

"Richard! Tess!" The deep melodious voice was unmistakable. Tracy and his wife turned to greet Vitamin Flintheart. "I'm so glad you were able to attend our little performance."

Tracy almost didn't recognize the old fellow. Vitamin wore a simple white robe, and carried a staff in place of his trademark cane. A satin sash wrapped around him read "1950." A long false beard hid most of his face, and rubber cement added a few more wrinkles to Vitamin's already age-lined face. The only thing that gave him away was his mustache, which was carefully trimmed and lightly waxed with the ends curled. The aging actor, who was now Sparkle Plenty's agent, was in his element tonight.

"You look wonderful, Vitamin," Tess offered.

Vitamin bowed with a flourish and said, "Thank you, dear lady." He took Tess's hand and with an extravagant gesture from his free hand, quoted in his best Shakespearean voice:

"O, she doth teach the torches to burn bright! It seems

she hangs upon the cheek of night as a rich jewel in an Ethiop's ear—beauty too rich for us, for earth too dear!''

Tracy watched Tess's face go blank. From long experience, the detective had learned that Vitamin Flintheart was sometimes in need of a translator. He leaned over to his wife and murmured in her ear, ''I believe Vitamin is saying that you look lovely tonight.''

She brightened and nodded. Turning back to the old fellow, Tess said graciously, ''Thank you, Vitamin.''

Eyes twinkling, Vitamin said, ''I shall be doing my part for the benefit tonight. In addition to organizing and emceeing the event, I shall also be sharing my talents as a thespian with you all. I shall close the show, of course, which shall begin with a rousing musical performance by my client, young Miss Plenty. I pray you'll be moved by my interpretation of a soliloquy from *Richard II*.''

Tracy felt his heart sink. He had a great deal of affection for Vitamin, but had never been able to enjoy the old ham on stage. Still, Tracy managed to summon up some phony enthusiasm and said, ''We'll certainly look forward to it.''

Maybe he'd get that call on his wrist radio after all, sometime during Vitamin's monologue.

The lights in the lobby dimmed twice in close succession, indicating that the show was about to begin. ''Ah! I must depart,'' Vitamin apologized. ''The stage calls out to me!'' With another bow to Tess, he hurried away.

People began to flood the theater, so the Tracys quickly found their way to their seats.

''Front row seats!'' Tess exclaimed. ''How did Pat manage this one?''

Tracy chuckled. ''Oh, I imagine he had a little pull.'' He looked around the theater for Sparkle's eccentric parents, Bob Oscar ''B.O.'' Plenty and ''Gravel'' Gertie. The house was full, but he didn't see them. They would stand out like a pair of sore thumbs if they were anywhere in the theater.

How a couple as odd-looking as B.O. and Gertie could have produced a child as lovely as Sparkle was beyond Tracy's understanding. B.O. was a gangly bewhiskered scarecrow of a man, and Gert, in sharp contrast to her flowing blonde hair, had a face like a Halloween witch.

Sparkle had inherited her mother's golden locks—in fact, she had been born with a full head of hair—but unlike either of her parents, she had the face of an angel.

The pre-schooler had recently become quite the singing sensation. Her mother had taught her to play the ukulele, and the child surprised everyone with her ability to memorize and play almost any song she heard. A few appearances on Ted Tellum's "Kid Talent" TV show made Sparkle an overnight TV star.

Vitamin Flintheart, acting as her agent, soon had her set up with her own television program. All was going wonderfully for the Plentys until that madman T.V. Wiggles kidnapped Sparkle and nearly killed B.O.

Of course, the Plentys might just be watching their little girl from the wings. B.O. had been keeping a close eye on his daughter ever since the experience with T.V. Wiggles. Tracy regretted only slightly that Wiggles was killed attempting to escape justice. He liked to see criminals put behind bars to pay for their crimes, as Blowtop had been. But he'd cry no tears for the likes of T.V. Wiggles—a higher justice had passed sentence on that lawbreaker.

The only thing that was more satisfying for Tracy than seeing criminals put away, was seeing those who were once on the wrong side of the law reform and become solid citizens. B.O. Plenty and his wife Gravel Gertie were a case in point. Now if only B.O. could learn to remember Tracy's name. The old coot was always calling him "Macy" or "Bracy" or some such thing.

The house lights were lowered, signaling that the show was about to begin. Tess leaned over and whispered,

"This place is packed except for the two seats to my left."

Before Tracy could respond, the red velvet curtain parted and Vitamin Flintheart shuffled out into the spotlight. Tracy had to admit that Vitamin made a marvelous Father Time.

"Friends, Romans, countrymen, lend me your ears," he boomed. As a trained actor, Vitamin needed no microphone to project his voice. With a grand sweep of his hand he continued, "For it is your ears . . ."

At the rear of the theater, a door slammed open.

"Consarn it, Gertrude. Don't dawdle."

Vitamin froze in mid-gesture at this rudeness, as all the patrons in the theater turned to see a gawky character with a mop of uncombed hair and an even more unruly beard, wearing a tuxedo jacket two sizes too big, and trousers six inches too short. He wore white socks and big brown work boots. On his arm was his wife, wearing a pastel-green gown, more appropriate for a high-school prom than this society function. Her long blond hair framed bug eyes, a pointed nose and chin, and a bucktoothed, gap-toothed grin.

"Hesh up, B.O.!" Gravel Gertie hissed.

B.O. Plenty continued as if he hadn't heard his wife's plea—and maybe he hadn't. Perhaps B.O. mangled Tracy's name—and the rest of the English language—because he was a mite hard of hearing. "We almost missed our leetle tyke's first song."

Fortunately, they arrived at their row, and Tess waved to attract their attention.

"Plague-take-it," B.O. grumbled as he stumbled to his seat. "It's too consarn dark in hyar." He lowered his voice a bit and greeted Tracy. "Nice to see you showed with the missus, Mr. Lacy."

Vitamin cleared his throat to bring the attention back to the stage. "For your ears will hear wondrous sounds and your eyes will see marvelous sights tonight when Miss Sparkle Plenty and her ukulele take the stage. Please welcome her with applause as generous as your contributions to the Orphans' Fund.''

With a flourish, Vitamin faded to the left as Sparkle, wearing a little pink dress and a satin sash saying "1951," entered from the right wing and took center stage. Though she was not yet four years old, the child walked out on the stage as if she owned it. With her ukulele in tow, she shot a sweet smile at this audience full of powerful and wealthy citizens, and before she even sang a note, she had them all in the palm of her tiny little hand.

Although Tracy had adopted Junior as his own son, the detective glanced at his Tess and wondered if someday they might also have a little girl like Sparkle to call their own.

"Two Sons From Tucson . . ." sang little Sparkle. When she came to the end of the first verse, she put her ukulele on her head and sang the chorus, which drew hushed but enthusiastic applause.

When she was finished, little Sparkle looked out at her rapt audience and announced, "My next song is for all the little young'uns out there what don't have folks. That's who this benefit is for." She launched into a moving rendition of "You Made Me Love You," which brought a tear to the eye of everyone listening—including her father, who blew his big bulbous nose into his handkerchief and muttered, "Cain't help blubberin'."

Suddenly a murmur rippled through the audience as the curtains of the left wing moved slightly. A meek-looking Vitamin Flintheart, still dressed as Father Time, shuffled out on stage.

"Dad-blame it all," B.O. muttered loudly. "What in blazes is that varmint Ironheart doin'? Ain't he got no better manners than a lowdown dog? What kind of idjit would innerrupt a preformer on the stage? I got half a mind to git up there and whale the tar out of that dad-gummed Flintstone." He stood up, pushing up the sleeves of his oversized jacket.

Tracy put an arm out to restrain his friend. "Stay in your seat, B.O."

Everyone in the audience gasped in unison as a big, blond, broad-shouldered man with a face like a bulldog's followed the old actor onto the boards, holding a cigar between his tightly clenched teeth and a gun in his massive hand.

"Blowtop." Tracy said it like a curse. This was the man who had almost destroyed his family—the man who had destroyed his home—the revenge-seeking, explosive-tempered brother of the hired killer Flattop. This was Blowtop Jones, who should have been spending his New Year's Eve locked in a prison cell, but now here he was, big as life, holding Vitamin Flintheart hostage.

Sparkle Plenty had stopped singing. Her head was turned in Blowtop's direction and her ukulele hung silently by her side. A frown marred her kewpie-doll face.

Tess clutched her husband's arm. Out of the corner of his eye, Tracy caught Gertie gripping B.O.'s arm as well.

"My baby!" wailed Gertie as Blowtop nudged Vitamin toward the microphone where little Sparkle stood.

"Happy New Year's, folks!" Blowtop bellowed. Vitamin moved toward Sparkle in an effort to protect her, but the ruthless criminal stopped the old man with a sharp nudge of the gun. "The beneficiary of this benefit has just changed from orphans to me, Blowtop Jones. If you'll just pass your jewels and wallets to the end of the aisle, my helpers will collect your valuables. We've already taken care of the box office and the police officers on duty outside. I have armed men guarding all the exits, so don't even think about trying to escape."

On cue, Blowtop's cronies, dressed in winter coats and stocking caps, with scarves covering their faces, worked their way down the aisles, urging people to hand over everything.

"Don't forget those watches, men," Blowtop chuckled. For emphasis, he strode over to the child star and dragged her by the arm back to the microphone.

"While they're giving to a good cause," Blowtop snarled to Sparkle, "why don't you sing for the folks like you're supposed to? They came here tonight to be entertained, so just go on with the show."

Little Sparkle's jaw jutted out stubbornly like a true Plenty. "No," she said, laying her ukulele down and crossing her arms. "I ain't a gonna sing. Not so long as you're pointing a gun at my friend, Mr. Ironheart."

"I said play, child!" Blowtop said, jabbing his gun in Vitamin's ribs hard enough to make the old actor jump. *"Play or I plug the old ham!* Woo-gosh!"

Still frowning, and shooting her dirtiest look at Blowtop, brave little Sparkle began to sing: "Come and sit by my side, leetle darlin' . . ."

B.O. Plenty moved restlessly in his seat, then leaned over to Tracy and said, "Consarn it, Mr. Macy, do something! That Blowstack ain't got no right to talk to the tyke that a way."

Tracy shook his head slowly and said, "Just sit back, B.O. Sparkle and Vitamin are better off if we just let the thieves take what they want and leave. There's nothing we can do while Blowtop holds them hostage with that gun."

B.O. raised his voice and wailed, "Oh, if I could get my hands on that vile dog, holding my little girl as a sausage. And Mr. Bracy too cowardly to withhold the law."

"B.O. . . . ." Tracy began, but he was interrupted by one of Blowtop's minions, a fat man whose rheumy little eyes were all of him that wasn't covered by winter garments.

"Hand over your valuables, folks." The fat man had a squeaky little voice.

Tracy emptied his pockets, and gritting his teeth, handed over his wedding ring.

The chubby thief gestured to Tess and said, "Hand over that pearl necklace."

"But they're not real," she lied, putting her hand protectively over the anniversary gift.

"Hand 'em over before I tear 'em off o' you," he snarled.

Tess turned to her husband for help, but he just patted her arm and said, "Do as he says, dear. Don't make any trouble."

"Oh, Dick. Your anniversary present." A tear slipped down her cheek as Tess unclasped the necklace and handed it reluctantly to the ruffian.

"Effen I jest had my shotgun," B.O. grumbled to Gertie, loud enough for Tracy to hear, "I'd show that Dacy a thing or two about protracting your family."

Sparkle sang "Honeysuckle Rose," "Rag Mop" and "Ghost Riders in the Sky." By the time Sparkle began "The Dying Cowboy Blues," Blowtop's men had finished bagging the valuables and were starting to leave. Blowtop remained onstage and scanned the audience as Sparkle sang, "Fer I'm a young cowboy an' I know I must die . . ."

Blowtop's fat flunky, the last remaining in the theater, passed by the front row again on his way out. His eyes fell on Tracy's wrist radio.

"Hand over the watch," he said to the detective.

Blowtop must have overheard his crony. He stepped to the edge of the stage and squinted through the stage lights at the front row.

"You there in the front row," Blowtop screamed, waving his gun. *"I told everyone to hand over their watches. I hate it when people don't follow orders. Hand it over!* Ugh! Gosh!"

Sparkle, startled by Blowtop's outburst, stopped singing.

Blowtop gave no sign of recognition as he looked right at Tracy. The stage lights must be blinding him, Tracy thought.

B.O. Plenty made an impatient noise. "Confound it,

Macy. I knew we shouldn't've gone and coordinated with Blowdup.''

Tracy stood and held up his two-way. ''This isn't a watch, Blowtop,'' he called out. ''This is a handy little invention known as a two-way wrist radio—and every member of the city police force has been listening in on this whole ordeal.'' The fat flunky, panicking, made a break for the nearest exit.

''Dick Tracy!'' Blowtop spat, his ugly face twisting up in hateful remembrance of the man who'd caused the death of his brother, Flattop.

''You see,'' Tracy continued, ''my concert tickets were a gift from my co-workers, and the favor they asked in return was that I leave my two-way on so they could listen to the concert while they were on duty tonight.''

Blowtop leaned out over the edge of the stage and peered out. ''I've been wanting to even the score for my brother, Tracy. I guess tonight's the night—out with the old . . .''

Tracy remained calm. ''I don't think you want to add murder to the list of new charges you'll be facing. By now, this place is surrounded and all your goons will have been taken into custody. Give it up, Blowtop.''

Blowtop Jones pushed Vitamin away and took two steps back. An audible sigh rippled through the captive audience, but quickly turned into a collective gasp as the vicious criminal swept little Sparkle up and held his gun to her head. Vitamin Flintheart stood silently near the right wing curtain, just within Blowtop's sight.

''Keep away from me,'' Blowtop snarled. *''I hate it when a plan doesn't work! I'm not going back to jail, Tracy!* Woo-gosh!''

Tracy shook his head sadly and said, ''I didn't think you'd sink that low, Blowtop. Why don't you put the child down?''

''I hate it when someone tries to tell me what to do!'' Blowtop backed up, waving his gun. *''Everyone stay back!''*

Tracy felt helpless. He tried to scan the wings for signs of back-up, but it was too dark back there to discern any movement.

Blowtop continued to move back with his little hostage tucked under his arm, but just as he turned to make a run for it, Vitamin Flintheart stuck his long staff out and tripped the desperate man. Blowtop and his gun went flying in different directions. In the same moment, Tracy vaulted onto the stage.

The gun skittered across the wooden floor and landed center stage. Blowtop hit the stage hard, with his hostage landing on top of him. Sparkle sunk her baby teeth into his hand and Blowtop let out a yelp. The child star, still clutching her ukulele, squirmed free from Blowtop's grasp. Grunting, Blowtop began to stagger to his feet.

B.O.'s unmistakable voice called out, "Dad-gum it, child, twang him with yore zither!"

Sparkle raised the instrument over her head and brought it crashing and splintering down on the criminal's skull.

"Right proud of the leetle tyke," bragged B.O.

Tracy tackled Blowtop as the criminal tried to scramble to his feet again. Blowtop pushed Tracy back and dove for his gun. Tracy staggered, then regained his footing and caught Blowtop before he could reach the weapon. He grabbed a fistful of Blowtop's shirt, spun him around and decked the thug with a right cross.

Sam Catchem entered stage left with two uniformed officers, confiscated Blowtop's gun, and tossed a pair of handcuffs to Tracy.

"He's your collar, Tracy," Sam said, a wry smile on his freckled face. He nodded to the uniforms, and they took positions on either side of a sullen Blowtop Jones.

Tracy cuffed Blowtop and grinned at Sam. "Did you and the boys enjoy the show?"

"Sure did," Sam replied, "and say, I think I have something for you here." Sam pulled a pearl necklace and a pair of wedding rings out of his pocket. "Took these off of a fat slob that walked right into our arms. Thought you might like 'em back."

"Thanks, Sam. You're a pal."

Tracy's partner nodded. "I have my moments."

Vitamin took center stage and announced to the audience, "Dear patrons, thanks to the remarkable police work of my friends Richard Tracy and Samuel Catchem, we shall be able to proceed with the evening's entertainment. One of our fine lads in uniform has informed me that all the culprits have been apprehended, and all of your possessions have been safely recovered—as have the box office receipts for the Orphans' Fund. A round of applause for our boys in blue."

Tracy and Sam, embarrassed by the attention, received a standing ovation from the crowd as the uniformed officers led a grumbling Blowtop offstage.

"Samuel!" Vitamin bellowed. "Since you are the only one of us wearing a timepiece, would you be so kind as to let us know if the New Year is nigh."

"Hunh?" Sam replied.

"He wants to know what time it is." Tracy interpreted.

"Oh. I'll be darned. It's exactly midnight!"

Vitamin turned to Sparkle. "Then my dear, 'tis time for your special song."

"But dag-nab it Mr. Ironheart, I done busted my uke over that bad man's haid."

"Then you shall have to sing *a capella*, dear child."

"But she ain't *got* no accordion!" B.O. hollered. Gertie held her husband's arm and gave him a look that told him he had misunderstood Flintheart.

Sam exited the stage, and Tracy hopped down to his seat to return the pearls and wedding band to Tess, who threw her arms around him and kissed him, saying "Happy New Year, sweetheart!" as Sparkle began to sing.

"Auld Lang Syne" had never sounded more beautiful than when sung by B.O. and Gertie's little girl, and the only sounds to be heard in the Towne Theater were the crystal-clear voice of Sparkle Plenty and the sniffling and sobbing of her sentimental pa, who muttered in apology, "Sorry, Mr. Macy. Cain't help blubberin'."

ROCKABILLY

by
F. Paul Wilson

Detectives Helmsly and DeSalvo had formed a two-man Committee to End the Noise.

"That racket's gotta go, Tracy," DeSalvo was saying.

"Yeah," said Helmsly.

Tracy couldn't look at these two without thinking of Abbott and Costello—Helmsly as the former, pudgy DeSalvo the latter. In fact they once did the "Who's On First" routine at a PBA talent show. But they were good cops, even if they were a little rough around the edges.

"You know we like the kid as much as anybody," DeSalvo said, "but either he takes his jungle-bunny music somewhere else or one of us goes in there and accidentally sits on his pipsqueak phonograph."

Tracy put down the newspaper. The news from Hungary was pretty depressing—martial law and mass arrests since the Soviets marched in—and the presidential campaign at home was boring, with Ike and Nixon looking like shoo-ins.

He stared at DeSalvo. He didn't like the jungle-bunny

reference, but he let it slide. A lot of people were getting pretty worked up about this new rock and roll music the kids were playing, calling it jigaboo jive and nigger music. He'd even heard some preachers and teachers on the radio calling it the Devil's music. Tracy didn't know about that. All he knew was that it wasn't his kind of music.

The trouble started when Junior brought his little, fat-spindled phonograph into the locker area off the squad room and started playing these funny looking pancake-size records with big holes in the middle—"forty-fives," he called them. There were times when the music coming out of that tiny little speaker made Tracy want to try a forty-five of his own on that thing—something .45 caliber.

Obviously Tracy wasn't the only one bothered by it. DeSalvo was still carrying on.

"Bad enough we have to listen to it half the day workin' on the Wonder Records case, but we'd like a break when we come back to the squad room."

"Okay," Tracy said. "Send him out here. I'll talk to him."

"Thanks, Tracy," said Helmsly. "Peace and quiet again, huh?"

"Peace on earth," Tracy said.

Tracy thought about Junior as he waited for him to appear. He was a little concerned about some of the changes he was seeing in the boy. The most obvious was his hair. Junior was starting to look like some of the JDs they were picking up on car thefts and in gang rumbles on the north side. What was next—a studded black leather jacket and engineer boots? Tracy would have to draw the line there.

Not that Junior wasn't a good kid—he was the best. But Tracy couldn't help feeling uneasy when he saw him looking like a young hood.

And listening to hood music.

Ye gods, that rock and roll stuff was enough to drive

any sane man up the wall! Junior played it endlessly at home. You couldn't pass his bedroom on the second floor without hearing twangy guitars, thumping drums, and wailing voices. Tess seemed to tolerate it better, even claimed to like some of it. But it set Tracy's teeth on edge. Especially that Little Richard fellow.

"Hi, Tracy," Junior said as he opened the door to Tracy's office. "You wanted to see me?"

"Yes, Junior. Sit down a minute."

Tracy was at once fascinated and repelled by Junior's hair. What formerly had been a wild red shock was now a carefully combed masterpiece of . . . . what? The kid had let it grow and now it was Brylcreemed to within an inch of its life. Parted high up on each side, combed toward the center and a little forward so that some carrot-colored curls hung over the forehead; the sides were slicked back above the ears to meet at the rear of his head in what was being called a D.A.—and it didn't stand for District Attorney.

Tracy didn't like any of it.

"This music you've been playing. Do you like it?"

Junior's freckled face lit with enthusiasm. "You bet! All the kids like it."

"Surely not all of them."

Junior's smile broadened. "You know that Elvis Presley song you hate—'Hound Dog'?"

Tracy winced. "How can I forget? You play it a hundred times a day."

"Well, it's the number one song in the country right now."

"There goes the country. Can you tell me why?"

"It's cool. It's a gas."

Tracy laughed. "Ah! That explains it. And that's why you listen to it all day long?"

"And all night too. At least till I fall asleep."

A thought struck Tracy.

"Would you consider yourself an authority on rock and roll, Junior?"

The kid shrugged. "Sure. An expert even."

"Good. I want you to look at something."

Tracy called to DeSalvo to bring him the evidence in the Wonder Records case. DeSalvo came in lugging the box.

"Hey, Junior," he said as he placed the box on Tracy's desk. "This is the kind of stuff you listen to. Maybe you can have them when the case is done."

Junior's eyes lit as he peered into the box. He glanced at Tracy. "Can I look?"

"Sure," Tracy said. "Handle them as much as you want."

Junior fished out a stack of 45's and shuffled through them like cards. Tracy noticed the kid's enthusiasm fading.

"Aw, these are all copies."

If the statement startled Tracy, it shocked DeSalvo.

"How do *you* know?" the detective said.

"Just look at the labels. 'Long Tall Sally' by Mark Butler, 'Blueberry Hill' and 'Ain't That a Shame' by Kevin Coyle, 'Maybellene' by Buster Squillace, 'I Hear You Knockin'' by Eleanor Robinson, 'Eddie, My Love' by Diane Gormley, 'Sh-Boom' by the Flat-tops? These aren't the real records. I *have* the real records, the ones that were done first—and best—and they're sung by Little Richard, Fats Domino, Chuck Berry, Smiley Lewis, the Teen Queens, and the Chords."

Suddenly Tracy saw what Junior meant.

"Oh, I get it. You're saying these are copies because they're sung by different artists than the originals."

"Right. They're put out for radio stations who want to play the top hits but don't want to play the originals."

DeSalvo ran a hand through his thinning hair.

"Why on earth would they want to do that?"

"Because all the originals were sung by Negroes," Junior said, looking DeSalvo straight in the eye. "Some folks call it jungle-bunny jive and so the big stations won't play it unless it's rerecorded note for note by white guys."

Tracy could see that Junior's sense of fair play was deeply offended, and he had to admit the kid had a point.

"That's not the kind of copying we're concerned with here," Tracy said before DeSalvo could reply. "The president of Wonder Records, Mr. William B. Cover, came to us with a complaint that someone is pressing perfect copies of his records and then selling them to all the stores in the city."

"If they're perfect copies," Junior said, "how did he find out?"

"Sales reports," DeSalvo said. "He read where a store reported sales far above what he'd shipped to them. He checked further and found out it was going on all over town."

"Serves him right," Junior said under his breath.

"No talk like that, understand?" Tracy said. "Whether you approve of what Wonder Records is doing or not, it's perfectly legal. Bootlegging copies of his product is not."

Junior looked down. "Sorry. You're right."

"We know it's an inside job," DeSalvo said. "Mr. Cover is positive someone's 'borrowing' his masters and pressing the copies."

"Borrowing?" Junior said.

"Yes," Tracy said. "None of the masters is missing, but Cover says someone must be pulling them one set at a time, pressing off the copies in a secret plant, then returning them. He says that's the only way the crooks could make such perfect copies."

DeSalvo snapped his fingers. "Say! What if we put Junior inside and—"

Helmsly burst in before Tracy could tell DeSalvo to forget it. "Just got a call from the Wonder Records. They found William B. Cover dead in his office."

Tracy was on his feet. "Foul play?"

"Strangled."

"Find Sam," Tracy said. "Tell him to meet me down at the Wonder offices."

As Tracy pulled into the parking lot at Wonder Records, he marveled again at the design that had made it one of the city's landmark buildings. The upper two-thirds of its north wall had been designed to look like the top of a phonograph. The huge black disc representing a record was the most arresting feature. A giant tone arm rested beside it; once every five minutes it would swing over and land on the disc. The disc itself didn't spin, but the bright orange Wonder Records label at its center did, giving the illusion that the whole gargantuan record was turning on its spindle.

Inside, Sam Catchem was waiting for him on the top floor. Cover's office took up most of the level. There was a small lobby outside the elevator vestibule where a receptionist's desk guarded the passage to a set of oak double doors. These opened on a suite of richly appointed rooms. In the rearmost office a team from Forensics was dusting everything in sight while a pair of morgue attendants waited for the signal to load the sheeted body onto their stretcher and take it down to the meat wagon.

Tracy went down on one knee beside the body and pulled back the sheet. He'd met William B. Cover only once before, at headquarters. A bluff, hearty man of about fifty with thick brown hair and apple-red cheeks.

"Strangulation didn't do much for his complexion," Catchem said in his usual laconic tone, talking around the lighted cigarette that dangled from the corner of his mouth.

Tracy had to agree. The big red cheeks were now a dusky blue mottled with tiny purple hemorrhages in the skin.

"What have we got, Sam?"

"One dead rock and roll record mogul, done in with the cord from his telephone."

"How long?"

"Still got some warmth left in him. I'd say about two hours. How about you?"

Tracy pressed the back of his fingers against Cover's throat. Not completely cold yet. He glanced at his watch.

"I'll go with that—which puts time of death right in the middle of lunch hour. Witnesses?"

"None."

"No secretary by the door?"

"Yeah, but there's a private elevator at the back end of the suite. According to his secretary—who found the body, by the way—he often brought his new talent in and out via that route. Seems he liked to keep them secret till he went public with them."

"She never heard anything?"

"I don't know. She was still pretty hysterical when I got here. She's down on the next floor. Maybe she's pulled herself together now."

Tracy threw the white sheet back over the corpse and nodded to the morgue attendants to take it away.

"Let's see what she can tell us."

The receptionist was Carolyn Typo, a pert brunette, young, barely out of secretarial school. She was shivering like someone with total body frostbite. After a few soothing remarks and reassurances, Tracy got to the point.

"I understand, Carolyn, that you saw no one enter Mr. Cover's office."

"That's right," she said, nodding and sobbing. "They must've come up the private elevator."

"Do you remember hearing anything strange, any sounds of a struggle?"

"No struggle, but they were talking pretty loud in there. In fact they were arguing."

"Did you hear any of the words?"

"Mr. Cover said something like, 'You'll never work in this town again, or in any other for that matter!' "

"Did you hear the other voice?"

"Yes, but I didn't understand what he was saying. Neither did Mr. Cover, I guess, 'cause he kept saying, 'What he say?' I guess the other man was foreign or something. Every time the other man spoke, Mr. Cover would ask over and over again: 'What he say?' ''

In the far recesses of Tracy's mind, a bell of recognition chimed faintly. He shook it off.

"Would you recognize that voice again?"

"Oh, yes."

"Good. There might come a time when we'll need you for that. But right now, I want you to go down to police headquarters and make a complete statement."

After the receptionist had been led away, Tracy turned to Catchem. "Who's the number-two man around here, Sam?"

Catchem checked his list.

"Hyram Figh. His office is on—"

"Did someone say my name?" said a short, slim, dapper man standing nearby. He appeared to be in his mid-twenties.

"I'm Detective Tracy, this is Detective Catchem, Mr. Figh."

"Just call me Hy. Everyone does."

"Okay, Hy. Do you have any knowledge of any associate of Mr. Cover's who doesn't speak English?"

"No. Not a one."

"How about some new act he might have been auditioning?" Catchem said.

"Well, I do know he was pretty excited about a new rockabilly quartet he was secretly rehearsing in one of our recording studios."

"What on earth is 'rockabilly'?" Sam said.

"Hmmm." Hy scratched his chin. "I guess you could best describe it as a hillbilly white kid singing rhythm and blues to a rock and roll beat."

"Oh. Thanks. That clears it up perfectly."

"Any time. Anyway, W.B.—we called him W.B.— was grooming this quartet to cut the first all-original recording in the history of Wonder Records. He'd always said the key to a hit rockabilly record was to make the lyrics unintelligible. He told me he'd found a singer no one would *ever* understand. Said the kids would go crazy wondering what he was saying. They'd play the song over and over on jukeboxes all over the country, trying to figure out the lyrics. He was *very* excited."

Again that bell rang in Tracy's brain, louder now. He glanced at Catchem, who shook his head.

"I know what you're thinking, but it ain't possible."

Tracy turned back to Mr. Figh.

"Thanks, Hy. You've been a big help. Please don't leave town for the next few days. We may have some other questions for you."

"Anything I can do to help. Anything. Just call."

As the young executive headed for his office down the hall, Tracy turned to Catchem.

"Who does that sound like to you, Sam?"

"Mumbles," Catchem said, lighting another cigarette. "Who else? But Mumbles is dead, remember? He drowned over a year ago, and almost took you with him."

"I know, I know. But it fits so perfectly. A guy no one can understand: that was Mumbles. Sings with a quartet: that was Mumbles. Crooked enough to have been 'borrowing' the Wonder Records masters and making illegal copies of Wonder hits—"

"I know," Catchem said. "Mumbles. But he drowned, he was buried, and neither of us believe in ghosts."

"And violent enough to kill when cornered," Tracy said. "That would fit Mumbles too." Tracy pushed back his yellow fedora and scratched his head. "Yeah. A crazy thought."

"No argument there," Catchem said. "But until Mumbles shows up, what say we get back up to the murder scene and see if we can find anything to point us toward a *living* suspect."

* * *

Tracy couldn't sleep. The William B. Cover murder wouldn't permit it. Finally he gave up trying. He left Tess slumbering peacefully in their bed and wandered down the hall to Junior's room. He put his ear against the door and listened. A radio was playing low. He knocked and stuck his head in the darkened room.

"Got any rockabilly records?"

The light came on and Junior sat up in bed.

"Sure. Want to hear some?"

"Just a couple of samplings. And real low. We don't want to wake the sleeping, let alone the dead."

Junior hopped out of bed and pulled out his record box. He showed Tracy the labels with the titles and artists, and played snatches of the songs.

They all sounded pretty much the same to Tracy. Junior ran through "Blue Suede Shoes" by Carl Perkins, "Tongue Tied Jill" by Charlie Feathers, "Ooby Dooby" by Roy Orbison, "Be-Bop-a-Lula" by Gene Vincent . . .

"Enough," Tracy said. "That's all I can take. But thanks for the lesson, Junior."

He tousled the kid's hair affectionately, the way he used to, but came away with a hand coated with grease. Wiping his palm on his pajama pants leg, he returned to his own bedroom.

And still he couldn't sleep.

Mumbles . . . was it even remotely possible that he was still alive?

Tracy thought back to July of last year when he and Mumbles had been caught in that salt marsh at high tide. Tracy had survived but Mumbles had drowned because he wouldn't—or couldn't—let go of the loot he had dug up. Tracy racked his brain now trying to remember if he or Sam or anyone for that matter had officially identified the body. They'd found it strapped to the barrel of jewels, they'd shaken their heads and said that Mumbles' greed had finally killed him, then they'd sent the body off to the coroner—tagged as Mumbles.

Tracy dragged himself back to the present. This was

fruitless. All it did was distract him from zeroing on a real suspect in the Cover murder.

And yet . . . rockabilly, with all its hiccuping vocals and nonsense lyrics, was almost custom made for Mumbles, wasn't it? If he were alive, he could very well have been rehearsing in the Wonder Records recording studios—

Tracy bolted upright in bed.

Rehearsing! Wouldn't they be recording those rehearsals? At least parts of them? After all, the quartet in question was slated to be a recording sensation. Wouldn't W.B. have wanted to hear what they sounded like on vinyl?

Tracy was out of bed again, this time reaching for his clothes. Those tapes might break this case.

The all-night security guard at the main entrance let Tracy in and directed him to the recording studios on the tenth floor.

Tracy said, "On the way in I noticed that the big record player isn't working," Tracy said.

"We turned it off in mourning for Mr. Cover. The big Wonder record won't play again until after his funeral."

"I'm sure he'd have appreciated that."

Tracy headed directly to the recording studios. All the tapes and masters in W.B. Cover's office vault had been accounted for this afternoon, so Tracy figured that the mystery quartet's rehearsal tape, if it existed, might still be in the studio.

But which studio? There were eight of them on the floor.

He realized he should have brought Sam along to help go through the hundreds, perhaps thousands of tapes that were stored here. But better to let Sam sleep so he'd be fresh for the morning. Tracy hadn't been getting any sleep anyway.

Where to start? He decided to begin at the end. As he walked down the hall toward Studio H he heard a noise.

He stopped and heard it again. A clatter . . . very faint. Coming from Studio C.

Tracy pulled his snub-nosed .357 and edged the door open.

The studio was a shambles. Empty tape cannisters were everywhere, the entire studio was festooned with tangled garlands of recording tape. As Tracy watched, a ten-inch reel, trailing a shiny brown ribbon behind it, sailed across the room and clattered against the wall.

To his left, out of sight, he heard someone shouting.

"Fina fug inape!"

A chill crawled over Tracy's skin. He knew that voice. But it couldn't be. Without thinking, he shoved the door open and stepped inside.

There were four men in the room. Three of them— one wearing a gray fedora, one with a knitted cap, and one bald and bareheaded—were tearing through the studio's tape library. But it was the fourth, standing in the center of the studio floor, who seized Tracy's attention. Short, medium-framed, close-cropped blond hair, heavy-lidded eyes, dark eyebrows, and a small, thin-lipped mouth.

"Mumbles!"

The man's eyes widened. "Syoo!"

Tracy shook off the shock of seeing Mumbles alive and covered the room with his pistol. He realized he'd made a rookie-level error: no back-up. But he had the drop on them so maybe he could pull this off.

"Hands up and into the middle there—all of you!"

They hesitated, looking to Mumbles for direction.

"Doozee sz," Mumbles said.

"What he say?" whispered the one with the knitted cap.

"What'sa matter? You deaf?" the bald one replied. "He said 'Do what he says.' So let's do it."

They joined Mumbles in the center.

"Now—everybody facedown on the floor."

When he had all of them down he could use the wrist

radio to call for back-up. This would be a good collar, even if it wasn't by the book.

Three of them went facedown on the rug. Only their leader refused to comply.

"You too, Mumbles," Tracy said.

Mumbles stepped to his left behind a microphone on a chrome stand. He stayed on his feet.

"Newt beoo, Trce."

"What he say?" said the knitted cap.

Baldhead said, "He said, 'I knew it'd be you, Tracy.' "

Tracy said, "How did you survive that tide? That's what I want to know, Mumbles. And who did we bury if it wasn't you?"

"Yoofih grout, cppr."

"What he say?"

"Shuddup," said the fedora.

"Down, Mumbles," Tracy said.

Mumbles' stare was coolly defiant.

"Nway, cppr."

Tracy approached Mumbles warily, keeping the three on the floor in full view.

"I'm warning you, Mumbles. Don't try anything foolish. You're now the prime suspect in the W.B. Cover murder. And if that isn't enough, you'll be tried for Cinn's murder and as an accomplice in the George Ozone murder. Now *get down on that floor*!"

Mumbles sidestepped, keeping the mike stand between Tracy and himself.

"Kz maz, cppr."

Tracy reached out to knock the mike stand out of the way. The instant he touched it, he knew he'd been suckered. He heard the buzz, felt the electric current shoot up his arm, saw Mumbles' sneering face dissolve in a cascade of blinding white, yellow, blue, and orange explosions.

Then everything went black.

* * *

Tracy awoke slowly, to the chilly caress of a city-flavored October breeze, to the sound of faraway voices, and to the throb of a thundering headache. He opened his eyes and immediately snapped them shut against the sudden, overpowering rush of vertigo.

He took a deep breath. For a moment there, he'd almost thought—

Tracy opened his eyes again. To his left the sun was rising. The dark, sleeping city was spread out above him . . .

No—*below* him. He was upside down—trussed up and being lowered by his ankles on a long rope from the roof of the Wonder building. He could feel the grooves of the giant record logo jouncing against his back as he was lowered along the north wall.

Voices filtered down from above. He picked out Mumbles' voice immediately.

"Hole air."

"What he say?"

"He said to hold it there. C'mon. We'll tie it to this vent stack here."

"Hey, that's pretty swell, Mumbles. You got him right over the dent where the needle hits. When the arm comes over it'll nail him good!"

"Lemring amurwep innacor!"

"What he say?"

"He said, 'Let them bring that murder weapon into court!' "

There was laughter from above.

"Swaj blow," said Mumbles and the voices faded out.

Tracy's hands were tied behind his back. He probed the depth of the pit in the surface of the giant record where the tone arm's "needle" impacted twelve times an hour. A deep pit. He glanced over at the metal spike that served as the needle. It wasn't sharp, but it had to come down with considerable force to wear a pocket like this. Force enough to punch a hole in Tracy's gut.

But the laugh was on Mumbles. The giant phonograph had been shut off.

Just then Tracy felt a hum through the back of his head. The giant record vibrated as the label at its center began to turn. To Tracy's right, the tone arm shuddered to life.

Mumbles had turned on the power!

As the arm began to lift, Tracy began to swing his body left and right. Soon he had a bit of a pendulum motion established. The arc was small, but he hoped it would be enough to give him a fighting chance to be out of harm's way when the tone arm came down.

It was swinging toward him now, looming over him. He augmented his pendulum motion with a quarter roll to the right just as the needle slammed down onto the record.

Missed me!

Now he had a couple of minutes to work at the ropes around his wrists. The left was not looped quite as tightly as the right. He made an all-out bid to pull it loose, clenching his teeth against the pain as the upper layer of the skin over his wrist tore away. He groaned and broke out in a cold sweat as something popped inside his wrist, but suddenly his left hand was free. Seconds later the right was also free.

Using mostly his right hand, Tracy pulled himself up inside the tone arm. He twisted himself around to an upright position and wedged his body into the metal struts of the supporting framework. His legs and ankles were still trussed up like a roast but he left the ropes where they were for now. He had to close his eyes and let this sick feeling pass. Good to be right side up again, but his left wrist was swollen and puffy and throbbing like an elephant's migraine. At least he still had his wrist radio. He flicked the transmitter switch.

"Headquarters, this is Tracy. I'm at the Wonder Records building. I need immediate back-up. Repeat: immediate back-up requested. Do you copy?"

But when he switched to receive, he heard only static. He tried again with similar results. Maybe he'd damaged the radio getting out of the ropes. Maybe just the receiver was out of commission. He hoped that was all.

Because things were a bit dicey up here.

Voices . . . from far below. Angry shouts. Tracy peeked down at the gesticulating forms in the parking lot below. He realized with a grin that they couldn't see him from down there. Couldn't even see the rope. They probably thought he'd escaped.

Well, in a few minutes they'll be right!

He went to work on the rope around his legs, doing the best he could without putting too much stress on his left wrist.

Just then the tone arm began to rise. He heard the motor groan with the strain of lifting his extra weight. The arm was just starting back toward its rest position when something snapped in its base. The motor screeched and died as the arm jolted partially free of its supports and tilted at an angle.

Tracy hung on by his fingertips, then got his feet braced against the framework again. Renewed shouts rose from below as he realized his hiding place was now exposed in the growing dawnlight.

He saw two figures, one blond, one bald-headed, dart for the rear of the building. It looked like Mumbles and one of his gang were coming back up to finish the job— probably by way of W.B. Cover's private elevator.

Tracy redoubled his efforts on the ropes, but they resisted him. If only he could use both hands!

Moments later he heard a clank above him. Mumbles was there, grinning maniacally as he leaned over the edge of the roof and hammered at the tone arm's remaining supports with a tire iron.

Tracy felt the structure twist and sag further. Any second now it would go, taking him down with it. And still the knots on his legs resisted him. If he could just free his legs he could climb up the arm and at least give himself a fighting chance.

And then Tracy heard a wonderful sound: sirens.

So, apparently, did Mumbles' companion.

"The cops, Mumbles. Let's get outta here!"

"Ntlee fls!"

"Are you crazy, Mumbles?" Baldhead said. "What're you doin'?"

Tracy glanced up and saw Mumbles swing his leg over the edge of the roof and begin kicking at the tone arm's base.

"Dmthns tuck!" Mumbles said.

The sirens were getting louder but every kick sent increasingly violent shudders through the arm. Its base was edging free of the support. A few more good kicks . . .

Tracy yanked on the rope that ran from his ankles up to the roof. Still tied. Suddenly he was glad he hadn't been able to conquer those knots.

Far below, Tracy saw the two other members of Mumbles' crew running for their car. Looked back up toward the roof to see Mumbles hanging from the edge of the roof by his arms, ramming both feet against the base of the tone arm.

Suddenly it twisted loose, but in twisting it caught Mumbles' foot. Mumbles lost his grip on the parapet. Baldhead made a grab for his arm but it was too late. Tracy dove free of the arm as it began to fall. The metal screeched but Mumbles' scream was louder as man and tone arm plummeted to earth.

Tracy was hanging upside down again, the blood rushing to his head. He saw the tone arm crash through the hood of the getaway car as it pulled away, saw Mumbles bounce off the car roof and land in a broken heap atop the trunk.

"That crazy bastard!" said Baldhead from above. "All because of you."

Tracy angled his neck to see the man's angry face glaring down at him. A knife snapped open in his hand.

"No reason why you shouldn't join him, cop."

As Baldhead began to saw at the rope, Tracy stuffed his right hand into the pocket the needle had made and clutched one of the record grooves with his bum left, hoping he might be able to hold on but knowing deep in his gut that there was no way in hell he could.

Suddenly there was a shot. Tracy looked up and saw part of Baldhead's scalp explode in a spray of red. Then the body slumped over the parapet. Warm blood began to drip on Tracy.

Sam Catchem's face appeared over the edge of the roof. "You all right, Tracy?"

"Just fine, Sam. Enjoying the view."

Catchem lit a cigarette. "Yeah. Me too. You know, I was listening to a preacher on one of the news shows last night. He was warning the kids that hanging around these rock and roll joints would bring them nothing but trouble. Looking at you makes me think he may have a point."

"Pull me up, Sam. Now."

"Yes, boss."

As he was being dragged upward across the grooved surface of the giant Wonder record, Tracy stared down at Mumbles' inert form and . . .

No—not inert. His arms and legs were moving—not much, but moving all the same. He was alive. Tracy shook his head in silent wonder. Mumbles' luck never seemed to run all the way out.

Well, at least now they had a good chance of finding out who was really buried in Mumbles' grave: They could ask Mumbles himself. Either way, though, Tracy would have to get an exhumation order. But that could wait.

At least until this afternoon.

THE CURSE

by
Ed Gorman

He was not sure when the blue sedan had started following him. Sometime around Colliersville, probably, where Tracy had pulled into a trucker's diner for an egg sandwich and a cup of coffee.

Now he was back on the narrow two-lane blacktop that wound through the rolling hills and deep valleys you found only upstate. Ordinarily, Tracy would have entertained himself by watching the countryside roll by, the fat harvest moon tinting the September cornfields with gold, lights in distant farmhouse windows looking snug and comfortable, lazing cows mooing on the soft Indian summer breeze.

Tonight, however, Tracy had to keep both hands planted firmly on the wheel and his gaze set rapt ahead. The rain was coming in silver sheets that struck the windshield with the force and sound of hail. It was one of those vicious summer rainstorms that unnerve you just because of their unexpected—and unseasonal—ferocity.

The interior of the car was unpleasant. It was raining

too hard to roll the window down, so the air was hot and moist. Even the air conditioning didn't cut into the clamminess. The windows were steamed up and Tracy had to keep wiping a patch of the windshield clear. Before the rainstorm struck, Tracy had been listening to a tape that was a salute to the big bands. That was still Tracy's favorite era of music. Hearing Bob Crosby and the Bobcats' "Big Noise From Winnetka" was just as thrilling tonight as it had been back in 1939.

For the third time, the car behind him came shooting over a hill, pulling up too close given the slickness of the asphalt, and then falling abruptly back. The person following him was an amateur, overcompensating when Tracy vanished from sight by flying over the hill, then applying the brakes when he realized Tracy could easily see him.

Reaching inside his black suitcoat, Tracy jerked the .357 Magnum from his shoulder rig and set it on the seat. He was ready.

In all, the pursuit went on twenty-eight miles through the relentless rain. Several more times the driver behind lost Tracy, then shot forward as if through a time warp.

Tracy, who was driving up to see an old police friend of his who was gravely ill in a hospital, had been on this stretch of highway often enough to recall the two-pump gas station that lay on the right side of the road approximately five miles ahead. His idea was to lure his stalker there and find out just what was going on.

No lights shone in the rain. The station, a relic of the thirties, was shaped like a cottage except for its deep slanting roof. Fishscale-pattern shingles managed to look dirty even in the downpour. In the wash of his headlights, he could see the large red padlock on the front door. The owner had gone home long ago.

Tracy pulled up to one of the two gas pumps, killing his lights as he did so. Taking the .357 mag from the seat, he shrugged into his trenchcoat, pulled the brim of his fedora lower, and walked out from under the protection of the island overhang.

The rain hit him like rubber bullets, echoing off his hat, soaking into the fabric of his trenchcoat. The rain smelled fresh; the ground smelled muddy.

A quarter mile west, he could see the headlights of the car that had been following him. They shone through the gloom like tracer rounds in an endless nocturnal war.

He walked over to the far side of the gas station and crouched behind a dumpster that smelled of car oil and transmission fluid.

He had his weapon pointed at the spot where he estimated the stalker would pull up. Given the nature of his job, Tracy had a hundred enemies. He was curious about which one this would be.

The blue sedan obliged him by pulling off the asphalt, rolling along the gravel drive and stopping at almost the exact spot Tracy had in his gunsight.

The car sat there, lights still on, rain silver and slanting in the beams, the sound of the radio muffled behind the sound of the engine loudly idling. Tracy couldn't see who was inside. The steamy windows prevented that.

First the radio went off. Then the headlights. Then the engine.

All Tracy could hear for long minutes was the noise of the rain banging metallically on the roof of his car and the stalker's car. He was getting hot inside his trenchcoat. His mouth tasted dead and warm. He wanted a drink of water or a piece of gum.

The door of the stalker's car opened. A tall figure emerged, wearing a trenchcoat and fedora much like his own. From here, Tracy could see that in the figure's right gloved hand was a large silver handgun.

By the time the figure came around the front of the car, Tracy knew it was a woman. The steps were tentative, almost mincing, in the downpour, and the sway of the hips beneath the bulky material of the coat was unmistakably feminine. This didn't surprise him. He was sure he had as many female enemies as he did male ones.

Tracy got off one shot. Even in the rain, the muzzle flashed yellow-red and the acrid odor of gunsmoke filled his nostrils.

The shot tore a piece from the overhang. It was sufficient warning for the woman. She started to dive for the protection of her car.

Tracy raised himself upright and said, "If you throw your gun down, I won't fire any more." He paused. "But I want to see you toss it out here on the gravel."

He couldn't see her. She was somewhere behind the driver's side of her car. She was better than Tracy had assumed. Her first shot missed his left shoulder by a quarter of an inch.

He put two quick ones into her fender. He heard her scream and scramble toward the back end of the car.

Over the next two minutes, she returned fire three times. None of the shots came close to hitting him. He came out from behind the dumpster and started walking to her car. Every few steps, he'd fire a round just to keep her at bay.

He was five feet from the rear of the blue sedan when he saw her jump up and aim her .38 right at his face.

All he had time to do was pitch himself to the ground and start rolling. If he lay still, she'd have an easy target. When he was even with her bumper, he rolled himself to one knee, ducked under her frantic gunfire, and put two shots in the middle of her chest. She slumped against the trunk immediately, her gun falling to the gravel. She began moaning, saying words that were not audible through the hissing downpour, and crying in a way Tracy recognized at once. It was the sound people made when they knew for sure they were about to cross over to the other realm.

From his pocket, he took a flashlight. He walked over to the woman and put the beam in her face.

Her hat had fallen off and now he could see her

shoulder-length blond hair and her classically beautiful features. Even in dying, her face was almost painfully lovely to behold. He had no idea who she was.

"I'm going to call an ambulance," he said.

"No," she said. "It's too late for that." She started to slide from the trunk to the gravel. Tracy helped her so that she could lie on the ground beneath the overhang, out of the pounding rain. Like a huge flower, dark red blood had bloomed over the front of her yellow trench-coat. A glistening stream of blood was also beginning to escape from the corner of her soft lips.

The strength of her grasp surprised him. She took his wrist and pulled him close to her. "I want to thank you, Tracy," she said.

"Thank me? For what?"

She smiled and in that moment he saw the madness in her blue eyes. "For killing me. Just the way I planned it." Blood was becoming so thick in her mouth, she could scarcely form words. "Purse," she managed to spit out. "Tape."

She died, then, Tracy cradling her blond head in his arms.

"Who the hell are you?" he said, even though he knew there'd be no answer. "Why did you want me to kill you?"

The ambulance came from a small county hospital. Both the driver and the attendant were women bulky in their white jumpsuits. Like Sheriff Olsen, the man whose jurisdiction included this lonely stretch of county road, the women looked very angry and suspicious when Tracy admitted he'd killed the woman.

Unlike Olsen, the women obviously did not believe Tracy's tale of being drawn into a shootout and learning only afterwards that he'd been trapped into killing her. The women glared at him even while the white, boxy ambulance was wheeling out of the drive. Tracy didn't blame them. He knew how suspicious this looked.

Olsen told him to stay in touch, that there'd be an inquest and further questions, then bid Tracy goodnight.

Tracy hadn't told Olsen about the cassette tape he'd found in the woman's purse. He figured that was between himself and the dead woman.

In the car two hours later, continuing his drive to see his old friend, the rain little more than a mist now, Tracy put the tape into the deck and listened.

The woman's voice was as lovely as her face had been.

"I am Kendra Long, the daughter of Charles Long, a man you shot to death three years ago while trying to arrest him for holding up a bank in which a guard had been killed. I'm not making any claim that my father was innocent. He spent his whole life being a criminal.

"But when you killed him, Tracy, you doomed me to a life of wanting vengeance. All I could think of was killing you. I alienated my husband and two little girls because my obsession with vengeance took the place of everything else. I could no longer love; I could only hate.

"Most people don't understand that hatred binds even more strongly than love. I could not let go.

"I spent six months following you. Learning your habits. Waiting for the one right moment.

"My plan at this time was to kill you and then return to my family.

"But gradually I began to realize that in a very real sense, my life was over. I had given it all up to kill you. So twice, I tried. Once I was about to send you a letter bomb and the other time I was about to shoot you when you were on vacation in Mexico.

"But both times, something stopped me. And after the second time, I realized what it was. It was not you I wanted dead; it was myself. Hatred had already killed my mind and soul so the killing of my body was little more than a formality.

"And how fitting that you'd be my executioner, Tracy. Just as you'd been my father's executioner.

"You will never forget me, Tracy, no matter how hard

you try. You'll remember what it was like seeing me die; my face, the sounds I made. You'll know what it's like killing an innocent woman.

"Just as you cursed me, Tracy, now I've cursed you."

And that was it.

Blank tape passed through the heads silently.

She'd said what she wanted to say. Nothing more.

A pearl-colored dawn stretched across the black line of horizon as Tracy pulled into the small town where his friend lay in the hospital.

He kept thinking of the one word that Kendra Long had used to describe him—"executioner."

Tracy was not a man given to much doubt about the morality of his calling. Sometimes to catch killers, you had to become a killer yourself, and you could not allow yourself the luxury of doubt.

But as he climbed from his car in the hospital parking lot, sunlight beginning to stream through the rainclouds, he realized that Kendra Long had had her vengeance indeed.

In a very real way, in a way that would trouble him and occasionally sap him with doubt if he was not careful, Dick Tracy had been cursed.

THE LEO'S DEN AFFAIR

by
Francis M. Nevins
and Josh Pachter

The timing was perfect. Dick Tracy had just punched the down button when an upward-bound car disgorged a distracted and sleepy-looking Sam Catchem, who stepped out without looking and plowed full-tilt into his crime-busting compadre. Both detectives toppled to the linoleum and shot rueful looks at each other before they burst out laughing.

"Another fine mess you've got me into," Tracy quipped, helping Catchem to his feet. "Glad none of the Squad saw that."

"I'm late," Sam apologized. The clock on the corridor wall read seven minutes after midnight. "Sorry. My Crimestoppers Chronometer needs a new microchip or something." He adjusted his bow tie in the mirror-bright brass of the elevator door. "What kind of a case is so important we have to lose a night's sleep?"

"Assault and art theft in the high-rent district. A priceless painting by Jesús Zumarraga, vanished. Just like that." He snapped his fingers, and as if on cue an inverted arrowhead glowed red above the bank of elevators and a cage door slid open.

"Sounds like a job for the Major Crime Squad all right," Catchem agreed. "Any chance our old buddy Art Dekko's back in town?"

"First thing I checked," Tracy said. "The little weasel moved to Canada a few years ago, and the Toronto Mounties caught him. Right now he's doing five-to-ten at the Mimico Correctional Centre. Anyway it's not his style. When did Dekko ever make a work of art disappear like a prop in a magic trick?"

In the basement garage they signed out an unmarked Major Crime Squad sedan and Catchem took the wheel, wrestling the heavy black Buick up the ramp to street level. Scowling, he cut in front of a night bus—"Damn drivers're still threatening to strike at eight in the morning if they don't get that pay raise," he grunted—and sped west across the garishly neoned cityscape as Tracy briefed him from scrawled notes.

"It happened at the Oxford House," he began. "That's a high-rise on Parkmoor that they converted from apartments into condos a few years back. Bigshot lawyer was slugged from behind. When he came to, a painting worth anywhere from three to five million wasn't hanging on his wall anymore."

"Did he see who did it?" The brakes screamed as Sam hung a hard left into Parkmoor Drive.

"He *smelled* who did it. Or at least that's what he says. The man he accuses is his ex–law partner."

Catchem wagged his head in mock sadness as they rounded a curve of the drive and a steel-and-glass tower studded with specks of light loomed up in the sedan's windshield. "He smelled the guy who beaned him, huh? Beautiful. The nose knows. Still and all, why am I complaining, right? Sounds like a nice normal straightforward case, as our cases go."

"True," Tracy agreed. "If lions are your meat."

"Lions?" Sam flung his chief a scowl of incredulity. "Here in Yuppie Acres?"

"Figure of speech." An amused look stole across Tracy's square-jawed countenance. "The name of the missing painting is *Lion and Cub*. The lawyer it was taken from is Leo Risinger Jr. Guess what room it used to hang in."

Catchem said nothing, swerving into the parking crescent in front of the Oxford House. The big Buick shuddered to a halt.

"His den," Tracy told him.

The lobby was a low-key sales pitch. Its richly-glowing paneling and buffed parquet floor, its elegant mirrors and designer couches whispered their seductive messages in unison: *Buy a condo. Live the good life. Dig deep.* The only sour note in the chorus was the night doorman, an obese creature of shifty eyes and furtive gestures, the kind of person who looked as if he would buttonhole a passing stranger in the street and offer him the short-term rental of a woman. A tag clipped to the breast pocket of his uniform jacket read ALDEN CURRY, ENTRY ADMINIS-TRATOR. He oozed out from an alcove as the two detectives strode across the lobby. "Can't leave your car in the crescent," he croaked. "You're blocking a fire lane."

But the moment Tracy flashed his shield and Major Crime Squad ID, the doorman metamorphosed from obstructive functionary to servile flunkey desperate to please. "Oh, of course! The Risinger case, right? That's unit 19-E, officers. You won't be needing my passkeys, the other detectives and Mr. Risinger and Miss Wood-ward are still up there. My God, what a jungle this city is! Robbery, assault, smuggling, forgery, rape, murder, vandalism—"

"And this is the *right* side of the tracks." Catchem cut off the hoarse litany of felony offenses. With Tracy a step ahead, he made haste to the elevators at the rear of the lobby.

"Strange toad," Tracy remarked as the carpet-walled cage lifted them. "Wonder why he was so eager to, ah, curry favor with us?"

"I know the type," Sam growled. "Brain rot. He sees the world as a never-ending cops-and-robbers comic strip."

"But we streetwise real-life cops know better, don't we?"

"You betcha," Catchem said. "The world's no comic strip, it's a pile of boring routine cases with paintings that vanish like magic, and victims that smell the perpetrators, and lions."

"Just like they taught us in the Academy," Tracy chuckled. "Come on, this is our stop." The cage door swished back and they stepped out into the corridor of the nineteenth floor.

The digital clock on the credenza in Risinger's den read 5:17. Tracy and Catchem had talked with the precinct cops and with Risinger and with Stella Woodward, the lawyer's former office receptionist and current live-in lady. They had talked with the other owners of nineteenth-floor condominiums and with the building manager and again with the obese and fawning doorman. They had called the Major Crime Squad and arranged for Lizz Grove and Lee Ebony to check out the former law partner whom Risinger accused of assault and art theft. They had prowled for more than an hour around the room from which the *Lion and Cub* had disappeared. The first streaks of dawn were spreading across the sky, but not a ray of light had yet been shed on the crime in Leo's den.

"What say we run through it again?" Catchem yawned and leaned back in the brown-leather executive swivel chair behind the teakwood desk. Ceiling-high shelves stuffed with lawbooks lined the two long walls of the den, broken only by a single door which opened onto a large cozy living room. On the short wall facing the desk the cream-colored paint was visibly less faded over a patch roughly three feet wide by two feet high, the dimensions of the framed painting that had hung there until shortly after eleven the night before. The wall at Sam's back was blank, except for a second, closed door directly behind him.

"Risinger and Woodward went out to dinner around 7:30," he began, glancing down at his notes. "No confirmation on that yet from the doorman who had the shift before Curry, but the two of them agree on the time, and there's no reason to doubt their story. Anyway, they got back here around a quarter past ten. Curry went on duty at eight and he verifies their arrival." Catchem gestured towards the living room, of which a wedge could be seen through the open door. "Risinger poured himself a Drambuie and made coffee for her, and by 10:45 they were in bed."

The murmur of soft voices reached them from somewhere in the unit: Risinger and his lady. The precinct cops had long since gone off to other duties, other crimes.

"A while later, around 11:30, Risinger decided he couldn't sleep. He got up, put on a robe and came in here to do some paperwork. He sat down at the desk, facing the door to the living room, which he'd left open. A few minutes went by uneventfully. No one came into the room. Then suddenly he got a whiff of this El Stinko cologne he recognized from behind him. Before he could even turn his head, he was conked. And when he came to, the painting was gone."

"Like magic." Tracy frowned. "Because none of the other residents on this floor saw anyone carrying a big framed painting through the corridor, or a rolled-up canvas either. And worse, Curry swears that no one could have gotten a frame or a canvas out of the building without him seeing them, and he didn't spot a soul out of place all night. Which means the Zumarraga must still be in the building somewhere. But where? The manager told us that all the unit owners moved in before Risinger brought the painting home from the office, so we know no art thief bought in just to get close to the target.''

''And as if all that's not bad enough,'' said Catchem, ''there's also the question of where the thief was when Risinger came into the den. He must have been in here already: if he'd come in *after* Leo, he'd have been seen or heard. Only there's no place to hide in this room. So, since Risinger was hit from behind, the thief *must* have been waiting for him in there.'' He got up from the swivel chair and went to the door in the blank wall behind the desk, inserted into the lock the key Risinger had given him, pulled the door open. From floor to ceiling the doorway was blocked by a tower of bulky cardboard cartons.

''Unit 19-D.'' Tracy took up the recital, beginning to feel like half of a vaudeville team. ''A studio. Unoccupied for months because nobody wants to buy a one-room condo. Risinger's been renting it to store office files since his partnership broke up, until the decorators finish with the new place he's moving into with his solo law practice. The studio's looked like this for at least four months, every square foot of wall space including the space against that communicating door blocked by cartons full of old law files. There's open space in the center of the room, and Risinger goes in and out when he has to via the studio's front door, off the outside hallway. The communicating door we're staring at simply couldn't have been opened from inside the studio because first of all the doorway's blocked and second of all the door was locked and Risinger had the only key.''

''Makes you wonder if he's telling us the truth,'' Sam said. ''After all, there's no love lost between him and his ex-partner.''

''But nobody,'' Tracy argued, ''would be dumb enough to set up a frame which was clearly impossible on its face!'' He sighed, stifled a yawn, snapped his notepad shut and got to his feet. ''Let's have Leo back in here. I want to hear him roar again.''

* * *

In fact, Leo Risinger Jr. wouldn't have roared on the worst day of his life. He was a slender, mild-mannered man, dark-haired and deeply tanned, and even with the swath of bandage taped to the back of his head he projected the image of a languid mandarin in his velvet dressing gown. He sat on the divan with his petite and lovely woman beside him and budged not an inch from his story.

"I know what I smelled." His cultured drawl spoke of Groton and Yale, of gourmet dinners and fine wines and art galleries and chamber music. "I had to inhale it every working day from the time I joined Dad's firm until I walked out six months ago. It was Machismo. No one in the world uses it anymore except for Katz. The company that used to make it went bankrupt two years ago and the penny-pinching boor bought up a lifetime supply at a quarter a bottle."

In an earlier interview, around one in the morning, Risinger had explained the background to them. In 1962, a merger had taken place between the law practices of Leo Risinger Sr., who represented the American interests of various European artists, and a young labor lawyer named Thomas Katz. Leo Junior's description reminded Tracy of *The Odd Couple*: his patrician father dealing suavely with museums and collectors on behalf of *his* clients, while the uncultured Katz counseled dock workers, city employees and common laborers. Both halves of the new firm had prospered, and it was not uncommon for the Risinger & Katz waiting room to simultaneously house a distinguished sculptor, the head of a prominent gallery, and a grease-faced backhoe driver with a grudge against his boss. Leo Junior had joined the firm after graduating *cum laude* from Yale Law School, but he got along poorly with Katz and, after his father's recent death, had taken steps to dissolve the partnership. "Katz got the office and the law library," he had told them, "and I took Stella." Stella Woodward had been hired as a receptionist only six weeks before the dissolution of the firm.

"You got the Zumarraga, too," Tracy had reminded him.

"It wasn't the firm's property." Risinger's voice had risen just a trifle as he defended himself. "It belonged to Dad personally, he'd just kept it hanging in his office all those years. It's called *León y Cachorro.*" Tracy had noticed that his Spanish inflection, like everything else about him, was impeccable. *"Lion and Cub,"* he had translated. "Lion. Leo. Dad and me. Zumarraga painted it and gave it to Dad when I was born, forty-one years ago. The birth of a son means so much to Spaniards, you see. And I was born on August second, which makes me a Leo that way, too."

"So your father had a Zumarraga original hanging among his law diplomas," Tracy had said, "and Katz never realized what it was worth until you dissolved the partnership and claimed it."

"Zumarraga and Dad had a falling out long before Dad merged with Katz, but the painting was a gift. Dad didn't have to return it just because the artist wasn't his client anymore. He kept it hanging in his office even after the merger. Considering what a cultural ignoramus Katz has always been, it's understandable that he had no idea of the picture's value."

"And now that Picasso and Miró and Dalí are dead," Tracy had pointed out, "and Zumarraga's considered the greatest living Spanish artist, the picture is worth three million minimum. Its value will skyrocket when Zumarraga dies, and he's over eighty now." A look of mild amazement had stolen for a moment across Risinger's detached features, as if he felt that a detective, even the world-famous chief of the Major Crime Squad, had no business knowing anything about the art world.

And now, almost five hours after that first interview, the investigators and the victim and the victim's lady were talking again about the painting and the theft and the prime suspect.

"Katz was upset when he found out how much it was worth?" Catchem asked.

"Outraged would be a better word." Stella Woodward's voice was as delicate as the tinkling of wind chimes. "Mr. Katz is the tantrum-throwing type. I was still with the firm when he learned about the painting's value. I heard the fights he had with Leo about it."

"How I stood that oaf for fifteen years, I'll never know," Risinger shuddered. "Let alone how Dad put up with him for twenty-five."

"Oil and water?" Catchem suggested.

"Make that Courvoisier and Kessler's. And remember, Katz comes out of the old labor-union tradition of self-help violence. He'd have had no scruples about taking the Zumarraga by force."

"Ah," Tracy cut in. "But would he have taken it in *this* way? A simple, straightforward man by both of your descriptions, yet we're supposed to believe that he hid himself where no one could possibly have hidden and made the painting and frame disappear as if by magic. That's not the old labor-union tradition, that's detective-story stuff. And even if Katz *was* smart enough to have set up the theft, how could he have been so stupid as to carry it off while wearing a cologne that's not even manufactured anymore and is identified with no one else but him?"

"I know what I smelled," Risinger repeated stubbornly, his long thin fingers teasing the sore spot at the back of his regal head. "It was Machismo. It was Katz."

The phone on the teakwood desk chirped discreetly. Catchem scooped up the handset, listened silently for two full minutes, then gave a disgusted grunt which Tracy, having heard it before, interpreted to mean that something else had gone haywire. Sam flung down the receiver and flashed a long-suffering look at his chief.

After perfunctory goodbyes to Risinger and Stella

Woodward, the detectives made their way out of the unit and the building. Catchem remained silent until they were in the Buick and on their way downtown again.

"What a case," he said at last. "First we beard Leo in his den, and now we've got to go bell the Katz. Tom Katz, no less."

"The phone call?"

"From Lizz, at the Interworld Hotel. Hey, you ready for some hot news? They've settled that transit dispute. No strike after all."

"I'll bite," Tracy said. "Have you been reading an invisible newspaper, or have you got an invisible radio plugged into your ear?"

"Neither. Lizz gave me an on-the-spot exclusive. The Interworld's conference suite is where the negotiators for the union and the Transit Authority have been slugging it out. They've been at it nonstop since six P.M. yesterday. Had their meals brought in, nobody left the room except for two-minute trips to the john. And guess who was captain of the union's negotiating team?"

"Katz?" Tracy hazarded.

"No one else. He was in that suite till after three this morning. Lizz and Lee talked to the whole, ah, kit and caboodle of them as the session was breaking up, and found out Katz spent the night around a table with a dozen witnesses, half of whom hate his guts and would love to see him take a fall for robbery. Even *they* say he was there the whole time. We can't break an alibi that strong." He expelled a noise that was half a sigh and half a groan. "Sometimes," he confided, "I think we *are* a couple of comic-strip cops, and there's some kind of a demon cartoonist out there, plotting these damn cases just to torment us." He swung onto the ramp for the elevated highway, which pointed like an arrow towards the convention district.

"I know the feeling," Tracy told him.

* * *

The clock behind the registration desk of the Interworld Hotel read 6:34. Bleary-eyed waiters shuffled about the restaurant area of the vast lobby, setting up an opulent breakfast buffet. Tracy and Catchem kept their eyes fixed on the elevator bank. When a cage door whispered open and a squat paunchy man in his fifties emerged, they crossed the marble floor to intercept him and showed him their badges. Thomas Katz was freshly shaved and wearing a clean shirt, but his rumpled suit and bloodshot eyes showed that the night's hard bargaining had taken its toll. He dropped onto a circular velour couch and planted his monogrammed pigskin overnight case between his size-12 feet.

The detectives sat one on either side of the lawyer and sniffed the air soundlessly. Tracy's nose told him that Katz was wearing some kind of cologne but he couldn't identify the brand. Catchem leaned towards him and muttered "Russian Leather" in his ear.

Katz's scowl was not what Tracy expected to see on the face of a man whose union client had just closed a deal for hefty wage hikes, but the detectives' call to his room from the house phone in the lobby had brought him down after less than three hours' sleep and that, Tracy reflected, might account for the man's displeasure.

"Okay," he growled when they had explained the situation to him, "so the picture's been ripped off from Risinger's condo and the little wimp blames me, huh? Well, I'll make it short and sweet. Leo's lyin'. Lyin'! Haw haw haw."

Tracy tried not to wince. No wonder Risinger dissolved the firm, he thought. But the pun did show that Katz wasn't fazed by his former partner's accusation.

"I saw a couple women cops talkin' to the Transit Authority boys after the meetin' broke up. Pinto ponies. One black and one white. Haw haw haw. Now I see what it was all about. They were checkin' if I had an alibi. Right?"

"You're right," Catchem admitted, "and you do. But

that doesn't mean you couldn't have sent out a munchkin to do the dirty work *for* you.''

A munchkin wearing Machismo? Tracy asked himself.

"Hey, listen. I could stand on my rights and tell you to go to hell,'' Katz said. "But I'm in a good mood this mornin', see? So you just go ahead and make your unfounded and maybe even slanderous allegations, and I'll sit here and listen like I got nothin' better to do. Or is there anything you wanna *ask* me?''

"We'd like to ask you about your after-shave,'' Tracy said, and fought to hide a grin when Katz blinked like a boxer who had just taken a surprise hit in the solar plexus.

"You're not wearing Machismo this morning,'' Catchem chimed in. "Your trademark. The stuff you bought up a warehouse full of when the manufacturer folded.''

"A warehouse full!'' Katz bent over almost double with laughter, and half a minute went by before he came up for air. "I pay taxes to have cops ask me questions about my cologne?'' he gasped. Then he straightened up and wiped a tear from his eye with the back of his hairy hand. "Okay, what the hell,'' he said, shifting position on the circular couch to face Tracy squarely. "Sure, Machismo was sort of my trademark. I wore it all the time, even kept a couple bottles in my desk so I could freshen up before business dinners, you know? But that was all before last month. Now I'm tryin' to unload my whole supply.''

"Why's that?'' Tracy asked.

"I'm 58 years old,'' Katz said heavily. "Age catches up to different guys in different ways, I guess. Some get ulcers, some go bald, some can't have fun in bed with women any more. Me, I started gettin' allergic to stuff never bothered me before. My face began to break out somethin' awful and I had the doc run some tests. Last month he told me it was the Machismo that was causin' the problems.''

"You can prove that, I suppose,'' Tracy asked.

"He sent me a written report. I can dig it up if I have to."

Tracy believed him. "When was the last time you saw Risinger?"

Katz's bulldog features grimaced in recollection. "Maybe two months back," he said, "when we signed the final papers breakin' up the firm."

"And since then?"

"Since then? Listen, if I saw that stuck-up creep on the street I'd cross over to the other side so I wouldn't have to look at him. The only thing me and him have got to talk about is *nothin'*."

"So he wouldn't be likely to have known about your allergy to Machismo?"

"Probably not," Katz conceded, only then catching the drift of the interrogation. "Hey, dammit, that proves he made up that story about smellin' the stuff! The little punk's tryin' to frame me!"

"Why would he want to do that?" Tracy asked. "You wound up with the office suite and the lawbooks. Did he think you were taking the, er, the lion's share of the firm's assets?"

"The lion's share." Katz grinned. "That's *funny*. Haw haw haw. Not bad for a copper." Then he sobered and rubbed his chin, pondering Tracy's question. "Hell, I guess Leo was satisfied with the split. It's just that that snooty little clown and me've rubbed each other the wrong way since the day he came to work with his old man. Now Leo Senior, God rest him, he could run that artsy-fartsy number too, when he had to—but when it was just the two of us and he could let his hair down, he was all right. Underneath the crap he was a real man. Not like the brat."

"Courvoisier and Kessler's?" Tracy suggested.

"More like Budweiser and Perrier," Katz said.

As Tracy expected, the lawyer's pronunciation of the French word was awful.

* * *

It had been a long frustrating night and the Inter-world's breakfast buffet was rumored the finest in town. Tracy and Catchem decided to fuel up before going back to Headquarters. Sam piled his plate with a basted egg, a hunk of cheese omelet, bacon and sausage links and home fries and crab Rangoon and a toasted bagel with cream cheese. Tracy settled for roast beef hash and peach fritters, but once back at their table he picked absently at his food with a faraway look in his eyes and didn't seem to hear any of Sam's small talk.

"Suppose Leo's not lying," he broke into Catchem's monologue.

Sam swallowed the melange of comestibles in his mouth. "Um-fm," he remarked sagely.

"Suppose," Tracy went on, "Katz isn't lying either."

"I'll bite," Catchem quipped, laying his fork down. "What are you driving at?"

"Not driving at," Tracy corrected him, pushing his chair back. "Driving *to*. Back to the Oxford House. Right now."

By 9:30 they were in their places and at 11:22 they slipped out of their hidey hole with .357 Magnums drawn and made their arrest. They caught the thief with the framed Zumarraga canvas in one hand and a claw hammer in the other. Under his arm was a mailing tube addressed to a post-office box in Kingston, Ontario. He offered the detectives no resistance, just sighed wearily and assumed the frisk position with his hands braced on the cartons stacked against the wall of unit 19-D.

"You should have seen the look on his face when we stepped out from behind that pile of boxes," Catchem chortled. They were seated on either side of Chief Patton's desk at Headquarters. "He thought he'd seen the last of us and then all of a sudden there we were. Thanks to Tracy. He figured out the whole thing over breakfast."

"It all fit together so beautifully," Tracy said, "once I stopped assuming that either Risinger or Katz had to be lying and asked myself what if they were both telling the truth.''

"He turns out to be Winston Trimble, the most notorious art thief in Canada," Catchem explained. "A protégé of our old sparring partner Art Dekko. He's usually as trim and nimble as his name but he put on fifty pounds of blubber for the part of Alden Curry.''

"Just like De Niro did for *Raging Bull*," said the Chief, who liked to think he was a movie buff.

"It was a good disguise," Tracy said. "Stella Woodward was in it with him, of course. Turns out they're married; Tina Trimble, her real name is. The Zumarraga was still hanging in the Risinger & Katz offices when they first came down here after it, so Tina wangled herself a job as receptionist right there on the scene. But before they could make their move, the firm broke up and Leo shifted the painting home to his condo. But Tina didn't miss a trick. She made a quick play for him and Leo, bless his heart, invited her to move right on in. Meanwhile, Trimble went on his De Niro Diet, set himself up a phony identity as Curry and landed the night doorman's job at the Oxford House.''

"With access to all the passkeys," Chief Patton remarked.

"Exactly," said Tracy. "They had to wait a couple of months before the job came open, but then they were in no hurry. They were sitting on a decent stake from their last caper, and they figured the Zumarraga was worth the wait. Then, once Trimble was settled in on the job, they concocted a scheme to steal the painting in a way that would throw dust in everyone's eyes long enough for them to close out their Curry and Woodward identities and get back to their home base in Canada by separate routes. On her last day at the office, Tina lifted a bottle of Machismo from Katz's desk. Then they settled back to wait some more, until the perfect opportunity rolled around, and last night turned out to be it. Or so they thought. Anyway, while Leo and Tina were out at dinner, Trimble sneaked upstairs, let himself into 19-D, the studio, with a passkey and spent half an hour shifting the boxes that were blocking the communicating door enough so that later on he could use *that* passkey to let himself into the den of 19-E.

"After the happy couple had returned and puttered around for a while, and Risinger had gotten out of bed to go work in the den, Tina used the extension phone in the bedroom to ring down to her husband with the signal to get cracking. So Trimble sneaked back upstairs and into 19-D again, slapped Machismo all over his face, used the communicating-door passkey to get into the den, and waited just long enough before slugging Leo to make sure he got a good whiff of the after-shave. Then he took the painting from 19-E back to 19-D and hid it in one of those big cardboard cartons—which he'd emptied out during his earlier visit, redistributing its contents in a couple other boxes. The carton where he stashed the painting was above eye level, but he taped it shut anyway, playing it safe, then put the studio back the way it was and went back to his alcove downstairs, with a short pitstop in the john to wash the Machismo off his face. All told, he was gone from his post no more than about seven minutes. If any of the building residents had happened to pass through the lobby during that time and wondered where he was, well, he could always say that he'd had to go to the bathroom, which was the truth, sort of."

"So then after Risinger reported the assault and theft and we turned up," Catchem continued, "Trimble threw some more dust in our eyes. He passed himself off as an idiot police buff, and we fell for it, for a few hours anyway, and wound up overlooking what an obvious suspect he was."

"He came back to 19-D this morning to pick up the painting," Tracy concluded, "and that's when we grabbed him. He tried playing dumb for about five minutes, but when he saw it wasn't going to wash he gave it up and laid out the whole chain of events for us.''

"So," Patton beamed, "Leo and his lions live happily ever after.''

"And those *lions*!" Catchem shook his head sadly. "I wish you'd've seen that painting, Chief. Three to five million bucks worth of brown, with a big green blob on the left and a little green blob on the right.''

"Zumarraga's *Lion and Cub*." Tracy kept his voice uncritical. "A modern masterpiece. Oh well," he sighed, "what's a cop supposed to know about art anyway?''

HOMEFRONT

by
Barbara Collins

It wasn't easy being married to Dick Tracy. The long hours he put in, the stress that went with his job—not to mention the danger—couldn't help but filter down to his wife. But Tess accepted the situation, and did what she could on the homefront to take the pressure off. Even in the worst of times, when she was worried sick about her husband's safety, she couldn't *imagine* her life any other way. She loved her little family.

And she loved her little house. It wasn't expensive, or located in one of the most exclusive suburbs; but it was comfortable and cozy—a haven for her husband to come home to and relax, after a hard day "chasing down crooks," as their young son Joe would say.

She especially liked the large kitchen, painted in soft pastels, and made sure that it was always neat and clean, with fresh-baked goodies on the counter for her husband and Joe. For it was in the kitchen that the family was able to gather—away from their busy schedules—at the large oak table, sharing a (even if she did say so herself) wonderfully cooked meal.

Like the breakfast they were having right now.

"Could I have some more bacon, dear?" Dick asked, seated at the table, dressed in a navy suit, white starched shirt and red-and-black tie. "And coffee?" The morning sun, streaking in the kitchen window, fell across his dark hair, making it shine.

Tess, spatula in hand, stood watch over the pancakes that were cooking on the griddle; the bright yellow apron tied around her slender, shapely figure was almost the color of her hair. "More bacon, dear. But you know what Dr. Locher said about that second cup of coffee."

"Can I have more pancakes, mom?" asked Joe, seated across the table from his dad. He was a handsome boy of ten, with his father's black hair and mother's blue eyes. Dressed for school, he wore a tan sweater, brown corduroy pants and maple-syrup mustache.

"All right, Joe. But *please* don't drown them in syrup. It's too much sugar."

Tess put another pancake on Joe's plate, and after replacing her husband's coffee cup with a glass of juice, sat down to her own now-cold breakfast. Underneath the table, Chester, the family cat, purred, weaving in and out of Tess's legs.

"Those were nice papers you brought home from school yesterday." She smiled at Joe.

"Thanks," he said, swallowing a mouthful of food.

Tracy studied Joe across the table. "Son, are you still having trouble with those boys on the playground?"

Joe looked down at his plate. His lips formed a thin line.

Tess's eyes flashed. "If those bullies continue to bother you, I'll speak to the principal!"

Tracy folded back a section of *The Chicago Tribune* he was reading. "Uh, son, remember what I taught you last week?" he said quietly, his gaze on the newspaper.

Joe's face lit up. "You mean about that left hook to the jaw, dad?"

Tess's fork paused in midair. "Dick! I will not have you teaching our son how to fight!"

Her reaction was met with silence.

She put the fork down. "Dick, I don't want Joe to think *fighting* is ever the answer to a problem."

Tracy, now about to take a sip from the juice glass, looked over its rim at Joe; father and son's eyes locked across the table. "Sometimes you have to do what you were taught not to do," he said.

Tess stood up, and began to clear away the plates. "Well, I *don't* like it! And I'm going to talk to the principal about those boys." She put the dishes in the sink and sighed.

Tracy got up from the table, taking some plates with him, setting them on the counter. Then he put his arms around his wife's waist.

She looked up sadly into his eyes. "They pick on him because of who he is, you know."

"Everything will turn out all right," he said with a small smile. "Have a little faith in your son." He kissed her on the forehead. Then he took his trenchcoat and hat from a coat-tree by the kitchen's back door.

"What are your plans for the day, honey?" he asked, putting on the coat, hat already on.

"Well," Tess said, wiping her hands on a dishcloth, "I need to go to the grocery store, and pick up the clothes at the cleaners. Oh, and there's a *big* sale at Wilson's Shoe Store today."

"Dear, can I ask you something? It's a question every man is dying to know the answer to."

"Yes?"

"Just how many shoes *does* a woman need?"

She looked at him with wide eyes, as if explaining something to a small child. "Dick, it's not a question of *how many* shoes. It's the *money* I can save by getting them *half off*!"

"Some mysteries remain unclear"—he smiled wryly, pulling her close to him, kissing her sweetly on the lips— "even after you've heard the solution. See you tonight around six." Then he went out the kitchen door, which led to a double garage.

After seeing Joe off to school (he walked, since the school was only four blocks away), Tess hurriedly finished cleaning up the kitchen. She was about to go out the door when the phone rang. Some man wanting to talk to Dick about speaking on crime prevention for some club or other. Dick accepted these requests from time to time, but lately, due to his unpredictable schedule, he'd been turning that kind of thing down. She told the man to call again, after six, when her husband would be home. Then she grabbed her purse and headed out the back door to her own car.

It was almost three o'clock in the afternoon when Tess pulled the car back into its spot in the garage. She hadn't meant to be gone so long, but at the shoe sale she'd run into an old girlfriend. After making their purchases (Tess, three pairs of shoes; girlfriend, two) they decided to go to lunch at The Sugar Shack, a Caribbean restaurant that had just opened. It took a while to get seated, and then served, but it was worth the wait. The food (Tess had jalapeño linguine with shrimp; her girlfriend, curried lamb on rice) was wonderful. But it was during the appetizer of fried banana chips that Tess wondered whether or not she'd turned off the burner on the stove. The burner she'd left the frying pan on. Oh, well. She'd be home soon.

After saying good-bye to her girlfriend, Tess rushed to the grocery store. And it was in the deli section, while picking up lox and bagels, that she wondered whether or not she'd locked the kitchen door when she left. As she stood in the checkout line, she chastised herself for being so careless. And to think she helped prepare home protection tips for her husband to use in his lectures on security! She could see the *Chicago Tribune* headline now:

DICK TRACY'S HOME BURGLARIZED! Tess cringed at the thought as she paid the bill.

And now, going up the short walk from the garage to the back door, arms full of dry cleaning, groceries and shoes, she was just sure she *hadn't*! She set the shopping bag of shoes down to one side on the stoop, freeing a hand to try the knob. It *was* locked! With a sigh of relief, she used her key in the door, opened it, and stepped inside.

The late fall afternoon sun now cast dark shadows over the kitchen; that was probably why Tess didn't see the man in the corner, over by the coat-tree, as she set the groceries on the table.

"Good afternoon, Mrs. Tracy," he said. Quietly.

This startled Tess so, that she knocked the sack over, spilling its contents onto the table.

"I *hope* I didn't *frighten* you," the man said, smiling, stepping out of the shadows. He was about twenty-five, dressed in torn bluejeans, jean jacket, and a T-shirt that read PROPERTY OF JOLIET PRISON. He had blond hair, a small pug nose, full lips.

And a forehead that had more folds than a fat lady.

She recognized him at once, although they'd never met. She tried not to reveal that in her expression; she buried her fright and unleashed her indignation.

"What are you doing in my house?" Tess asked angrily, clenching her fists because they were shaking.

He took a few steps toward her. "I came by to see your husband, and found the door here unlocked. So I thought I'd wait inside." Then he added with a friendly smile that Tess knew was anything *but*, "Hope you don't mind."

"Well I *do* mind!" she snapped.

He reached out, closing the half-open kitchen door. "You know, you should be more careful when you leave the house. And this oughta be a dead-bolt lock."

"Who are you?" Tess demanded. *But she knew.*

"The name's Brow. Same as my dad. Anyway, that's

what my friends call me.'' His eyes narrowed. ''My enemies, too.''

Many years ago, this boy's father had died escaping from her detective husband's grasp; and more recently the young Brow's homicidal girlfriend had lost her life in a violent run-in with Dick.

Tess could feel herself beginning to sweat. ''If you want to see my husband, I'm afraid he's out of town for the week on business,'' she said, making her voice sound matter-of-fact.

He moved closer to her, clicking his tongue, shaking his head slowly. ''Too bad. Wanted to ask him to speak at a club I belong to. Parolee's group.''

Oh, my God, thought Tess, it had been *him* on the phone! Even though her pulse was racing, suddenly she was tired of this cat and mouse game. ''*What* do you *want*?'' she demanded, surprised by the toughness of her own voice.

''What do I want?'' he said slowly. ''What do I want?'' he repeated, backing her up against the stove, his breath smelling of liquor. *''I want Dick Tracy dead!''* And with that, the Brow pulled out a switchblade from the front pocket of his jeans; it flashed open, the sharp edge just inches from her face.

Inside she tried to remain calm, but outside she could feel her body shaking. *This is all my fault! I told him when Dick would be home. I forgot to lock the door!*

She swallowed. ''Look . . . You don't want to do something that will send you back to prison. If you go right now, I promise you this *never* happened. Just go.''

''Lady, I don't care if I go to the electric chair. I have nothing to live for. Dick Tracy saw to that!''

At that moment Chester jumped up on the table, to check out the spilled groceries. Tess's eyes darted to the cat, then back to the Brow.

''Oh,'' he snorted sarcastically, ''is there someone behind me?''

"No," she said nervously, eyes darting to the cat and back, "there's no one there."

"You think I'm going to fall for *that*? You think I'm *stupid*?"

"No," she said, looking at a spot a little closer now, and back. "It's just the cat."

Did she detect something in his eyes? Doubt? Stupidity? *Yes! He's going to look! He can't help himself!*

As he spun around, so did Tess, grabbing the handle of the skillet on the burner. And when he turned back with a smug little smile on his face, she wiped it off with hot bacon grease.

He howled, dropping the knife, covering his burning face with both hands. That's when Tess lifted the skillet, bringing it down on his head, sending him crumpling to the floor in a silent heap. Then she kicked the knife across the room, where it sailed under a counter.

She fled the kitchen, taking the stairs up to her bedroom two steps at a time. She pulled out the top drawer of the bureau, where Dick kept his socks. And a loaded .357. *How many arguments had they had over that gun? Please don't keep it in there. What if Joe would play with it? Does it have to be loaded? Where was it!* Her hands flew through the drawer's contents, waiting to hit metal, but coming up socks.

"You lookin' for this?" growled the Brow, who was standing—rather, leaning—in the doorway, one hand holding the .357, the other his aching head. His face was covered with red splotches from the hot grease, like a teenager with terminal acne.

Tess backed up, terrified, against the bed.

The Brow, pointing the gun, came toward her. "You really shouldn't keep a loaded gun in the bedroom. It might fall into the wrong hands."

Tess began breathing hard, panic building. He was standing so close to her that she could feel the hard barrel of the gun pressed against her stomach. The smell of bacon grease was strong.

"I should've known Dick Tracy'd have no *slouch* for a wife," he sneered. "You're quite a woman." His eyes focused on her heaving chest, then back to her face.

Oh, no! thought Tess, *he's not going to . . . dear God, this can't be happening to me!*

The Brow, gun still held against Tess, reached out and caressed a strand of her blond hair, then ran the hand down the front of her blouse.

"Yes sir," he smirked evilly, "Dick Tracy is one lucky dick."

Tess's mind raced. *What am I going to do? How am I going to get out of this?* She felt her heart thumping in her throat. Now the aroma of bacon grease mixed with the booze was making her sick. Suddenly that wonderful Caribbean meal, still in her stomach, wasn't so wonderful. She fought the building nausea. But when his hand began to unbutton her blouse, Tess thought, *why fight it?*

She threw up all over his hand and front.

"*Jesus*, lady!" the Brow yelled, jumping back, letting the gun barrel drop downward. He tried to hold the shirt out away from his skin, with the fingers of his free hand. "Yuck! And this is my favorite T-shirt, too!"

Tess, having dropped to the edge of the bed, sat, too weak to take advantage of the moment; but she had accomplished what she'd hoped.

"That does it!" the Brow said, angrily, stripping off the shirt, throwing it on the floor. "I'm gonna tie you up in the kitchen!" He put the jean jacket back on; then, with gun still pointing, he grabbed Tess by the arm, pulling her out of the room and roughly down the stairs. She knew she'd have bruises on the arm, but it was nothing compared to the nightmare that might have taken place seconds before. She forced her mind not to think about it.

In the kitchen, the Brow moved the large oak table off to one side, setting one of the chairs in the middle of the room, and Tess in the chair. Then he produced twine from a pocket of his jacket and tied her hands behind her, and each of her legs to the chair. He stepped back to survey his work. He smiled. Then frowned.

"You got any tape?" he asked, almost politely. "I forgot the tape."

She glared at him. "You're *nuts*! And when my husband gets home, he's going to *kill* you! You're going to be as dead as that *girlfriend* of yours!" Tess knew she shouldn't have opened her mouth. But she felt helpless. And maybe, just maybe, if she said it, it would become true.

The Brow's face contorted in rage; he lifted one hand to strike her but it was stopped in midair by a knocking at the front door.

Tess's eyes flew to the clock on the kitchen wall. *Joe! He was home from school!* She started to scream, "Joe, run!" but the sound was muffled as the Brow slapped his hand over her mouth. He reached out and grabbed the dishcloth on the counter nearby, and stuffed part of it in her mouth, wrapping twine around her head to hold it in place.

The knocking persisted, louder, along with a small voice heard through the door, "Mom? Mom?"

The Brow grinned at Tess, who was struggling with her bonds. "Expecting someone? Little Dick Tracy Jr., perhaps?"

He left the kitchen. After a moment, Tess heard the front door open and the Brow say, "Well, hello, big guy. Come on in. I answered the door because your mother is tied up in the kitchen."

"Who are you?" Joe asked suspiciously. Then the front door closed.

Tess turned her head and rubbed the towel hard against her shoulder; the rope, which wasn't secured very tightly, fell down around her neck.

"He's bad, Joe! Run!" Tess screamed. She heard a scuffle and then the Brow howl, "Ouch!"

With all her strength, Tess scooted her chair toward the door leading to the hallway, so she could see. The

Brow, towering over the boy, had ahold of one of his arms; but Joe was kicking furiously away at the man's shins.

"Left hook to the jaw, Joe!" yelled Tess. "Left hook to the jaw!"

But as valiantly as he tried, Joe could not escape the man's grasp, and he was dragged into the kitchen, placed in a chair, and tied up like his mother. Only now their mouths were covered with mailing tape the Brow had found in a kitchen drawer.

The fear Tess had felt before was nothing compared with what she felt now. Now that her son was in danger. She *must* remain calm. She *must* not let Joe sense how utterly desperate she was. She kept her eyes cool as she stared into her son's. She was thankful that he appeared more angry than frightened.

Time crawled on. Once, when the Brow left the kitchen to use the bathroom, Tess slid her chair over to Joe, turning her back to him, stretching to reach his ropes, her wrists raw from rubbing. But the Brow returned, pulling her back to her spot, wagging his finger menacingly at her.

"Yes sir," the Brow was saying to Joe, "you're going to have a ringside seat when your daddy comes through that door and I shoot him in the head!" He grinned, producing the .357 from out of his waistband and Joe's eyes went wide with horror. "I lost my daddy to yours. Now we're gonna even up the score."

Tess's heart ached.

It was dark outside. Within the house only a few lights were on, those in the living room and kitchen. Tess hoped something would appear odd to Tracy when he came home; something would tip him off that things weren't normal. The Brow had drawn the kitchen blinds to prevent Tracy from looking in and seeing his wife and son tied up; but then, most evenings when it got dark, Tess would close them anyway. She looked anxiously at the clock on the wall: 5:45.

Suddenly, the crunch of car wheels on cement broke the deadly silence. Headlights danced across the kitchen blinds as a car pulled up the drive and into the garage.

Tess stiffened in her chair, her heart pounding. The Brow moved into position between Tess and the boy, pointing the .357 at Joe's head in a warning to Tess not to make a sound.

A car door slammed. Footsteps scuffled on the side-walk—Tracy's footsteps—his Florsheim shoes slapping the pavement.

Dick, Dick, thought Tess, *you've always said we've been married so long you can read my mind. Please, dear God, read it now! Don't come in! Go back! Go back!*

Tracy was on the stoop, keys jingling as he searched for the right one to the door.

The Brow leaned forward, eyes gleaming, mouth frozen in a hideous grin, anticipating the kill. Tess strained at her ropes, blinking back tears. Both held their breath, waiting for the sound of the key in the lock.

But it never came.

Outside, the wind rustling the branches of the trees was the only noise.

Seconds ticked by. The Brow blinked, confusion clouding his face, adding even more creases to his forehead. Tess looked at Joe and beneath the tape, his mouth was smiling.

"What the . . . !" yelled the Brow, as suddenly the house plunged into darkness.

For a moment Tess was blind. But then, as her eyes adjusted to the darkness, she could see the Brow, standing a few feet away.

"Okay, pig," the Brow half-whispered, "you wanna play a little game? We'll play a little game." Then he moved slowly, quietly across the kitchen, disappearing into the darkness.

Tess fought an urge to push herself over to Joe; she

was afraid the noise might make the Brow shoot toward them.

The silence was unbearable!

A shot rang out, so close by, it made Tess and Joe jump in their chairs. That was the last thing Tess heard before she fainted dead away.

"Tess . . . Tess . . . Tess." The voice sounded so distant. Her husband's voice. She opened her eyes and tried to focus on his face, but a light shining behind him was too bright. Were they in heaven?

"Tess! Everything's *all right*!" Tracy was holding her, and now she realized she was sitting on the kitchen floor. She reached out and grabbed him, feeling his warmth, letting the smell of his after-shave fill her lungs. Then she sobbed into his chest.

"Mom!" said Joe, putting his arms around her, too, "don't cry. Dad got him. He's tied up in the hall. I even got to call it in on the Two-Way." He was talking so fast now. "Oh, I *wished* I coulda seen it! When that bad guy went outa the kitchen, *POW, THUNK*, a karate chop to the neck! Way to go, Dad!"

Tracy cupped Tess's face with his hands, wiping the tears gently with his thumbs. "Are you *hurt*?" he asked, searching her face, eyes brimming. She knew what he meant. She shook her head no, managing a weak smile, and he held her tight.

"Oh, Dick, I tried so hard to send you a message! To warn you not to come in!"

He pulled back from her, looking into her eyes. "Yes. And you did."

Her mouth opened in astonishment. "Then . . . you read my mind!"

He shook his head, smiling at her. "No, you left three pairs of new shoes outside the kitchen door. I knew something *had* to be wrong, so I went in a basement window I found unlocked."

"Oh, dear Lord," Tess gasped, a hand to her lips,

remembering she had set them down to open the door, and never had time to retrieve the package before the Brow cornered her.

Tracy helped Tess up off the floor, and turned to his son. "You were a brave little boy, Joe. And I'm proud of you." He looked closer. "Say, is that a black eye you got there? Did *he* give it to you?"

Joe grinned from ear to ear. "Nope," he said, "I got it on the playground."

Tracy put his hand on Joe's shoulder. "Looks like it's going to be a bad one."

"Not as bad as the one I gave the *other* guy, dad."

Father and son embraced, laughing, and Tess sighed but then joined in, slipping her arms around both of them.

In the distance, a police siren wailed, coming closer . . . closer.

THE PARADISE LAKE MONSTER

by
Wayne D. Dundee

It looked like the last thing in the world Dick Tracy wanted was exactly the thing he was going to get—a new case to work on.

The famous detective had gone up to the remote lodge on Paradise Lake, alone, unannounced, with some very simple goals in mind: to breathe in plenty of fresh air, to do a little fishing, to relax and generally recharge his batteries. He'd made the decision—somewhat impulsively, a rare trait for him—to tie one of several overdue personal days he had coming from the department in with what promised to be a slow weekend and create the opportunity just to get away for a while. It marked the first time he'd ever taken a vacation—even a mini-version such as this one—separate from Tess and his son. He felt a little funny about that, but it was only for three days, and Tess had been all for it, had even helped him pick out a new rod and reel.

And now this had to happen.

"This" was a murder—not just any murder, but one

bizarre enough and challenging enough that he knew there was no way he could not get involved, no way he could remain in the background and not provide assistance to the local authorities. Especially when they were practically begging for his help.

"Well, Detective Tracy, what do you make of it?"

The question came from a lanky, weathered, middle-aged man who had introduced himself as John Nolan, the sheriff of Paradise County. It was Nolan who had first approached Tracy shortly after his arrival at the lodge—as he was still unpacking his things in the cabin that had been assigned to him, as a matter of fact—and asked, somewhat apologetically, if he could trouble him for his advice on a matter.

Sheriff Nolan had led the way on foot only a short distance from the lodge, up a long, wooded hill and then partway down the slope of the opposite side to a spot where the trees gave way to a sandy embankment that angled sharply into the lake. The two men now stood on the lip of the embankment, gazing down at the torn and bloody body that lay sprawled on the sand with its feet in the gently lapping water.

Tracy grunted. "It's a nasty one, that much is for sure. Have you determined who the victim is?"

"You'd never know it from what's left of his face, but the clothes and that battered hat laying off to the side there—ain't much doubt it's old Manny Wolf."

"A local?"

"That's right. One of our local characters, I guess you'd call him. He was an Indian who lived alone in the woods in an old shack. Never bothered anybody, except maybe once in a while with the tall tales he'd lay on kinda thick. A shame to have this happen to him. I aim to catch whoever—or whatever—did that to him, Detective Tracy. That's why I'm asking for your help. We ain't had a murder in these parts in fifteen years, and that was before my time as sheriff. So here I am as rusty as an old tin pail when it comes to investigating anything like that, but it turns out I got probably the world's most famous detective staying only a few hundred yards from the murder scene. You can understand why I have to try and take advantage of that.''

Tracy absently nodded his understanding. His narrowed eyes were busy scouring the immediate vicinity around the body. ''Those odd prints in the sand all around him,'' he said, ''what made them?''

Nolan shoved his cap to one side and scrubbed at his bristly hair with a knuckle while he scrunched up his face. ''Well, uh . . . that's the other thing.''

''What other thing?'' Tracy wanted to know.

The sheriff straightened his cap and squared his shoulders and tried to meet the inquiring gaze of the big detective, but couldn't help feeling—and sounding—a little foolish as he said, ''Have you ever heard of the Paradise Lake monster?''

Tracy gave a brisk negative headshake. ''No. Tell me about it.''

Nolan cleared his throat. ''Well, it's one of those legends that's been around for a hundred years. Heck, maybe two or three hundred for all I know. Long as anybody can remember anyway, there've been stories that this lake has some kind of mysterious creature living in it that folks catch sight of from time to time, usually at night or around dusk. Ain't no big dinosaur thing like that Lock Ness critter over in Scotland. Those that have seen it claim this is, well, kind of a man-fish, a thing that can stand upright, about seven feet tall when it does, all scaly and bumpy, with webbed feet and hands and claws and teeth like a barracuda. Kind of a waterlogged Bigfoot, if you get the picture.''

''Are you telling me,'' Tracy said, ''you believe this man-fish is what killed the old Indian down there?''

''What I'm telling you is that those tracks around the body ain't from no animal or human like I ever saw. And you'll notice they're the *only* tracks anywhere on that sand—except for mine when I made my way down to examine the body. What's more, the way Manny was ripped to shreds and battered like he was, that ain't the mark of no animal ever seen in these parts either. And I'd sure hate to think they're the mark of anything human.''

''Unfortunately,'' Tracy said, ''there are far more human monsters on the loose in our world than the other kind you described. I can attest to that.''

Nolan nodded solemnly. ''That's why I need your help. Ain't no shame in a man admitting to his shortcomings—and dealing with weirdo murderers is one of mine. I want to do right by old Manny there. I don't want to screw up because of my inexperience.''

''You'll need to get those wounds carefully examined for trace elements—animal, human, chemical, whatever they may contain. Also scrapings from under the victim's fingernails, in case he had the chance to struggle and did some damage to his attacker.''

''The county coroner's on his way here now with a couple of his men. They should be able to handle all those things, even if they have to send lab samples to a bigger facility.''

Tracy thought longingly of the vast resources so routinely available to him in the city. It was ironic, but the two-way wrist computer, with its various accessories, that he wore on his person each day while on duty was very likely better equipped than the whole of Nolan's department. Tracy's first inclination was to regret not having brought any of his equipment along (nothing, that is, except the .357 Magnum he was seldom without and which rode even now at the small of his back under his shirt). The omission of the rest had been very purposeful—after all, this *was* supposed to be a vacation. And even though the remoteness here probably would have prohibited any linkup with the central computer at headquarters, the self-contained features of his wrist unit still could have told them many things in a matter of seconds. But then, on second thought, the prospect of delving into a case purely the old-fashioned way—searching for basic clues and motivation, operating on good old cop instinct—held a strange appeal. The famous city detective actually caught himself smiling with grim satisfaction at the challenge.

"Have there been any recent sightings of this man-fish monster?" he asked.

"Been a whole spate of them, as a matter of fact," Nolan answered. "That's always been the pattern. Go a few years with nobody seeing any sign of it, then there'll be a rash of sightings in a close span of time. Once it gets started, of course, there's a lot of pranks and nonsense goes along with it."

"The monster ever killed before?"

"No, never that I remember hearing of. Just scared the heck out of whoever was unlucky enough to spot it."

"You should get plaster casts of at least a couple of those prints."

"Okay. I've got a kit for that. Never had call to use it much, but I've got a couple deputies who should be able to handle the job."

"Aside from this monster business, what about the victim? He have any enemies, anything worth stealing or inheriting if he was suddenly dead?"

"That's a laugh. Like I said, he lived in a shack in the woods and existed on what he took off the land and out of the lake and from a few odd jobs here and there for what little cash he needed. I don't think the shack even belonged to him, he just squatted there. Sure can't picture anything from his lifestyle worth stealing or bothering over—and I don't know anything about any relatives he might have around anywhere. Nor can I think of any enemies he ever made."

A rustle of footsteps coming down the grassy slope behind them announced the arrival of the county coroner's crew, led by one of Nolan's deputies.

"You've got plenty here to keep you busy over the next couple hours," Tracy said to the lanky sheriff. "Be sure to take all the measures we discussed. I'll get out of the way, go back to my cabin, finish getting settled in. You can bet I'll continue to mull all this over, though. Check with me later, we'll talk some more."

Nolan nodded obediently. "Fair enough. Much obliged, Detective Tracy. I really appreciate the help."

"This monster stuff is all hogwash! That poor old Indian wasn't killed by no monster—leastways not the kind you're talking about. It's all the work of that damn Harmon Bluster, I tell you, all part of his obsession to put me out of business."

The speaker was burly Tony Bates, owner and proprietor of Paradise Lake Lodge. He, in the company of Dick Tracy and Sheriff Nolan, was seated at one of the rough pinewood picnic tables outside his lodge's main dining hall. The day's final sliver of sunlight, sinking in the spring sky behind towering pines and rugged cliff peaks, cast long, gloomy shadows over the scene.

"Oh, for crying out loud, Bates, listen to yourself," Nolan replied. "You're the one who's obsessed—obsessed with the notion Harmon Bluster has nothing better to do than cause trouble for you."

"Are you denying all the things he *has* done to try and force me to sell this lodge? Ruining my reputation with the town businessmen so I could no longer get credit on goods and services . . . Using his influence on the bank board to force them to refuse my loan extension . . . The anti-tourism ads he's run in all the surrounding newspapers . . . The small fortune he spent on lobbying the state legislature so the new highway swung west of here instead of coming close to Paradise Lake . . . Do you want me to go on?"

"But all of those things are a far cry from murder," the sheriff pointed out stubbornly.

The two men glared at each other. Into the silence, Dick Tracy said, "Harmon Bluster . . . why does the name sound vaguely familiar to me?"

Nolan made a gesture with one hand. "Oh, sure, you must have heard of him. Famous author, the one they're calling the Ernest Hemingway of the last half of this century. Big, opinionated, ultra-macho type, wrote all those gutsy, sexy action dramas they turned into popular movies—*The Blonde with the .44 Magnums; Kill Me, Passionately; I Baptize Thee in the Name of Blood.* Remember those?"

Tracy nodded. "Okay. Now I've got him placed."

"Only he hasn't written anything worth beans in the past dozen years," Bates said bitterly. "That's why he hangs out up here at his place on the north end of the lake, practically like a recluse except for the occasional celebrity he flies in to hunt and fish with him, and the bimbos who come around to keep him company. Oh yeah, and that flaky, college-hopping son of his—the one he had by that flaky Broadway actress who ended up blowing her brains out a few years back."

"That's a pretty harsh picture you paint, Bates," Sheriff Nolan said. "All of those things may be true enough, but the man has a right to his privacy. He prefers the peace and tranquillity of Paradise Lake the way it is, not the way it's likely to get if your lodge is successful and others like it crop up and start bringing in a flood of tourists. Lot of folks around feel that way. They're entitled to their opinions."

"I don't mind opinions. What I mind are Bluster's high-handed tactics," Bates said through clenched teeth. "But this time he's gone too far and you've *got* to do something, Sheriff."

"Murder's an awfully serious charge, Mr. Bates," Tracy observed. "And if it's you Bluster is out to get, why would he kill innocent, uninvolved Manny Wolf?"

"That's just it—Manny *wasn't* uninvolved. You've heard about the recent monster sightings, right? Well, Manny was convinced they were all a big hoax, that the real monster had nothing to do with any of it. Oh, he believed in the Paradise Lake monster all right. He'd lived around these parts for years and even claimed to have seen it himself. That's what made him so determined. He was convinced this latest hubbub—the sightings, the footprints turning up everywhere—was all somebody's idea of a joke, poking fun at the real thing. He planned to use his knowledge of the area and his Indian ways to track down whoever this jokester was.''

Tracy frowned. ''I don't see the connection. What does any of that have to do with the trouble between you and Bluster, or the notion Bluster was responsible for Manny's death?''

''Don't you get it? It's Bluster who's behind all the monster sightings in the first place—probably using special effects tricks he learned from some of his Hollywood buddies. The idea of the monster showing up all around this end of the lake was supposed to scare people away from staying at my lodge. When Manny Wolf set out to expose the hoax, he had to be gotten rid of. And what better way than to make his killing look like the work of the monster and dump his body practically on my property—scare away even more of my customers!''

Sheriff Nolan shook his head sorrowfully. ''Lord knows you've had your share of grief, Bates, and I sympathize with you, I really do. But you're reaching awful far here and you're borderline slanderous with some of your accusations. I got to warn you to be careful with how hard you push this thing.''

Bates's reply was interrupted by his pretty wife, Janet, emerging from the dining hall, wiping her hands on her apron and looking worried. ''Excuse me, everybody. I hate to bother you right now, Tony, but we've got a drain stopped up in the kitchen and it's making a terrible mess with all the dishes we've got to get done. Won't you come and see if there's anything you can do?''

Bates stood up. ''No problem, honey,'' he said, through clenched teeth again, his scowl burning into the sheriff. ''It's not like I was getting anything accomplished out here.''

The couple withdrew, Bates clomping angrily, Janet looking uncertain and even more worried.

"I really do feel for that guy," Nolan said after them. "What with money problems and lousy weather, he's had two real bad seasons in a row. If this coming summer don't turn it around—and in a big way—he's likely to lose it all."

"Do you think there might be anything to what he claimed?" Tracy asked.

Nolan looked somewhat startled. "Do you?"

"You know the participants far better than I do. I'll admit Bates's scenario sounded a little farfetched. But consider this: Is it any more farfetched than the idea of a killer man-fish striking out of the depths?"

The sheriff ran a bony knuckle along the line of his jaw. "Yeah, I see what you mean. Keeps getting more and more complicated, don't it?"

"Was your coroner able to come up with anything?"

"Preliminary results show old Manny died from a massive blow to the head. The clawing and shredding came after that."

"Any results from the claw marks or fingernail scrapings?"

"Still working on that."

"Did you get a cast of the footprints like I suggested?"

"A couple of them, yeah."

"Something just occurred to me—has anyone ever done a serious study of this lake monster of yours? An in-depth news team, a research group from a university or anything like that?"

"Well, yeah, as a matter of fact. Four, five years back, back during the last rash of sightings, some college professors and a bunch of his students came here and camped on the shores of the lake for a couple weeks. They strung up all sorts of sound and video equipment, ran round-the-clock watches, really went all out. Nothing ever came of it, though."

"Were there footprints then? Did they make any casts or take any photographs of them?"

"Sure there were footprints. Always are. All the things those kids done, they must have taken some kind of record of them."

"I think you should get hold of whatever they got. Run comparisons with what we found this afternoon."

"Okay. Good idea."

The two law officers were quiet for a time. Studying Tracy's craggy silhouette as the famous detective gazed thoughtfully narrow-eyed out over the lake, John Nolan felt a swell of pride to be working with this man. He felt awed by him, knew he was probably making a poor impression of his own, stumbling around in a kind of hero-worship stupor the way he was. But he couldn't help it. Much as he wanted to solve the case and bring the killer swiftly to justice, he was in no hurry for this association to end.

"So," Nolan said at length, "do you think I should pay a visit to Harmon Bluster and, uh, you know, try to feel him out a little about some of Bates's ideas?"

"Probably wouldn't be a bad idea," Tracy agreed. A bemused twinkle settled in his eyes as he glanced over at the lanky sheriff. "Would you mind if I tagged along?"

Nolan cleared his throat. "Well, uh, no. Heck no. That'd be all right with me."

Tracy grinned. "Okay, it's a date then. For tomorrow morning. On the way maybe we could swing around by Manny Wolf's shack, have a look there, too, while we're out and about."

"Sure," Nolan said. "Sure, I was planning on doing that anyway."

The Bluster estate sprawled over a hundred-plus acres, wrapping around most of the northern end of Paradise Lake. The place was accessed by a long crushed-gravel drive leading off the county blacktop and passing through massive stone pillars supporting a wrought-iron arch boldly displaying the letters HB. The main house was an impressive mix of stone and wood with an expansive cantilevered porch jutting out over the water.

"Quite a spread," Dick Tracy observed from his vantage point in the passenger seat of the county cruiser that Sheriff Nolan steered up the drive in a rolling cloud of gravel dust.

"Sure is," Nolan agreed as he worked the wheel easily. "A far cry from Manny Wolf's old shack just a few miles back, eh?"

The two lawmen had spent a depressing half hour at what had been the deceased Indian's home, a ramshackle bare wood hut all but overgrown by a stand of thick timber that cast the place permanently in dusklike shadows. As the sheriff had predicted, they found no evidence of anything that would have made Wolf's death profitable to anyone. His meager stock of canned goods and his pitiful array of personal effects could all have fit in a common paper bag with plenty of room to spare.

The only surprising thing the visit had turned up were the library books carefully stacked on the kitchen table alongside a reading candle. With subject matter ranging from popular folklore to theater crafts, they stood as mute testimony of how the man had passed his lonely hours and also served as a comment on his unexpected depth. Nolan had dutifully gathered up the books for return to the library, and they were riding in the back seat now toward that end.

The cruiser crunched to a halt on the edge of an oval parking area, and Nolan and Tracy got out. Both squinted against the day's brilliant sunshine. On the drive up they had noted the activity on the long, sturdy pier that thrust out from the sandy private beach. They walked in that direction.

A broad, canopied pontoon boat was docked at the pier, and the scurry of activity that had caught the lawmen's eyes involved the efforts of five people getting the craft loaded with provisions for an excursion onto the lake. The individual apparently in charge—judging by the amount of noise he was making and the way he was throwing his thick arms about in exasperated gestures—was a beefy, bearded man in his middle to late fifties wearing bright Bermuda shorts and boat sandals.

"Morning, Mr. Bluster," Nolan called to him as he and Tracy scuffed across the sand.

Bluster wheeled about and looked down at them. From the cock of his head he probably was scowling, but it was hard to tell because of the mirrored sunglasses he had on.

"Sheriff!" he boomed in the same gruff baritone he'd been giving orders with. "What in tarnation brings you up this way? And who's that with you?"

"This is Dick Tracy, Mr. Bluster. He's—"

"*The* Dick Tracy?" Bluster cut in.

"That's right," Tracy answered for himself.

"I've heard of you."

"And I've heard of you, Bluster."

"Ever read any of my books?"

"Can't say as I have."

"Well, I never saw you conduct a criminal investigation either. So I guess we're even." The big man rumbled with laughter over the idea. He stopped abruptly and addressed Nolan again. "We're about ready to shove off here, Sheriff. What was it you were saying brings you around?"

"I need to ask you some questions, Mr. Bluster."

Bluster strode down the gangplank onto the pier. He moved very agilely for such a big man. "This an *official* visit, Sheriff?"

"I'm on duty, if that's what you mean. Detective Tracy here is assisting me on a matter of grave importance. We only need a couple minutes of your time."

One of the other people stepped off the boat, a tall, raw-boned man with straw-colored hair and a rolling gait. "What's the hold-up, Harmon? We got her all loaded up. Me and them fillies are ready to get out on the water and soak us up some of this bodacious sunshine.''

"Them fillies" the raw-boned man spoke of were a pair of curvacious, bikini-clad young women leaning attentively on the rail of the pontoon boat who giggled breathlessly at such a homey reference to themselves.

"The hold-up, Clint," Bluster said to his friend, "seems to be the fact that I'm being investigated by the famous detective, Dick Tracy."

"*The* Dick Tracy?"

"Uh-huh. We've already been through that. He's the big square-jawed fellow on the right. Trust me, even though it is a bit disconcerting to see him in dungarees and hiking boots instead of the much vaunted fedora and trenchcoat we've been hearing about and seeing in news photos all these years."

Tracy grinned easily at the ribbing. "No more disconcerting than it is to see your friend there without his six-guns or Stetson," he said. "He *is* Clint Flint, the Hollywood cowboy star, right?"

The raw-boned man, barefoot and knobby-kneed, clad only in swim trunks, grinned back a little sheepishly. "Reckon you got me, Detective Tracy. Reckon you caught me with my pants down."

The two bikinied girls giggled some more at that.

"Regardless of the fact I seem to be up to my ears in celebrities," Sheriff Nolan reminded everybody rather crisply, "I *still* have some blasted questions I want to ask."

All faces turned to him.

Appearing somewhat taken aback, Harmon Bluster said, "By all means, Sheriff. The floor is yours."

Nolan hitched up his belt. "That's better. Now, in case you haven't heard, we had a murder down around Paradise Lodge yesterday."

The bikinied duo gasped audibly.

Bluster smacked his right fist into his left palm. "I knew it! See, that's the kind of trouble that comes around a nice peaceful place like this when you start catering to outsiders looking for nothing but fun and frolic. I've been saying all along that lodge will bring nothing but grief to this area."

"It wasn't one of Bates's tourists who got killed. It was Manny Wolf."

"That old Indian? The one who lived off by himself in the woods?"

"None other. This is the first you're hearing any of this?"

"It sure is. Clint and his fillies showed up for the weekend and we been too busy catching up on old times and partying to pay attention to much of anything else. How did the Indian get killed?"

"I'll get to that in a minute. I want you to think back now . . . over the past couple weeks have you seen or heard anything unusual on or around the lake?"

"What kind of 'unusual'?"

"Anything. Whatever comes to mind."

"Nothing comes to mind. I don't know what you're talking about."

"How about your son over there? He's been staying with you all during spring break from college, hasn't he?" As he asked this, Nolan jerked his chin to indicate the fifth member of the boating party, a slender young man standing near the far rail of the pontoon craft, quietly stocking an ice chest with cans of beer and soda from cardboard containers.

Without turning, Bluster bellowed, "Sean! Step over here, son. Sheriff wants to ask you some questions."

The young man emerged somewhat timidly from the shadow of the boat canopy, the paleness of his frail body contrasting sharply with the rich tans of the scantily clad females and the ruddy complexions of his father and Clint Flint. He said, "I'm sorry, Sheriff, I g-guess, I w-wasn't listening. W-what was it you wanted t-t-to—"

"Dammit, boy, quit that stuttering," Bluster barked. "You know you can do better than that when you take a mind to. This is an official police investigation, no place for you to come across like some stumbling, mumbling idiot.''

Although he held it in check, Tracy felt an immediate surge of anger in himself for this treatment of the boy. He noted John Nolan's jaw muscles clenching and unclenching visibly as well, and even the two superficial beauties on the boat rail went a little tense.

Calmly, Sheriff Nolan restated his question for Sean Bluster, asking whether or not the youth had noted anything unusual over the past several days.

When Sean answered to the negative, his father promptly and agitatedly jumped in. ''Now what in blazes is this all about, Sheriff? I want to know how that Indian was killed!''

Still keeping his voice flat and calm, Nolan said, ''It looks like—or at least it was *made* to look like—he was killed by the Paradise Lake monster.''

As the cruiser rolled away from the Bluster estate, Tracy said, ''Well, one thing is certain. If they were acting—which at least one of them, of course, is allegedly capable of doing—they did a mighty convincing job of it. The news of Manny Wolf's murder seemed to come as a complete surprise.''

Sheriff Nolan grunted. ''There's one more thing that's certain—our little visit and the news we carried sure put a crimp in their 'party hearty' weekend. Those two bug-eyed girls are going to be too busy seeing monsters every time they turn around to be fun company for anybody until they're hundreds of miles away from here. Don't ask me why I get so much satisfaction out of that, but I do. Bluster, that crude, pompous jerk . . . All this time I've been so impressed by him, so impressed by having him living in my county. Then I saw how he treated his own kid . . . ''

''Even though Bluster and his son were aware of the lake monster legend,'' Tracy said thoughtfully, ''neither of them claim to have seen any sign of it during these past couple weeks when there have been so many sightings elsewhere. Is that common—during your past sighting 'phases'—to have the monster appear more in one area of the lake than another?''

Nolan shook his head. ''I'm not sure. Guess that's something else I'll have to check on. Of course, if Tony Bates's idea has any substance, then that would explain why this time the sightings have been mostly around his end of the lake.''

''Are you starting to think there might be something to Bates's claim after all?''

''I don't know. I guess I'm so sore at Bluster maybe I'm *hoping* there is.''

''You know, there's another side to that we should consider.''

''What do you mean?''

''Well, we know what Harmon Bluster stands to gain by causing trouble for Bates. What about what Bates stands to gain by causing trouble for Bluster? If Bluster were to get run out of the picture—on charges of this monster/murder business, for instance—Bates would get a ton of free publicity for his lodge, would remove the thorn that Bluster has been from his side, and should have clear sailing from there on out, right?''

''Holy mackerel. You mean maybe Bates is behind all this monster stuff—including the murder—so he can rig it to be blamed on Bluster in order to get rid of him?''

''Anything's possible.''

Nolan heaved a long, ragged sigh. ''You know, it's a real honor to be working with you, Detective Tracy, but, no offense, I got to say there's a down side, too. Man, you're *always* thinking. Trying to keep up with you makes my brain ache.''

Tracy laughed. ''Well, I've got just the thing for that, Sheriff. You drop me back at the lodge. I'm going to set to work and squeeze in at least one afternoon of fishing no matter what. That should give both our brains a rest. How does that sound?''

"The lodge it is, Detective Tracy. The lodge it is.''

Harmon Bluster answered the door just as Sheriff Nolan was raising his fist to knock a third time. The author's expression was as dark as the starless sky that had descended over Paradise Lake.

"You!'' he said at the sight of his visitors. "Haven't you two done enough for one day? You've frightened away my house guests, you've turned my son into even more of a quivering jellyfish than he ordinarily is. You're not welcome here.''

"This badge,'' Nolan said, "makes me welcome wherever I decide to go. If you'll step aside, Mr. Bluster, we need a few minutes of your time.''

Bluster looked stunned as Nolan, with Dick Tracy at his heels, brushed past him and entered the house. "This is an outrage,'' he growled. "I'll *have* that blasted badge of yours for this, John Nolan. I'll—I'll—''

"Careful, Mr. Bluster,'' Nolan said calmly, "you're starting to stammer.''

The three men stood in a tiled foyer with wide doorways opening on either side of them. To the left a plushly furnished living room, to the right a sturdy den paneled in dark wood with mounted animal heads and fish and polished gun racks lining the walls. In the midst of these familiar trappings, Bluster managed to compose himself enough to say, "All right, what is the meaning of this?''

Nolan held up a folded paper. "I have here an arrest warrant for the murderer of Manny Wolf.''

"What the devil does that have to do with me!?'' Bluster demanded.

"I was fixing to tell you just that. Better yet, since it was Detective Tracy who did most of the work, I'll let him have the honors.''

Tracy began casually. "This is an impressive spread you have here, Bluster. The house, the land, the lake—

front. A spread so vast that it holds secrets even from you.''

"Not very damned many," Bluster growled.

"You're familiar with the maintenance shed on the western fringes of your property, the one down near the water's edge?''

"I know the place. My workmen use it to store tools and supplies when they're taking care of that end of the property, fences and drainage ditches and the like.''

"Has anyone used it recently?''

"Not in a while, no.''

"You're wrong, Bluster. Someone—or maybe I should say some*thing*—has been using it quite a lot lately. I was out on the water doing some fishing this afternoon and I happened to work my way up around this end of the lake. As I was doing some casting in the shallows near the shed, I couldn't help noticing the heavy concentration of footprints on the muddy ground around it. Nothing so unusual about that, except their size and shape—exactly the size and shape of the ones I'd seen around the body of Manny Wolf, the footprints attributed to the 'monster' that killed him.''

Bluster frowned. "Surely you can't hold *me* responsible for that? You said yourself my property is vast, that the shed is on the far reaches of it.''

"Based on what Tracy saw," Nolan said, "I was able to get a search warrant, and earlier this evening we paid a visit to the shed. We found the Paradise Lake monster there—at least the current version of him. Or part of him, I guess I should say.''

"You're not making any sense!" Bluster said irritably.

"They're talking about me, Father.''

The voice came from the stairway at the end of the hall that led straight off the foyer. Sean Bluster stood there, three quarters of the way down the steps, one hand on the banister, the other hanging at his side. His tone had been surprisingly strong and sure, minus any hint of his earlier stuttering.

Bluster's head was pivoting back and forth as though his controls were short-circuited. "I don't get any of this!" he wailed.

His son came the rest of the way down the steps. "How did you know it was me, Detective Tracy?" he asked.

"I continued with the logic that Manny Wolf had already started," Tracy explained. "I got to thinking about those library books we found in his shack, about how two of them were folklore studies on this part of the country—including chapters on the Paradise Lake manfish, which fit in with Wolf's vow to get to the bottom of these recent sightings—and how one of them was a behind-the-scenes look at theatrical makeup and costuming. My first take on the latter was that it tied in with Tony Bates's belief that one of your father's Hollywood friends might be helping create this monster scare; but then I realized Manny's book had been on theater illusion, not movie special effects. That got me to thinking about something else Bates said, when he mentioned your late mother was a stage actress and you were a 'college-hopper.' "

"*That* part I know about," Harmon Bluster muttered. "Me and my wallet know about it all too well."

"Tracy did some phone checking when he got back to the lodge," Nolan said, "and tracked your college career back through all those schools, Sean. He found out you didn't get kicked out of them like everybody believed. On the contrary, you moved on of your own accord—moved on after you had become the star of their various theater arts departments and had mined each one for all it had to teach you. You established quite a reputation in the college theater ranks as a wizard of difficult staging and special makeup and costuming."

"I never heard about any of that," the elder Bluster said.

Somewhat wearily, his son said, "You never heard, Father, because you never chose to listen. I wasn't a jock,

I wasn't a rocket scientist, I wasn't any of the things *you* wanted me to be, so you didn't want to hear about any of the things *I* wanted to be.''

Nolan went on. ''During our search of the toolshed, we found certain pieces of the 'monster' get-up bearing the stamp of the theater department of your current school, Sean. That's pretty strong circumstantial evidence. The fingerprints we were able to lift should clinch it beyond any doubt.'' He paused, then almost gently asked, ''You want to tell me why you did it, why you started this whole monster scare thing?''

Without meeting anyone's eyes, Sean said, ''I kept hearing how badly my father wanted Bates's lodge out of business, how he wanted all tourism kept away from Paradise Lake. I struck upon this idea how I could maybe accomplish a double goal. How maybe I could *finally* do something to meet with my father's approval by reviving the Paradise Lake monster and frightening away Bates's customers, forcing him under, and at the same time demonstrate the theatrical skills I wanted to make my life's work.''

''Oh, my God,'' Bluster said softly.

''And Manny Wolf?'' Nolan pressed. ''How did he get killed?''

Tears welled up in Sean's eyes. ''That was an accident, Sheriff. You've got to believe me. Mr. Wolf surprised me that evening at the maintenance shed, just as I was putting on my monster costume—the one you found there today. He began calling me names, threatening to expose me. When he tried to grab me, I jerked away. Somehow he fell—he was an old man, not really as strong as he looked. He fell and crashed his head against a post. I'd never seen a dead person before but I knew immediately he'd been killed. And then . . . then . . . even though it made me sick to my stomach—I knew what I had to do. I used the claws of the monster suit on him and then . . . then I took him by boat down near Bates's lodge and dumped him on the shore, making sure I left plenty of tracks around him.''

Sean began sobbing at the completion of his confession. His father looked as if he had somehow collapsed in on himself. His big hands trembled and a couple times they started to lift, as if he would reach for the boy. But he never did.

Nolan cleared his throat and said, ''I have to take you in now, Sean.''

Harmon Bluster suddenly bolted and thundered clumsily into his den. ''No! I won't let you take my boy!'' he bellowed.

He seized a heavy rifle from one of the gun racks and started to swing around with it. But Dick Tracy, a half step behind him, halted him in mid-turn by pressing his lightning-drawn .357 Magnum against Bluster's ribs and saying, ''Hold it right there, mister. No need for any more foolishness. The time for displays of fatherly concern on your part are long past.''

At that point the big man disintegrated into a series of loud, racking sobs of his own.

His son watched him with a blank expression as Nolan motioned in the two deputies who had been waiting outside and one of them shook out a pair of handcuffs for the boy.

Dick Tracy called his wife, Tess, from the lodge later that night. Although he would tell her all the details when he returned home, for the time being he avoided worrying her and skipped any mention of the murder case he had helped close. When she asked how the fishing was, he simply told her it had been a little slow so far but he had one more day before heading back and he hoped to make the best of it.

After he hung up the phone, Tracy stood for a long time at the window of his cabin, gazing out over the inky nighttime waters of Paradise Lake. He thought about the man-fish legend and wondered what basis of fact there was behind it. In any event, he figured the legend would endure. And that was okay, he couldn't see the harm in that. After all, it wasn't the threat of spooky old legends that worried him; it was the thought of the monsters that lurk inside each one of us, waiting to break free.

NORDIC BLUE

by
Barry N. Malzberg

It was quiet in the Major Crime Squad when the call
came in. However busy Central Headquarters could become in the crazy July heat, the offenses were minor—
lots of verbal threats, hacksaw jobs against animals, car
fires. Juveniles doing juvenile things. Tracy was taking
advantage of this slack time to catch up on paperwork
and think about his upcoming vacation. Vermont was far
away from hacksaws, he hoped, but then there was that
New England temperament—

"Funny call, boss," Lizz Grove said. "A real strange
one."

"Strange what?"

"Strange call."

Tracy shrugged. "We're paid to take strange calls."

"Death I mean."

"Huh?"

"I know the air conditioning is on, boss," Lizz said.
"Get with it, will you? There's a dead body out there."

Tracy came slowly into focus. Lizz's intensity could

be gripping but sometimes she oversold. Part of the temperament. "Is it a murder?"

"I don't know. Maybe. An Officer Grun called, said he had found a dead body and reported it to the Chief. Patton turned him to us. You know him?"

"The Chief?"

"I know you know the Chief," Lizz said. "Grun, I mean."

"It's a big department. Can't know everyone, Lizz, it's expanded with the times." Tracy looked at Lizz and decided not to think any more about expansion. "Who is the deceased? How did it die? Male or female? Death by violence? Gunshot or auto wreck?"

"That's the strange part," Lizz said. "Grun says the man froze to death."

"Froze? In the middle of July?"

"That's what he said."

"It's ninety-six degrees out there, Lizz."

"The hottest summer on record. Grun says that the guy—it's a male, about forty, he thinks—is frozen stiff. No ID, hidden behind some weeds in the empty lot on Great Depot Avenue, three blocks north of the university. Want me to take the case?"

"No," Tracy said. "That's okay." He grabbed the yellow fedora, put it on.

"Kind of hot for a hat, don't you think?"

"Not if some guy is getting frozen out there."

"I can take it, you know. Might be interesting. Sam and I can go on—"

"You have more of a paper backlog than I do. *I'll* take Sam."

"Wouldn't you know," Lizz said, with a dramatic sigh. "The boss pulls rank."

"What's rank for?" Tracy said. "Where's Sam?" He stood. "I've got to go and lumber after that guy—"

"I'll call down," Lizz said. "I think he's in the barracks or maybe he's bowling. The nightclub is closed, you understand, or he'd be up there with the showgirl."

"Enough," Tracy said. He adjusted the hat. "Enough repartee, Lizz. You've proven you're smart."

"And you've got a live one," Lizz said. She waved at Catchem who, Samlike, seemed to have shown up in a corner of the room. "I think he's coming to get an autograph, boss."

Tracy shrugged. "A live one, Lizz? You probably mean a dead one."

"A dead who?" said Sam, now within earshot.

"A dead stiff," Tracy said.

In the topmost condominium of a certain high-rise building in the most upscale portion of the city, Crystal Freezum stalked icily across the room to answer the signal knock. She was as always dressed in white, a white as pure (she thought) as the snows of yesteryear, as the heart of the city, as the stricken innocence which she carried so gracefully within her. A white so pure it had glints of Nordic blue. Spending the day at home—as she tried as often as possible now to manage—she wore a long dress that glistened in motion and snapped at every ray of light, sent little scurrying knives of cold through her with each delicious curl. Her hair, white as the dress, as her pure and glistening heart itself, hung in multiple spirals to her shoulders, snow-cloaked icicles in the dead of winter.

She opened the door to her two minions, Hugh and Huge Alpine. Arms crossed, caps dangling from their fingers, twinlike but not (as she knew) nearly twins, cousins in fact from opposite branches of the same deadly family, they grinned obsequiously at her. Hugh was the one with the brown eyes, she knew, and Huge was the one more in love with her, but aside from these small facts which Crystal sometimes had difficulty keeping in mind, it was hard to sort them out; in some anterior connection, that dangerous family had curled around itself and produced these doubles from antique and now probably cement-ensconced parentage.

"Did you get rid of the body?" Crystal said.

Her voice, because of an unfortunate childhood accident that had all but severed her vocal cords and had pinched them beyond repair, filled her little pure white heart with rage and loss, had a high-pitched, chimelike quality that was as penetrating as the sound of Cheyne-Stokes breathing, that gulping, surging shriek with which near-cadavers were apt to take their last breaths. Or perhaps like the sound of shattering ice.

"That we did," Hugh said. Like his cousin, he was six two. Were it not for their obsequiousness, the men would have seemed to loom threateningly over the slender, yet ebullient figure of their love. Both gaped at her, Huge slightly more enamored but Hugh also devoted in his way, she the object of their fantasies as Crystal knew so well, and both willing to do her bidding, no matter into what cold and dark circumstances their devotion might lead them.

"And no one saw you?"

"No one," Huge said. "You are truly beautiful."

"You left nothing behind?"

Huge gulped. "Nothing behind?" he said. "But you have—"

Hugh put a large elbow into Huge's ribs. "Concentrate, cousin," he said. "No, we left nothing behind but the body itself."

"Excellent."

"I am truly in love with you," Huge said sincerely. "If I could just take a moment—"

"Not now," Crystal said sweetly. "Later. You are both good boys." She reached up to pat Huge's pallid cheek, then Hugh's. Her hand was cool against their heated faces and they seemed to shiver. It might have been lust or because the air conditioner kept Crystal's rooms so delightfully cold. Probably lust, she thought. Which was useful but meant that both of them, particularly Huge, had to be carefully watched.

"Good boys," Huge said. "We are not boys. I mean we are boys but we are men too—"

Hugh used his elbow again. "Stop it," he said. "Remember where we are."

"We're with Crystal, aren't we?"

"All right," Crystal said. "That's enough for now. I want the two of you to go back to the plant and try to see that no one else learns where I live. I do so hate to keep killing people."

"But can't we stay here with you?" Huge asked.

Hugh gave a little sigh of exasperation. "No one stays with Crystal," he said to his cousin. "Even I know that, isn't that right?"

"That's right, Hugh," she said. "It's a rule we have. A little rule."

"It's not fair," Huge said. His lip trembled.

His cousin took Huge's arm and tugged him toward the door. "Come on," he said. "Miss Freezum wants to be alone now."

"Tomorrow?" Huge said hopefully. "Maybe we can talk more tomorrow?" His little eyes radiated sudden warmth and Crystal shuddered.

"Tomorrow we'll discuss it," she said.

Reluctantly, Huge responded to Hugh's incessant little touches and followed his cousin toward the door. Crystal sighed, followed them, opened the door while they waited patiently, and then helped propel them into the luxurious, carpeted hall. "Good-bye," she said unnecessarily. Crystal locked the door behind them, then double-locked it, flowed across the stark white rug to the white couch, located neatly at the center of the bright room. She liked white. It was the only color she would, given a choice, have had around her except for an occasional Hugh- or Huge-colored figure, or maybe an occasional touch of blue to better set off the white and the fetching pallor of her person. Some people, the rude and disrespectful police in particular, that bunch who had almost captured her back in the previous administration when she had gone masked as the Snow Queen, said that was because she had a dark heart, a heart she wished to conceal. That was nonsense. Crystal was pure inside, pure and driven, pristine and of excellent morality. As a result of her surveys she knew that she came as close to purity, of an ethical perfection, as anyone in this rotten, corrupt city. Particularly the police. She was white with a fetching touch of blue at the core, white to the very center, and that was as she would stay. Aloft on a high pure raft of light.

Tracy and Sam Catchem came to a sharp stop beside the lot on upper Grand Depot. It was a bare, stark tableland, cleared for renewal five years ago but blocked by arguments between at least three citizen groups, each of which had the right answer for development and was willing to stay in court indefinitely to prove it, and it would have been empty now as almost always, but for the blue-clad figure of Officer Grun who stood looking at the sky, seeming intent upon disassociating himself from the object at his feet. A few East-End kids, barefoot in shorts and sleeveless shirts, ringed the perimeter, just taking in the scene. They did not seem interested in coming closer, an unusual position for East-Enders in deep summer.

The heat dove like a cloak around Tracy as he stepped from the car and the youngsters waved at him. "Hey," one of them said, "I know you. I've seen you on TV."

"No you haven't," Catchem said. "That was some other guy."

"I did so," the kid said. "Other places too."

"He's trying incognito," another said, pronouncing the word correctly. "He's in disguise, maybe. He doesn't want us to know. But *we* know all right."

"There's been a murder, right?" a third kid said. "That's a murdered body at the cop's feet."

"We don't know yet," Tracy told him. "We're trying to start an investigation."

Catchem nudged him. "Stop politicking," he said.

"There's a murder all right," one of them said. "Dick Tracy doesn't show anywhere on the beat no more unless there's been a murder."

"He does too," a defender said. "He comes around no matter what happened if something's really wrong and only he can help."

"Ah, that's baloney. He's a bigshot, too big to come out on the beat."

"You're a liar. You don't understand anything."

The two seemed ready to fight, dead body and cop in the distance or not, but Catchem stepped forward and separated them. "Cut it out or we'll run you in," he said. "Or you can stay back and form a ring. That way you'll be helping out in the investigation."

"Yeah, sure," one of them said. "We'll keep people out. Anyone comes in, we'll break heads."

"You can take separate sides," Catchem said. "If you need more help, I'll call the precinct and bring in reinforcements."

"We don't need no help."

"No help at all."

The kids moved off with authority to patrol the perimeter.

"Good going, Sam," Tracy said. "Keep 'em busy, give a little authority, and they'll let us do our job."

"Everything I know I learned from you," Sam said. "Except how to be on TV."

They walked toward Grun. As they got closer now, Tracy could feel the freeze in the air, a sudden density in ninety-six-degree weather—and he knew it wasn't from a sudden, welcome cold front.

"Feels like a deep freeze locker got left open," Sam said.

They reached the body, nodded at Grun, who seemed happy to turn away and face the patrolling kids, a hand thoughtfully but probably unconsciously on his gun. The body of the early-middle-aged man lay on its back, rigid and with arms raised as if to deflect a sudden assault. The face had a stunned but quickly congealing aspect. The grass close around the body was brown and crisp, ashen like grass in early February, and a strip of patchy brown led from the street to this resting place.

The dead man's eyes were open, filled with remnants of cold terror, with flakes of ice still melting in the July heat, streaking his cheeks like tears. Grun was standing about two yards away, made no move to come closer as Tracy knelt beside the corpse. The cop seemed to shudder, put a hand on the holster of his pistol as if to be warmed.

"Look at this, Sam," Tracy said, palpating the flesh. "No more than a quarter of an inch of this guy is flexible."

Catchem crouched to substantiate what Tracy said. "The rest of him is frozen solid," Sam said. "He's like a piece of beef, dumped from the deep freeze outside after two years in the locker."

"How long has he been here?" Tracy said to the patrolman.

Grun stopped stroking his holster, stroked his watch. "Half an hour, forty-five minutes maybe. I don't know *how* long it was here before that. A couple of those kids out there found him, put the squeal in, saying they'd found a Popsicle man."

"They don't look too disturbed by it now," Tracy said.

"Nothing disturbs these guys. They live in the projects, stuff like this is entertainment."

"They say anything when you came here?"

"They didn't say he was a relative," Grun said disgustedly. He shook his head. "This is a lousy detail."

"Aren't they all?"

"Not all," Grun said. "I've seen you on TV. You can get up in the world."

Tracy shrugged. There was a lot of that now. He had never intended it to be that way but law and order was always a good company image so nothing to be done. He looked at the body again as Sam, crouching, stared intently as if for some subterranean, unremarkable clue. The man had been dressed in a conservative gray suit, now faintly damp, a white shirt and patterned scarlet tie with an archangel at the center. There were small spots on the raised trumpet. The shoes, wing-tips, were perfectly buffed.

"An ordinary businessman," Sam said. He stood heavily, sighing, slapping dirt from his thighs and then rubbing his hands together. "Just a guy out there with a smile and a shoeshine. But he feels like he's been in the butcher locker for a year."

"No," Tracy said, "you're wrong, Sam. This is a flash freeze job. It's not evenly iced throughout, there isn't the same consistency."

"An instant coffee job, then."

"Can I be relieved?" Grun said. "Could you get some reinforcements?"

"Stand your post," Tracy said. "The fingers are thawed enough so we can get prints, I think."

"You do that," Sam said. "I'll take over for Grun if he wants to take a break."

"Be professional," Tracy said. "Both of you. You've got a dead body here but that's no reason to let standards erode." He pulled the tiny steel probe from the side of his two-way wrist computer and delicately took a scraping from the corpse's congealed skin, then lifted a miniscule particle of earth from directly beside the body. While Grun and Sam looked on with bemusement, Tracy ran a quick analysis, then another, and shook his head. "That's peculiar," he said, "and it's quite disturbing, too."

"What?" Sam said.

"I expected to find increased traces of CO_2, but they aren't here."

"Why did you expect that?"

"Something I read in a report a few years ago about a perp called the Snow Queen. They called her that partly because of a coke connection and partly because she had an unusual M.O. She left iced corpses in her wake. She froze them with liquid CO_2."

"I think I remember her," Sam said.

"I only joined the force two years back," Grun said. "You can't know everything from the start. I do reading and research, though."

"You think this could be the same perp?" Sam said.

"I don't know. It could be. Crystal Freezum is her real name. She may have shifted from CO_2 to nitrogen."

"That would be twice as deadly," Sam said.

"Not necessarily, but it would be more than twice as quick. One shot of liquid nitrogen would freeze a man's heart to his ribs."

Tracy fed a query into his wrist computer and waited for the readout. "I do lots of research," Grun murmured. "It's important to try to keep up. I didn't join the department to be on TV but to be a good cop." Sam coughed, kicked the ground.

Tracy decided to let it go. The computer beeped, and delivered the readout. "Just as I suspected," he said. "Crystal Freezum is at large. She left her previous surroundings bearing a close resemblance to a set of igloos and the local authorities don't know where she went."

"But we do," Catchem said.

"Yes," Tracy said. "She's in town."

In the distance, they could hear the siren from the meat wagon, coming closer. The watch kids at the perimeter were stirring, showing signs of real interest, and Grun was staring at his shoes.

"Technology is a wonderful thing," Tracy said, but he didn't know if he believed it.

On the way back to headquarters Tracy alerted Lizz, asked her to check with area hospitals and clinics to see if there had been July cases of frostbite or hypothermia. That meant explaining about Crystal Freezum, but it turned out Lizz knew already, had intercepted the information coming in on the wrist computer, had already put inquiries into progress. "Devious," Lizz said. "She's heartless, acquisitive and vicious. You should see the stuff that's turning up. She'd as soon freeze as look at you. But the Eastern cops couldn't prove a thing and they had to let her go."

"Did they get her arraigned?"

"Arraigned but out; the grand jury wouldn't hold her."

"I hate Miranda," Sam said suddenly. "I hate what's happened here. It's not like the old days. Grand juries, Miranda, warrants, the Fourth Amendment. So a lunatic like this can run around icing people."

"Remember, Sam," Tracy said, "we have no evidence. Just suspicion." But his heart wasn't in it. Sam was right, the old times were best. Not that there was any less crime of course. "Lizz," he said into the speaker, "I want you to tell Lee to check with the electric company. By the time we get back there, I want to know who has run up exorbitant bills lately, anyone, anywhere in town. If it's an old account that has gone sky-high or a new one that's out of line. Got that?"

"On the way," Lizz said, and cut off. Tracy sat back, let Sam drive, felt the tension ease a little. He had a good team. The problems had never been with the operation, only with the courts and the press.

"Why check the electric?" Sam said. "I don't follow."

"You have any idea how much power it would take to turn nitrogen into liquid?"

"A lot."

"You bet. You'd have to get the temperature down to maybe two or three hundred degrees below zero. That's Fahrenheit. Someone running a refrigerator that hard would tally up a whopping debit in a fairly short time. And talk about heavy duty equipment—"

"Could she get hold of something like that?"

"For the right price."

"Technology is great," Sam said. "Isn't it a wonderful thing?"

"Was having the same consultation myself, before," Tracy said.

At headquarters they found that Lee Ebony was having computer hangups with the electric company but Lizz had learned of two hospital patients treated for arctic or high-altitude ailments within the past month.

"One of the guys had frostbite," she said, "as bad as if he'd fallen off Mount Everest in January. Both hands came off. The other had a case of hypothermia so severe that his body temperature was down to nearly seventy degrees when he came in. He nearly died."

"Where are the patients?"

"The amputee is still in the hospital. He doesn't show too much interest in getting out, either. The other got stabilized and sent home. I've already phoned the guy, and he doesn't want to talk. So we're going to see the hospital guy instead. It's all set up."

"You don't let the grass grow, do you?" Tracy said. "One might think you were ambitious, Lizz."

"Someday," she said, "one or both of you guys are going to retire, and what's going to happen to crime detection then? The hospital guy is one Arnold Ringfelder. I mean, we could get stubborn with the other one at home, Donald something or other, but why don't we try this one first? It's hard to say you won't take questions if you're lying in a hospital bed."

"Where are we going?" Sam said, coming over from some business in the squad room. "We got an appointment?"

"I'm driving," Lizz said.

"Is she taking over?" Sam asked.

"Give her a few years," Tracy said. "We'll jump. But you have to read us our rights first."

"I don't get it," Sam said.

"They never do," Lizz said.

"Who are *they*?" Sam said.
"It was different in the old days," Tracy said.
They stared at him.
"I didn't say *better*, mind you. I said *different*."

Arnold Ringfelder, given a private room at Metropolitan because of the interesting nature of his condition, was an old, gray, wrinkled combat veteran. He told them all about the "combat" part of it, was most specific. The Bataan death march was bad, he said, but this was worse. This was *much* worse and at least you could understand the Japanese, kind of figure their motive. The Japanese wanted you dead and out of the way but *this* one—

"I was just walking my dog," he said, "that's all I was doing. And now, look at me." He held up his bandaged stubs. "And I can't feed myself. And my dog's dead. Who would have thought it would get so cold in July? And so fast, even for an old man like me?"

"Where did this happen?" Tracy said.

"On Hawthorne," Ringfelder said, "up near the developments. You know? I see you know. It was so hot, so hot and then it was colder than a witch's nose in a blizzard. Except for the shoes and socks it would have gotten my feet too. Next thing I knew I was in the hospital in a tub of warm water." Ringfelder peered at them. "There was a guy running around, had just passed me, some crazy jogger. He went down too. What happened to him? He make it?"

"He'll make it," Tracy said. "He just doesn't want to talk much."

"Don't blame him. He's got all his stuff with him?"

"You mean hands and feet?" Tracy said. "Yeah, I hear that."

"Let's go," Sam said. "I feel cold all of a sudden."

Lizz, standing by the window, looking at the little shimmers of heat bounce against the fogged pane, said, "I bet we'll find out where there was a sudden power outage. In fact, I'm sure of it."

"Sure of what?" Ringfelder said. "Who's going to take care of this for me? What's the real outage?"

"We'll talk to you later," Tracy said. "Thanks for your cooperation."

"Oh sure, sure. I always cooperated. My dog didn't make it, you know. They scraped him off the sidewalk I hear. Wire-haired terrier, six months old. You got a dog for me, detective? You got anything?"

Tracy said, "You've been very kind," and led them to the corridor. Lizz was talking earnestly into her wrist device. Tracy could hear the words *vicinity of Hawthorne near redevelopment, current check.*

"Urban redevelopment," Sam said. "It's a changing world."

"Sometimes," Tracy said. "Other things never change."

Lizz signaled him. "They've pinpointed the outage," she said. "High-rise and apartment. A system-wide drain."

"That's good work," Tracy said. "Can you take us there?"

"We're on the way," Lizz said.

They put the unmarked car in public parking across the street from the Towers and walked across the tree-shrouded avenue; there were no sentry kids here and no stark lots but rather a kind of insulation from the landscape, which Tracy had always associated with Miranda. Miranda and luxury high-rise had come in at about the same time and both seemed a way of shielding the population from harder facts in any uneasy way. With Miranda, perps could make believe that they were citizens just as the Towers residents could deny that they were in a bleak and overpopulated city, a city that would need every bit of luck it could find in order to make it out of the century. The doorman came to attention seeing them, then seemed contentious as Sam showed ID. "Guests must be announced," the doorman said. His little face contracted. Tracy felt he would have been better off with the sentry-kids.

"Apartment 15-K," Tracy said. "No announcement."

The doorman looked unhappily at Sam's credentials, shook his head. "I don't know if the three of you—"

Lizz gave him a dazzling smile, removed her own ID with a flourish and put it very near his face. "Oh yes you are," she said. "You're very sure."

"Who's in 15-K?" Tracy said.

"We're not permitted to release information on tenants—"

Tracy leaned over the doorman's shoulder, looked at the building roster spread out on the sign-in sheets behind. "As I figured," he said to the others. "It's our gal."

"Didn't even change her name," Lizz murmured.

"Arrogance of the class," Tracy said. They walked past the doorman. "I'd advise not phoning ahead," he said. The little man gaped, then looked solemn. The elevator was waiting for them.

"Maybe you should stay down here, Sam," Tracy said. "We could use backup."

"I'll stay, boss," Lizz said.

"No," Sam said, "I don't think so. This is my job, let's do it." He motioned them toward the elevator. "We'll just have a talk here, my pal and I," he said. The doorman looked unhappier yet. Tracy eased Lizz into the elevator, then hit the floor number, one of those systems that responded with infrared to heat. The car glided in the shaft. By the time the indicator light hit 7 Tracy could smell it.

"Ether," he said.

"Just a trace," Lizz said. "But we're closing in on it."

As they rose the smell became more penetrating. When the doors came open it clung dense and sickening, little gaseous loops in the air.

"It's enough to make me think Crystal Freezum has graduated from cocaine to methamphetamines," Tracy said.

"She's making speed?"

"My conjecture would be ice," Tracy said, guiding them from the elevator. There were only two apartments in the narrow hall, 15-E to their left and 15-K dead ahead. Deception in the lettering. Privacy for the citizens. "The profit margin would be higher on that."

"The effects last twenty hours instead of the twenty minutes that crack gives you, isn't that right?"

"Exactly," Tracy said. "I think the frozen guys are a byproduct." He knocked on the door.

"Byproduct of the icemaking?"

"Probably," Tracy said. He tensed as the door opened slowly. In the frame were two gigantic young men, identical twins it seemed. Over their shoulders Tracy could see a gnarled, middle-aged woman peering at them. The smell in the apartment was almost overpowering. The gnarled woman had a ladle in her left hand.

"Hold it," Tracy said. "Police. Just don't move."

One of the twins backed down the hall, toward a curled hose that was tacked against the wall. The other twin backed with him, then reversed, came deliberately at Tracy. He went for his gun but not quickly enough and suddenly he was pinned against the wall. Lizz was struggling with the woman, the ladle flashing in the air. The twin with the hose yanked it off the wall, turned toward him.

Convulsively, Tracy fought past the blocking hand of the man nearest him, got the .357 Magnum out. "Don't do it," he said, "don't do it!" but the twin didn't listen. Tracy shot him in the chest and the man collapsed, the hose flapping free, dangling in his hands, then falling to the floor where it made faint hissing sounds.

The other man shrieked and came at Lizz. She tried to get her own gun out but the man was on top of her. Tracy, turning to fire, was tangled in the hose and fell to his knees, feeling a kneecap give painfully, then used the body of the man he had shot as a lever to struggle upright. Lizz was flailing around, the woman with the ladle was shrieking. Tracy knew that he could knock the other twin out of action but only by risking a shot at Lizz. The woman was tugging at his elbow in a dangerous and distracting way. Tracy flailed for balance.

Sam appeared in the door and shot the twin neatly from behind, getting him in the middle of the shoulder blades. He fell with a thump, pinning Lizz until she crawled free.

"I knew I should have come here from the start," he said.

"You did good, Sam. You did fine."

"Backup, Tracy. You need backup now. We're getting old."

"No one's old," Lizz said. She gasped once, inhaled. "The times are changing, that's all. Got to move with the times." They stared at the huge bulk of the two men sprawled in the hall, the tangled stink of sweat and blood mingling with the ether.

"They were terrible people," the woman said. She put the ladle down neatly, arose, stared dull-eyed at Tracy. "You saved me from them," she said. "I was just trying to protect meself when the fighting started. I was real glad to see you."

"Who are you?"

"I'm Crystal's Mum. Oh, terrible things have happened. This isn't the girl I raised. She was a sweet girl, sensitive, shivered a lot—"

"Where is she?" Tracy said.

"She left last night. She said she had some business and would be back by morning. But she's not back, is she? She ran away. Her own mother can't trust her."

Sam looked at his gun, put it away. "We have to call in," he said. "Look at this mess."

"Go on, Sam, use the phone."

"We can do it by computer," Lizz said.

"Both. Do it both. I want a record of the call," Tracy said. He crouched, looked earnestly at the tiny woman. "I want you to think where she might be," he said. "We don't want to hurt her, we just want to talk."

"She did buy me a fine ladle, didn't she? And these two nice boys to help me, she said, until I found out what they were and told them. All I had to do was watch this for her. Follow. Follow the recipe. It wasn't much work but I don't like having all this ether around. It smells strange, doesn't it?"

Lizz put something into her wrist computer, turned it around and got out handcuffs.

"You don't need those," the woman said. "I'm not part of this. She made me do this. I'm her old Mum, I had to help my daughter, didn't I? I'm a victim. I'm a battered old Mum, that's what I am."

Lizz stood, uncertain. Tracy said, "She's a trafficker and a thief and there are two men who almost died, one of whom will never lift a fork again. We want her. We want her bad, battered Mum or no."

"Me too," one of the enormous twins said. He looked up weakly from a curled position, then turned slowly on his back. "I want her real bad. Where is she?" He raised an arm. "Oh there," he said to the woman, "oh there, there you are. But Crystal, why, *why* are you—?"

His breath poured out in a huge, deathly gulp. The old woman quivered against Tracy. "Shut up," she said. "Huge, shut *up*!"

"Too late," the large man said and died.

"You fool!" the woman said. She staggered, lurched forward, tried to kick the man but the other, also apparently not quite dead, grabbed an ankle and brought the woman to her knees.

"A kiss," he said, "one last kiss—"

The woman flailed and cursed. But Tracy had her in his grasp now and held her. "Oh Crystal," the abandoned twin said, raised a supplicatory arm.

The woman managed a kick this time. The twin sub-sided.

"I think I understand this, boss," Lizz said. "I think I see what she was doing. Let me tell you—"

But Crystal, nearly unseeing, tearing at her clothes in a rage, hammering against the wall in her dishonest fury, didn't seem interested in an explanation. Willing as Tracy and the ever-patient Sam would have been to share it with her.

OLD SAYING

by
John Lutz

One of the men in the booth of the Waterfront Czecho-slovakian Cafe looked exactly like Charlie Chaplin. Across from him sat a medium-sized, stern-faced man wearing a felt hat square on his egg-shaped head. A few strands of blond, strawlike hair sprouted out from each side of the hat. His ears stuck out, his eyes were faded and blue and wise, and his mouth was a horizontal slash that barely moved when he spoke. Outside the window, the waterfront fog moved in over the docks in a gray pall; it was the kind of morning that grounded seagulls.

The wise-eyed man in the felt hat sipped coffee from his mug with what seemed to be infinite appreciation, as if he needed the hot, strong liquid as an antidote for the gloom beyond the window. He said, "Putty, you take care of that matter down in Louisiana?"

The Chaplin lookalike touched his forefinger to his mustache and nodded. "It's done, Maxim. That old family mansion was a cinch. Everyplace we hit is—when it comes to the kinda stuff we want, which ain't all that valuable.''

Maxim took another sip of coffee. ''The Old South money barons who inherited the estate might disagree. Beauty is in the eye of the freeholder.''

''True enough, Maxim, but what I'm talking about here is intrinsic value. I mean, they'd turned the joint into a museum, so what do they care if something's missing? They weren't ever going to sell it anyway.''

Maxim sighed. ''I'm afraid, Putty, you have a very materialistic outlook.''

Charlie Chaplin smiled. ''Seems to me we share the same outlook.''

''Right now we do,'' Maxim admitted. ''But I want money to attain the freedom to pursue my personal and worthy goal of unlimited time for reflection. You, I'm afraid, want it so you can retire to Paris and live the gaudy, crass life you think your acting career should have provided.''

''I don't see a thing wrong with that.''

''You have little experience with the very dangerous Paris underworld. Remember, Putty, the crass is always meaner on the underside of the French. Speaking of which, have you cased the museum in Paris?''

''Sure, Maxim, and it should be no problem. We oughta do the job there, then hit the Chicago museum the next day. But right now, we oughta get to work before the morning slips away.''

''Best not to be hasty,'' Maxim warned. ''It's the early worm that's devoured by the bird.''

Charlie Chaplin suddenly sat up straighter and peered out at the fog. ''Hey, here comes Fin.''

The restaurant door opened to admit a strong breeze that carried the fishy scent of the ocean, along with a lean-waisted, muscular man wearing only sharkskin trousers and a striped T-shirt despite the cool morning. He had a bullet-shaped bald head and an underslung chin. His round black eyes, set so wide they were almost on the sides of his head, didn't change expression as he smiled to reveal a row of pointed teeth. The blunt rounded head, the underslung jaw, the glinting sharp teeth, made him look remarkably like a shark that had somehow found its way onto land and learned to dress like a human.

Fin said nothing as he slid into the booth next to Putty and ordered an Eastern Bloc omelet, orange juice, and coffee.

"Everything ready for today's operation?" Putty asked him.

Fin's black, expressionless eyes slid sideways to fix on him. "Keep your voice down or the waitress might overhear," he whispered.

"She doesn't understand English," Putty assured him. "She's from Czechoslovakia."

"I don't trust Europeans," Fin said. "In fact, there's nobody I trust."

"Me, either," Putty said, "which is why I asked if you did your part and have everything ready to go today."

"Don't worry about *my* part, mate, you just take care of your own end of the poop deck, eh? And any funny business and you'll regret it. Lotsa folks are scared of me, and if you two aren't, you're making a mistake."

"You're the one who oughta be scared about trying to pull any kinda double cross!" Putty shot back. He gave Fin as menacing a glare as Charlie Chaplin could muster.

Maxim shook his head sadly. "It's a mistake to fright among ourselves."

Putty, who actually was afraid of Fin, silently finished his coffee, as Fin's order arrived and the pretty blond Czechoslovakian waitress smiled and hurried away.

Fin stared at him and squeezed his juice glass until it cracked, then, with his sharklike smile, drank the remaining juice. Like the predatory fish he resembled, he could, and would, consume almost anything. He put down the glass in disgust. "Stuff's warm. I thought there was ice in it, but it was just broken glass. Kinda scratched my throat going down.''

Maxim gazed at the remaining orange juice with its glimmering shards of glass that caught the morning light. ''All that glitters isn't cold.''

Fin ignored him and devoured his omelet in two huge bites.

Putty glanced at his gold pocket watch and looked concerned. ''We better get outa here soon, or . . . ''

''Not to worry,'' Maxim assured him. ''We understand the gravity of your problem.''

Fin tossed down his steaming black coffee, then bit the metal cap off a salt shaker, chewed, and swallowed. ''So much for breakfast. Let's be on our way then, mates. Hey, waitress!''

He stood up and swaggered toward the door. Putty waddled after him in Chaplinesque fashion, leaving Maxim to pay the Czech.

On the other side of the window, the three men disappeared into the fog: One who looked like a cracker-barrel philosopher, with his poorly cut clothes, his wise, seamed face, and his straw-colored hair sticking out from beneath his hat. Another who looked like a great white shark. And one who strongly resembled Charlie Chaplin, only his face seemed suddenly oddly distorted.

They didn't know the waitress had worked for years in a shopping mall international food court and spoke seven languages. As she watched her three suspicious customers leave, she decided to tell her boss what she'd overheard.

The owner of the Czechoslovakian Waterfront Cafe, Sid Abromowitz, scratched his wide head as his waitress, Carrie Cupp, told him about her three customers and related the part of their conversation she'd overheard.

Then he dried his hands on a gray dish towel and hurried to the wall phone near the potato processor. He called Police Headquarters and talked to his friend, policewoman Lee Ebony, who seemed only vaguely interested in what he had to say but told him she'd pass the information on to *her* boss.

When Chief of Detectives Dick Tracy and his partner Sam Catchem arrived at the restaurant within half an hour, they were plenty interested.

"This Maxim and Fin I don't know," Tracy said, "but I've got a pretty good idea as to the identity of Putty."

Catchem nodded. "Putty Puss!"

Abromowitz looked puzzled. "Vat is this, Putty Puss?"

"His real name's Harley Niav," Tracy said. "He's an actor whose disfigured face was restored in an experimental latex and silicon plastic-surgery procedure. For an hour at a time he can manipulate his features into looking like anyone he chooses, and with his actor's skills he can easily manage a successful impersonation. But after approximately an hour, his face melts and sags like warm wax. No matter who he looks like, he's always dangerous."

"And not one of your best friends," Catchem added, swallowing so hard it caused his bow tie to jiggle.

Tracy shrugged and looked at Abromowitz. "I gave Putty Puss some trouble once, and he wants to give it back."

"Ziss is true?" Abromowitz asked, wide-eyed. "He can change his features at vill?"

"Check," Catchem said.

"Vat?"

"Only for an hour at a time," Tracy reminded everyone.

"The one he called Maxim seemed to be the boss," Carrie Cupp said.

Tracy nodded to her. "And you were right to tell *your* boss about what you overheard, young lady. Those men are most certainly the criminal element." He moved away a few steps and used his wrist computer to contact

Headquarters, then left instructions for the entire Major Crime Squad to be in his office in half an hour.

"Think something big is going down?" Catchem asked.

"If Putty Puss is involved," Tracy said, "it's big, even if we can't take the overheard conversation at face value." He thanked Abromowitz and Carrie, then headed for the door at a brisk pace.

While Catchem drove to headquarters, Tracy used his wrist computer to access FBI and Interpol computer data banks, as well as local police files. He wanted to learn more about Maxim and Fin, and he wanted to learn it fast.

The other two members of the Major Crime Squad, policewomen Lizz Grove and Lee Ebony, were waiting in the office when Tracy and Catchem arrived. Lizz was a curvaceous brunette about thirty, tough and competent. Lee Ebony was an attractive black woman, also about thirty, and the newest member of the squad. Tracy removed his yellow snap-brim fedora and stood behind his desk.

Lizz looked eager for action. "What's the deal, Chief?" she asked Tracy.

Tracy laid it all out for them and watched their faces become grimmer as he spoke. They knew the case might turn nasty, and they wouldn't be jousting with amateurs.

"Lizz," Tracy said, "I want you to find out what you can about this man Fin. Take Junior to that Czech cafe and get the waitress to describe the men in detail—not the one who looks like Charlie Chaplin, though." Junior was Tracy's adopted son, and one of the best police artists in the business. Soon the squad would have a good idea of what Maxim and Fin looked like. "Lee, I want you to get whatever information you can on Maxim. There's nothing on either of them in the files, so they must be extremely competent criminals, or they've changed their identities. We do know they're involved with Putty Puss, so they're pros.''

The two policewomen nodded, then hurried from the office.

''What about us?'' Catchem asked.

Tracy sat down behind his desk. ''If museum thefts are occurring, the loot's being sold to fences who handle that kind of merchandise. We're going to check on any activity in the illegal art market. If we find the fence, Sam, we can work backward and catch the thieves, building an airtight case as we go.''

''Brilliant!'' Catchem said.

Tracy stood up and plunked his hat back on his head. ''Just solid, honest police work, which is what the criminal element fears most.''

But after checking with informants all day, Tracy and Catchem were sure there hadn't been an unusually large number of stolen museum pieces sold lately.

''Maybe this stuff's being snatched for one of those wealthy eccentric collectors,'' Catchem suggested.

''Maybe,'' Tracy agreed. ''Our next step is to contact museums around the country and see if we can compile a list of items that might be missing from their collections. That'll take time, but when we have our list, we might be able to construct a profile of the collector who could be in the market for such hot merchandise.''

Catchem nodded with approval and got busy.

While computers and fax machines communicated between museums and headquarters, Lizz checked in by wrist computer communication.

''Chief, the one they call Fin is a tough number,'' said her voice from the tiny speaker. ''He's an able seaman and diver, and they say he killed the entire crew of a boat in the Bermuda Triangle. Anyway, I found out where his boat, *The Shark*, is usually docked, and went there. *The Shark* put out to sea this morning, not long after the conversation in the restaurant, and is still gone from its slip. The old salt who watches over things at the docks told me it's been leaving every morning and staying out much of the day. He said he's seen men fitting Fin and Maxim's descriptions on board, and a man who looks like Charles Laughton.''

''What makes you think the old salt is reliable?''

''He's a seasoned Navy veteran, Chief. I'd like to hang around and see when the boat returns.''

''All right, but be careful, Lizz.''

''This isn't the Bermuda Triangle,'' she said haughtily.

Tracy switched off the wrist computer and lowered his arm, wondering what went on at sea when *The Shark* left port. Whatever it was, he was sure he wouldn't like it.

A mile and a half off the coast, *The Shark* bobbed gently on gray-green waves. It was a small tugboat that had been converted for use as a diving station. At anchor now, the boat rode bow into the wind as an on-deck compressor chugged away. An air hose, communication line, and winch cable lay over the side and disappeared into the choppy water.

Maxim and Charles Laughton were sitting at a table on the bridge, playing two-handed bridge and snacking on peanuts. Fin was standing on deck and staring at the sea, absently eating peanuts still in their shells. He licked a finger and jabbed it in the air.

''Wind's kicking up!'' he said loudly.

''What's that mean?'' Laughton asked.

''Means we gotta get back to shore soon, you landlubbin' sand crabs. Ain't even a bird brave enough to fly in this murky gray sky.''

''It's an ill wind that blows no one gull,'' Maxim remarked.

''So get yourselves down here and help me hoist the gear!''

''I feel seasick,'' Laughton said.

''And we're in the middle of a rubber,'' Maxim pointed out.

Fin swung his muscular body up the ladder to the

bridge and rolled his head to the side, as if about to snap at the air. "Don't expect me to bow to that kinda excuse," he said with a stern look. "You might be the boss in this caper, Maxim, but remember who's in charge on this boat!" To emphasize his point, he ate the cards, thus ending the bridge game.

The three men scrambled down the ladder to the deck and got to work. Fin worked the electric winch, and soon the lead-gray helmet of a deep-sea diver's suit broke the surface.

"Careful, now," Maxim said, glancing at the sky. "There are such things as police helicopters, and what we don't show can't hurt us."

"Helicopters don't fly in this kinda weather," Fin said with a sharklike sneer. He took a bite of the steel cable that had already been reeled in, as if it were a strand of licorice, then speeded up the action of the winch.

Within ten minutes, *The Shark* had the wind at her stern, blowing a stream of black diesel exhaust out before her, and was chugging persistently toward land.

"After they left the boat," Lizz told Tracy, "I snuck down to the dock and put an electronic beeper on the hull where they'll never notice it."

"Good work," Tracy said. "Now we can chart *The Shark*'s position by radio signal when it's at sea."

"The boat seems to be fitted out for deep-sea diving," Lizz said.

Tracy stroked the point of his chin and looked thoughtful.

"Any luck with the museum thefts?" Lee Ebony asked.

"Yes and no," Catchem said.

"There have indeed been a series of thefts from a number of museums all over the country," Tracy said. "And several museums in France. Few of the objects stolen have been relatively valuable, dating back only to the mid-nineteenth century. What's even more curious is that none of the stolen items has turned up with the fences who convert such loot to cash for the crooks.''

''Darn strange,'' Lee Ebony said.

''Lizz,'' Tracy said, ''check tomorrow's weather report.''

''I already did, Chief. It's going to be a cloudy day.''

''The FBI has a silent helicopter that uses satellite technology to photograph through cloud banks and then construct computer-enhanced pictures,'' Tracy said. ''I'll call Inspector Trailer and request it, and try to find out what Maxim and his men are up to on *The Shark*.''

But the next day, even before the helicopter photographs were processed, Lizz threw open the door to Tracy's office. ''Sorry to interrupt, Chief, but you better come quick and see this.''

Tracy apologized to his wife Tess and cut his phone conversation short, and he and Sam Catchem hurried into the squad room.

''There,'' Lizz said, pointing to the small TV mounted on a wall bracket. ''The evening news.''

Tracy could hardly believe what he was seeing on the flickering screen. There was a local anchorman interviewing Maxim, Fin, and a regular-featured, very average-looking man who appeared vaguely familiar and might have been every actor who ever played the husband in a television commercial. The three criminals were nattily dressed, though Maxim's suit fit him loosely and couldn't disguise his bumpkin-philospher look. Vaguely Familiar was preppy; he wore a button-down collar and had his sweater slung cape-like across his shoulders with the arms knotted in front. Fin appeared sleek in a tailored sharkskin suit. The three of them looked . . . well, respectable. Tracy knew it was an act.

''About the treasure,'' the interviewer was saying.

''The French freighter *Lampoon* sank a mile and a half off the coast in a violent storm in the summer of 1869,'' Maxim said. ''It was carrying art objects and cotton.''

The interviewer moved closer. "And you, Mr. Fin, and Mr. . . . ."

"Smith," said Vaguely Familiar.

". . . actually located the wreckage and sent down a diver for the art objects."

"Exactly," Maxim said. Fin merely smiled. The interviewer hastily moved back to where he'd been standing. "Of course, most of the objects aren't of much value," Maxim continued. "They're almost generic, interesting more because they represent the period when the ship went down, rather than because they have artistic merit. Like this ante-bellum tea set." He motioned with his arm, and the camera moved away to show an array of mid-nineteenth-century objects spread out for display on a table. Swords, muskets, samples of currency, flatware, crystal figurines.

"And did you raise all the treasure from the ship?" the TV journalist asked.

"We left some down there," Fin said. "Only raised what struck our fancy."

"We don't know much about art," Maxim explained, "but we stowed what we like. Of course, everything that was on the *Lampoon* is still the property of the French government. We only located the wreckage and raised the treasure for the fun of it. We're adventurers."

"Then you stand to make *nothing* out of your enterprise?" the interviewer asked incredulously.

"Perhaps we'll write a book," Maxim said, "all about a sunken treasure and three men in a tug."

"You can bet there's no sunken ship down there," Lee Ebony said. "Probably there never really was a *Lampoon*."

"I don't get it," Catchem told Tracy. "That's gotta be the museum loot, but if they're pretending it's legit and they gotta give it all to the French government, what's the point? You think they really did it all so they could write a book?"

"Con men don't wait for royalty statements," Tracy said, "they write them."

Lizz handed Tracy a large brown envelope. "Here, Chief, a messenger just brought this for you."

Tracy opened the envelope and examined its contents, the computer-enhanced photographs of the morning's activities on board *The Shark*. Catchem, Lizz, and Lee Ebony gathered around as he thumbed through the photos. They merely showed the three men on deck, manning equipment that ran cables and pumped air to the deep-sea diver below.

"You wondering the same thing I am?" Tracy asked Catchem.

"Yep. Who's the fourth man down below in the diving suit?"

Tracy shuffled the photographs until he saw one of the diver being hoisted from the sea onto the deck. "I think I know," he said. "Let's get this photo back to the lab and have it enlarged as much as possible. Lizz, in our files there's a professor of naval history who's an expert on French shipping. Check with him at Harvard and see if the *Lampoon* really existed, and if so, what happened to it."

Lee Ebony looked surprised. "I'm sure there's no ship. They just made up that story to explain where the museum loot came from."

"I think there *is* a ship down there," Tracy said. "This case is deeper than we imagined."

An hour later they met in Tracy's office. Traffic hummed softly outside, and off in the distance a police siren was yodeling. A patrolman passed by in the hall, the hard rubber heels of his big shoes *thunk, thunk*ing on the tile floor.

Lizz was excited and puzzled. "The report from Harvard was just faxed in," she said. "There really *was* a *Lampoon*, and it sank in a storm approximately where Maxim described. It was sailing back to France with a cargo of cotton and carrying various art objects in an exchange between museums."

"Except that most of the objects Maxim put on display are museum objects *now*, but were merely commonplace at the time the ship sank."

"That's right!" Catchem said.

"And look at this." Tracy laid the enlarged photograph of the emerging deep-sea diver on his desk. "Look closely at the window in the diving helmet and tell me if any of you know that man." He was smiling as they all leaned over his desk.

"Chief!" Lizz cried.

"Exactly," Tracy said. "There is no face inside the helmet, because the diving suit is empty."

Sam Catchem's bow tie bobbed as he scratched his head in confusion. "But why—?"

"Fin must have run across the wreckage of the *Lampoon*," Tracy said, "and the three crooks didn't want to surrender the treasure to the French government. So they cased various museums and stole a substitute, *less valuable* treasure to surrender, one made up of fairly common objects impossible to identify specifically. The real treasure on the *Lampoon* was already secretly raised, probably by night, and is no doubt stashed somewhere on land. *The Shark*'s daily trips to the treasure site, supposedly to send a diver down, were just for show, so passing ships would substantiate that diving occurred and a so-called treasure was brought up at the time Maxim claimed. Probably they even planted some of the stolen museum loot down below on the *Lampoon* for French government divers to find; that'd make their story even more believable."

"Why, the whole caper's diabolical!" Catchem explained.

"It sure is, Sam. But then, so's Putty Puss and anyone he'd associate with in order to work a con."

"What now, Chief?" Lizz asked.

Tracy grinned. "Our crooks won't be able to stay away

from the real treasure for long. We follow them to wherever it's hidden. Then we nab 'em!''

It was easy enough to tail Maxim from the plush midtown motel where the three crooks were now staying. Lee Ebony was the one on stakeout at the time. She followed as Maxim traveled by cab to where the genuine recovered treasure was stored.

When she phoned in and told Tracy where to meet her, he was surprised. But while thinking about it in the speeding unmarked squad car driven by Sam Catchem, he decided it made sense.

What better place to hide treasure than in a storage warehouse? It was where divorcing couples stored the furniture, where people with too much sentimental junk stashed it when they ran out of space at home. Not much of astronomical value was stored at such places, so it would be among the last spots where anyone would look for nineteenth-century treasure. Especially if that treasure had supposedly been returned to the French government.

Sam parked the car and killed the headlights. Secure Storage really wasn't a warehouse, but was made up of fifty or so individual little brick buildings that looked like bunkers with overhead garage doors. The whole setup was surrounded by a tall chain-link fence topped by concertina wire. A wide gate, the only way in or out, was watched over by a uniformed security guard standing in a metal sentry shack not much larger than a phone booth. The shack was brightly lighted inside, and the guard was staring hard at a small television set playing a cops and robbers show. He hadn't heard the entire Major Crime Squad approach.

Tracy knocked on the shack's metal door and the guard jumped. Then he seemed to compose himself. He put on his uniform cap, turned off the TV, and stepped outside. "Help ya?"

The guard was in his late seventies, Tracy estimated,

wondering if the man remembered how to use the police Special holstered on his belt. Gray tufts grew out of his ears, and his eyes were faded and clouded with cataracts. The name tag below his silver watchman's badge said *Lester*.

Tracy flashed his shield at Lester. "A man went inside here about fifteen minutes ago. Average size, wearing a felt hat, about fifty years old—"

"That's old for a hat. Wouldn't make sense in this case."

"The *man*'s about fifty!"

"That'd be Mr. Jones," the guard said, his old eyes flashing in remembrance. "I had him sign in, see?" He held out a clipboard with the name "Jones" scrawled on it next to the noted time.

"This Mr. Jones?" Lizz asked, showing the guard a photo.

"That's the one," the guard said. "Ain't no doubt. I spent twenty years as a cop in Brooklyn, so I remember faces. He's in there with the other fellas that rent number 2-C."

"Really?" Tracy said. "This one of the others?" He showed the guard a photograph of Fin.

"Sure," Lester said. He spat what might have been tobacco juice off to the side, barely missing the toe of Sam Catchem's black shoe. "Be hard to forget *him*. That's Mr. Smith. He's the one driving the truck."

"They're intending to move the treasure!" Lee Ebony said.

"Treasure?" the guard said. "Then you got the wrong fellas for sure. They told me all they got in there is some hats they bought when a millinery shop went outa business."

"Better open the gate," Tracy said.

The guard ducked back into his lighted shack and pressed a button. The gate hummed open. "Somethin' not right about them fellas?" he asked.

"The way week-old fish ain't right," Sam Catchem said.

"How 'bout I come with you, then?" Lester patted the bulky revolver on his hip.

"No, you better stay here," Tracy said, glancing at Sam Catchem. "So you can stop anyone else who wants to enter. We don't want any civilians hurt. Now, where's storage unit 2-C?"

"End of that second row. Sure you don't need help?"

"I'm sure," Tracy said. "Let's go, squad."

They fanned out and crept along the row of storage units, keeping to the backs of the squat brick buildings. The lighting around the area's perimeter only served to make the shadows blacker.

Within a few minutes Tracy heard voices, something going *bump*! as it was hurled into the back of a truck.

"Careful!" a man's voice urged. "That's glassware that'll bring a fortune on the open market after my dear old mother dies. Which'll be next month, so we can explain how I came to possess it, along with all these other 'family treasures.' "

"You sure nobody'll suspect and blame us for the museum thefts, once they put two and two together?" asked a second man.

"Oh, they'll suspect, but so what? Relax, Fin. Money can buy happiness. Inheritance is bliss."

The other man emitted a chuckle cold as the North Atlantic.

Tracy signaled to Sam, then stepped around the corner, gun drawn. "You're under arrest!"

Fin had been about to load a large carton into the truck. When he saw Tracy he dropped it on the ground, and gold coins and various artifacts scattered from it. Maxim had frozen and was staring at Tracy's gun. Fin shoved him out of the way and started to run, then saw Lee Ebony behind him and hesitated. He began running again, and Maxim panicked and bolted in the opposite direction.

Tracy tackled Maxim, digging in a shoulder, and heard him say "OOOMPH!" as the breath exploded from him. *No fight left in this one.*

He placed handcuffs on the fallen Maxim, then straightened up and saw Sam, Lee, and Lizz wrestling with Fin. Sam had managed to get a pair of cuffs on him, but Fin merely bit through the chain.

Finally the three of them wrestled Fin to the ground and Lizz handcuffed his wrists behind his back. Lee Ebony fit her cuffs to Fin's ankles while Sam sat on him.

"Where's the other one?" Sam asked Tracy, breathing hard.

Lizz glanced around, then aimed her revolver at Fin and said, "How about it? Where's Putty Puss?"

Fin didn't answer. Tracy swung his gun around toward Maxim, who knew the better part of valor.

"He's acting as lookout!" Maxim said immediately. "Putty Puss didn't want to load the treasure without knowing if anyone was coming, and prudence was the—"

"Shut up!" Fin yelled.

"Haven't you caught on?" Maxim called over to his hand-and-ankle-cuffed partner. "Putty chose to save his own malleable skin rather than ours. He ratted on us. A snitch in time saves doing time. He decided that rather than turn up like a bad copper penny, he'd—"

"Yoiks!" Tracy said, slapping his palm to his forehead.

"*Copper* penny! Lester!" He ran full speed back to the guard shack.

The genuine guard was bound and gagged on the shack's floor, wearing only his underwear. He looked exactly like the guard Tracy had talked with earlier, only he wasn't, and Tracy knew it.

Putty Puss, in the guard's uniform, had escaped.

Tracy used his wrist computer to contact Headquarters and get an all-points bulletin out on Putty Puss, but he knew it was hopeless. By now Putty Puss would be someone else, and might even become one of the cops searching for him, before the dragnet was called off.

When he returned to the storage unit and the genuine treasure that had been raised from the sunken *Lampoon*, Sam was just finishing reading Maxim and Fin their rights. The paddy wagon arrived from headquarters and braked to a stop, and Fin was loaded inside, writhing and bucking like a landed fish. Tracy bent down and peered inside the box Fin had dropped, to see what it contained besides gold coins.

But in the confusion, Maxim had drawn Lee Ebony's gun from its holster and was pointing it at Tracy.

"Nobody moves or I blast your chief!" he yelled.

Everyone stood still.

"Now drop your guns!"

After a few seconds, every cop on the scene obeyed. Steel bounced off concrete as they dropped their weapons.

But when Maxim turned he found Tracy staring at him over the wide barrel of a nineteenth-century dueling pistol. "This isn't one from the ship," Tracy said. "It was stolen from a museum and Fin must have taken a liking to it because of its perfect condition. Want to bet he didn't load it?"

Maxim squinted into the darkness, trying to distinguish details of the gun. He knew that if he pulled the trigger and killed Tracy, Tracy would have time to return fire. The result would be two dead men, and one of them would be Maxim. He began slowly backing away.

"Another step and I'll pull the trigger," Tracy said. "Maybe nothing will happen. Maybe the gun'll explode in my hand." He grinned. "Or maybe . . ."

Maxim stood motionless, then lowered the gun. He knew the detective was willing to die in the line of duty. "All right, Tracy, it's a time for surrender, not flight to live another day."

The other detectives quickly grabbed and disarmed

Maxim, and wrestled him toward the waiting paddy wagon.

"What's he mean by that?" a puzzled, struggling Sam Catchem asked, as he bent one of Maxim's arms.

"He means that stone walls a prison make, and iron bars a cage," Tracy said, dropping the rust-caked and unworkable old dueling pistol back into the box.

Maxim stood up straight before letting himself be shoved into the wagon. "I never heard that turn of phrase," he said, "but I'll remember it. Once turned—"

The wagon doors slammed shut.

WHIRLPOOL, SIZZLE, AND THE JUICE

by
Ric Meyers

I

Her name was Victoria Timm and she was beautiful. She was a young woman made entirely of curved lines. Her forehead swept down, her pert nose swept out, the lines of her eyes swept open—then closed at the corners, housing what could have been sparkling blue marbles which darted this way and that, taking in the marvels of the gray, linear city.

Her mouth lines were sweeping as well, creating luminous lips always on the verge of a smile—powered by secret pleasures. Her chin was strong and curved, sweeping down to her smooth, elegant neck. From there, the curves were even more luxurious. They were strong and firm—yet soft and supple. A man could drown in them.

The expression on Vicky's face was partly innocent, but also partly knowing. It was the expression of almost all attractive young girls. They were humans trapped in special shells—respectful (and frightened) of their power. It was with that knowledge that Vicky covered her form in modest comfort. Her silky, off-white dress cinched at the waist, but billowed out elsewhere. The loosely pleated skirt caressed her legs as she strode down the street. The wind billowed the deep U-neck of the blouse, moving it like sand across a molded landscape.

Her low heels clacked on the asphalt, making her hair bounce. Her blonde mane also swept across her head. The yellow hair caressed her smooth, unblemished skin like a lover's touch. She kept it cut to a modest length, so it would not seem like a crown of fire. Instead, it rolled and loosely coiled, framing her features, like a calm sea on a beautiful beach.

Vicky didn't have to pretend not to notice the looks she got today. She honestly couldn't care. She went down the block with a special energy. She practically glowed with a special radiance. As always, people stopped, turned, and stared; or hazarded guilty glances. But today they could sense her happiness, not just be dazzled by her looks. For that alone she was grateful.

Everything was special today. The bleak city streets seemed exotic. The noisy, seething street activity seemed fascinating. The refuse and graffiti seemed quaint. Even the slums appeared rustic in the moonlight. Vicky Timm was looking at it all with different eyes.

She turned onto her block and stopped at her favorite open-air market.

"Hey, Miss Timm!" Kwang called, wiping barbecue sauce-soaked hands on his apron. The white cloth looked like a Jackson Pollock painting. "That stuff is plenty expensive! What happen? You meet rich doctor, huh?"

Vicky smiled as the proprietor approached. Kwang was a small, thin, jolly Korean who smiled so much and so wide that no one had ever seen his eyes. They were slits set in a permanent squint.

She continued to select the finest fruits and vegetables he had. "Now stop trying to marry me off," she said merrily, shaking a kiwi at him. "No rich husband, Mr. Kwang, a job!"

"Acting job?" Kwang said incredulously. He started gathering her selections, sharing her excitement. "On soap opera maybe?"

Vicky started to frown, her lower lip thick and soft. She continued to shop. "Well, no. Not on television. But it's a real contract, with a real company, headed by a very well known stage actor. I'm going to get some great training, and experience, and contacts!" She put two avocados together and looked heavenward. "And they're going to pay me for it too!"

"Finally!" Kwang said, having a time keeping up with the girl. "Maybe you move out of neighborhood, then. This no good place for pretty girl like you."

"Oh, Kwang," she replied, returning her attention to the crates of produce. "It's not so bad."

"It better once," Kwang said flatly. "Getting worse all the time. I have to come out every night, every few hours, with baseball bat . . . shoo pushers away. Not good for pretty girls living alone."

Vicky smiled down at the paternal little man. "Now, Kwang, nothing's going to happen to me . . ."

"Maybe not before," he said, not looking at her. He went on while weighing and bagging her selections. "It different now. I feel it. Nobody care. No more . . . control. The stuff they sniff and swallow and shoot . . . make them crazy. They do what they want to do . . ."

Vicky felt a chill. She resisted the temptation to hug herself. Instead she concentrated on preparing her own special celebration. "No more talk like that, Mr. Kwang," she chastised, fingers darting over the shining yellow crate of fat Florida lemons. "Or I'll have to take my business elsewhere."

Kwang laughed. "You no do that, huh, Miss Timm?" he called, reaching for a stubborn pomegranate which had rolled just out of his reach. He stretched across the counter for it, his fingertips just touching its smooth crimson skin. "Huh, Miss Timm?" he grunted. "Huh?"

Vicky reached for the biggest, fattest, shiniest lemon,

at the top of the bunch. She smiled, her mouth opening to answer him. A shadow fell across her.

Someone snatched the lemon out from under her fingers. The words caught in her throat. The lemon seemed to fly between her leaning body and the crate. She watched it fly, her bright blue eyes rolling down in their sockets. She was stunned when it suddenly snaked up and out of her sight.

She felt something at her mouth . . .

A hand fell on Kwang's outstretched arm. Fingers snapped around the Korean's wrist. The little man winced in pain as he was pulled off balance. His torso fell onto the counter, knocking three packs of candy bars onto the floor. They scattered around the feet of a well-dressed man.

Kwang stared. He recognized the shoes. They were three-hundred-dollar Italian loafers. He recognized the cloth of the expertly tailored suit. Smooth Hong Kong cotton. Like all good marketers, Kwang knew quality when he saw it.

"How about the money, pop?" said somebody.

"Miss Timm," Kwang grunted, trying to regain his arm and balance. "Miss Timm . . . !"

"Don't worry about the girl, pop," said the voice. "We got her money too . . . by now."

But they had more than her money. Vicky felt her teeth being pried open. Tart, acidic spray tickled her nose. Something raked across her palate and stung her tongue. Her mouth was filled with the lemon.

She bit down before it was pushed completely behind her lips. She tasted the juice which coiled down her throat. She coughed, bucked, but couldn't scream. She felt an arm tightening around her waist. She buried her fingernails in it, but felt only soft, luxurious silk.

"The money, pop," the voice told Kwang.

The little man struggled, kicking. "No!" he managed to bleat just before a hand slapped on the back of his head. His face was slammed into the counter.

The Formica filled his vision (little black boomerangs on a sea of yellow), then he felt the wood meet his skull. He heard the thwack of bone and wood. He felt the pressure as his brain sloshed against the front of his head. He was distantly aware of his nose bone snapping. Then it was mercifully over . . . and just beginning.

He felt backwards, his outstretched arm up, the pomegranate in it. The shock had numbed his mashed face, so he hardly felt the back of his skull hitting the shelf behind the counter. He slid to the coarse wood floor in a shower of green mouthwash, clear hair tonic, blue shampoo, red cough syrup, and pink laxative. Blood began to pour out of the tear in his forehead, bent nose, mashed lips, and ripped chin.

Still he was not unconscious. He looked up through the wash of crimson to see a man digging through the cash register. He was leaning over the counter, hunched down. His right arm was in the way, so Kwang couldn't see his face. But he could see the man's perfectly cut and styled hair, and the rest of his expensive suit.

Kwang was in shock. He always expected robbers to come, but never like this. He had always pictured them as young punks—drug addicts with greasy hair, torn T-shirts, and rended denims. What did this well-dressed man want with the few measly dollars in his cash drawer?

Kwang could no longer distinguish between the curtain in his brain and the very real sheet of blood that covered his face. All he knew was that he saw everything through a rippling wash of scarlet. The man on the other side of the counter stuffed his pockets with the Korean man's money, then turned toward the street.

For a split second, they stared at each other. The robber stood still directly in front of the grocer. Kwang opened his mouth to cry out, but the blood dribbled in, choking him. The little man contorted in place, trying to cry.

The robber's face was moving too. The wash covering Kwang's eyes wasn't causing it. Through the haze, the man's features seemed to be moving. They seemed to bubble, like pizza in an oven.

The robber hunched his shoulders and ran away.

Kwang collapsed, but then he was blinded by a bright yellow vision. No, it was not the day. It was his mental image of Vicky Timm. Her face was the sun and her lovely blonde hair was the sunbeams. He saw exploding red sunspots appear on her lovely visage. What did the boiling-faced man do to her?

Kwang forced himself up. He tried to call out, but the sounds were swallowed up by the exploding pain in his head. His fingers spasmodically grabbed the counter. He lurched to his knees, his jaw hitting the Formica. When the brain shellburst cleared, he saw a double vision. Two men, at the curb, in front of an idling van—one on either side of a shapely, contorting form. The men seemed to be barking at one another.

That did not last long. The man with the boiling face turned away and leaped into the van. Kwang's tortured eyes followed him for a split second, just enough time to see the van's driver turn toward him. Kwang reeled back. The driver's face was rippling. That's all the Korean could see: another man, in another expensive suit, with a face which coursed downward—like waves lapping at the beach of his chin.

Kwang was distracted by movement to his left. The girl was being hurled into the van by a third man. Same sort of expensive suit, shoes, shirt, and tie, but he was bigger than the others—obviously stronger and angrier. He threw the girl into the rear section of the vehicle, through the open side door. Then he looked around, seemingly hoping someone would try to stop him.

In that moment, Kwang saw his face too. The little man gasped in terror. These were the demons of his youth, dressed in the best of American finery. They were traditional monsters decked out in modern trappings. They were a sign of the apocalypse.

The third man's face was a whirlpool. It was a maw

with eyes, nose, and mouth set in its depths. The image stuck in Kwang's mind. It grew larger and larger, even as the third man leaped into the van and it roared away. It filled Kwang's vision until he fell into it. The Korean dropped deeper and deeper into the pit, until swallowed by blackness.

II

The man in the yellow snapbrim fedora turned toward the footlights. Once again, the regal old actor almost gasped at the man's sharp, distinctive profile. The man's face seemed to cut into reality, rather than reside or rest there. He seemed to be standing in front of the world, or on top of it, rather than in it. Everything was sharp lines with the man. His suit was black and severe. His tie was red and black and straight. The actor could practically smell the starch of the man's white shirt. He could imagine the weight of the substantial snubnose revolver in the weathered leather shoulder holster.

It did not pull the man down. His shoulders did not stoop with the weight of his responsibilities. As always, Dick Tracy's back was straight. He looked beyond the footlights into the gloom of the theater—as if he would find the secret of Vicky Timm's location there.

"Richard . . . !" Vitamin Flintheart cried out, sweeping toward the Chief of Detectives. "And the illustrious members of the press rhapsodize about *my* 'pro-feel'! If only I had your stature for just one night, just one performance . . . !"

"It wouldn't help us find your ingenue," Tracy said, mildly annoyed at the interruption. Ever since the actor had passed the age of sixty, it was hard to keep his mind on anything but his ego.

"Of course not," Flintheart blustered. "Of course. She was a diamond in the rough, Richard. I could feel it. It would only be a matter of a few performances. She would shine under my tutelage, Richard, positively spar-kle!''

Flintheart's oration was interrupted by Tracy's assis-tant. "Then we just have to make sure her light doesn't go out, don't we?'' He placed himself between the noted performer and his boss. "The other actors aren't much help, Tracy. Usual stuff about what a peach she is, but no info on where she might be, who might have taken her, or why.''

Flintheart looked upon the broad-faced man like an upstaging upstart. He was dressed for the part: pleated slacks, dark jacket, black shirt, bow-tie, and double-breasted vest. Perched on his head was a hard-brimmed, round-crowned fedora. He was smirking, but there was no humor in Sam Catchem's eyes.

"Outrageous!'' Flintheart exclaimed. "That a young girl can just be taken off the streets . . . whisked off the sidewalk for apparently no rhyme or reason! This city has gone insane, I tell you, insane!''

The bombastic speech was interrupted again, this time by a female voice coming from the audience. Both Tracy and Sam looked into the darkness.

"Yes?''

"The 'illustrious members of the press' are getting ugly,'' the woman explained. "I may not be able to keep them entertained much longer. You almost done here?''

Sam took the occasion to pull a cigarette out of his pack. "That outfit alone should appease them, Lizz,'' he said while lighting up. "I could look at your legs all night.''

Lizz Grove glanced down at the black minidress and stockings. "I'm surprised you can see anything through that haze you're sucking into your lungs,'' she replied mildly.

Tracy ignored the banter. He knew they were just blowing off steam—Sam literally. This was a nasty case, coming at the end of a very nasty month. "Almost through, Lizz. Keep them occupied a while longer. I don't want to overlook anything if I can help it.''

The policewoman nodded. They could now see the whites of her shining eyes. ''Will do,'' she replied, knowing how important this was.

''Try the can-can,'' Sam called after her. ''They should appreciate that.''

Even the actor could hear the woman's derisive snort.

''Very tough young lady,'' said Flintheart.

''Very tough old job,'' said Sam, looking back toward Vitamin's troupe. They had been having a late rehearsal when Vicky was abducted. Tracy could find no motive for any of them to have arranged kidnapping her. He had checked her background: there was no one to get a fat ransom from. Her surviving relatives all came from hard-working lower- and middle-income families.

''Perhaps you should call the reporters in, Richard,'' Flintheart suggested. ''Perhaps they will respond to an impassioned plea for assistance.'' Vitamin's left hand was over his heart. His right hand was aimed at the ceiling. ''Allow them to spread the word! Could it be that some-one out there''—he pointed that way—''has seen this poor girl . . . ?''

Tracy shook his head. ''Not yet, Vitamin. I'm afraid that's what her captors might want.''

Tracy walked away, toward center stage. Flintheart looked after him, then at Catchem, confusion infusing his craggy features.

Sam shrugged. ''Beautiful young girl gets snatched, essentially in broad daylight—no motive, no phone call, no ransom note. It could have been done for kicks.''

''Kicks?'' Flintheart repeated the word with multisyllabic distaste.

''A thrillnapping.'' Sam scowled. ''Used to be a body would kill a body just to get attention. Nowadays, some people will do anything, just for the hell of it.''

''Why, that's simply terrible!''

Sam shrugged, anything but indifferent. ''Just being

all they can be, like they see on television. Haven't you heard, Vitamin? It's the nineties. The 'Me-dia' decade.''

"I beg your pardon?"

"They're being trained, Vitamin," Sam said quietly, the cigarette smoke wafting under the brim of his hat. It danced sinuously toward the rafters. "For all the good it does, the news media is also advertising crime as a high-reward, low-risk job."

"That's preposterous!" Flintheart retorted, rallying to the defense of his fellow entertainers.

But Sam just smiled, starting to move away. "You said it yourself, Vitamin. The city is going insane. You've got to ask yourself: 'who's putting out the word?' " Then he was at his superior's side.

"The Korean grocer described them to a tee, Sam." Tracy said quietly.

"Not easy mistaking them, Dick. Whirlpool, Sizzle, and The Juice."

The Major Crime Squad had been chasing them for weeks. The Central Headquarters' computer had told Tracy's squad all they needed to know. The criminal trio had been friends since childhood. They had graduated from being grammar-school dropouts to high-ranking members of a street gang. But this city's melting pot had been on the boil since drugs mixed in. No matter how tough your gang got, there were always new gangs willing to be even more savage, even more insane.

The trio went to one rumble too many. The new kids on the block didn't just want to beat them—they wanted them punished. They wanted them marked . . . forever.

They kept the trio prisoner for two days in the back room of a diner. The Juice was lucky. He was just repeatedly beaten until every feature on his face drooled blood, pus, saliva, and mucus. He survived with bleeding gums—which always outlined his teeth in red—an eternally runny nose, and mashed eyes, whose sockets produced so much lubricant it ran down his cheeks.

It went much faster for Sizzle. His face was merely pushed into hot oil, then pressed onto a hamburger grill.

But Whirlpool was the pièce de résistance. The leader of the new kids took a nice sharp knife, placed it at the northeast corner of his face, and made a curlicue spiral to the center of his nose.

The new owners of the trio's territory left them in an alley. Somehow they survived. Somehow they got to a hospital. Somehow they checked out long before any of the doctors believed they could even walk. Somehow they got back to the neighborhood and blew the new kids away.

From that moment on, they had been playing hide and seek with the police, leaving at least a dozen robberies and assaults in their wake. Tracy was certain they were building a new power base. Who knew how many drugs they had already bought and sold? That was the problem: how to catch them, and how to prove it.

"But what would they want with Vicky Timm?" Tracy wondered.

Catchem shook his head sadly. "Don't look for motive anymore, Dick. There just might not be one."

Tracy looked at his associate. "Times have changed, my friend," he said evenly. "Motives have changed. They may have gotten slimmer, and stupider, but they're always there. Even if they took her because they were bored, that's still a motive and will still help us stop them."

He was interrupted by an insistent beeping coming from his wrist. Tracy raised his arm and looked at the device strapped there without special ceremony. His Two-Way Wrist Computer had become as much an extension of his arm as a watch would be to the average man.

He didn't have to identify himself. The image was crystal-clear and in full color. It was like looking into a window. Junior could see him and he could see his adopted son.

The red-haired young man started talking with little

preamble. "We've got a break, Dick. Sizzle called Channel Ten."

"Sizzle!" Sam exclaimed, joining in on Tracy's frequency with his own Two-way.

"What did he want?" Tracy asked.

"Air time," said Junior.

Sam glanced over at Vitamin Flintheart, who looked on incredulously.

"Air time?" Tracy repeated. "What do you mean, air time?"

"He wants Charity Chanel to do his life story."

"The Ice Pick?" Sam interjected. Chanel was the cool blonde anchorwoman on the local newscast, known to her peers by that nickname.

"Did he say anything about Vicky Timm?" Tracy asked.

"Not word one," Junior replied, "but the news director is a friend of mine. He sent me a tape of the call, but I had to promise not to involve him."

"You're breaking your promise, aren't you, Junior?" Tracy's words were quiet, but his tone and expression were full of admiration and thanks.

"A girl's life is at stake, dad," Junior said, just as quietly.

"Where's the tape?" Tracy continued briskly.

"I brought it to Diet Smith," said Junior. "I'm with him now."

The image on Tracy and Catchem's wrist computers broadened to show both Junior Tracy and the scientist/inventor/philanthropist. Diet Smith had taken over the broadcast. They sat in the old man's study. Behind them was a phalanx of electronic equipment.

"Sorry to get you up, Diet," Tracy said.

"Wouldn't miss it, Dick," the industrialist retorted. "Damn ulcer keeps me up anyway. Couldn't sleep with a girl's life on my conscience."

"What have you got?"

"Put the recording through the most basic of sound

sensors," the billionaire told him. When Diet Smith said "most basic," it usually meant on equipment even the Japanese wouldn't see for six months. "Pulled out two things. The sound of a plane, and the noise of a work crew."

"Near the airport," Sam guessed.

"Can we narrow it down any further?" Tracy asked.

"This baby can chop up the sound and layer it like a sandwich," Diet continued. "The tonal qualities say that the plane was descending, rather than ascending, and that the work crew was working underground rather than on the road."

"Sam," Tracy called, "we need to know the airport's landing patterns and the jobs Metropolitan Hydraulic is on tonight." Catchem was back on his own frequency and checking in even before Tracy returned his attention to the wrist-TV screen. "Hold tight, Diet, I'm going to use the Keyhole."

The Keyhole was Diet's newest innovation to the communication device. It allowed Tracy to keep two contacts on the screen at once. It was named in honor of what hotel dicks always used to get their evidence from. Tracy woke Pat Patton out of a sound sleep.

"What is it, Tracy?" he asked gruffly and groggily. "What's wrong?"

"We've got a line on Whirlpool, Sizzle, and The Juice, Chief. I think we'll be able to pinpoint their hideout in a matter of minutes."

Patton sat straighter at the mention of the trio's names. "Good. You can bring them in for questioning."

"I need a helicopter and some backup."

"Wait a minute, wait a minute!" Patton interrupted, rubbing his eyes. "What do you need all the manpower for? Just go and bring them in."

"They may have taken a hostage, Chief."

" 'May have'? What is this, Tracy?"

"Chief, we've got an eyewitness to an abduction!"

"I heard what you got, Tracy. You've got a material

witness in the hospital who hasn't regained consciousness since he was brought in. You're taking the hearsay evidence of a paramedic. I can't take that to a judge or the D.A. They'd throw me out of court!''

''Chief, these three have a long history of violent crime . . .''

''All unproven, Tracy. In the eyes of the law, they are innocent.'' Patton looked stricken, but he remained on the company line. ''I can't just give you carte blanche anymore. The Mayor's cut the budget, the unions're breathing down my neck, the pressure groups are all over me . . . !''

Catchem glanced at his immediate superior, almost expecting to see Vesuvius ready to blow, but he should have known better. As always, Tracy's jaw was set and his brow was unlined. If anything, maybe his eyelids were even narrower.

''Take it easy, Pat,'' he said. ''Take it easy.''

''These people have rights too, Tracy!'' the Chief cried, trying to rationalize his actions.

''I know,'' Tracy said reasonably. ''I'm only reporting in. We have a suspicion that the alleged perpetrators have taken a hostage, and are doing everything we can to ensure that the suspects are brought in without incident.''

''No probable cause, Tracy. No eyewitness testimony. No valid justification!''

''Yes, Chief,'' said Tracy calmly. ''You're right, Chief. The City Government dictates that the rights of the known, represented individual must take precedence over the unknown, unrepresented victim. I understand, Chief.''

''Tracy . . . !'' Patton looked as if he were about to collapse from both guilt and anger.

''Don't worry, Pat,'' Tracy said quietly. ''Go back to sleep.'' He tuned out the Keyhole.

''Got it, Dick,'' Sam quickly told him. ''Only one place the flight pattern and emergency water crew's work intersect.''

Tracy nodded, then gave his full attention to Diet and Junior. They couldn't hear or see Chief Patton, but they both read the detective's expression.

"Dad . . . " the young man started with concern, but the businessman interrupted him. He yawned and stretched elaborately.

"Man, what a beautiful night! Just the sort of night that would be perfect to test some new infrared devices. Do me a favor, will you, Junior? Have the boys down at the hangar get FAA clearance for some testing down at the shore. Tell 'em it'll be ecologically safe." Diet looked directly at the screen. "You don't mind if I step out for a little reconnaissance flight, do you, Tracy?"

Tracy was about to inform him of the dangers of night flying—especially near three psychopathic criminals—but who was he to trounce on the personal freedoms of an American citizen? Especially after all they had been through together.

"No," he said, smiling. "I don't mind."

Everyone turned toward the back of the theater as the exit doors flew open. A small mob of reporters flowed in, barely held back by the efforts of Lizz Grove. As always, they were already bellowing the names of everyone they recognized. The photographers were begging for "posed candids" by shrieking directions at the subjects, while the reporters were yelling any inflammatory question which came to mind—anything to get a reaction other than "no comment."

Tracy didn't disappoint. By the time they had surged down the aisle, he was standing at the stage "apron," looking down on them. He held his hands up and said one word.

"Quiet!"

Vitamin Flintheart admired his amazing projection. Everyone flinched, but then they could hear crickets chirping in the back rows. Before the chaos could start again, Tracy asked *them* a question.

"Is a reporter from Channel Ten here?"

The mob quivered, then a chillingly attractive blonde appeared. It was the Ice Pick herself, hair coiffed as if molded in plastic and makeup applied as if by laser.

The reporter's and detective's eyes met. Incredibly, the rest of the reporters, actors, and police watched, completely silent.

"Do *you* have a question for *me*?" Tracy asked her softly.

To the other reporters' amazement, Charity Chanel only stared back at him, then lowered her head. "No," she said.

Before all hell broke loose, Tracy again raised his hands. "I have a statement," he announced. Lizz saw his almost imperceptible motion for her to get out of the way. She headed for Sam's side.

Tracy looked back at the veteran stage actor. "Vitamin?" he said. "Tell them."

For a moment Flintheart was confused, but he never looked a gift stage in the wings. He found the klieg lights' hot spot and began his aria. "I want to tell you a story," he declared. "The story of an innocent girl and a city gone insane. A city? Nay. A society. A society which had lost its mind . . . !"

Tracy pulled his hat brim down tighter as he surged by his associates. "Let's go," he said intently. "Right now."

III

Vicky Timm's life was hanging by a rope. She stood before her captors, on her tippytoes, the thick, scratchy hemp tightened around her neck. She couldn't kick to maintain her balance: the monsters had cinched her ankles with a pair of handcuffs. She couldn't use her hands to loosen the noose: they were bound behind her back.

She had to stand as still as she could, choking, in the middle of the loft-like penthouse. Whirlpool, Sizzle, and The Juice circled her. The latter two examined her as if she were some sort of esoteric modern sculpture representing woman as captive. The former stared as if she were a chef's specialty. Vicky could only stare back, marveling at the open white space around her, and the huge wall of twenty-five-inch televisions looming above them all.

There were thirty of them, five rows of six each, stacked on each other, next to the one big, thick, steel sliding door. Each set was tuned to a different network— some even on channels that showed four images of four different programs. And even then, not every program on was represented. Instead Sizzle had concentrated on the news stations. Vicky was battered by twenty-four-hour docudrama, multiplied more than thirty times.

She gasped and gagged as The Juice distastefully tapped the taut rope. He looked up, watching it vibrate to the pebble glass skylight some thirteen feet above. He checked the knot around the window's latch: a simple metal handle with a small hole at the end. He glanced at the metal-tipped wooden pole which lay on the floor. That was the only way to open the skylight from inside. But if it swung down, Vicky Timm would be hauled up . . . and strangle to death.

"Ith this trip really nethethary?" the oozing faced man asked facetiously. Each time he spoke, the viscous liquid drooled into his mouth, making him burble and spit.

"It'sss okay, it'sss okay," Sizzle said quickly, his words hissing out of lips which couldn't bear to move too much. "The more outrageousss the act, the more interessst created in the public sssector."

Whirlpool smiled proudly on his associate, the curve of his lips mingling with one of his long scar lines, making it look as if the grin was fourteen inches long. "I'm glad you approve, little brother," he said. "Why waste time, I say. Show them who's boss right away."

"What are you going to do with her?" said The Juice.

"What do you think?" said Whirlpool.

They stood in their fancy suits, in their fancy building,

discussing the fate of the beautiful girl trapped between them.

"They catch usth here and they've got a witnessth," The Juice reminded him.

"They don't know where we are," Whirlpool sneered. He stepped over and put his arm around Vicky's shoulders. "Besides, she'll never testify. One flick of that latch up there . . ."

She could only tremble. Any other move might kill her.

The Juice walked away, grumbling and bubbling. Sizzle moved quickly to the other side so she would not topple over. The disfigured criminals sandwiched her between them.

"We sssaw you on TV," he hissed. "We sssaw that commersssial you did, and the guessst ssshot on that sssitcom. Yesss, yesss, we know all about you. We know all about all of you. But you're the firssst one we've ssseen in the flesssh. We had to take you. We'll get more coverage with you . . ."

"What are you talking about?" Whirlpool complained, his upper scar line arching down. "I wanted her, I took her . . . !"

"Whath's this?" The Juice exclaimed. He was standing with his back to them, at the phone table, pointing down at an open Yellow Pages. Sizzle moved quickly toward the televisions.

"What?" Whirlpool barked, alerted to the tone in The Juice's voice. They met midway between the captive and the blaring screens. Both men looked at Sizzle.

"Televithion stathions?" The Juice said ominously. "Channel Ten?"

Whirlpool grabbed the thick telephone book and hurled it in Sizzle's face. The pages fanned out, cutting him around the eyes. Sizzle grabbed his head, howling, and reeled back—almost slamming into the TVs. Instead he stopped in midair, held up by Whirlpool's fist clutching his shirt front.

"You called that blonde bitch, didn't you?" Whirlpool yelled.

Sizzle waved his hands. "Yesss, yesss, I had to, don't you undersssstand?" He talked more quickly than normal. "Look at all the ssstarsss of crime; Ssstark, Ssson of Sssam, the Bossston Ssstrangler! They all had great publisssity! They all had booksss and moviesss! But now it'sss a buyer'sss market! We have to move now to beat the russsh!"

He had regained his feet, and Whirlpool's grip had lessened. Sizzle could see the interest in his eyes. All three men had grown up loving and hating the images they had seen on their electric friend—their combination mother, sister, and babysitter. They had accepted that packaging of life. They had watched it make reality increasingly entertaining, and fantasy increasingly realistic.

Whirlpool let Sizzle go. He was right: why not become the superstars they deserved to be? Why else had they run this road? Fame and power, pure and simple. And television was the place to get it. As long as they continued acting insane, they would be world famous!

"Idiots!" The Juice cried. "Televithion stathions record their callths! They might've traced it . . . !"

Just then the front-door buzzer sounded. It made everyone, including Vicky, start. She wobbled on her medium heels, the rope creaking.

Sizzle started to move, his hand going inside his suit jacket. The Juice grabbed his arm.

"Don't anther it."

The three men stood stock still, looking at the door. Hundreds of feet up, inside one of Diet Smith's helicopters, his sensor technicians fed information to Junior Tracy.

"We're hovering over the brownstone now," Junior reported into the wrist computer. Through the new infrared radar equipment, the tech could see through the skylight as if he were standing on it.

Four stories below, Dick, Sam, and Lizz stood outside the front door, with no warrant of any kind. On Tracy's signal, Catchem pressed the doorbell again.

"Thanks, Junior," Tracy said. "Keep us informed." He turned to his friends. "Vitamin'll keep the press busy for a while. But as soon as they find us, this will turn into a media hostage circus. We've got to get that girl out now."

"Where is she?" Lizz asked.

Tracy looked up. A fat raindrop hit him in the left eye.

Whirlpool, Sizzle, and The Juice's heads spun toward the skylight as it rattled. The heavens were crying for Vicky Timm, tapping on the window. Their heads snapped back to the door as the buzzer sounded again.

"Blasth!" said The Juice. He slapped Whirlpool's arm. "You sthay here." He grabbed Sizzle's sleeve. "You come with me."

"What if it's the cops?" Whirlpool angrily asked.

The Juice smiled, liquid coursing around either side of his lips. "Then they'll have to announth themselths. That's the law."

Sizzle pulled the 9mm fifteen-round automatic out from under his fancy jacket. "And then we'll blow them away," he hissed.

Vicky's eyes widened—and not because she saw two of her captors leaving, or because she was alone with Whirlpool. It was because she felt something cold and wet on her throat. She felt it dribbling onto her dress. She craned her neck back as far as it could go without losing her balance. Her eyes rolled up in her head.

The rain obscured her view of the night sky. Instead she saw that the window had a leak. Water was pouring over the latch, then dribbling down the rope. It snaked through her hair, and dropped across her form. A puddle started to grow around her feet.

Her stance began to get slippery.

She opened her mouth, then saw Whirlpool staring at

the televisions, his back to her. Vicky had to ask herself: did she really want him to turn around?

She clamped her teeth tightly and bit her lip, trying to remain upright.

Downstairs and outside, Sam pressed the doorbell again while he pressed himself against the wall beside it. Lizz quickly prepared herself for action by putting her small purse's long strap over her head so it cut across her torso. Then she pulled another thin strap, which had been stapled to the back of the purse, around her slim waist. She tied the strap ends together so it made a belt and kept the purse tight against her side. Inside the black bag was her .38 snubnose and extra ammunition.

The Juice stood midway up the front staircase, holding a mini-Uzi semi-automatic he had gotten from his second-floor apartment. Sizzle had leaped to just inside the front door, the 9mm automatic tight in one fist, and a sawed-off shotgun clutched in the other.

"Who ith it?" The Juice called.

Catchem rolled his eyes and grit his teeth. "Police," he called back. "Open up!"

Sizzle stepped back, his eyes glittering. "Sssure we'll open up," he cried giddily, both hands wrapped around the gun butt. "Come on in!"

The last three words were drowned by the booming of the gun, which pumped projectiles through the solid wood. The door was pounded, splintering and cracking, as if repeatedly slammed with a giant fist. Sam and Lizz leaped off the stoop in opposite directions, landing on the sidewalk fifteen feet apart.

Tracy couldn't help but look back at the sound of the shots. But it was too late for him to return. He had already chosen his task. The sound of distant weapons echoed inside the empty neighboring building. Tracy said a silent prayer for his companions and raced even faster up the stairs.

"Didn't you hear?" Sizzle screeched, bringing up the shotgun. "I sssaid, 'come in!' " He blasted the rended door completely open. The wood exploded outward, littering the street, a shard catching Sam against the head. He went down on his back, hat and snubnose flying.

The Juice appeared through the smoke, his mini-Uzi leveled. He saw one man down, and a girl kneeling. The tiny machine gun swung toward the female.

Lizz got off one shot. The Juice felt a tug at his shoulder. He pulled the trigger. The pavement next to Lizz erupted. She tried to run away, but the concrete chips sliced into her ankles, bringing her down.

Sam saw her disappear between the pavement and the stoop, his hand awkwardly reaching for his gun. His fingers tightened around the brim of his hat instead.

The Juice saw something flying at him in his peripheral vision. He brought the mini-Uzi around, but the spinning hat went over his arms and into his face. The hard brim caught him at the upper lip. The surprise knocked him down more than anything else.

"Out of the way!" Sizzle bellowed, trying to get over him.

"No!" said The Juice. "Up the sthairs! Get Whirlpool, kill the girl, and get out of here!"

Sam bounded to the other side of the stoop. He looked down to see Lizz lying against a basement window, her stockings torn, her ankles bleeding.

"You okay?" he asked quickly, worried.

"Fine," she said with a grimace.

"I told you not to wear a miniskirt," he said, smirking grimly even as he moved away.

"Get them!" Lizz yelled after him. "Cover Tracy!"

Tracy was on the roof of the building next door. It was being renovated, hence the emergency water work earlier that evening. There was plenty of water up there. The rain came down around him, pouring across his hat and soaking him to the skin. It had already chased Diet Smith's helicopter away. Tracy looked from the sky to the skylight across the way. The only thing between him and it were piles of building materials and a fifteen-foot-wide alley.

Inside the penthouse loft, Whirlpool got tired of the two dozen late-night news programs blaring their tragedies into his head. He turned toward the girl with her shoes slipping across the puddle. He didn't see that. All he saw was her dress molding her form as never before.

"Now darling," he said, approaching. "Let's see just how much crime pays . . ."

Just as he touched her, there was a gun blast they could hear even above the TV speakers. Whirlpool raced out into the hall, looking down the stairwell. "What the hell is going on?" he boomed.

Sizzle stuck his head over the banister from the second floor. "Copsss," he yelled as Sam's head and arm appeared from the other side of the first floor. He got off one shot, chewing banister, before both criminals jerked their heads back.

Whirlpool hastily returned to the loft, closing the door behind him. "Cops?" he echoed, looking from the televisions to the phone to the girl. Finally he saw the water coursing down the rope. He looked slowly from Vicky's terrified face to the rain-covered skylight . . .

The roof door swung open, slamming against the steel wall beside it. Tracy stopped, midway across the twenty-foot-long plank he had placed from building to building. It was only two feet wide, but that was enough to get Tracy across, even with the wind and the rain.

"Cops!" Whirlpool screamed into the storm, marching angrily toward the edge of the brownstone. "Cops!" He wanted a gun bad, but all his weapons were in the third-floor apartment he called home. That was okay; he didn't need a gun to finish off this flatfoot.

Tracy bent his knees, firming his balance, as he reached for his own .38. Whirlpool was faster. He slammed both hands against the end of the plank and pushed it off the roof.

Tracy saw Tess's face. He saw his beautiful wife and

his young son Joe, as the plank slid over the edge of the brownstone and dropped.

Four feet.

Whirlpool had not pushed it hard enough. The plank end fell forty-eight inches onto an outcropping ledge just over the loft's side windows. Even so, Tracy was bounced up, and hurled down. His back slammed solidly on the wood, while his arms and legs swung on either side.

"More lives than a cat," Whirlpool muttered. "I'll kill you!" He leaned over the edge, reaching for the plank.

Tracy's bullet nicked his earlobe, sending him back. As he fell to the rooftop, Whirlpool saw the cop still flat on his back, but with a revolver in his hand, aimed between his knees.

"Fine," Whirlpool said to himself, rage filling him. "Fine! You want to live? Fine, but you'll never save the girl!" He started crawling quickly toward the skylight.

Tracy tried to get up. The plank shifted. One corner slid off the ledge. Tracy froze in place. He tried to slide down the plank, but his wet clothes seemed pasted to the wood. He peered intently over the building edge from his precarious vantage point. Dimly, on the roof made distant by the driving rain, he could see Whirlpool's arm reaching for the skylight latch . . .

Just a few millimeters too far. Whirlpool couldn't quite get his hand on the thing no matter how he stretched and strained. He ducked, glancing over his shoulder to make sure Tracy couldn't shoot him from there. He smiled, his lips disappearing into his scar. The water was a veritable curtain, almost completely washing the cop from view.

Whirlpool stood, emboldened. He stepped onto the skylight with one foot, and reached with one hand. The latch was just under his fingers when his foot went through the pebble glass.

Tracy heard the scream as Whirlpool's leg dropped into the loft while his other leg stayed on the rooftop. Incredibly, given his position and balance, he partially sat there, his crotch grinding against the broken glass. Whirlpool howled and flailed, but just couldn't get up.

The shards rained down behind Vicky, shattering on the teak floor. She almost jumped, strangling herself. Instead she looked up, watching a new waterfall mingling with blood, over Whirlpool's imported pant leg, sock, and shoe. It inspired her to even greater escape efforts.

The fact is, no matter how tight the rope, both hemp and flesh give. And the captive desperate enough to ignore raw, torn skin can get free. Vicky Timm's flesh was smooth, and her hands were small: small enough to match her wrist size if she pulled her fingers together.

She pulled and twisted and rubbed.

Whirlpool shrieked, yanked, and reached for the latch.

He grabbed hold just as Vicky pulled her bleeding wrist free.

The glass beneath Whirlpool gave way.

Whirlpool's middle finger went into the hole at the end of the latch as his body dropped. Vicky's hands went to the noose around her throat. She threw it off like a hated necklace as he fell, middle finger caught in a too-tight ring.

Both screamed as they landed. Vicky hit the floor on her side, her ankles still cuffed. Whirlpool jerked in the air, his toes just inches away from the floor. He hung there, by his now broken middle finger, screaming anew. Vicky's cries mingled with his as she dragged herself away through the glass, metal mesh, and water.

"Sizzle! Help me!" Whirlpool screamed. "Juice! Juice! Where are you?"

They couldn't hear him. Sam was pinned down on the stairway by Sizzle's guns. The Juice was in the cellar, trying to find a way out. Instead he saw Lizz's body lying against the outside of the basement window. She couldn't see him. She wasn't looking inside. All she saw was outside wall. The Juice held his mini-Uzi loosely, trying to decide what to do, the barrel aimed at the policewoman's heart . . .

Tracy was trapped. The plank shifted with every move, threatening to fall off at any second. He could hear Vicky's sobs. He could hear Whirlpool's howls. And he could only lie there, hoping to push the end farther on the ledge. It wasn't working. He felt the plank budge again . . . in the wrong direction . . .

Vicky dragged herself away from the contorting human chandelier, his toes just touching the widening pool of water as he kicked. Her body wracked, her ankles cinched, her eyes bloodshot, and her ears filled with the televisions' shouts, she crawled toward the door.

Whirlpool suddenly hung limp. He let all his weight hang from the latch. He no longer felt the pain; it had gone beyond that. Instead he let it feed his hate—all the hate he had ever felt: as a kid, as a teen, and as an adult. Society would pay. They would pay through their representative—Vicky Timm.

Whirlpool prepared himself for a gigantic tug which would free him—even if his finger was ripped completely off.

Vicky got her hands on the side of the sliding metal door. With almost all her remaining strength she slid it completely open.

Sizzle was standing on the other side, staring at her in surprise.

"Kill her!" Whirlpool screamed.

Sizzle brought his reloaded 9mm automatic down and pointed it right between Vicky's shining blue eyes.

He hesitated. Because rising up behind Whirlpool, in the skylight, was Dick Tracy.

He had stood up on the board. He had leaped. The plank had fallen. Tracy had slammed onto the building's edge. Even with the water and wind, he had held on. The stone scraped his fingers and tore his clothes, but he held on. And climbed . . .

Tracy ran across the rooftop, his gun already aimed.

His bullet went through the top section of the open sky-light window and into the hallway as Sizzle ducked behind the wall of televisions.

Each one of their screens started exploding out as Sizzle shot through their backs at the cop. With all the noise he couldn't hear Whirlpool screeching, or see him twisting in the air.

"Damn you!" the scarred criminal said, the words tearing from his raw throat. "Damn you, damn you, damn you!"

Huddling on the floor in the doorway as sparks and plastic showered down on her, Vicky couldn't tell who he was cursing—her, the cops, or himself.

She never found out because just then the entire sky-light window gave way, ripping out of its frame.

The huge broken pane swung in and flew down, colliding with the stacked televisions in a torrent of water. The entire wall of screens smashed backward into the wall as the liquid splashed inside them and against the electric plugs.

There was an eruption as if a twelve-foot-high flash-bulb were going off. Then there was a torrent of sparks and a cloud of steam. Before the lights went out they could see him: the man with the broiling face jerking in place, his entire body boiling amid the television sizzle.

Then there was only moonlight.

Vicky heard the policeman drop to the floor. She heard the scarred man's footsteps getting nearer and nearer. Then she felt his hands around her throat, the cold, wet steel of the window latch still stuck on his horribly twisted middle finger.

She scratched him. She raked her fingernails vertically down his encircled scar. She heard him grunt. She felt his fingers weaken. Her hands searched the darkness, finally finding the skylight window latch. She gripped and twisted.

She heard him scream. So did Catchem and Tracy.

Sam was practically in front of the man, but couldn't see him in the darkness. He swung his arm, catching Whirlpool on the side of the head.

Vicky felt a pillow of air hit her. Sam felt the man falling. Whirlpool dropped out of the door, hitting the banister on his side. He flipped over, and was gone.

The cops and girl didn't see it, but they heard it. Whirlpool dropped down the stairwell. His head hit the edge of a stair across the narrow hall, flipping him back. His right leg caught in between banisters, swinging him face first into another stair. The banister and steps pounded his body, mashing his muscle and breaking bone. From above it looked as if Whirlpool was falling into his own scar. Whirlpool died in the whirlpool.

The Juice heard him hit the floor above him. The building shook. The dust cascaded onto his head. The liquid carried it down, into his eyes, nostrils, and throat. He choked and stumbled, the gun going off. It tore up the wall and shattered the glass just above where Lizz was lying.

The wounded policewoman rolled over, pushed her arm through a hole in the pane, and aimed, her eyes having already adjusted to the dark. She pulled the trigger. The bullet did not have far to go in the small basement.

It sank into The Juice's chest, went all the way through, and popped out the other side. The tiny, flattened piece of lead twirled, did two small somersaults in the air, and fell to the cellar dirt.

IV

When Tracy got to him, The Juice was laughing. They were weak, blood-coated laughs, but laughs none the less. Tracy looked quizzically at the policewoman.

She shrugged. "Something about agendas," she told him.

Tracy kneeled next to the disfigured man the other two creatures had taken orders from.

"You the bossth?" The Juice asked. Tracy nodded. The Juice chuckled, more blood drooling from the corner of his mouth, among everything else.

"Take it easy," Tracy suggested. "The paramedics'll be here any second."

"What for?" The Juice demanded. "No way I'm going to jail . . . They're not going to do thith to me again." He tried to point at his face, but couldn't. Tracy could only watch him. It wasn't the first time he'd served as confessor to a dying criminal. It wouldn't be the last.

"We would have made it." The Juice laughed quietly. "Ith only we all wanted the same thing." He looked out the broken basement window. "Whirlpool wanted to have fun. He wanted to get away with anything. Sizthle? He wanted to be famouth. He wanted fame, like all hith heroes . . . Charles Manthon, David Berkowith . . ."

His eyes started glassing over. Tracy could see him going. "How about you?" he asked. "What did you want, Juice?"

"Me?" The Juice said in weak wonder, amazed that anyone cared. "I juth wanted to sthay alive." He looked directly at Tracy. "I wanted to live."

Tracy shook his head. "Too bad," he said. "You won't even get that."

The Juice's eyes flickered. What was that on the cop's face? Sadness? No, that was impossible.

Liquid streamed out of the criminal's broken eyes: some of it tears . . .

CHESSBOARD'S LAST GAMBIT

by
Edward D. Hoch

It was Sam Catchem who first brought Dick Tracy the news about Chessboard Briggs on a wintry January afternoon when the news reports were warning of an impending snowstorm.

"We picked up one of Chessboard's men early this morning," he reported, strolling into Tracy's office at headquarters. "He was trying to steal a car, but it was too cold to start the engine."

"Who was it?"

"Gazie O'Rourke. He was in prison with Chessboard." Chessboard Briggs had earned his nickname in that same prison, when a vengeful con had shoved him against the red-hot grillwork of a metal stamping machine, leaving a large brand like a chessboard across his chest. Chessboard Briggs wore it as a symbol of honor, and had been known to unbutton his shirt before committing one of his robberies or killings, just so his victim would be sure of his identity.

"Stealing a car is rather small potatoes for someone

like Gazie,'' Tracy remarked, ''unless he was planning to use it in a bigger caper. Let's go talk to him.''

Catchem led the way down the hall to the lockup, where prisoners were kept while awaiting interrogation or arraignment. He was wearing his usual black shirt and bow tie, and as they came up to O'Rourke's cell his lumpy, freckled face took on the familiar smirk that criminals had come to know so well. ''Hello, Gazie! You been robbing newsstands again?''

''Go to hell!'' O'Rourke told him, not bothering to stand up.

Tracy edged past his partner and signaled for the cell door to be opened. ''We've got a few questions for you,'' he said, entering the cell and seating himself on the bunk bed next to the prisoner.

''See my lawyer.''

Tracy ignored him. ''We want to ask you about Chessboard Briggs.''

''Who?''

''Wise up, Gazie. Chessboard's the one we want and you know where he is. Drop us a hint and we might go easy on the grand theft auto.''

But Gazie O'Rourke was too experienced to play games. ''You're the one should wise up, Tracy. The car didn't move. The most you got on me is breaking and entering, or maybe attempted theft.''

''With your record, that's enough.''

''See my lawyer,'' the little hoodlum said again, and Tracy knew the interview was over.

They left the holding cell and returned to the squad room. ''Well, we gave it a try,'' Sam Catchem said with a touch of fatalism. ''Who knows? Maybe Chessboard's gone south for the winter.''

''He'd have taken O'Rourke with him if he went.'' Tracy had an idea. ''Sam, what did Gazie have on him when he was picked up? An address book, anything like that? Maybe there's a phone number we could trace.''

Catchem went off to the property room while Tracy

phoned Chief Pat Patton. "Chief, this morning one of Chessboard's men was picked up trying to steal a car. Chessboard may have wanted it for a robbery. Have you had reports of anything unusual today?"

At the other end of the line Patton gave a good-natured laugh. "No, Dick, all the criminals are hibernating because of the storm. The big companies are all closing early so their employees can get home before it hits."

Tracy glanced out at his office window. A few wind-blown flurries were visible now, hinting at what was to come. "I hope you're right, Chief. I've got a funny feeling."

He hung up just as Sam Catchem returned from the property room with a big manila envelope. "Here it is, Dick. No address book, but there is one of those little pocket diaries."

Tracy opened it, seeking today's date. The only thing written there was *TTT*.

"*TTT*," Sam read aloud. "Mean anything to you?"

Tracy shook his head. "Not a thing." As an afterthought he added, "Except that they're my wife's initials."

Tess Trueheart Tracy was having a busy day. She'd been gone from her suburban home since morning, running a number of errands; now she was heading home at last, hoping she'd arrive before her son Joe returned from school. The warnings all day long of the impending storm had closed some schools early, although the suburban schools were still in session.

Glancing back toward the city in her rearview mirror, Tess noticed that the top of the Tribune Tower was already lost in the clouds. The flurries were growing thicker. For once it appeared that the weatherman was going to be right. She hoped Dick wouldn't have to work late tonight.

As she turned the car into her street, she noticed an

unmarked blue van parked in front of the house. Her first thought was one of annoyance that some workman from one of their neighbors had chosen this spot for a parking space. Then, pulling into the driveway, she realized there were two men in the front seat. Almost at once the driver started the van's engine and began backing into the driveway behind her. Tess felt a moment of fright as she pushed the button to open the automatic garage door. Then she was safely inside and the door was closing behind her.

She decided to call Dick at once if the van remained in the driveway. He'd often warned her not to take chances. She got out of the car and walked to the garage door to look out the window.

A voice behind her said, "Those are just friends of mine, Mrs. Tracy."

She whirled and found herself facing a burly man wearing a plaid shirt and fur-lined leather jacket. His arms hung loosely at his sides as he walked toward her. "Who are you? What do you want here?" She was backed against the door with no place to run.

His heavy brows shaded deep, dark eyes. He smiled slightly, revealing a missing tooth, and yanked open the front of his plaid shirt to show her a crosshatch of scars that covered his chest. "People call me Chessboard," he answered softly, "and I want you."

There was welcome news that afternoon. The flurries got no worse, and suddenly the storm warning was over. On Sam Catchem's little desk radio he heard the announcer say, "The latest storm update from the weather bureau states that the area of heavy snow is now expected to pass well north of the city. The storm warning has been downgraded for our area, and the worst we can expect is intermittent flurries for the next few hours. The Charity Awards Dinner will be held as scheduled, and the Community College will hold its regular classes."

"No snow after all," Sam told Tracy. "Just flurries."

"That's good. Come into the interrogation room. O'Rourke's lawyer has arrived, and we might as well get the formal questioning over with."

The little hoodlum was seated next to his attorney, a balding man named Cyrus Jacobs, who was known around headquarters for his skill at springing professional criminals from their cells. "Do you plan to charge my client?" he asked as Tracy and Sam entered the room.

"We certainly do," Tracy told him. "And if a larger crime is involved he'll be charged as an accessory before the fact. He could be looking at some serious prison time if he doesn't cooperate."

"I assure you Mr. O'Rourke is willing to cooperate. He will answer your questions to the best of his ability."

As for O'Rourke, he asked for a cigarette and settled back with a defiant sneer on his face. "You know my name and my record. What more can I tell you?"

Tracy held up the little appointment book. "What's this *TTT* written on today's date? I wouldn't want you missing an important engagement."

"I forget."

"Come on, Gazie. The state can give you a long time to refresh your memory."

"I told you I don't remember. Maybe it was a reminder to pick up my dry cleaning from Tommy the Tailor."

"Sure it was!" Sam Catchem responded wryly. "And you needed to steal a nice clean car to bring it home."

"Do you deny knowing Chessboard Briggs?" Dick Tracy asked, going back to basics.

"Sure, I know him. You get to know a lot of guys in stir."

"Have you ever had any criminal dealings with him?"

Cyrus Jacobs held up a hand and the two of them consulted in whispers. Then O'Rourke replied, "We see each other around town. I don't have criminal dealings with anyone. I'm on parole. I can't associate with known criminals."

"Why were you stealing the car?"

"I was trying to move it. I usually park there and it was blocking my space."

"Didn't you try to steal it for Chessboard to use in a caper?" Sam asked.

"No, sir."

They went on that way for another ten minutes, until Tracy finally called a halt. He pressed a buzzer and an officer arrived to take Gazie O'Rourke to the courthouse for arraignment. "You'll be free in an hour," Jacobs called after his client.

"Don't count on it," Sam grumbled. But he knew in his heart that the shady lawyer was probably right.

Outside the interrogation room Tracy was waiting for him. They checked on the voice stress analyzer contained in Tracy's Two-Way Wrist Computer, and received an immediate analysis of Gazie O'Rourke's answers. "Lots of stress," Sam Catchem confirmed. "Look at that! He lied about Chessboard and he lied about not needing the car for a caper. He—"

"Chief!"

They were interrupted by the sudden appearance of Lizz Grove, a tough, dark-haired policewoman who seemed unusually disturbed. "What is it, Lizz?" Tracy asked quickly.

"We have a report from one of your neighbors. He thinks he saw Tess being forced into a red van in her driveway."

"How long ago?"

"About thirty minutes. At first he wasn't sure he saw right and he tried phoning Tess. When there was no answer he called us."

"What's his name?"

"George Blake. He lives across the street from you."

Tracy's expression was grim. "There's no one named Blake across the street, or anywhere else on our block."

Sam could see he was remembering the *TTT* written in O'Rourke's date book.

* * *

Tess awakened with the odor of ether still fresh in her memory. She knew she was in some sort of moving vehicle, but it took her a moment to remember the blue van she'd seen in her driveway. Then she remembered the man named Chessboard as well. She tried to scream and realized she was gagged, tried to move and found that her hands and feet were tied.

The truck bumped along, and she wondered how long she'd been unconscious. Certainly no more than an hour, because she could still see daylight out the rear windows of the van. She thought of Dick, and Joe, and wondered if she would ever see them again.

Suddenly the van came to a stop. She guessed they were somewhere on a dirt road, from the roughness of the journey. Perhaps they'd brought her out here to kill her. The rear doors opened and she saw again the man who'd been waiting in her garage. Chessboard.

"Hello again, Mrs. Tracy," he said. "I'm sorry we had to kidnap you like this. Just keep calm and you won't be hurt." She tried to say something through her gag, but only muffled noises emerged. "We're going to leave you here for a time, but we'll be back." He closed the doors firmly. Soon she heard another car start up and drive away.

It began to grow cold in the van. She could feel it even through her heavy winter coat. Outside the light was fading, and that meant it was after five o'clock. She tested her bonds and they seemed tight. Then she let her gaze travel over the interior of the van. If there was anything she could use to cut her ropes, she had only minutes to find it. After that it would be too dark to see.

There were no loose tools anywhere, but the rough metal braces of the van's interior seemed promising. She began to maneuver herself into a position to reach them.

Dick Tracy reached his suburban home a few minutes before five o'clock. Sam had driven with the siren on, even though they both knew it was too late to do Tess any good. She would be far away by now, and all they could do was wait for the message they were sure Chessboard would send. Sam's lumpy face was grim as he drove, and Tracy was silent by his side.

"We'll find her," Sam said once, but it brought no reply.

At the house Tracy found Tess's keys on the floor of the garage, near the car. "She drove in," he decided, "and Chessboard was waiting for her. Here is where he must have grabbed her."

"They had to have a car waiting," Sam Catchem said.

Tracy agreed. "Of course. But probably not a red van like the phone call reported. Talk to the neighbors across the street and next door, will you, Sam, while I check inside? Ask them if they've seen anything of my son Joe."

He went into the kitchen and looked around, but nothing seemed out of place. Nothing—and everything.

Tracy took off his yellow fedora and leaned against the counter. If the call to headquarters hadn't been made by a neighbor, then it must have been made by Chessboard or one of his men. Why? Why had he wanted Tracy to know about the kidnapping as soon as possible?

Sam Catchem came back in a few minutes with young Joe along. Tracy was relieved to see his dark-haired son, who seemed to resemble his father more as he grew up. "I was at the Sayers', Dad. When Mom wasn't home I figured she got delayed."

"That's good. I'm glad you're all right. Your mother's away right now but she'll be back." He looked up at Sam. "Find anything?"

"There was a van parked in front of the house for a while, but it was blue, not red."

"Is something the matter with Mom?" Joe asked, perhaps catching the anxiety in their voices.

"She's just helping me on a case," Tracy replied. "She's fine. Would you like to have dinner with the Sayers tonight?"

"Sure! That would be great!"

"I'll call them and make sure it's all right."

Once Joe had been sent on his way, Tracy turned his attention back to Sam. "What do you think?"

"They've got her, all right."

"I can't sit here waiting for a call. Arrange with the phone company to have all calls to this number forwarded to headquarters. If I'm not there they can contact me on the wrist computer."

"I'll handle it, Dick."

Tracy walked into the living room and stood staring out at the familiar street. He felt helpless, without a clue to go on. The one clue they'd had—the letters *TTT* in O'Rourke's appointment book—hadn't been understood in time.

That was what he had to do—talk to O'Rourke again.

Sam drove him back to headquarters and went to get O'Rourke. As soon as Tracy sat down at his desk, Lizz told him Chief Patton was on the phone. He picked it up at once. "Hello, Pat."

"Dick, I just heard about Tess. I want you to know I'm assigning every available man and woman in the department to search for her. Sam Catchem already phoned in a description of the blue van and we're combing the city. If my wife and I weren't invited to the *Tribune*'s charity dinner tonight I'd be there with you."

"Don't worry, Pat. I know there are a lot of good people to help me."

He hung up as Sam hurried into the office. "Do you have O'Rourke?"

"Dick, you're not goin' to like this. Jacobs got him sprung on five thousand dollars' bail."

Tess had been working on the ropes, trying to fray and weaken them against the rough metal of the van's interior, for more than an hour. She was almost ready to give up when at last the strands loosened, weakened and then snapped. Her hands were suddenly free.

For a moment she just sat there with her back against the cold metal. Then she quickly bent to untie her ankles, removing the gag last of all. She opened the back doors and stepped shakily to the ground, surprised to see stars overhead. The snow had passed them by somehow, and it was a cold but pleasant night.

But where was she? Along a dirt road somewhere, with not a light visible in any direction. She walked around to the door on the driver's side of the van. Finding it locked, she returned to the back doors and climbed back in, squeezing between the seats until she was behind the wheel. The ignition was locked, of course, but she could still blow the horn.

She kept at it, beeping in various patterns, long and short, for a full minute. Then it occurred to her that Chessboard's hideout might not be that far away. Rather than summoning help she might be merely alerting her kidnappers. She stopped honking and climbed out of the van again. It looked like she had a long walk ahead of her.

Then Tess spotted the distant headlights coming toward her. The honking had attracted someone, but she had no way of knowing whether it was friend or foe. She hid quickly behind a bush and waited. The lights came closer and finally pulled to a stop not far behind the blue van. A man in a heavy winter coat got out and looked around. The fact that he did not immediately open the van to look inside encouraged Tess.

"Help me," she said in a clear voice.

"Who's there?" he asked, switching on a flashlight in his hand.

"I've been kidnapped," Tess told him. "I need to get to a phone."

"I heard you honking and came out to see what the trouble was. I've got a phone back at the house. Get in."

The man's wife gave Tess a glass of water while she called her house. Immediately the call was switched to headquarters and she heard Dick's voice. "Tess?"

"Oh, Dick! Chessboard kidnapped me and left me tied up in a van on a country road. But I'm free and all right now."

"Give me your exact location, Tess. I'll have a car there within five minutes."

The man gave her the address and she relayed it to Dick. Then she sat down to wait.

After Tracy had dispatched a car to pick up Tess he glanced at the clock. It was nearly six-thirty, and his apprehension was growing. "What is it, Dick?" Sam asked. "Tess is safe. You should be happy."

"They left her tied up in the back of the van."

"Yeah, that was pretty lousy on such a cold night."

But Tracy wasn't concerned about that. "Don't you see? They didn't even have a place to take her. The kidnapping was a spur-of-the-moment thing."

"Maybe," Sam agreed cautiously.

"But if it wasn't planned in advance, what were Tess's initials doing in O'Rourke's appointment book on this date?"

"I don't know," he admitted. "Maybe—"

"Maybe *TTT* didn't stand for Tess Trueheart Tracy at all. Maybe it stood for something else all along—a caper so big that when we arrested O'Rourke, our man Chessboard remembered the *TTT* in his book and realized we'd find it. He came up with the idea of kidnapping Tess before the real meaning of the initials occurred to us."

"What other meaning could they have?"

"I don't know," Tracy admitted. "It's evening now and nothing's happened yet. That pretty much rules out a bank holdup or payroll robbery."

"Heck, there's nothing happening tonight except the *Tribune*'s charity awards dinner."

"I know. Chief Patton and his wife are going to it."

"It's a big social thing. The ladies will be dripping in diamonds."

"That's not Mrs. Patton's usual—" Dick Tracy stopped

in mid-sentence and stared at Catchem. "Sam, where is the dinner being held?"

"At the newspaper. In the big private dining room at the top of the Tribune Tower."

"The Tribune Tower."

"Would Gazie have abbreviated that as *TTT*?"

"He tried to tell us it stood for Tommy the Tailor, didn't he?"

Sam's mouth was hanging open. "You don't think—?"

"Come on!" Tracy said.

Chessboard felt fine now that Gazie O'Rourke was out of jail and back on the team. He'd planned the caper for himself and three others, and the prospect of proceeding without Gazie had been bothering him all day. Now, as they entered the *Tribune* pressroom disguised as workers, the plan was right on schedule. They took the elevator in the pressroom up to the floor below the private dining room at the tower's peak. There they shed their pressmen's garments to reveal waiters' uniforms underneath. From their bags they extracted automatic weapons capable of spraying the entire dining room with bullets in a matter of seconds. Chessboard and Gazie would cover the diners from opposite ends of the room while the other two, Fritz and Lou, collected the jewelry from the women guests. There were one hundred guests at the charity dinner, probably fifty women, and he knew most of them would be wearing diamonds worth thousands of dollars.

They went up the fire stairs to the top floor and Chessboard picked up a serving tray near the door, covering his weapon with a napkin as he started across the crowded room. "Wait till I'm at those big windows at the other end before you uncover your gun. Then we'll both fire short bursts into the ceiling. That should get their attention."

He moved down the aisle between tables of diners, trying not to stare at the wealth of jewelry on display.

The others had thought him a bit crazy to attempt a robbery at the Tribune Tower, but he had more in mind than jewelry. This crime was certain to bring a wealth of publicity, in the *Tribune* itself and elsewhere. The others could wear masks if they wanted, but he'd make sure everyone knew this was the work of Chessboard Briggs.

He reached the far end and turned around, his back to the big floor-to-ceiling windows. The napkin came away and he raised the Uzi to fire a burst at the ceiling. There was an instant of utter silence in the room. He pulled open his shirt and announced, "My name is Chessboard and I've come for your jewelry. My men will—"

"Drop it, Chessboard!" a voice barked, almost at his side.

He turned to see a stocky man in a tuxedo pointing a snub-nosed revolver at him. "Who—?"

"Chief of Police Patton. You're under arrest!"

At the other end of the room he saw Dick Tracy burst from the elevator, his .357 Magnum already covering Gazie O'Rourke. Others were coming out of the stairwell. Suddenly there were police everywhere.

Chessboard smiled and swung his Uzi toward Patton. The chief fired once and the force of the bullet sent Chessboard spinning against the window behind him. He felt it giving away, and then in a shattering of glass he was falling, with only the frigid night air between himself and the street far below.

That was when some of the guests panicked and started screaming, but it took Tracy only a few moments to calm them. Sam Catchem was handcuffing Gazie O'Rourke and the other two when Tracy announced, "It's all over, folks. Everyone calm down and go back to your dinner. I'm sorry for the interruption."

Waiters were already covering the smashed window to keep out the cold when Chief Patton hurried up. "You were just in time contacting me on the wrist computer,

Dick. I was able to hide behind the drapes just as they came up the stairs.''

"I couldn't risk a lot of shooting with all these people here," Tracy told him. "I was hoping we could get them before that started."

"I guess Chessboard won't be bothering us anymore. You going down to look at the body?''

Dick Tracy smiled. "No, I'm going home to see Tess.''

LIVING LEGEND

by
Stephen Mertz

They hit the crack house hard and fast, a by-the-numbers bust executed with full force, the caravan of seven vehicles careening onto the block of tenement buildings that had been condemned by the city and were scheduled for the wrecking ball. It was 2:00 A.M. precisely, but there was pedestrian traffic aplenty along here, shadowy, frightened figures that scuttled into the night away from the piercing glare of headlights and flashing rooftop lights.

The "ram" led the caravan, an armored vehicle from the front of which protruded a ten-foot-long iron pole, giving the truck a tank-like appearance. The ram mounted the curb, climbed the front steps of the crack house without slowing. The battering pole burst apart the front door, the doorframe, and the surrounding masonry.

The last car of the caravan glided to the opposite curb. From the back seat, Tracy watched the SWAT teams pour from the cars, storming the house with commando precision.

From behind the steering wheel, Dan Sprague, honcho of the city's undercover anti-drug task force, pumped a round into his shotgun.

"Remember, Tracy, you're here on strictly observer status. Stay out of the way."

"I'll remember," Tracy said quietly.

Sprague's partner, Wil Garrett, a black man of line-backer proportions, occupied the front passenger seat. He checked the action of his Beretta automatic.

"Relax, Dan. You're wound too tight. Tracy'll follow the chief's orders."

The three of them wore plainclothes, and windbreakers with POLICE stenciled across the back.

Sprague was heavyset, muscular, in his middle twenties. The shotgun looked like a toy in his hands.

"It's not enough, busting down dope dens. They give us a goddamn living legend to keep out of harm's way while we're doing it."

"Just do your job, Lieutenant, and I'll do mine," Tracy said. "Good luck, men."

He watched them leave the car. Garrett had time for one apologetic backward glance and a shrug, then they angled away at a loping run and disappeared into the house.

Tracy was fifty years old, but he worked to stay in top physical shape through a daily regimen of exercise. He wore a .357 Magnum shoulder-holstered beneath his windbreaker.

The popping of handguns, alternating with the stutter of Uzis and MAC-10's, carried to him dully from inside the house, punctuated with indecipherable shouts, then the loud boom of a shotgun once, twice, three times in rapid succession.

"Observer status," he said to himself.

He scanned the buildings adjacent to the crack house, his gut knotted with frustration, with the urge to be doing something.

For a second he thought it was only wishful thinking

when something caught his attention, then he looked again and in the illumination of a nearby street light he saw the something beyond the line of vision of the policemen stationed in front of the house.

A window up on the third level had opened, someone had leaned out to stretch a plank across the ten feet or so separating the tenement buildings. First one figure, then others, scampered on all fours across the plank.

Tracy upholstered the Magnum and hit the pavement running toward the building next door. He motioned to the men in front of the crack house.

"They're getting away. Two of you cut around to the back. Someone cover me."

He charged into the building, taking the stairs inside three at a time until he pressed himself to the wall just below the first landing, the .357 up and ready.

Frantic footfalls thundered down from above.

Whether they headed out the front or the back, they would have to pass this landing on their way out.

He caught the first one across the mouth with a swipe of the Magnum, breaking bone, popping the punk onto his behind, splattering droplets of blood across two of the four black males, teenagers, crowding the steps on their way down.

They were heavily armed with pistols and Uzis but they froze in complete surprise as he stepped onto the landing to assume a two-handed shooter's crouch.

"Freeze. Drop your weapons."

Their surprise yielded to arrogance and belligerence. One, holding an Uzi, snarled.

"Who you jerking, old man? There's four of us and one of you. Let's burn his ass, homes," he said to the others, "and be gone."

"You'll take me down," said Tracy. "But I'll take at least two of you down with me, and the two who get away will be cop killers and there won't be anywhere for you to run. Or you can drop your weapons and your lawyers will have you back on the street in no time at all. Call it.''

The tableau held like that in this little corner of the world for a few more seconds, then the clatter of weapons dropping to the floor, one by one, set time in motion again and then the cops from below flooded in to take charge of the prisoners.

''Not bad for an old man,'' the kid who'd held the Uzi snickered as he was led past Tracy.

Tracy holstered the .357 and followed them down to the street.

An hour later in Chief Patton's office, Sprague sat in one of the chairs facing the Chief's desk, Garrett had the other. Tracy leaned against a windowsill, the lights of the city cold, multicolored, against the blackness beyond the window.

''Well, Dick,'' said Patton, ''what's your assessment?''

Tracy was aware of Sprague and Garrett eyeing him intently.

''If the mission objective was to put a kink in the gangs running that part of town,'' said Tracy, ''I'd have to say the operation was a success.''

''One more drug house out of business,'' said Garrett. They still wore their windbreakers.

''You're damn right it was a success.'' Sprague's voice was a bit shaky. ''The Hawks' man went down in that drive-by shooting last week, and I greased Cool Step, the Blood Devils' boss, tonight. Those were the rollers. They kept the peace and they kept the Jamaicans out. With those two bangers out of the way, what's left will fight among themselves. We can handle it from that angle.''

''Incidentally, Lieutenant,'' said Patton, ''considering the circumstances, I've gotten word that Internal Affairs will more than likely waive the usual suspension of duty after an officer has killed a man, despite your rather excessive use of force.''

"I don't like hoods," said Sprague. "I especially don't like it when they pull down on me."

"Three shotgun blasts to the head and chest," Tracy said.

Sprague bristled. "It takes excessive force to stop the Cool Steps of this world. Everyone in this room knows that. Whose side are you guys on?''

"Easy, Dan." Garrett spoke in a soothing baritone.

"Internal Affairs also wishes someone had actually seen him pull down on you," Patton said. "But the bottom line is that you men did shut down that operation and no one is going to miss Cool Step."

The city's poorest section, like all inner city barrios and ghettos across the country, was under siege from gang war bloodshed unlike anything experienced since the bootleg wars of Prohibition. Neighborhood teenage gangs fought over the distribution of crack cocaine. The two main confederations of gang alliances were the Blood Devils and the Hawks, an alliance comprised of dozens of subgroups, or sets, organized along neighborhood lines, made up of about thirty homeboys, or bangers, to a set.

The Devils and the Hawks each grossed more than one million dollars a week from the sale of illicit drugs.

"The thing is," Tracy said, "my assignment was to observe and assess tonight's operation from the point of view of looking for gape spots."

Too many anti-drug operations lately had gone sour. Someone, upper echelon, was working with one or both gangs from inside the department, feeding them information, selling out for a piece of the action.

"So all right," said Sprague. "Considering that the bust was a success, what did you find to criticize?"

"There's always room for improvement. You hit that street from different angles and you maintained radio silence; that was good. But you should have had those adjacent buildings covered. You should have been ready for some sort of escape route like the one they tried to use while you were taking care of Cool Step. And until we find out how the gangs have been getting their information, who their mole in the Department is, I suggest all meetings and briefings regarding undercover activity be impromptu, held at spontaneously selected locations, not here at Headquarters, in case they have us bugged.''

"You're not saying one of our men is dirty, are you?'' asked Garrett.

Sprague glared angrily. "That's exactly what they're saying. Don't you get it, Wil? We trade fire with the enemy, we put our lives on the line, and Tracy's got the gall to suggest that one of our unit is dirty.''

Patton cleared his throat. "That will be enough of that. Lieutenant, you and your men are to be commended for your bravery tonight and for a job well done. Now we must move quickly to exploit this vacuum in the gang leadership.''

"There's also word on the street of a new takeover,'' said Garrett. "Not the Jamaicans, not the Colombians. No one seems to know who. We'll have to run that down.''

Sprague glared at Tracy. "And with all due respect, we'll make a lot better progress if we're not busy nurse-maiding an extra hand.''

"I said that will be enough.'' Patton spoke sternly. "We're all on the same side here, Lieutenant. Don't take this review of your operation so personally.''

"Sorry, sir, it's hard not to. Will that be all?''

"It will. Give the men of your unit a personal well-done from me, will you?''

Sprague said he would. He and Garrett left the office.

"That Sprague is one of the angry ones,'' Patton said. "Sorry about that, Dick. Thanks for going along with them tonight, though next time you're sent on observer status, you'd better obey orders and *remain* on observer status. Tess would have my hide if you caught a bullet because I sent you somewhere you had no business being.''

"She's a cop's wife, Pat. She knows how it is. And I was glad you called me in. We've got to plug this security leak. One bad cop hurts us all.''

"Just the same, tomorrow you're back to your regular job heading up the Major Crime Squad. That's more than enough responsibility for a Chief of Detectives. We're going to plug this pipeline the gangs have into the Department, but right now I'd say we're dead-ended.''

"Whatever you say, Pat. If you need me, just give a holler.''

The following morning he awakened to the smell of coffee and the sound of crackling bacon from the direction of the kitchen. He was surprised to see that the bedside clock read 10:35. He showered quickly and, when he entered the kitchen, he was wearing the black suit with the red-and-black tie that Tess had set out for him. He encircled her with his arms from behind and kissed her as she labored over the stove.

"Morning, hon. Thanks for letting me sleep. Guess I needed it.''

She returned the kiss with her special smile. "Have some coffee, breakfast is coming up.''

"Joe get off to school okay?''

Joe Tracy was in the fourth grade. He wanted to be a detective like his dad when he grew up.

"Yes. Yes, Joe's okay.''

He thought he caught a catch in her voice, but then she was setting his breakfast before him.

"I don't like going a whole day without seeing my son.''

She sat across from him and buttered a hard roll for herself as he dug in.

"You know he understands how important your work is. How did it go last night?''

He decided not to tell her about his confrontation with the four punks.

"It was rough. There was a fire fight. A gang boss was killed, a couple more wounded."

"I'm so glad you were only there to observe."

"The man running the bust called me a living legend last night," he said in a bemused tone. "A punk called me 'old man.' "

"You're young enough to have a ten-year-old son. And if you're an old man, that makes me an old lady and I don't even want to consider that."

She was trying to be sunny but he could see in her eyes what he had seen before.

"What is it, hon?" He pushed away his plate. "That was a fantastic breakfast, but ever since I came in I've picked up that something isn't right. Is it Joe?"

"He's okay, Dick, but . . . something happened at school yesterday."

"What happened?"

"Joe overheard some older boys talking on the playground. One of the kids was offering to sell his classmates heroin. He said he'd stolen it from his father. Joe said the boy was bragging that his father was a dealer. But at the time Joe overheard them, he was with that little Connally girl he's got such a crush on. The older kids didn't know they'd been overheard, and Joe didn't want to start anything because he didn't want the girl to get hurt. When he went back by himself a few minutes later, he says they were gone and he couldn't find them. Isn't it terrible, Dick? We moved to the suburbs to get away from things like drugs. These kids are only ten and twelve years old!"

"Did he recognize any of those kids?"

"It's a big school. They weren't in his class. He only recognized the boy offering to sell the heroin, the one who said his father was a dealer. It was Sonny Medlow from down the street."

"Wayne Medlow's boy?"

"Not very surprising when you think about it, is it?"

"Unless the boy was making something up to impress his friends. Problem kids will do that."

"I know I should feel sorry for the man, bringing up the child on his own like he is, but he doesn't have a job and he never seems to be home. He's always leaving his son with Mrs. Knurd, the woman I told you about from the next block."

"The alcoholic?" Tracy frowned. "I wonder if Children's Services is aware of that situation. I know Medlow hasn't exactly been a boon to the neighborhood."

"He admitted at the last neighborhood meeting that he keeps an arsenal in his home. I don't like the man. I've even heard that he's deeply involved in a white supremacist organization."

"I've heard those rumors too, but you know how I hate neighborhood gossip. And no matter how abhorrent a point of view is, we have to tolerate it if no laws are being broken. But what Joe heard the Medlow boy say about his father being a drug dealer, well, that's different."

"What are you going to do?"

"I think I'll have a talk with Medlow on my way to work."

The lawn was overdue for a mowing: weeds everywhere, cigarette and cigar butts everywhere, and here and there an empty beer can.

Medlow yanked his front door open within seconds of Tracy's first press of the doorbell. He was of average height but a large build gave him bear-like proportions. He wore a crewcut, camouflage fatigues, and spit-polished combat boots. He held a can of beer. A lighted cigarette wagged from the corner of his mouth.

"Yeah, what do you want?"

Tracy paused before speaking when he saw the boy standing in the living room behind his father. Sonny was a chunky kid with long hair. His right eye wore a swollen shiner.

"What happened to your son?"

"He was in a fight at school this morning. Some other kid got in a sneak punch. They sent him home. What the hell is it to you?"

Tracy looked at the boy.

"Is that what happened, son? Don't be afraid. You can tell me. I'll protect you."

"What do you mean, you'll protect him?" Medlow demanded. "I don't care if you are a cop, Tracy, you've got no damn right coming to my home and—"

Tracy ignored him. "Tell me what happened, Sonny."

Medlow spun on the boy. "Yeah, Sonny, tell the nosy cop what happened."

Sonny avoided Tracy's eyes.

"It's, it's like Dad said. It happened on the way to school. When I got there, they sent me home."

"What were their names?"

"I don't know. I didn't recognize them. Can I go now, Dad?"

"Yeah, beat it. Don't go out of the backyard. Now, Tracy, what the hell do you want?"

"Hold it," Tracy said before the boy could leave. "Sonny, I've got to be sure. You can come with me now if you want to. You've got nothing to be afraid of. Tell me the truth. Did your father give you that black eye? Did he strike you?"

"Hey, what the—" Medlow started to protest.

"Stow it," Tracy said. "Tell me, Sonny, who did that to you?"

"Some boys on the way to school." The reply was a choked sob. "Dad didn't do anything. Now let me go, will ya!"

"This is your own home, son." Medlow narrowed his eyes, dueled with Tracy's stare. "You go on now like I told you. Don't pay any attention to our nosy neighbor."

"Just remember that I am your neighbor," Tracy told

the boy. "You know where I live. There are laws to protect children. You come to me anytime."

The youngster scurried from sight.

"Now, unless you've got some official business here, cop, I suggest you get off my property."

"There are laws against child abuse, Medlow."

"Yeah, and I haven't broken a one of them."

"See that you don't."

Tracy turned, strode back to the car. He felt Medlow's eyes at his back every step of the way.

"Bradley Funeral Home."

"Let me speak with Mr. Bradley."

"Uh, sir, if this is about our services, Mr. Diggum is our Funeral Director—"

"I said I want Bradley."

"Yes, sir. Just one moment, sir."

Several clicks and another voice came on, spitting out run-together words with the staccato rhythm of a submachine gun.

"Yeah, this is Buzz. Whaddaya want? Who is it, who wants to talk to me? Come on, say something."

"Do you recognize my voice?"

"Yeah, Wayne, of course I recognize your voice. Why shouldn't I recognize your voice? What do you think I am, stupid or—"

"Don't use names, goddammit!"

"Okay, yeah, right, no names, right. Okay, so what do you want? What's shaking? Why the call during business hours? What is it? Come on, tell me, what is it?"

"We've got trouble. Could be big trouble. We're gonna have to do something about it, fast."

He thought about the encounter all the way into the city.

He was driving in later than usual, his schedule thrown off by last night's special assignment. He was used to the rush-hour traffic. The sparse, early-afternoon flow on the freeway moved smoothly, allowing him to dwell on the matter of Wayne Medlow.

He had gone over to Medlow's in order to size the situation up, to get a handle on what kind of man he was dealing with. The instant he saw Sonny's black eye he knew exactly what to make of Wayne Medlow.

Child abuser.

The question now was: how best to deal with the situation.

His primary concern was the boy's welfare. He knew it would be extremely difficult for the vastly understaffed, overworked agencies charged with investigating incidences of child abuse to act in a case where the victim refused to cooperate; a legalistic, bureaucratic nightmare, and the victim's rights were all too often placed at the bottom of the list.

He had not brought up Sonny's offering to sell heroin to his schoolmates. It was not difficult to construct a likely scenario. The father had discovered that some of his heroin was missing and he knew who had taken it. He had struck Sonny, Tracy was sure of that. He was also certain that Medlow did not know his son was going around school bragging to other kids that his father was a dealer. If he had known, Sonny would probably be dead, or at least a lot worse off than having one black eye. And Medlow would have behaved far differently toward a policeman who showed up at his front door, especially if the policeman happened to be a neighbor. If Medlow was a dealer and knew he might be under suspicion, he would have put on a cooperative front, not been so openly confrontational.

The problem was a lack of solid proof. Legally, Tracy had nothing to go on.

Given that hard fact, he had decided on the spot at Medlow's house that the child's best interests would be served at this point by not mentioning anything about the playground conversation overheard by Joe. He had no desire to put Sonny in more jeopardy than the boy was in already.

As he steered his car into the underground parking lot of Central Headquarters, he was still considering what he should do about Wayne Medlow.

He walked into the offices of the Major Crime Squad to find Sam Catchem and the rest of the unit swamped with the endless official paperwork that is the reality of police procedure. It was a busy but uneventful day, purely routine, spent in the office.

He did find time for a quick phone call home, promising Tess he would be home that night in time for dinner and putting in his request for her meatloaf and potatoes dinner, one of his favorites. They did not discuss his visit with Medlow. She would wait for him to bring that up after he came home, when the time was right.

Around five o'clock, while Sam was out to dinner before pulling night shift and after the others had already left for the day, he was clearing his desk prior to leaving, when Dan Sprague walked in.

"Say, Tracy, I, uh, just wanted to apologize for last night. For, uh, some of the things I said in Patton's office. He was right. It wasn't personal, you were just doing your job. Guess I was a little more stressed out than I realized after greasing that punk. Even on the street, you don't kill a man every day. Anyway, I'm sorry."

He extended his hand across Tracy's desk. They exchanged a firm handshake.

"We're in a tough line of work, Lieutenant. It can get to a man."

"I especially apologize for that living legend crack and all that. You're still one of the best, or I wouldn't feel so lousy about it. Thanks for your help, by the way."

"I did what I had to do."

"Guess I just get frustrated that things aren't as cut and dried as when you were new to the force."

"Aren't they? I'm hardly out of touch with the streets.

Enough real life crime comes through this squadroom every day.''

''I'm just saying it's a hell of a game we're being asked to play. The criminals outgunning us on one side, the feds come in and take all the credit, and the watchdog groups birddog us every step of the way just waiting for a legal loophole to get these criminals off the hook when we do arrest them. You're right, sometimes it gets to a guy. That's what happened last night.''

''Apology accepted,'' said Tracy. ''We'll say no more about it.''

Wil Garrett appeared in the doorway.

''Hello, Tracy. Lieutenant, that call we were waiting on just came in. That buy on the lakefront is on. It's set to go down in fifteen minutes.''

''Then we'd better hustle.'' Sprague moved toward the door. ''Excuse me, Tracy. Thanks for your time. This could be lead on that new source we've been working on.''

After they were gone, an edgy restlessness came over Tracy and would not go away.

Tess stepped from the kitchen and brought a cup of coffee across to where he sat in a darkened corner of the living room. He had placed one of the kitchen chairs so he had a good view, around the edge of the drawn curtain, of the Medlow residence across the street and halfway down the block.

He lowered the infrared night-vision binoculars and accepted the coffee with a smile.

''Thanks, hon.''

She returned the smile. ''You remind me of Jimmy Stewart in *Rear Window*.''

''For a man who doesn't like to hear neighborhood gossip, I feel like the neighborhood snoop.''

He'd made it home in time for dinner, and the three of them had enjoyed a traditional family meal with lively conversation dominated mostly by little Joe's wisecracks.

Every word was music to his ears, and for a while the edge of restlessness within him simmered on low and almost disappeared.

Wayne Medlow's pickup was gone—there were no lights on in the house, he'd noted when he drove by on his way home. The house had been visible from where he'd sat at their dining-room table during dinner. Toward the end of the meal, he'd noticed truck lights pulling into the driveway. It was too dark to see anything more from where he sat, but moments later the Medlow house lights went on.

After dinner, Joe had asked for help with his homework. He needed to be quizzed on facts he expected to be tested on the next day. Tracy offered to help.

While Joe was getting his books ready, Tracy helped Tess by drying some dishes, at which time he quietly asked her to keep an eye on the Medlow place and call him if the pickup left.

During the course of their going over Joe's homework, Joe had said, "I did like Mom told me, Dad. I didn't mention to anyone what I heard at school yesterday."

"Good boy, Joe. Did you happen to hear anything about Sonny Medlow being involved in a fight on his way to school this morning?"

"Gosh, no, not a thing. Any time there's a fight, the word gets all over school. Dad, do you think what Sonny said about his Dad being a drug dealer is true?"

"I don't know, son."

"I wish there was something I could do."

"I know how you feel, believe me, but your place is safe in your home at night and being a kid at school, not catching criminals. I know you've done some amateur detecting in the past, but this is different. I don't want you anywhere near any of this."

"Dad, I already promised Mom that I wouldn't get involved."

He grinned and ruffled the boy's unruly hair. "Okay, then, let's get back to this homework."

Later, after saying goodnight to his son, while Tess oversaw Joe getting ready for bed, he had positioned himself for a more concentrated surveillance of the Medlow place.

As he sipped the coffee, Tess asked, "Anything?"

"Mrs. Knurd stumbled her way up to the front door about five minutes ago. That means he's getting ready to go out. He must bother with a sitter just to keep up appearances and not draw attention to himself. By the way, Joe said there was nothing at school today about Sonny being in a fight."

They had discussed his encounter with Medlow.

Her eyes grew flinty. She stared over his shoulder, through the break in the drapes, at the house down the street.

"Then you were right. That son of a bitch beats his child."

"That's why I'm treating this so low-key," he told her. "That boy's safety, his life, is in our hands. As a parent, Medlow has rights. This has to be handled with a feather touch so none of those rights are violated. If they are, and if he is abusing his son, then it could turn back on Sonny when we aren't there to help."

"I just wish you weren't going into this without any backup. At least you're wearing your Wrist Computer."

"Yes, but I'm not going to use it to call headquarters on this until the time is right and I have something concrete to go on. I tell you, the way the courts are, if I use official channels on this with nothing solid to go on, and if Medlow is up to something and is busted, a smart lawyer will find a way out and we'll lose the bust."

"You should at least tell Sam what you're up to. That Medlow is a dangerous man."

He brought the binoculars back to his eyes.

"So am I, angel. I take Medlow, if he is polluting this neighborhood, as a personal affront. I just want to check him out as best I can on my own. If I still think he's clean, there's still the matter of Sonny. Whatever kind of

a case I can put against this guy, I want it to be airtight.''
Then he saw something up the street. "Uh oh, looks like
we're on.''

He saw Medlow climb into the cab of the pickup. He
set the binoculars down, stood and quickly donned his
fedora and trenchcoat.

Tess went with him to the door.

"Honey, be careful."

He gave her a quick kiss.

"You know I will. You and Joe rest easy. Don't wait
up for me."

"You know I will," she said.

Medlow headed onto the freeway system, going west.
Tracy maintained a surveillance position, choosing to
hold back with the pickup's taillights well ahead of him.

He considered briefly if his following this man might
not be a case of that edgy restlessness getting the better
of him. What if Sonny had been lying about his father
being a dealer, had lied to his schoolyard friends about
having heroin for sale? What if the boy had been in a
fight that morning and Joe simply hadn't heard about it?
What if Medlow was just a guy who didn't like nosy
neighbors and who was now on his way to meet a friend,
maybe a girlfriend?

Eventually, across town, the pickup left the freeway
and, some blocks later, turned into the parking lot of the
Bradley Funeral Home, a modern, sprawling one-story
structure set back from the road in a well-heeled section
the city.

The funeral home's parking lot extended around behind the building. The pickup disappeared from Tracy's
line of vision.

He pulled to the curb, doused his lights, left the engine
on idle, giving things time to settle, wondering what
Medlow was doing at a funeral home.

He decided to find out.

He cruised past the building.

In addition to the neon sign spelling out the name of the business, which he'd read from the next block, the front grounds, landscaped, were tastefully lighted. The parking area and the grounds alongside the building were in shadow. The Bradley Funeral Home appeared closed for the evening.

He drove to the end of the block, turned right and backtracked along an alley.

He braked when his headlights reflected off the chrome of Wayne Medlow's pickup, parked next to a late-model luxury car. He killed the headlights and the engine and unholstered his pistol. He left the car, moving soundlessly, not latching the car door behind him.

He advanced on the building, gained the shadowy rear wall and paused, debating his options.

There was a lighted basement-level window farther along the wall, just the other side of the parked vehicles. Staying against the wall, he started toward that window.

He was nearing the vehicles when a figure emerged from the shadows, barely discernible in the darkness.

"Hey, what ya doing, what's going on, what the hell's happening? Come on, tell me, I want to know."

Tracy had the .357 tracked on the voice but he held his fire. He sensed more than heard the incoming attack from behind. He started to turn and in that instant knew he had been snookered. His last thought was that he should have listened to his wife, should have listened to Tess, should have played this one with backup.

The blow caught him behind the right ear. The explosion of pain was the last thing he knew before a widening hole of nothingness swallowed him . . .

Medlow emerged from the shadows. He pocketed a leather-covered sap.

Buzz Bradley scurried over. Buzz was shorter than average, a wiry ball of energy wearing thick-lensed glasses, and with a mouth that seemed to be spasming even when he wasn't talking.

Medlow looked down at the unconscious Tracy.

"I'm glad I stayed out here to watch after I got here. He must have trailed me all the way from home. I figured something might be up after he came snooping around this morning."

Bradley's head zipped back and forth as if trying to look in every direction at once. At the same time, he knelt and rolled the motionless figure onto its back.

"Holy, moly, do you know who this is? I can't believe it, I can't believe you just KO'd the famous Dick Tracy. I don't believe it, I don't—"

"Slow down, Buzz, slow down."

"Slow down, he says, slow down. My man, the neighborhood could be crawling with cops right now, don't you realize that? I know it, I can feel it, we gotta—"

"If this was a bust, Tracy wouldn't have come in his own car, prowling around all by himself. This is some lone wolf deal, him being here. I don't get it, but that's what it is."

"We still gotta do something, we gotta act, we gotta take steps, we—"

"We'll take him inside. We're all alone here, right?"

"Yeah, of course—"

"We're taking him downstairs."

"Downstairs?" Buzz's babble slowed. "The crematorium?"

"The crematorium." Medlow nodded. "The famous Dick Tracy is about to vanish from the face of the earth."

"Oh, I don't know, Wayne, I don't think we oughta do this, killing a cop, you know, I don't—"

"Shut up, Buzz. There won't be any way for anyone to connect it to us even if they suspect. Come on, you grab his legs."

"Catchem."

"Sam, this is Tess."

"Hi, hon. What's up?"

"Sam, have you heard anything from Tracy?"

"When, tonight? I thought he was at home with you, taking a well deserved night off."

"He was, but . . . oh, Sam, I'm worried."

"Let's hear it, kid."

She told him everything, about what Joe had happened to overhear at school, about Sonny Medlow, about Tracy's unofficial surveillance of Sonny's father.

"He told me he wouldn't take any chances. He told me not to worry. But, Sam, I am worried. Is there anything you can do to check up on him?"

"I'll get right on it."

"Thanks."

"Any time. Now get off the line so I can get to work on it."

He regained consciousness with a jolt of agony that raced through him, emanating from the spot where he'd been sapped. Impulse made him want to touch the spot. When he tried to move his hand, the next wave of awareness washed over him and he realized he was on his back, securely tied down, a prisoner, virtually unable to move. He had that groggy, cotton-between-the-ears feeling that told him he'd been out for a while.

He was bound to what felt like a slab of plywood, the approximate width and length of his body.

He became aware of other things at the same time: a smothering warmth, the crackle of flames very close by, and a conversation in progress.

Sorry, Tess, he thought.

There was a bitter taste in his mouth. He kept his eyes closed, gave no indication of having regained consciousness.

"I'm just not sure we should do it, not sure at all, really, Wayne, not sure 'cause I don't like it, not one teeny weeny bit do I—"

"Shut up, Buzz." Medlow's voice. "You'd be bankrupt by now if I hadn't seen the possibilities in this inheritance of yours."

"Yeah, great, a rich uncle leaves me a funeral home, just what I need but yeah, I guess maybe you were right, Wayne, we are going to clean up, I know we are, that's a fact, yes sir. Kind of funny, ain't it, at least I think so, and—"

"Right. So we're all set for the first shipment tomorrow and you want to let this cop blow it and bust us and send us away?"

"It's just that, I dunno, Wayne, when a guy kills a cop, they always get him, they always—"

"That's because there's a body for them to work with, you babbling goofball. There's evidence that a murder's been committed. With Tracy, the evidence that we killed him will go up in smoke." Medlow chuckled.

Tracy opened his eyes. "Better listen to your friend, Wayne."

Medlow's grin was not very nice.

"Well hello, Tracy. Welcome back to the world of the living. Too bad you can't stick around."

An open furnace door, a foot or two from the end of the board, the raging fire in the furnace, was the source of the heat.

The board to which he was bound rested on a conveyor mechanism of metal rollers designed to feed the deceased into the fire for cremation. He fought down the wave of despair that coursed through him.

Tess. Joe . . .

The jittery man with the crewcut and glasses said, "All right, Wayne, all right, okay, I see it, you're right like you always are, don't I know it, okay, so we gotta do what we—"

"Do it, then," Medlow snarled. "The hell with talking."

Tracy felt the wood slab beneath him jolt as Buzz started sliding him along the rollers, closer to the furnace, inch by inch.

Buzz continued babbling. "Yup, cop, yeah, go ahead

and scream but it won't help you one little bit, no sir, hear that, not one little bit, so go ahead and—''

''What's the deal?'' Tracy asked Medlow in as calm a voice as he could muster. *There must be a way out of this,* he told himself. There *has* to be. ''I can see where some of your victims might prefer death to hearing this motormouth, but I'm the curious type. Don't I at least get to know why you're doing this?''

He recognized Medlow's type. Being in charge wasn't enough for him. There was an arrogance, too, that would make him want to brag. It was all Tracy had to work with.

And it did work.

''Okay,'' said Medlow. ''Hold it a minute, Buzz.''

The progress of the soles of Tracy's shoes toward the mouth of the furnace ceased.

''Hold it?'' Buzz snapped. ''What do you mean, hold it, why should—''

''Shut up, Buzz. Tracy, I'd like you to meet Buzz Bradley. I guess it's only right a condemned man should know who it is iced him. Or maybe in this case, I should say *burned* him.''

''So tell me what I've stumbled on to here. Shouldn't that be a last right for the condemned?'' The nearness of death had brought his senses fully awake. He worked at his bonds, but he was securely bound, not with the regular apparatus for feeding the deceased into the fire but instead with chains locking at his side, pinning his arms to him. His ankles were chained together.

''What is this about?'' he pressed Medlow. ''Some sort of white supremacy craziness? Is it worth killing a cop over?''

''I think so.'' Medlow grinned. ''Here it is, Tracy, short and sweet. My pal, Buzz here, he inherited this place. He wanted to sell it, but I saw the potential right away. Buzz isn't the undertaker type, exactly, so we hired a staff and a funeral director and they run the place, but

Buzz can come and go as he pleases. He's got the run of the place, especially after hours.''

"Shoulda sold it," Buzz chattered, "but I guess it's in the blood, know what I mean, anyway, I shoulda—"

Tracy recalled what Joe had overheard Sonny tell his friends.

"Heroin. You're a couple of ghouls. You're using this place to smuggle in heroin."

"You know what a big deal the drug war is," said Medlow. "But all of the action is focused on Latin America. Funding is still tight, you oughta know that, too. They had to reassign money and manpower from somewhere else, and that somewhere else was the old pipeline in from Asia, the Golden Triangle: Burma, Laos, Thailand. I made connections there when I was in the Nam. I was smart even back then. I knew there'd be a day. I got it to the West Coast, but from there back to here was something else. The drug war has the Feds watching interstate transportation real close.''

Tracy fought down his revulsion. He had to keep this conversation going, had to find an angle to play this, buttons to push on this guy to make Medlow change his mind about killing him. There had to be a way.

He felt heat through the bottom of his shoes. His nostrils twitched with the stink of the soles smoldering.

"Bodies shipped here for burial from California. Do you make your own corpses, too?''

"Sometimes," said Medlow. "You'd be surprised how much pure, uncut heroin you can hide away inside a cadaver that no one wants to inspect in the first place.''

"The bodies are shipped to here. I thought you white supremacy guys were into racism, not peddling dope to school kids. You're the new drug source they've been talking about on the streets. What good can come of something like this, Wayne? You've got a child of your own.''

Medlow's grin was ear to ear.

"Do you know a better way to keep the niggers and

spics in their place? Get them hooked on smack and crack and they'll stay in their ghettos and the barrios where they belong forever."

"Wayne, we gotta stop talking about it and do it if we're going to do it," Buzz buzzed. "Maybe he was followed, we got to do something and do it quick before—"

"Okay, do it," Medlow said. "Trying to buy time was a trick that won't work, cop. So long. Take your time, Buzz. I want to hear him scream."

Tracy heaved himself against his bonds. They would not give. Buzz commenced sliding him along the metal rollers. The heat at his feet increased. He writhed in his chains, determined to go out struggling. Beads of sweat ran in rivulets down his face.

The sudden shattering of glass from the painted-over basement window erupted at the same instant as the door to the crematorium was sent bursting inward off its hinges by a powerful kick from outside.

Three figures stormed in: Wil Garrett gained entry through the window, hitting the floor with panther-like grace, the MAC-10 auto pistol he held tracking on Buzz Bradley.

"Hold it right there. Back off."

Medlow whirled toward Dan Sprague and Sam Catchem, who stormed through the doorway. Medlow's right hand instinctively dove beneath his jacket for concealed hardware even before he saw the faces of the intruders.

The shotgun in Sprague's hand boomed once, twice, three times, resounding like cannon fire within the confines of the crematorium, and all three loads caught Medlow in the chest, lifted him from his feet, toppled him into a sodden, misshapen heap in the corner, the wall behind him a mural of bloody, glistening swirls.

"Sam, get me out of this thing!" Tracy shouted.

Catchem rushed over to pull Tracy well back from the heat of the furnace.

"Keys," he snapped at Bradley.

Buzz Bradley was suddenly speechless. His eyes were wide. He was slack-jawed, fixated by the gory remains in the corner. He handed Sam the keys with a jittery hand.

Sam unlocked the chains and Tracy sat up. The first thing he did was to untie and remove his shoes, which still smoldered. When he stood, he found it to be not too uncomfortable. The floor of the crematorium felt clammy beneath his stocking feet.

"Whew, that was getting a hotfoot the hard way. Thanks, men."

"Thank your wife," Sprague said. He pumped another round into the chamber, turning from the remains of Wayne Medlow. "She started to worry about you. She called Sam."

"I thought of you working so close with Sprague last night," Catchem continued. "I gave him a call. Tess told me Medlow's name. When I told Sprague, he knew right where to come and the three of us beat it over here."

"Dan thought just the three of us should come here," said Garrett, keeping his pistol trained on Bradley. "There wasn't time to round up the rest of the squad."

"Thanks, men, for saving my life," Tracy said. He turned to Sprague. "I don't mean to sound ungrateful, Lieutenant, but would you mind explaining to me how you knew Medlow would bring me down here?"

"Just put it together, that's all. We've had this operation under surveillance for months, letting them set it up so we could shut them down when they went to work."

"No, you haven't. I went over all of your active files, remember, prior to last night's bust. I would have recognized Medlow's name if I'd come across it." Tracy turned to Garrett. "Were you aware of this operation before tonight?"

Garrett frowned. He studied his partner.

"Can't say as I was."

"It's intel I developed on my own," said Sprague.

"What does it matter? Are you crying tears over that scumbag Medlow? Forget it. He's just one more dealer out of the way, permanently."

"Just like you took down Cool Step last night," Tracy said. "You've pushed your luck too far, Lieutenant."

Garrett kept his pistol trained on Bradley, who was still at a complete loss of words, and threw an uncertain glance at Tracy. "What are you getting at, that Sprague is dirty?"

Tracy did not take his eyes from Sprague. He was aware that the holster under his jacket rode empty. Buzz or Medlow had relieved him of his .357 while he was unconscious.

"That's exactly what I mean."

"You'd better have some proof of all this," Sprague said. "This is crazy talk."

"I think we'll find the proof if we dig. You've been the gang's connection inside the Department. You couldn't say no to the dirty money. You must have made a deal with Medlow. You took out Cool Step and probably that other gang boss we thought was a drive-by shooting, and that cleared the way for this new source to move in that everyone was talking about. You're not a very trustworthy guy all around, are you, Lieutenant?"

Sprague snorted and started to turn away. "I don't have to listen to this."

"Yes, you do," said Catchem. He had not holstered his revolver. "And keep that shotgun aimed at the ground. In fact, maybe you oughta just set the thing down."

"Maybe I ought to tell you to go to hell. Tracy's in shock from what just happened to him, is all I can figure. He doesn't know what he's saying."

"You decided to go with Medlow because there were less risks and the pipeline from Asia was probably just a starting point," said Tracy. "But tonight when Sam told you about me following Medlow, you put two and two together. But you overplayed your hand. You thought on your feet and you made the wrong decision. You decided to cancel out your arrangement with Medlow the same way you had canceled out Cool Step. You knew you could always line up some more graft, but if you let Medlow do me in, the spotlight would be on the whole department. You figured you'd be in the clear with Medlow out of the way. He wouldn't have confided in a moron like Buzz Bradley, he only needed Buzz for this place, and you'd have looked good for having saved my life, not a bad cop at all. I should have suspected something on that raid. There's always something wrong when a cop uses excessive force. You tried to smooth it over today, saying it was work stress, and that was smart. Not like tonight. You should have let them kill me. Now I'm going after you."

"I still haven't heard anything like proof."

"It's there. You wouldn't have been worried unless there was evidence somewhere that you've been on the take. Computer searches will uncover where you've buried the money."

Sprague's face became almost unrecognizable, the desperate snarl of a trapped beast, and he started to yank the shotgun up into firing position.

Tracy had caught the telltale flicker in Sprague's eye that warned him of exactly what Sprague was about to do. He brushed aside the shotgun with his right arm, grabbed the barrel and pushed the gun ceilingward. It boomed and plaster swirled like snow. He jerked the weapon from Sprague's hands and, in the same movement, hooked a foot behind Sprague and shoved forcefully with his other hand. Sprague fell to the floor, scrambled around to start up again and stopped when he found himself staring into the muzzle of the shotgun aimed between his eyes.

Tracy jacked another round into the chamber. "Hold it right there, son. You should have known better than to tangle with a living legend."

* * *

Less than ten minutes later, Tracy, Catchem and Garrett stood off to the side and watched Sprague and Bradley being loaded into separate squad cars for the ride downtown. Buzz still had not gotten around to saying anything, as if Medlow's death had rendered him mute.

Garrett shook his head as the taillights of the cars disappeared around the building.

"I can't believe it. I always thought Sprague was one of the best."

"Maybe he was, once upon a time," Tracy said. "It's hard to think of a man betraying his trust when he's your partner."

"At least we nailed them," said Sam. "Good work, Tracy."

"Good work," Tracy echoed. His voice sounded weary to his own ears. "So I proved there was one more cop who could be bought. I take no pride in that. Now I have to go home and ask Tess to help me tell a young boy that his father is dead. I'll be in first thing in the morning to fill out the reports."

"I'll cover this tonight for you," Sam said.

"And whatever the consequences," said Garrett, "thanks, Tracy."

He accepted that with a nod. Then he turned and strode off into the night, toward his car.

NOT A CREATURE WAS STIRRING

by
Max Allan Collins

The child was dead.

Tracy knelt over the slumped, crumpled form in its neat-as-a-pin blue-and-white snowsuit; he touched the boy's bruised face. The child was in a ditch, in a culvert, feet in, head out. Flakes of snow as big as half-dollars were drifting to the earth, and the countryside nearby was blanketed white like something off a Christmas card.

But in this ditch the snow mingled with cinders and soot and the boy looked as dirty as he did dead, even as snowflakes kissed his white face and dissolved into moisture.

Sam Catchem, his hands sunk deep into his topcoat pockets, his breath smoking, stood next to Tracy. His rumpled, freckled face was plainly mournful. He did not lean down to see the dead child better; he didn't seem to want to.

"About your boy's age," Catchem said.

Tracy nodded. His eyes were slits in a face as blank as the blacktop road nearby. "About," he said.

"Joe's a little older."

"No," Tracy said, and shook his head. His eyes were fixed on the small corpse. "This child is older than all of us."

"Huh?"

He stood. "You can't get older than dead."

Up on the blacktop, the ambulance awaited, its lights swiveling, casting streaks of blue light into a clear, cold night. Several squad cars were there, one city, one sheriff's department, as well as the farmer and his wife who'd spotted the little body, before dark.

"Fourth child," Catchem said, "in as many weeks. All boys. All about five, six years old."

Tracy said nothing; he just stared at the boy.

"Strangled," Catchem went on. "With one powerful hand."

Tracy sighed and began up the embankment.

"No apparent sexual assault, at least," Catchem said.

Tracy nodded to the ambulance boys, who'd been waiting with their stretcher and tiny body bag. They went down to the culvert.

"The bastard's going to do this again, you know," Catchem said.

"No he isn't," Tracy said.

Everybody called him the Fat Man, but his three hundred pounds were remarkably solid on his six-foot frame. To glance at him, you'd take him for jolly; but there was cruelty in the Fat Man's eyes, and something else: something not wholly sane.

His features, however, were so benevolent, people often failed to notice—at first—the wrongness in his gaze. His hair was prematurely snow-white, thinning on top, long on the sides, tied back in a short ponytail; his beard was white, neatly trimmed. He had apple cheeks, touched with apple-red, a substantial yet rather pug nose, and a big, wide smile—albeit yellowed and sans eye-teeth, emphasizing the front teeth and canines.

He'd held many jobs during his forty-five years, hard physical work, mostly: he was a veteran of foundries, shipyards, warehouses. He never lasted at any of them long, because he inevitably either stole something, or hurt someone. For that reason, he'd had many names, various sets of fake, forged IDs; and he'd lived everywhere, or at least in every major city in the States, including Hawaii and Alaska, and Canada, too.

He had the wanderlust, all right, but now as he was getting older, he was tiring of boxcars and flophouses; for all the petty theft in which he'd engaged, for all the drunks he'd rolled, women he'd mugged, he had nothing to show for it. Years of hard work, and what had it gotten him?

He didn't drink, he didn't smoke—except occasional weed—and, other than enjoying a good meal, had no vices to speak of. Except for the little boys.

The Fat Man was no pervert, not in his eyes. The little boys were part of a scheme, a master plan. There was nothing deviate or sexual about it, as far as he was concerned. He'd always got worked up, when he did robberies; he'd always got stiff in his pants, when he invaded somebody else's home. Didn't everybody?

The wind, the snow, flecked his face as he stood on the street corner, ringing the bell. It was late morning in the Loop. Shoppers passed by and only occasionally stopped to toss coins or even more rarely paper money into his pot. People just didn't have the Christmas spirit this year, the Fat Man had come to realize; sometimes he didn't know what the world was coming to.

A little boy and his mother passed by, exiting the big department store in front of which the Fat Man had set up his little tripod with pot. It didn't say "Salvation Army" on it, it didn't say anything at all; there was nothing to indicate any charity—but nobody noticed, or anyway cared. And some suckers *did* give. This boy's mother didn't. Rich bitch, in her fancy clothes; fur collar. An animal died for her to be fashionable and warm, the Fat Man thought disgustedly.

The little boy was perfect. The mother was obviously well-to-do. But today was wrong.

The Fat Man didn't know why, but he'd limited himself to Fridays. Every single one of them had been on a Friday; today was Saturday—he'd already done one, yesterday. And the funeral wasn't till Monday—so he might as well work the smaller con, today, and pick up a few dollars.

"Mommy," the little boy said, tugging his mother's arm, as he noticed the Fat Man. The little boy was about seven, a round-faced, bright-eyed child in a tiny camel's-hair coat that must have cost a small fortune. "Mommy, mommy!"

"What, dear?" The mother was in a hurry, but never in too much of a hurry to stop in her tracks and attend her spoiled brat. The Fat Man rang his bell, smiled, thinking about how people were scum.

"We should give some money," the little boy said. "It's Christmas and there's poor people in the world."

"Okay, dear," the mother said, digging in her purse.

She trotted impatiently over to the kettle where the Fat Man stood ringing his bell, and tossed in a quarter. It rang against the metal. A rich bitch like that, and a lousy quarter. Jesus!

The mother then hauled the little boy away; down the street, getting lost in the falling snow and the swarm of holiday shoppers. His small face looked back brightly and his little white smile was shy. "Bye, Santa—bye!"

"Ho ho ho!" said the Fat Man in the white-trimmed red suit, and his bell rang in the chill afternoon. "Ho ho ho!"

"We're glad you're willing to head up the task force, Tracy," the weary, balding detective said. His name was Simmons and he was a detective on the Homewood force. He and half a dozen other detectives and two sheriff's deputies from adjacent counties were seated at a long conference table in the Major Crime Squad's war room at Central Police Headquarters. Chief Patton sat at the head of the table; Tracy stood studying a map that had been tacked to the wall.

On the periphery stood the other members of the Major Crime Squad: Sam Catchem, Lizz Grove, and Lee Ebony. The two women were physically similar, attractive young women in rather severe dark suits designed to subdue their charms in favor of a businesslike demeanor. Lizz was in her early thirties, with a detached expression born of experience. Lee Ebony was in her mid-twenties, a black woman who, latest addition to the team that she was, was alert and eager.

But neither Lizz nor Lee—nor the two men for that matter—were immune to the horror of this crime. Prolonged exposure to the seamy side of life—which Grove, Catchem and Tracy had had, and then some—was no cushion for child murder. Lee Ebony, when she went through the murder scene photos, had wept. Nobody held it against her.

"Gentlemen," Chief Patton said to the visiting detectives, "I think we're all wise not to get bogged down in red tape and territorial rights. We've got a serial killer who has struck in three suburbs and in the city itself."

"He may be clever enough," Tracy said, turning away from the map with its four pins stuck in it, at various points representing the murder sites, "to hope to muddy the waters by spreading the murders around, as it were."

"It's a potential bureaucratic nightmare," Simmons said, shaking his shiny head.

"Only if we let it be," Tracy said, a forefinger gently raised.

"What I would suggest," Chief Patton said, gesturing with open palms, reasonably, "is that you turn all the murders over to Tracy and his team—and they'll interface with investigators in each of your cities, and counties, at the appropriate times."

One of the sheriff's deputies, a thin, dark man named Martins, said, "That doesn't sound like a task force to me." There was no irritation in his voice, but clearly toes had been stepped on.

"What *I* would suggest," Tracy said, "is that an investigator from each department work out of our office. With us." He nodded toward Simmons. "When one of my people is investigating the crime in Homewood, for example, you'll be along."

"What about the rest of us?" another detective asked. He was a heavy-set fellow named Schlemon, out of Naperville.

"You'll be here dealing with the various tips and confessions that are going to start pouring in," Tracy said, "when the papers get wind of this cooperative effort."

Lizz said, "We should encourage that, by the way—set up a Hot Line number."

"There's already a reward from the local Crimestoppers group," Catchem reminded them.

Tracy nodded. "Are we in agreement, then? Can we proceed as a task force?"

There were nods and murmurs of agreement all around.

"We need a name," Simmons said.

Catchem snorted. "How about the 'Let's Nail the Psychopathic Son-of-a-Bitch Task Force'?"

There was a smattering of wry laughter.

"We'll make it the Christmas Killer Task Force," Tracy said, with finality.

"Why?" Simmons asked.

"Because Christmas figures in," Tracy said matter of factly. "Each of these children was with his mother, shopping at a mall or a major department store. They were separated, in various ways, and the child was lost in the Christmas crowds. Forever."

Everyone nodded. Several sighed.

"Besides," Tracy said, with a tight smile that really

wasn't a smile at all, "I intend to stop the psychopathic son-of-a-bitch *before* Christmas gets here."

The Fat Man sat on the threadbare couch of his dingy two-room apartment and counted his money. Next to him on the couch, at his right, was the kettle; on his left was a leather pouch into which he was dropping the coins. At the moment he was thumbing through the greenbacks he'd collected in a long, cold day's work. Fifty-one bucks in bills; maybe another twenty in change. Cheap bastards.

He wore the red pants from the Santa Claus suit, and the upper part of him, including his enormous belly, was encased in the pink of longjohns; his socks were black and holey. He was smoking a small pipe filled with hash. His apple cheeks beamed. Despite the small haul of the day, he knew he was getting richer.

When this was over, he'd have a hell of a stake. Maybe open up a small business of some kind. An adult bookstore would be nice. Maybe he could fence stuff out of the back, or start dealing dope. Leave all this petty theft behind and be a solid, respectable businessman.

He put a rubber band around the bills and rose slowly, the hash making him drowsy, and moved over to the tiny plastic tree on the television. Several strands of red and green lights winked on the little tree; some aluminum angel hair shimmered there. On the TV screen, the sound turned down, the news was on; an image of a car crash was replaced with that of the boy the Fat Man had most recently killed.

He placed the cash under the tree where many more rubber-banded wads of money lay—the proceeds of the expensive goods he'd been peddling to fences these past weeks. He stood rocking on tiny feet that seemed barely to support his weight, smiling, smoking, looking at his money.

He kept the cash hidden under a floorboard when he went out; but when he was home, after a day's work, he carried the bills from their hiding place to the tree, where he arranged them carefully, like so many presents to himself.

How he hated Christmas. That had been the worst time, at his house. His father was a brute who drank and beat his underfed skinny son, and the three similarly underfed skinny daughters. The skinny little boy's mother was fat, and the drunken father hated her for it; she got beat worst of all.

There were no Christmas presents in that house. It was a house—or rather shack—where Santa Claus never came. Except for one year when Mama bought them a few toys, but Pop, when he found out, beat her for ''spoiling the brats.'' Really, he beat her because buying the toys meant she was holding out money on him. Money he could've drunk up.

Not that Mama was a wonderful person. She caught the skinny little boy abusing himself, when he was eleven or twelve, and she beat him with a belt, worse than Papa ever did, almost. Told him sex was a sin, told him it was ugly. She was right about that. The skinny little boy, who had grown into the Fat Man, felt no particular attraction to men or women. His great pleasures in life came from eating, stealing and hurting.

For several years now, he had parlayed his resemblance to Saint Nick into an effective Yuletide con, dressing up in the Santa suit and ringing the bell next to the kettle outside various department stores and within malls. He stayed on the move, working one place a day, sometimes two, so that nobody caught on.

He despised children, but had to pretend otherwise; they always came up to him and pestered him, calling him Santa, or accusing him of not being Santa, asking if he was the real Santa's helper, wanting to pull his beard and see if it was real—all that crap. He stood ringing his bell, wishing he could wring their necks.

Then, at the beginning of the season this year, just before Thanksgiving, outside a particularly posh department store, he noticed a mother dressed to the teeth, accompanying a nose-in-the-air brat wearing a brown leather coat, and the idea came in an instant.

Or at least, it came in the instant during which the brat's stuck-up expression melted upon seeing Santa Claus. The boy was probably six, and still believed.

"Santa!" he said, eyes sugarplum-bright. "Santa—are you going to bring me my pony?"

"Ho ho ho," the Fat Man had said. "Ho ho ho!"

"The victims have a lot in common," Lizz said, pointing to pictures that were tacked to a bulletin board in the war room. Fortunately these pictures of the boys were not death photos, though seeing the portraits—studio photography, all—was sad enough.

"Wealthy parents," Lee Ebony said, nodding.

"Six years or under," Catchem said.

It was early Saturday evening, with Christmas a week and a day away, and the task force members from the suburbs had gone home. Only Tracy and his team remained; they'd not been out in the field yet.

The long day had been spent going over the files on the four homicides. Forensic evidence was skimpy: a few strands of red cloth, a few more of white wool, had been found at two of the killings respectively. Each child had been strangled by a single powerful hand, presumably but not necessarily the hand of a man.

On Monday, the detectives would start talking to the parents of the victims, and begin trying to retrace the steps of the last day of each child.

"We have white kids," Tracy said, sitting on the edge of the table, "from all over the city." He ticked that fact off on a finger; proceeded to do the same for the facts that followed. "We have rich kids—or anyway kids whose parents are relatively well off. We have young kids—kindergarten or pre-school, but no toddlers. Always boys. Always out Christmas shopping with their mothers."

"Always on Friday," Catchem said.

"You can count on serial killers to be two things," Tracy said.

"Sick," Lizz said, finishing his thought for him, "and cyclical."

"Right," Tracy said. "And as far as I'm concerned, the significance of Friday is limited."

"Limited to what?" Catchem asked.

"Limited to," Tracy said, "we got till next Friday to catch him."

The Fat Man hadn't planned to do it more than once. But he hadn't planned to *like* it, either. When he strangled the first boy, he'd felt that familiar stiffening, followed by the warmth, the wetness of release.

He'd suffered guilt afterwards—not for the killing, but for the sexual emission. But the guilt passed, and as the Fat Man did not deny himself any pleasure, he began to think of doing it again.

When the first haul proved enormously lucrative, he decided to continue. The police would think they were dealing with a serial killer. They would not, the Fat Man knew (and it was a thought he relished), suspect that they were dealing with a criminal mastermind, a world-class thief.

"It will just take a moment," Tracy told Tess.

Tess, his wife of many years, a lovely blonde with delicate features, smiled bravely and nodded.

From the back seat, Joe—their mid-life son, who was now ten years old—said, "Come on, dad! They'll be sold out of 'Hatchet-Jaw,' if we don't hurry!"

Tracy turned and looked back at the boy. "Who says you're getting Hatchet-Jaw for Christmas?"

"Dad, it's such a cool game. You've played it at the arcade with me! Scott has the home version, and it's really great—truly *awesome* graphics!"

"I'm not crazy about you spending so much time planted in front of these video games."

Tess reassured her son. "Maybe Santa Claus'll bring it to you."

"Santa Claus," the boy said, derisively. "Yeah. Right. Him and the Easter Bunny and the Tooth Fairy. They'll all chip in."

Tracy shook his head, smiled, climbed out of the car and walked through a snowbank to a shoveled walk before an impressive, Colonial-style house. These folks had money, Tracy thought; but today they were the poorest people on the planet.

He knocked.

A sad-eyed, red-haired woman of about forty, in black, answered. "Yes?"

"Are you Mrs. Jeffries?"

"No. Mrs. Jeffries is my sister. I'm afraid she's not seeing anyone right now."

He showed the woman his badge. "Is Mr. Jeffries here?"

"I'll get him. Step inside, would you, please?"

Tracy stepped into the entry way.

Jeffries, a handsome, haunted-looking man in his thirties, approached and offered his hand. He wore a white shirt and a black tie. "Mr. Tracy," he said, obviously recognizing the well-known detective. "An honor to meet you."

The men shook hands.

"I was pleased to hear you'd taken charge of this investigation," Jeffries said. "Would you like to come in? Can we get you coffee . . . ?"

"No, Mr. Jeffries. I had hoped to speak to your wife, today, because . . . well, I know the funeral is tomorrow, and I thought, perhaps . . ."

Jeffries shook his head, smiled tightly. "I'm afraid Maggie isn't in any shape to . . . well, as you can imagine, she's taken this rather hard. Bobby was our only child, you know. And we can't have anymo— Uh . . . anyway, she's blaming herself." He shook his head again, made a clicking sound in his cheek. "She's been sedated."

"I understand, Mr. Jeffries." He gave the man his card. "My work number and my home number are both on there. If you wish, call me this evening, and I'll come back. The sooner we can do this, the better."

Jeffries nodded. "I understand. Do you think you can catch this creature?"

"Yes."

"You sound confident."

"I am."

"Mr. Tracy, my son was a good boy. A sweet boy. He never hurt a soul. How could anyone harm a sweet child like Bobby? What kind of sick son-of-a-bitch could do that?"

"I don't know, Mr. Jeffries. I've been at this a long time, and I never cease to be surprised at the depths human beings, at their worst, can sink to."

Jeffries shook his head, stared at the floor.

Tracy put a hand on the man's shoulder. "But you can't dwell on that. There are also heights that human beings rise to. Sometimes human beings can be as good as your Bobby was."

Jeffries smiled a little, and nodded. "I know. I know. But Mr. Tracy—at their worst, people can be . . . ghouls. We've had reporters hounding us. TV cameras in our front yard. I talked to the father of the little Reynolds boy, the boy who was killed last week. Do you know that the day of the funeral, somebody broke into their house and looted the place?"

"Unfortunately, that's common. Thieves watch the papers for funeral notices, and hit the place while the family is away."

"Ghouls! Goddamn ghouls . . . "

The man was shaking his fists.

"Take it easy, Mr. Jeffries."

"I . . . I'm all right, Mr. Tracy."

"I'm a father, too. I understand. Can I give you a little advice?"

"Certainly, Mr. Tracy."

"Quit holding it in. Start crying, now. You owe it to yourself. And to Bobby."

Tears began streaming down the man's face and he nodded and swallowed. Tracy went out.

At the mall, Tess went off by herself and Tracy and Joe shopped together for the boy's mom, stopping at a cosmetic counter for perfume, then getting a salesgirl's help picking out clothes. Out in the central area, Tracy was standing at the gift-wrapping booth, paying, when he suddenly realized Joe was no longer at his side. He looked over his shoulder and saw his son standing over by the fenced-in "lawn" of gold-flecked cotton-snow surrounding the throne where the mall's Santa sat. A line of kids was waiting; a little girl was on Santa's lap.

Joe didn't believe in Santa anymore; hadn't for a couple of years. Nonetheless, the boy was standing looking at the man in red and white with the fake beard, looking at him yearningly. Ten years old, Tracy thought, and the boy's already lost some of his innocence.

Still, Joe wasn't so old that he couldn't get caught up, for at least a moment, in the myth, in the spell, in the magic of Santa Claus. The thought made Tracy smile.

Then it made him frown.

On Monday afternoon, the Fat Man went to the Jeffries house. He was dressed as Santa Claus. In his hand was a large tin can with the words "Help the Homeless." He went to several houses on the suburban street where the Jeffries family lived, and collected donations. There weren't many homes on this street, however—Jeffries had dough, and he had the big house and the big lawn that that kind of money could buy.

This afternoon, the Fat Man knew, the Jeffries were at a big, expensive funeral. They were Catholic, according to the obit in the paper, and the boy (Robert, his name was) would receive a full Mass. Plenty of time to fill Santa's sack—and the back of Santa's battered panel truck, which he would pull into the garage once he'd swung open the door from within.

He would go in through a window in back (after he clipped the phone line—most alarm systems were tied in that way), fill his laundry bag with smaller valuables like jewelry, cash and art pieces; and figure out exactly what he was going to take of bigger items, before moving the truck inside.

What had made his plan so masterful was that he'd hit a number of other homes, on the days of funerals, in the last month, so that the fact that the families of the slain boys were among these robbery victims wouldn't seem significant.

But it had been those robberies, the ones of the parents of the dead boys, that had been the most profitable. Because he'd gone after little boys who were obviously from rich families. Like the one whose distracted mother had stopped at a perfume counter and didn't see her son making awed conversation with Santa, who'd stepped inside from the cold for a moment, from his charity-kettle stand. Or the one whose mother stepped into the ladies' room, leaving her boy to wait just outside; or the mother at the mall gift-wrapping booth who didn't notice her boy wandering away, his attention caught by a bell-ringing Santa; or the mother who was making a call in a pay phone just inside the door of a department store, while her boy's attention was caught by Santa on the street corner nearby.

They'd all been wealthy, at least by the Fat Man's standards, and he liked hurting them. Hurting the children first, and then, like today, hurting the parents.

The window, which he broke with his gloved fist, opened onto the kitchen; but he soon moved into a large, plushly furnished living room, dominated by a big, real evergreen whose lights twinkled and whose elaborate decorations were storybook perfect. Other Christmas touches made the room festive: here a holly wreath, there a poinsettia plant; a nativity scene shared the mantel of the brick fireplace with framed family photos and three carefully draped, knit green stockings with names sewn in red thread: MOM, DAD, BOBBY. A fire crackled below. Odd. No one home, and a fire going . . .

"Get your hands up," a voice said. "Right now."

The voice was deep, and it meant business.

The Fat Man turned and saw a shovel-jawed, slit-eyed guy in a black suit and red-and-black tie. He wore a yellow fedora and had a .357 mag in his fist. He looked like a kid's idea of a detective.

But the Fat Man knew this was no kid's fantasy: this was Dick Tracy himself.

The Fat Man had no weapons. He never carried a gun, and though he used a knife, had none with him. This was his day to steal, not to hurt. All he had to fight back with was himself, and a surprising quickness.

He flung the empty laundry bag at Tracy, whipping it through the air, and it caught the detective's wrist and the gun went flying toward the big tree, which seemed to swallow it. Then the Fat Man charged Tracy, lowering his head and running him down, like a car plowing into a pedestrian.

Tracy was on his back with the enormous fat man in the Santa Claus suit on top of him. The man smelled bad, and his Santa Claus face was looking down at Tracy with a contorted expression, which made for a bizarre effect: this guy was like the Santa Claus in the old-time Coca-Cola ads, only decayed—several teeth missing, the rest yellow, the eyes hard and crazed and bloodshot.

And massive rough-gloved hands were sliding around Tracy's throat.

Tracy was pinned beneath the man, but one of his arms was free, and he slammed a fist into Santa's side, once, twice, and again, and again, but it seemed to have no effect, and as those fingers gripped and squeezed, and as Tracy's world began to go red, he wondered if Sam, Lizz and Lee—posted variously outside the house—had heard the clatter.

The detective summoned his will and his strength and he directed a solid fist into the side of Santa's head, aiming for the man's ear—and striking the mark.

Santa howled, his weight shifted, his grip loosened, and Tracy lifted and dumped the fat man off him, to one side, like a big sack of cement. He rolled to one side, and the fat man, recovering, came after him; but Tracy swung a foot up and caught the bastard in the groin.

The fat man curled into himself, silently screaming. He was one red ball, his pink balding skull presenting a target Tracy couldn't resist. He slammed a fist into the skull, and the fat man toppled, backward, like giant bowling pin.

There was no time to try to recover the gun; it was lost in the tree and the presents underneath. Tracy fished his handcuffs from his suitcoat pocket and snapped one onto the wrist of the fallen fat man, who was on his back, his face distorted with rage.

But the other hand, balled into a fist the size of a softball, plowed into the side of Tracy's face, knocking the kneeling Tracy onto his side. The big man lumbered to his feet and, with both fists raised, moved like a tank toward Tracy, who scrambled back. He felt the heat of the fire on him, realized the fireplace was nearby, and his fingers found the fireplace utensils in their stand. His hand curled around an iron poker, and he swung the poker into the fat man's belly, cutting him in half.

Tracy stood, and swung the poker like a golf club, catching the doubled-over fat man in the back of the neck, and the man plowed into the brick fireplace head-first. The fat man fell with a *whump* in a heap on the hearth.

Tracy bent and pulled the arm with the cuffed wrist around behind the guy to meet his other wrist, but Santa came suddenly alive, and bucked Tracy off.

The fat man was getting to his feet when Tracy charged

him, knocking him back onto the hearth. The fat man's head was inches away from the fire, but he reached up maniacally and got his hands around Tracy's neck again and started to squeeze. Hard. Tracy's fingers fumbled for the poker, instead found its mate, a small shovel. He swung the shovel back, and brought it down savagely, and flattened the fat man's face.

The hands fell away.

Tracy, swallowing, got up. His breath was heaving. He stumbled back and got his balance and looked down at the fat man. The fat man's eyes were open wide, staring at nothing. The bones and cartilage of his nose had been shoved up into his brain. His white beard was spattered with blood; his mouth was a pulpy mess. He was deader than a Christmas goose.

Sam and Lizz were inside, now; the fight, which had seemed to go on so long, had been only a minute or two at most.

"When we didn't hear from you by Two-Way," Lizz told Tracy, "we thought we better come in."

"Good decision," Tracy said, still catching his breath.

Catchem was looking at the fat body sprawled on the hearth. "Looks like Santa here came down the chimney the hard way," he said.

Tracy sat on the edge of the sofa. His face was touched with red here and there—his own blood and the fat man's. He sat there and looked at the Christmas tree. Its lights sparkled; angel hair shimmered; round shiny decorative balls of green and red reflected.

"Are you okay, boss?" Lizz asked him, a gentle hand on his shoulder.

Tracy's battered, bloodied face, which had settled into a blank mask, broke into a smile. "Never better. How often do you get exactly what you want for Christmas?"

BESTSELLING BOOKS FROM TOR

THE BEST IN SUSPENSE

THE BEST IN SCIENCE FICTION

THE TOR DOUBLES

Two complete short science fiction novels in one volume!

☐ 53362-3 A MEETING WITH MEDUSA by Arthur C. Clarke and $2.95
    55967-3 GREEN MARS by Kim Stanley Robinson   Canada $3.95

☐ 55971-1 HARDFOUGHT by Greg Bear and $2.95
    55951-7 CASCADE POINT by Timothy Zahn   Canada $3.95

☐ 55952-5 BORN WITH THE DEAD by Robert Silverberg and $2.95
    55953-3 THE SALIVA TREE by Brian W. Aldiss   Canada $3.95

☐ 55956-8 TANGO CHARLIE AND FOXTROT ROMEO $2.95
    55957-6 by John Varley and   Canada $3.95
    THE STAR PIT by Samuel R. Delany

☐ 55958-4 NO TRUCE WITH KINGS by Poul Anderson and $2.95
    55954-1 SHIP OF SHADOWS by Fritz Leiber   Canada $3.95

☐ 55963-0 ENEMY MINE by Barry B. Longyear and $2.95
    54302-5 ANOTHER ORPHAN by John Kessel   Canada $3.95

☐ 54554-0 SCREWTOP by Vonda N. McIntyre and $2.95
    55959-2 THE GIRL WHO WAS PLUGGED IN   Canada $3.95
    by James Tiptree, Jr.

Buy them at your local bookstore or use this handy coupon:
Clip and mail this page with your order.

Publishers Book and Audio Mailing Service
P.O. Box 120159, Staten Island, NY 10312-0004

Please send me the book(s) I have checked above. I am enclosing $_____
(please add $1.25 for the first book, and $.25 for each additional book to
cover postage and handling. Send check or money order only—no CODs.)

Name _____

Address _____

City _____ State/Zip _____

Please allow six weeks for delivery. Prices subject to change without notice.